THE GREENING

a novel of romantic suspense...with a touch of magic

Book 1 of *The Green Man* series

To Barbara—
Thank you and happy reading!
Veritas!

Sharon Brubaker

The Greening is a work of fiction. Names, characters, places and incidents either are the product of the author's imagination or are used fictitiously. Any resemblance to actual persons living or dead, events or locales is entirely coincidental.

2nd Edition

ISBN: 1497544920
ISBN 13: 9781497544925

ACKNOWLEDGEMENTS

Many thanks to Peggy and her wonderful pen! Thank you, Laura Gordon, at http://bookcovermachine.wordpress.com Thank you to Meredith Keating and Brandon Boas of Grunge Muffin Designs (www.grungemuffindesigns.com) for a fabulous website, creative fire with the multitude of projects.

Thank you Ms. Griffith from long, long ago, for planting the original seed for this book. Many thanks to my family and friends near and far. Thank you to our 'Bayside' neighbors.

For more information on Sharon Brubaker's books, visit www.sharon-brubaker.com

TABLE OF CONTENTS

CHAPTER ONE

To everything, there is a season, a time for every purpose under heaven: a time to be born and a time to die. — Ecclesiastics 3

Death choked Sylvia. She childishly ran out the back door slamming it with a satisfying bang. She ran down the steps, away from the crying and weeping people. They were mourners for Gran.

It had taken her almost an hour to make her way across the living room, and out to the kitchen, where escape lay. Old family friends gave clinging hugs, and too many strangers cursorily stopped to hug her, and clutch at her, telling her what a beautiful person Gran had been.

She breezed past the kitchen table which was laden with food that her mother called funeral baked meats, brought by well-meaning friends of Gran and neighbors. The sight of the food made her nauseous. She thought the custom barbaric. How could she and her mother ever eat all that food – especially the casseroles that had begun to glaze over with a plastic-like sheen?

She ran. Sylvia ran down to the shoreline and stopped to take deep, steadying breaths of the spring air and she stared blindly at the horizon.

It was one of those perfect days of May that is clear and bright where the puffy clouds hung perfectly still as if they were suspended on fine transparent strings in the bowl of blue sky. At first, she couldn't feel any breeze. Yet the trees chattered above her, with a zephyr that made them active and pushed a lone sailboat, its sails pregnant with the wind, moved lazily up the bay. The air smelled sweet and green, and she breathed it in with the scent of the water.

Sylvia was angry with herself. At the last visit, she should have realized how serious things were with her grandmother's health. She berated herself that she should have seen how cancer had robbed the sparkle in her grandmother's eyes and filled them with pain. They had all gotten used to Gran's wispy new hair that was growing in with small white curls. The chemotherapy had taken away the long, snow-white tresses that her grandmother had braided and pinned up elegantly each day. But still, Sylvia had been confident the remission was continuing. How could she have been so obtuse? Gran's attitude through her illness had been that the cancer was a "bump in the road." She knew Gran had not been afraid of death. She was at peace and told Sylvia so, but somehow Sylvia had not equated Gran's discussion to an impending death. Sylvia gave leave to the anger and walked around the yard, giving the leaves around the yard short, bitter kicks and clenching and unclenching her fists. Sylvia knew in her heart that her grandmother had wanted her to finish her final semester in college. Gran had told Sylvia she was just fine a few weeks ago when Sylvia was getting prepared for finals and graduation. Sylvia ambled through the yard, continually kicking a leaf or two away until she reached a small stand of trees where her grandmother had long ago planted spring bulbs. The damp, matted leaves covered the ground with a blanket and the yellow-green spiky leaves of long gone daffodils lay prostrate on the ground. No one had bothered to clean-up the old leaves or tie up the daffodils' greens the way Gran used to so that they looked like little dolls standing in a row. Sylvia scuffled through them and breathed in their delicious scent of the crumbled leaves as well as the scent of the newly warmed spring earth.

Gran had been chipper in her phone conversation with Sylvia even two weeks ago. She told Sylvia not to worry about her and how she hoped Sylvia could spend a few days with her after the big event. Gran said she was trying to get healthy enough to manage the ride to the college. Sylvia now knew that her mother, and Gran, had purposely not told her how ill Gran was, or the fact that Gran was in hospice care the last few weeks. Unbeknownst to Sylvia, Gran, and her mother made the decision for Gran to stay at home in her last weeks of life rather than going to a hospice facility. She kept telling herself it was good that Gran wasn't in great pain and went quietly in her sleep. Yet, Sylvia still felt guilty and resented not being able to say good-bye. She felt cheated and empty without this closure. One of Gran's last wishes was to see Sylvia graduate from college, but she never had the chance. Sylvia forced herself to go through the ceremony for Gran more than herself because of Gran's wish that the funeral to be delayed if needed so that Sylvia could participate in the graduation.

She continued to scuffle along through the grass and leaves still wet with dew, uncovering the ripe smell of damp earth and grass. Her shoes went from damp to the chilled, feeling the wet on her stocking toes. She didn't care. She kicked sharply at a bit of particularly matted leaves when her foot hit something solid. She looked down at the pile of leaves and persistently kicked away at them to uncover an oddly shaped bit of wood. It was something that wind, water or insects had created and it almost looked like a mask with holes for eyes and a mouth.

Suddenly the zephyr kicked up the leaves as well, and Sylvia saw something like a great, green angel arise in the spot where the mask had lain. Sylvia stood frozen to the spot watching as a face of living wood took shape from the mask-like object, and rose to six feet with leaves flowing over limbs. Her mouth dropped open as the being spoke.

"Sylvia," a rich baritone came from the creature's lips. "Do not be afraid. You are part of the pattern."

Her mouth hung slightly open. Sylvia didn't know whether or not she should be afraid. Deep down, as surreal as this experience was, she was not afraid. But the figure faded as quickly as it had come. She stood again wondering, did she imagine things due to the stress of Gran's death?

Gran had always firmly believed in fairies and angels and had communicated her beliefs to Sylvia away from her mother. It was their secret that Gran talked to the plants in the garden as if each had an accompanying fairy. Sylvia was charmed as a child and her Gran had made it a fun activity to leave out cakes and milk for the fairies at various times of the year. A childhood friend once teased her that Gran was a witch. Sylvia had been surprised and hurt by the comment. Gran was just 'Gran' to her and very special.

Sylvia stooped, flicking a long, chestnut braid over her back and picked up the wooden mask, turning it over and examining it curiously. The great, green, angel being she saw was different from the ethereal fairies she believed in as a child. Feeling slightly foolish Sylvia put it up to her face and looked out at the water through two of the larger holes. It seemed like an ancient Greek mask to her as she held it close to her face. The air shimmered as though looking at the horizon on a hot summer day. Her face tingled a little where it had touched her face and she rubbed at her cheek absentmindedly.

Sylvia was used to Gran always picking up the odd shell, driftwood, and stones or beach glass and sharing them with her. As a child, she and her grandmother would make up stories about each found treasure. Many of the picked up treasures found their way back to windowsills and coffee tables in her grandmother's home where they could admire their stark beauty. Gran used to argue that if Georgia O'Keefe, the famous painter could pick up and adore natural treasures, so couldn't she? Sylvia remembered the stout way Gran would defend her treasures to her mother, Mary. Mary hated those little bits of things and would immediately discard any that made their way into Sylvia's room. Sylvia had become clever at hiding her pieces of treasure. Gran would have loved this piece of wood. She tucked the wooden piece inside her suit jacket, hoping it wouldn't make a mark on her dress, as she planned to put it somewhere special. She thought it might help her get through the next few weeks.

"Syl—vi—a," her Mother's anxious voice made its way across the yard.

Guiltily, she tugged the jacket tighter around the wooden mask as if her mother knew it was there. She turned towards her grandmother's house with a sigh. Her mother was on the deck waving to her.

"Come back, please," her mother called to her.

Sylvia raised a hand in acknowledgment and trudged toward the house. She stepped into the kitchen and was confronted by her mother.

"Oh, Sylvia," her Mother admonished, "Just look at you! Your shoes! They're soaked!"

Sylvia glanced down at her dress shoes now soaked with the remaining dew. She sighed audibly and made an effort not to roll her eyes. Her mother regularly treated her as a child of seven or eight years' old. To keep peace she obediently took off her shoes and set them near a register where heat pumped gently on this cold spring day. Sylvia warmed her damp, chilled toes, standing stolidly and refusing to let her mother see that she was chilled as well.

"They'll be fine, Mary," a quiet voice said to her mother. Sylvia turned to see her grandmother's friend, Marian patting her mother on the arm. Marian came over to Sylvia. "But, Mary, I wanted to ask you what you wanted to do with some of the leftover food in the dining room. Could you take a look-see and let me know what you want to keep and what you want to throw away? There are still a few mourners enjoying the spread. Perhaps if they see us start to clean-up, they'll give you a chance to catch your breath."

"Just make sure your shoes are completely dry before you polish them," Marian advised Sylvia. She came over to her and patted her arm, whispering conspiratorially, "And then there won't be any stain if they're really wet," she said, "you can stuff them with newspaper to retain the shape."

She had not had a chance to really get to know Marian with the confusion and grief of the past few months, but Marian was one of those people that Sylvia liked immediately. Sylvia smiled at her gratefully for distracting her mother. Sylvia vaguely remembered meeting Marian a couple of times during her childhood, but Marian had moved away. Sylvia thought she went to live in England for several years. Her voice still carried a slight trace of a British accent along with a few idioms that made Sylvia smile. Marian had moved back to the area in the past few months while Sylvia was finishing her degree. Marian had been helpful to Mom as Gran battled her cancer. Sylvia liked Marian's kind green eyes and soft white curls.

Marian had followed her mother into the living room and Sylvia tucked the piece of wood on top of canned goods high up in the pantry and returned to warm her toes on the register.

After her toes had felt sufficiently warm, Sylvia padded into the living room. Pasting on a smile, Sylvia thanked the last few remaining mourners along with her mother. When they returned to the kitchen, Marian was wrapping up the remaining food and putting it away. Sylvia looked at it with distaste and picked up paper plates and plastic silverware. She placed them in the trash while her Mother gathered coffee cups and loaded the dishwasher. They were silent as they cleaned up, none of them trusting the high pitched emotions that would surely leak out if they spoke. Finally, when everything was back in order, Marian gave them a quick hug. She told them to call her if they needed anything and that she would be in touch. Sylvia leaned her head heavily against the frame of the screen door and watched Marian pull out of the driveway in her ancient Volvo wagon. When she closed the door and turned around, her Mother had disappeared. Sylvia glanced in the living room, dining room and study. Not finding her mother she started to go upstairs but stopped and listened. At the stairs, she heard a sound. Sylvia listened to the sound of sobbing coming from an upstairs bedroom. Sylvia felt herself well up with tears, but she couldn't cry. Not yet. She only felt very, very weary. Sylvia tiptoed slowly up the stairs and went into her grandmother's bedroom. When Sylvia sat on the bed, she shivered involuntarily. All the medications and any signs of Gran's illness had been whisked away in the last week. The room seemed hollow without Gran's presence, but it still held her favorite scent of Devonshire violets. Sylvia breathed in the smell. She shivered still more from shock than cold. Grabbing the quilt from the bottom of the bed, Sylvia wrapped it around her and rocked back and forth slowly on the bed, looking at the room. She loved this bedroom with its crisp white walls and curtains and accents of soft, bright blue. Growing up she had found any excuse that she could to come into Gran's bedroom and snuggle in bed with her. Gran had never turned her away. Sylvia remembered the comfort of snuggling up to her grandmother's large, warm body, and the reassuring arm around her if she was frightened by a nightmare or a strange sound in the dark. She would whisper into Sylvia's hair how much she loved her and what a special girl she was. Unable to keep her eyes open any longer, Sylvia curled up on the bed and slept.

It was dark outside when she woke up. Sylvia was disoriented at first; she didn't know where she was. The soft lap, lap of the waves against the shore blew in the window softly rustling the curtains with the cool night breeze reminding her she was at Gran's house instead of her apartment at the college. The house was dark and quiet. It was much darker here on the bay than the college campus and it startled Sylvia. She lay quietly for a moment, getting used to the dark and the sounds around her. Shivering from the cold spring night air, Sylvia closed the window as quietly as she could before she took a sweater from Gran's closet and put it on hugging herself. She tiptoed out of Gran's bedroom and peeked in the room across the hallway. Her Mother was sound asleep. Sylvia tenderly pulled a blanket up and over her Mom, who sighed but continued sleeping.

Sylvia's stomach growled loudly so she tiptoed out of the room of her sleeping mother as quickly as possible. She realized she hadn't eaten much the whole day and she padded quietly down the stairs and turned on the light.

The bright kitchen light immediately clicked on and Sylvia squinted hard, momentarily blinding her in its bright fluorescent glare. She walked to the refrigerator and stared at the bevy of plastic wrapped items crowding the shelves. Sylvia pulled open a corner of plastic wrap on a cold meat tray and helped herself to a small handful of meat slices and cheese.

With snack in hand, she walked into the dark living room and out the French doors to the deck. There was no moon. Stars glittered in their blanket of velvety blue-black, and the water peacefully lapped at the shoreline. Somewhere in the distance, an owl hooted and from far away, she heard the sounds of people far down the beach or on their boat. She couldn't tell which. Down here on the water, there were no streetlights. It was pitch black. A little cool breeze came off the water and she wrapped the sweater around her more tightly. She wondered if a rain storm might blow up. The air smelled damp and different from the usual clean watery scent of the bay.

Sylvia sat, feeling minuscule and vulnerable in the darkness. She was a little spooked from the inky blackness of the night. Sylvia stood up like a silent ghost and went inside. Walking inside to get warm again she remembered the mask-like object she had found earlier that day. At first, Sylvia wondered where she had left it. She glanced around the kitchen and looked in the living room, and finally entered the study where she and Gran had deposited many of their natural treasures over the years.

Finally, Sylvia remembered she had hidden it on the top pantry shelf. She walked silently out to the kitchen and took it down from the soup and vegetables, holding it gingerly and returned to the study. Something was different on the wood. A small perfect leaf had sprouted from the wood jauntily decorating the forehead of the mask. Sylvia stared at it in amazement turning it over and over, wondering if a stray seed had lodged in a crack somewhere. Baffled as to how the leaf had grown, Sylvia realized she was too tired to figure out the mystery. She put the mask on a shelf in the den vowing to examine it more in the morning with a clearer, less sleepy head

It was the smell of coffee drifting upstairs the next morning that woke her. Turning abruptly in the now new bed, she nearly fell out. Her bearings were lost and it took a minute until she figured out once again where she was. The brilliant light of the morning bathed the room in a clear, bright light. Sylvia looked away from the boxes in the corner and went quietly downstairs to find her mother sitting at the kitchen table running her finger absentmindedly around the rim of the coffee mug, staring into space.

"Morning, Mom," she crooned, dropping a kiss on her Mother's head.

Her Mom raised up her head. "Hello," she answered.

Sylvia heated milk in the microwave and added coffee and sat down. The house seemed cold and empty this morning. Gran had been an early riser and usually was up and about for a couple of hours when Sylvia or her Mother visited. She was always cheerful, often humming, and many times baking muffins or something yummy early in the morning. Gran had told Sylvia many, many times that morning equated joy to her. She couldn't understand why everyone didn't want to get up early and greet the day, much to the annoyance of her husband and daughter for years and years. She told Sylvia that it took her a long time to figure out that she needed to fill the solitude with the joy of her own making and did so with walking, gardening, and baking until everyone else roused. Sylvia had joined her on several early morning jaunts, sniffing the fresh air enthusiastically when they stepped out the door to greeting the world. But, memory was a memory and those days seemed long ago.

Sylvia sat down with her mother at the small drop leaf table, smoothed the placemat with one hand and traced around it with the edge of her finger mimicking her mother's pattern of tracing the edge of her coffee mug while sipping her coffee.

After a few moments, Sylvia broached breakfast. "Do you want something to eat?" she asked her Mom.

Her Mother glanced at her and shook her head. "No," she murmured. "I'm not really hungry."

There was something about her mother's tone that caused Sylvia to cock her head and stare at her. Her Mother ignored the stare, got up to get more coffee, and sat back down again, looking rather grim, Sylvia thought.

"I'm not sure where to start," her Mother said faintly, staring at her coffee cup.

"What do you mean?" Sylvia asked puzzled.

"This may be a surprise to you," and she paused, "but Gran left this property to you," her Mother informed her. Her mother glanced up and looked into Sylvia's eyes.

"What?" Sylvia asked incredulously as she was now suddenly very much awake.

Her mother nodded, "You heard me," she said, the grim expression set firmly on her face now.

"But," Sylvia interjected and then stopped. She didn't know what to say. Her eyes swam confusedly with unshed tears and with a medley of emotions at what her mother told her.

"You know Gran," her mother began, "and her New Age sort of thinking. She felt that you needed some time and somewhere—to find your path, or gift or something. That's what Gran said," her Mother told her with a slightly bitter edge to her voice. "She knew you didn't have any career plans..." her mother broke off halting the sarcasm that had oozed into her tone.

Sylvia's choice of a Liberal Arts degree had prepared her for little and had always been a point of argument between them, but Gran had always been supportive that she would find her 'gift' as she often told Sylvia. Gran had argued with her mother that the Liberal Arts degree gave Sylvia a background in several things and that really, in the end, it didn't matter. Sylvia knew her mother expected her to go into banking as she had after her father died, but Sylvia couldn't stomach the thought of being with all of those suits. She had never known her grandfather. He had died before she was born. Her father had followed suit with his Type A personality and had a heart attack when she was nine.

It was after her father died that her Mother started working her way up the banking ladder and found that she loved it. Sylvia had absolutely no interest in banking or finance. The thought of the business track in high school and college made Sylvia's blood curdle. Instead, Sylvia had been shipped to Gran's house for holidays and summers. She felt she had grown up more here than in the pristine suburban home she and her mother shared outside of Philadelphia. Now she wondered if it had been a point of jealousy between them. Her mother looked as though she was counting to one hundred before continuing and gaining control over her emotions. It was a strategy she often used.

"I thought I would help you clean things up and get some of Gran's things packed for charity," her Mother said changing the subject, "and then I can return in a few days to get things straightened out with the lawyers."

They sat again in silence, allowing Sylvia to let the news sink in.

Finally, her Mother said, "You could sell it, you know. You could invest the money and you would be set for retirement." She paused for a moment and said uncomfortably, "I had always thought to rent it out," she told Sylvia, "you know, for an extra income property."

Sylvia tried to control the emotions on her face this time as she knew this was a typical reaction and thought of her Mother – the almighty dollar winning out. She was surprised, too, by the slight touch of bitterness that had risen in her mother's voice. But, Sylvia couldn't bear the thought of selling Gran's home.

Her voice squeaked a little as she answered, "I love it here, I couldn't sell this place, I…I" she stammered and stopped not able to continue for the lump in her throat.

Her mother sighed heavily and stared down at her coffee cup still running a finger around and around the rim. Apparently she was at a loss for words or did not want to start an argument with Sylvia.

Sylvia stood up and took her coffee out onto the deck. She couldn't think. The morning light was pearly and the bay a powdery deep blue. Its rippling water exuded calm and she stared for a long time. This house had always been a haven of peace for her. Gran insisted on it, often proclaiming the quiet neighborhood a 'paradise.' From upstairs she heard a door slam shut and the sound startled a great blue heron that had stood silently watching for its own breakfast. It took off with a complaining "Kaa-aack" in its rusty, scraping tone. Sylvia giggled involuntarily and relaxed a little and breathed a sigh of relief. She didn't want her mother to come out to lecture her. Her own house! *This* house. It was one of her favorite places in the world. A spot of excitement grew in her. Looking out at the bay, she silently thanked Gran for her wonderful gift.

CHAPTER TWO

Hold onto what you believe,
Even if it is a tree which stands by itself.
Hold onto what you must do,
Even if it is a long way from here.
Hold onto life,
Even when it is easier than letting go.
Hold onto my hand,
Even when I have gone away from you.
--Pueblo Indian verse.

Sylvia stepped back into the house and warmed her hands on her coffee cup poured from a fresh pot her mother had made. Cocking her head she listened and heard the shower and decided to look at the mask again. Sylvia gasped when she saw it. Instead of one leaf, it was now covered in leaves—tiny, perfect oak leaf shaped leaves, almost like a wreath. Sylvia picked it up and held it to her face to peer through the two eye-like holes. It gave the room a greenish cast. It was almost like looking at the wavering white-hot haze in the summertime, but this haze had a green cast to it and it made the air shimmer and move as she looked through the eye-like openings. Sylvia stared out of the window and saw a flash of greenish-white light, but jumped when she heard a shrill "Eeek!" Turning, with the mask still up to her face, she saw her mother standing in the doorway looking horrified.

"What is that?" her mother asked with distaste clearly in her voice.

Sylvia took off the mask from her face and rubbed at the tingling sensation that remained where it had touched her skin.

Wonderment tinged her voice when she said, "I found it outside yesterday and thought it was interesting," Sylvia answered her Mother. "It's sprouted these incredible leaves," she told her.

Her mother looked at the leaves and asked with trepidation, "It's not poison oak is it?"

Sylvia hadn't thought of that but definitely would not admit it to her Mother. She briefly wracked her brain trying to remember what poison oak looked like.

"No, I don't think so," Sylvia said. She placed it carefully back on the bookshelf.

A knock at the kitchen door made them both jump. Her mother went to answer it and Sylvia leaned against the doorway from the hallway into the kitchen. It was Mrs. Peters from down the street, bearing a plate of muffins. Her mother had frequently referred to the woman as the local gossip.

"Good morning," she said cheerfully. "I thought you would like some of these."

"Thank you," replied her mother. "You shouldn't have," she said politely and offered for Mrs. Peters to come in for a cup of coffee.

"Oh, no thank you," she said. "I'm on my way to church and I thought I would drop some muffins off to you. I need to deliver some to old Mr. Brown just down the road. He has liver cancer you know and he won't last much longer. Another funeral soon," she said shaking her head sadly.

The silence hung uncomfortably for a moment, as Mrs. Peters realized her faux pas until Sylvia spoke up. "Thank you for thinking of us," she said.

Mrs. Peters smiled and waved gaily as she went back to her car. Sylvia took the muffins from her mother and breathed deeply. "These smell wonderful," she said. "I think they have chocolate chips in them."

Sylvia went to refresh their coffees while her mother pulled out plates and napkins.

"I know you don't like her very much, Mom, but it was nice for her to do this," Sylvia said, "and these are a treat."

Her mother nodded in agreement refraining from an acerbic comment on the neighbor.

"I suppose we should pack up Gran's clothes for charity today so that you can move some of your things in," she told Sylvia when she had finished the muffin, "since the house and its contents are yours, lock, stock, and barrel. You might as well keep all the household goods and sort through them at your leisure," she suggested.

Sylvia nodded in reply, not trusting her voice. The reality of Gran's death shot through her like an electric current. She put her things in the sink and went up to shower. When she was dressed, she found her mother hovering in the doorway with some boxes. Her mother packed dresses and clothing from the closet while Sylvia emptied drawers folding nightgowns, lingerie and sweaters into the boxes. She pulled out one of her favorite sweaters of mottled green, blue and brown hues and kept it aside for herself. It had been a favorite of Gran's and Sylvia held it up to her cheek. Sylvia placed it at the head of the bed and continued to pack. They worked silently and methodically together.

The telephone rang, startling them both. Her mother reached to the bedside table to answer it. It was Marian calling to invite them to her home for lunch. After chatting briefly, her mother gratefully accepted the offer for a much-needed break. Her mother stacked the boxes neatly in a corner of the room and labeled them for charity.

Marian had given her mother directions to her home a few miles south of Gran's house bordering state park land. Sylvia's mom turned up a sandy tract that read "Oak Forest Lane" on a small sign. Small, white "Private property" signs bordered each side of the tract and "No Hunting" banners were blazoned on trees as they slowly drove up the road.

Her mother stepped on the brake quickly, jerking them both forward in their seats and exclaimed, "Just look at that house!"

Sylvia craned her neck to look around a small skirting of trees to see a magnificent home. It was the largest modern built log cabin home Sylvia had ever seen. It had an enormous wrap around front porch and gorgeous windows reaching from the first to the second floor.

"This is quite the private, little community," her mother remarked. "I wonder who lives here."

They passed a couple of other magnificent homes, driving slowly and gawking while following Marian's directions that led them to the end of the tract. Marian's house dated back to the mid-19th century. The two stories of Georgian red brick had some of the original windows. A bricked terrace off to the side had apparently been added, yet looked tasteful with its black wrought iron furniture. Faithful to the name of the street, oak trees surrounded the property with a large, apparently ancient tree in the side yard. A fenced meadow bordered the side and back of the house with the forest edging it. Sylvia wondered if it had been a farmhouse at one time.

When they approached the front door, Sylvia stopped in her tracks staring at the bronze knocker of a strangely carved head with leaves disgorging from its mouth and eyes. Sylvia stared at the blank wooden eyes for an extended moment. She thought it looked familiar, but wasn't sure why. Tentatively she reached for the knocker and knocked softly.

"Oh, Sylvia," her mother said exasperatedly. "Marian will never hear that."

Her mother took the knocker and rapped loudly on the large oak door. It was a moment before Marian opened the door while Sylvia continued to stare at the knocker. Her mother gazed around impatiently until they heard footsteps approaching the door.

"Come in, come in," Marian said as she answered their knock and led them into a large main foyer filled with an antique sofa, mirror and drop leaf table.

"I thought it would be cozier to eat in the kitchen," Marian said as she led them through a formal dining room with a huge country kitchen complete with fireplace and a small love seat to sit on.

"Can I help you with anything?" her mother offered.

"Oh, no," Marian answered. "I have everything under control. Have a seat."

They sat at an oak table with huge claw and ball feet. It gleamed in the light of a small fire crackling in the stone fireplace. Sylvia looked around the room. Warm mustard yellow walls filled the kitchen with light and warmth. Oak cabinetry was everywhere and Sylvia was surprised to see Marian open what looked like cabinet doors and see the refrigerator. She had only seen the like in high priced home magazines. Braided rugs were placed at convenient intervals on ceramic tiles that looked like roughly hewn multi-colored bricks. The overall effect was sunny and peaceful. Marian brought over a tureen of soup. When she lifted the lid of the tureen, Sylvia stared. The soup was orange and definitely not a tomato-y orange.

Marian chuckled at her expression. "Carrot," she said. "Curried cream of carrot to answer your questioning face," she continued and smiled in the direction of Sylvia.

"Hmmm, it's delicious," her mother, remarked when she tasted the soup that Marian had ladled into shallow bowls.

Sylvia took a tentative taste and was surprised that she liked it. She loved curry but had never ventured to try it for anything other than Indian or Oriental food. Her face gave away the look of pleased surprise.

"Good," Marian replied, "I'm glad you like it. It's one of my favorites," she commented at Sylvia's look of surprise. She passed a plate of whole grain bread and thinly sliced ham for sandwiches.

"I know it's silly of me to have a fire this late in the year," she remarked, "but, it keeps the chill off in this big old house," she said. "And it has been an extremely cool spring," she remarked. "Don't you think so?" she asked them.

They chatted about the weather for a few minutes until Sylvia's mother mentioned her amazement of the private community and the gorgeous homes on the lane.

"Yes," Marian agreed. "It's a beautiful community. It's quiet and most of the residents want it that way. Most of them travel frequently and are seldom here to enjoy their homes. Sometimes I think we should call this "Restless Oaks," she chortled at a private joke.

While they were eating dessert, Sylvia excused herself. They were reminiscing about her grandmother and Sylvia didn't want to listen. She excused herself and stepped out from the kitchen door to the patio. The air was cool in the shade of the enormous oak. Sylvia moved into the warm sunlight. The meadow was filling with green. Sylvia wondered where Marian's property ended and the state forestland began. An opening in the trees looked like a path.

It seemed to beckon to her. Inadvertently she started to walk to the forest path when her mother's voice pulled her back to the present.

"Syl," she called. "It's time to go."

Sylvia slowly turned and saw her mother and Marian standing on the stone patio. The windows in the house seemed to blink at her in the sunlight. Feeling as if she was in a dream, she blinked back at the house and at her mother as she walked towards the two women.

"I'm sorry we need to eat and run," she heard her mother's voice tell Marian. "But, I'm afraid I need to get back to the city. I'm going back to work tomorrow." She continued voicing her frustration of juggling to get things packed up, the house cleaned and getting back into the swing of work.

Sylvia approached them and also thanked Marian for lunch.

Marian turned to her and smiled. "I'm glad you could come," she said. "Will you be coming back soon?" she asked Sylvia. Her voice seemed to radiate calm and peace.

Sylvia nodded, but her mother answered.

"Mom left the house to Sylvia," her Mother told her. "We'll need to settle things in the next week or two. It really needs a good cleaning..." her voice trailed off as Sylvia interrupted.

"I thought I could bring down some things in the next day or so," Sylvia said. "But, I'm not sure what I'm doing yet."

"I could spare some time to help you out if you would like," Marian answered.

"Thank you," her mother answered before Sylvia could. "I know I've been dying along with Mother the past few months," she stopped and sighed. "I'm almost relieved it's over and I'm anxious to get back to work. I know I'll feel better knowing Syl had someone to touch base with," she said.

Startled by her mother's statement, Sylvia felt a spark of anger. Her mother was glad that Gran had died? She was shocked and couldn't believe what she had just heard.

"Give me a call when you come back," Marian told Sylvia. She gave her a hug and looked at her quizzically. As petite as Marian was, she took Sylvia's shoulders and forced her to turn her attention to her.

"It will be all right. It's hard to understand right now," she almost whispered. "You both need your time, space and way to grieve."

Sylvia nodded mutely in response and went to the car where her mother had already turned over the engine. Sylvia climbed in silently and gave Marian a small wave goodbye.

CHAPTER THREE

I arise today, through strength of Heaven,
Light of Sun, Radiance of Moon,
Splendour of Fire, Speed of Lightning,
Swiftness of Wind, Depth of Sea,
Stability of Earth, Firmness of Rock
--Ancient Celtic Prayer to the Guardian of the Forest
The Thistle and the Bee, Clan MacInnes Society, Inc. Newsletter,
July 2001

They stopped back at Gran's house to pick up their overnight bags and lock up. Sylvia was silent as her mother drove them back to their home in suburban Philadelphia. Her mother didn't seem to notice but chatted to Sylvia about upcoming projects. Mary complained happily about all of the things she needed to do before she went back to work, wondering out loud as to what she would wear to work the next day.

When they arrived home, her mother went off to organize and Sylvia went back to her room. Not a speck of dust or dirt was apparent on the pristine silvery gray carpeting throughout the house. Gray and blue walls complemented the glass and chrome tables in the living room, modern dining room and sterile kitchen. All the glass and chrome made Sylvia feel as though she lived in a slick, high-rise office building instead of a house. Sylvia liked old things. She escaped to her room where she plopped on the bed, kicked off her shoes and wriggled her toes. Her bed was carved oak and had been her grandmother's when Sylvia was a child. She loved to touch the oak and run her fingers over the carved designs in the headboard of acorns and oak leaves. It felt solid and comforting.

Sylvia sighed, thinking of the last few days. The fact that her Grandmother's death seemed surreal was nothing compared to the fact that she left the house to her. Sylvia and Gran had had several conversations about how she had felt more at home at Gran's house than with her mother, but she never imagined that Gran would leave the house solely to her. She fervently wished Gran had talked to her about it before she became so ill instead of it being a surprise. She could imagine Gran smiling and her eyes crinkling up with laughter at Sylvia's confused state. Thinking too much of Gran made her well up with tears. Yet, she still didn't feel ready to cry. She got off the bed and looked around the room to think of what she needed to pack. Feeling a bit stupid it finally dawned on her that her car was packed to the gills with the trappings of her life from her last couple of years at school. She and her roommate Gwen had shared an apartment this last year and they had sold most of the furniture to the incoming students, but her household goods, stereo, computer, and clothes were stuffed in the car and in the garage. She could drive down and unload the car and pick up the rest another day.

Relieved, she padded barefoot out to the kitchen where her mother was at the kitchen table making lists and taking notes. Her day planner was open and several files were stacked on the table.

When Sylvia entered the kitchen, her mother glanced up. "Hi Syl," she said. "Are you getting hungry?"

"Sort of," Sylvia replied.

"Me too," her mother said. "Should we send out for pizza? La Roma's have some great new pizzas—Chicken Caesar and Greek Delight," she said and added, "They deliver too."

"Hmm," said Sylvia, "Both sound good. What's on the Greek Delight?"

"Black olives, feta cheese, red onion, marinated artichokes," her mother told her. "I can't remember everything, but it's splendid."

"Perfect," Sylvia replied. She looked up the number in the phone book, dialed and placed the order.

"Thirty minutes," she told her Mom when she hung up the phone.

"Good," her Mother replied. "I can finish this up before it arrives."

Sylvia went back to her room and went through the closet and drawers to see if she wanted anything specifically for Grans. It had been so long since she had spent a significant time at home that her room felt slightly alien. Still beloved, but not completely hers as it had been in the past. It was a strange feeling. As the 'man without a country,' she mused, or at least until things were settled with Gran's home. She packed a small duffel bag with some summery clothes and a few of her favorite books until the doorbell rang.

By the time she went back to the kitchen, her mother had paid for the pizza and on the table and was pouring two glasses of chilled white zinfandel. As they ate, she told Sylvia that she would try to get an appointment with the attorneys in the next few days to take care of the paperwork.

"Gran's house could use a good spring cleaning," she told her. "I didn't get a chance commuting back and forth. The hospice workers were wonderful, but they only took care of the basics," she said.

She refilled their wine glasses and continued. “If you could take the remainder of the clothes to charity—a shelter or something, it would be helpful,” she told Sylvia.

Sylvia nodded. “Sure,” she replied.

Her mother had drained her second glass of wine before she asked Sylvia, “Do you think you’ll be looking for a job in the next couple of weeks?” Her mother tried to sound casual, but anxiety tinged her voice.

“I guess so,” Sylvia said honestly. “I really hadn’t given it much thought, yet,” she admitted.

Her mother had sighed a deep sigh before she continued. “I worry about you,” she told Sylvia, “You live in such a dream world, Syl.”

“Give me a chance, okay?” Sylvia answered trying not to sound like a petulant teenager.

“All right,” her mother said, sounding resigned.

They cleaned up silently to avoid an argument. Sylvia went into the family room to surf through channels until she grew sleepy. Her mother did not join her. She said goodnight about an hour later as she walked past the kitchen table, her mother’s head bent over paperwork in the light. She murmured a ‘good night’ to Sylvia as she walked past.

The next morning her alarm buzzed at her impatiently. Sylvia hit the snooze button three times before she groggily reached up to turn it off. She stumbled, yawning out into the kitchen where her mother was putting finishing touches on lunch she was taking to work. Sylvia helped herself to a cup of coffee and leaned against the counter.

“Morning, Syl,” her mother greeted her. “I was just going to come in to say goodbye. I wanted to get an early start this morning.”

Her mother continued, “I’ll transfer some funds this morning into your account so that you can buy groceries and left you a little cash on the table,” she told her.

Surprised, Sylvia replied, "Thanks," and endeavored to look more awake than she felt.

Her mother gave her a quick hug and a kiss on the cheek and headed for the car. "Be careful driving," she told Sylvia. "And call me when you get to Gran's," were her last words to Sylvia. Sylvia nodded and took her coffee to the living room window to wave goodbye.

Sylvia was anxious to get to Gran's house as soon as possible. She quickly showered and dressed in jeans, t-shirt, and sandals and put her duffel bag into her packed car.

Halfway to Gran's, Sylvia turned from the main highway to travel two-lane roads to the bay. She wasn't in a hurry and enjoyed driving through the green tunnels created by overhanging trees. The sunlight dappled through the leaves creating a golden green thruway. She blasted some of her favorite Celtic music and cruised.

When she arrived at Gran's, no *her* house, she stretched after the drive and looked at the bay. It was a perfect day—sunny, warm and bright. The water sparkled. The cool weather had been replaced with an intense warmth that wasn't too hot with the breeze blowing in. The bay was empty except for one sailboat lazily wending its way from the bay to the river. Sylvia knew that most of the boaters were weekenders in the area.

Sylvia pulled her bag and some boxes and opened the kitchen door. Emptiness assailed her and she took a deep, steadying breath and entered. Everything seemed dull and empty without Gran's presence. Starting upstairs, Sylvia went around and opened up all of the windows and doors to let sunlight and fresh air in.

When she entered the study at the front of the house, a faint aromatic woodsy smell greeted her at the doorway. Looking for the source, she noticed the mask was lush with growth. She picked it up and propped it against some books so that it stared out into the study as she opened the windows. She noticed a strange flickering of light on the curtains and when she turned around, she nearly fainted. A weird green light bored through the eye-like openings of the mask. Sylvia gulped, staring fixedly while warm hazel eyes replaced the light and full deep lips moved to speak. It was like the green angel she saw a few days ago, but this time, it was just the face in the mask. Suddenly, Sylvia started to shake. She backed up to the desk and put a hand out to steady herself.

"My God!" she exclaimed in a stage whisper.

The hazel eyes twinkled and a voice like liquid mahogany chuckled, "Some think so..." From somewhere inside the mask, the deep voice emanated and it vibrated through her body. Sylvia could do nothing but stare and gape at the mask, not sharing in his or its amusement.

The face turned serious again and it said, "Hello again, Sylvia," the voice said in a rich, warm tone.

At first, she could not speak. Her mouth gaped open, trying to form the words, but nothing came out. Finally, in a faint voice, she stammered, "Who... what?" she had difficulty getting any words to form.

"I am the Green Man," the deep voice continued. "I have returned."

CHAPTER FOUR

Let there be peace in the sky
And in the atmosphere,
Peace in the plant world and in the forests;
Let the cosmic powers be peaceful;
Let there be fulfilling peace everywhere
-Atharvaveda

The eyes closed and the eyes and mouth disappeared and returned to the leafy, mask structure as quickly as it had come. Sylvia continued to stare at the mask unsure whether she was awake or dreaming. She felt frozen to the spot, clutching the edge of the desk in one hand, hands seemingly glued in place. She couldn't take her eyes off the mask. Wild thoughts of weird science fiction films and alien invaders flitted through her thoughts. She thought she was going crazy. She thought she imagined this. She thought she was going crazy. Finally, she shook her head to clear her mind and walked tentatively towards the mask. No eyes stared back at her. No voice spoke. It looked exactly as it was before. What was happening?

Was she going crazy? She shakily and bravely reached out a hand to touch it gingerly. It took a couple of attempts before she picked it up, and carefully propped it up against the books again, and backed to the desk. Reaching backward, she pulled the desk chair out and sat down without taking her eyes off the mask. The phone jangled near her elbow and she nearly jumped out of her skin. It rang a couple of times before she could get her hands to stop shaking and answer it.

Marian was on the other end. "Hello, Sylvia," she said in a cheery voice.

"H-h-hi," Sylvia replied a little shakily.

"Are you all right?" Marian asked, concern in her voice.

"Uh, yeah, I mean, yes," Sylvia told her. "I'm all right. I just walked in a minute ago."

"Do you need help with anything?" Marian queried.

Sylvia answered, "No, I think I'm okay. I need to unpack a bit and figure out where I'm going to put things."

"Why don't you plan on coming over for dinner?" Marian asked her.

"All right," Sylvia agreed. "What time?"

"Would 5 o'clock be too early?" Marian asked.

"No, that would be great," Sylvia told her. "I'll see you later."

She hung up and could not decide if she had imagined the episode with the mask or not. Skirting the edge of the study, she avoided the mask and walked out to the car. She made several trips, unpacking boxes and stacking them in the kitchen. She put her computer boxes near the door to the study but did not go in. The voice kept echoing in her head. The face kept appearing in her mind's eye. She put her stereo in the living room, set it up and put on a lively Celtic CD letting it blare through the house clearing some of her anxiety. When the car was unloaded, she decided to take a break and do some basic grocery shopping. She glanced through Gran's pantry and noticed that it was as skeletal as the refrigerator.

At the grocery store, she picked up milk, yogurt, peanut butter, cereal, bread, eggs, pasta, sauce, some chicken breasts and a lot of low-fat frozen meals. Starving, she added cookies, pretzels, ice cream, olives, cream cheese, bagels and some lunchmeats. Sylvia glanced at her full cart while waiting in the long checkout line flipping through magazines and scanning the entertainment rags. In her mind, Sylvia could hear her mother's voice admonishing about not going to the grocery store hungry. Oh, well, next time, she thought as she opened a bag of chocolate chip cookies in the car and started to eat a few on the way home. Sylvia rationalized the snack because she hadn't eaten any lunch. Glancing at the time, she realized she would have to unpack the groceries quickly, shower and change to make it to Marian's by 5 pm. She took a detour to the liquor store to pick up a bottle of wine for Marian and a bottle of wine and some beer for her own refrigerator.

The phone was ringing when she got out of the car and she rushed to unlock the door to answer it, vowing to purchase an answering machine as soon as possible. She had forgotten to charge her cell phone and it was plugged into the wall in the study. She sighed when she answered it. It was her mother.

"Hi, Syl," her mother said. "You made it ok? I wasn't able to get you on your cell phone. How are things? What have you been up to?"

"Fine, fine," Sylvia answered a little out of breath, "I just walked in the house from the grocery store, Mom. Sorry, my cell wasn't charged and I left it here inadvertently. I can't talk long, I'm headed to Marian's for dinner," she announced.

"Oh, good," her mother said. "Please give her my best."

"I will," Sylvia said.

"Did you pick up something to take?" her mother inquired.

"Yes, Mom, of course," Sylvia said hoping she kept the defensive tone out of her voice successfully, "I picked up a bottle of wine to take over."

"Oh, good girl," her mother replied.

Sylvia made a face at the phone before answering, "Mom, I need to go so that I can unpack the groceries and change."

"Okay, okay," her Mother said. "Take care. I'll give you a call tomorrow to let you know when we can meet with the attorney. He was in court today."

"Okay," Sylvia replied. "I'll talk to you tomorrow."

Sylvia unpacked the groceries leaving a bottle of red wine in the front seat. Nervously she glanced into the study, but still hesitated to go in. Briefly, she considered putting the mask outside, but she still didn't want to touch it. Turning from the study, she went upstairs to shake out a shirt so that it didn't look too wrinkled and went to shower and change.

She arrived at Marian's, wine in hand promptly at 5 pm. The doorknocker, she realized, looked just like the mask that had spoken to her earlier. She tentatively put out a hand to grab the knocker. She knocked once lightly and then more loudly two more times, continuing to study the knocker thinking of the mask that had come alive earlier that day.

Marian opened the door. "I see you've found my Green Man," Marian said. "Isn't he wonderful?"

All Sylvia could do was nod silently in agreement afraid if she opened up her mouth it would gape like a codfish as it had earlier that day. She followed Marian into the house. If you put eyes on her mask of leaves, it would be an exact copy of the face on Marian's door. Marian had called it a 'Green Man' the same as the mask identified itself in that rich baritone that still rang in her memory. She followed Marian silently through the house into the kitchen. Marian thanked her for the bottle of wine, opened it and proffered a glass to Sylvia. Sylvia accepted and they sat down on the love seat in the kitchen.

Marian asked, "You look as though you have something on your mind."

When Sylvia didn't answer immediately, Marian prodded, "Sylvia?"

"The face," Sylvia gave a nod in the direction of the front door, finally able to speak, "on your front door...what did you call it?" she asked.

"A Green Man," Marian replied. "Have you seen one before?"

"I have one," Sylvia said faintly. "Well, sort of," she said. She told Marian about the unusual mask made of leaves but left out the part that it came to life and spoke to her.

"I would like to see that," Marian said with genuine interest, "Um, I'm sort of a collector of green men. When Hugh and I were in England, we saw several in the churches and local sculpture. They're all over Europe, here too in the States, I think."

"You're welcome to come and see it," Sylvia told her. "It's not like a planned topiary or anything, but it's unique. This is very..." she hesitated as she searched for a description. Sylvia shrugged. She took another sip of wine before asking, "What is the Green Man?"

Marian laughed a little before answering. "He's a lot of things to a lot of people," she said. "The Green Man is a ancient, mysterious and very powerful figure...pre-Christian. He represents a 'Father Earth' figure, representing renewal and rebirth. Here in the States, you see him in a lot of garden sculpture and in architecture. But, throughout Europe, you'll see him mostly in churches connected or on pub signs named after his visage. He's connected with King Arthur, Robin Hood and Sir Gawain and the Green Knight. He is in many forms in many cultures. He is Al-Khadir in the Muslim faith or 'the green one.' He's the guide to Moses, which is quite an interesting thought. Apparently 'the green one' accompanied Moses up on the mount to collect the ten commandments. There are other stories about him as well as an all wise and "all knowing" guide. A guide, at least, for those who are perplexed," she chuckled. "I could use a guide to that many times! But, I'm not as familiar with the religion or culture. I pretty sure what I've told you is correct, but I'm not an expert on Al-Khadir. Other's feel the Green Man is more pagan," Marian paused before she added, "That's a description, in a nutshell," she finished with another chuckle.

Sylvia and Marian sat in thoughtful silence. The buzzer went off on the stove and Marian went to fix their plates.

"Can I help you with anything?" Sylvia asked.

"Just bring the wine and glasses to the table, thanks," Marian told her. "Oh, and you can take these salads to the table too."

Marian had prepared a small pork roast in a savory orange sauce with roasted vegetables along with a salad of torn greens with vinaigrette.

"This is delicious," Sylvia told her. "I've lived on quick meals for so long, that I don't know how beautiful a home-cooked meal tastes. Thank you."

Marian said. "It's nice to be able to cook for someone other than me for a change."

"How long have you been alone," Sylvia asked hesitantly, not wanting to be rude. She had lost all memory of what Gran had told her of Marian long ago.

Not offended, Marian answered, "My husband died about two years ago. We were living in England, but I wanted to come home. So, here I am," she said and made a gesture of raising her hands.

"This is a lovely house," Sylvia told Marian.

"Yes," Marian answered, "I love it here. It feels a little large to rattle around in sometimes, but it's home. Hugh and I spent a lot of time rehabilitating this old place when he taught at State. It holds a lot of happy memories."

They continued with their dinner in a companionable silence until Marian asked, "What about you? What are your plans?"

Sylvia chuckled a bit sardonically. "I haven't had any," she told her. "Gran thinks," she paused uncomfortably before she corrected herself, "Gran thought I needed to find my path. Mom, on the other hand, wants me to find a job ASAP."

"What about Sylvia?" Marian asked gently.

Sylvia shrugged, not answering and not really having an answer.

"You won't have a problem finding a job," Marian assured her. "Do you have any ideas?"

Sylvia shook her head. She hadn't a clue so she changed the subject. "This vinaigrette is excellent! How did you make it?" she asked after she took a bite of the torn greens.

"Oh, just a few herbs from the garden," Marian told her. "I never know if it will come out right or not. It's a fun, continuing experiment," she chuckled.

"I would love to learn how to make it," Sylvia said.

"Not a problem," Marian told her and offered. "Why don't you join me tomorrow to pick up some plants? I know I'll be purchasing herbs as well as flowers to plant. Anyway, it's going to be too lovely to be indoors and housecleaning," Marian said.

"All right," Sylvia agreed, never one to want to keep things as pristine and dust free as her mother did.

Marian served a warm fruit cobbler with ice cream for dessert. Sylvia felt warm and comfortable as they cleaned up and took their coffee out to the terrace. She understood how Gran and Marian had become good friends. After this evening, Sylvia felt as though she had known Marian all of her life.

The early evening light was silvery gray and lilac that hovered like a fine mist. It was light enough to see for a few minutes, but the darkness gathered with the long shadows of the trees blending into the quickening twilight. The trees were dark silhouettes against the sky. Leaves had sprouted on some, but several trees had their budding branches create stark, inky black lines that cut the early evening sky into puzzle-like pieces as it deepened from blue to lilac to gray.

"Oh," Sylvia breathed. "This is lovely."

"Yes, it is," Marian agreed. "I love..." she started when the phone rang. "Excuse me," she said and she trotted to the house.

Sylvia sat, watching the pockets of darkness grow deeper in the forest and spread out into the meadow. Fireflies blinked on and off in the meadow giving her a show. Sylvia leaned her head back and stared at the sky. When a star or two appeared the childhood rhyme of "Star light, star bright" popped into her head. Sylvia chanted it under her breath, but at the end, did not know what to wish for.

"I'm so sorry," Marian said as she returned to her seat on the terrace interrupting her wish making thoughts. "That was Owen Anderson," she said. "He's an old family friend who's been recently employed by the Thurmont Company. He'll be spending a few weeks here while he relocates." Marian slapped at a couple of mosquitoes. "The bugs are beginning to come," she said. "Let's go inside."

"I should be going," Sylvia said as they returned to the kitchen and placed their coffee cups in the sink. Thank you for an excellent dinner."

"You're very welcome," Marian told her. "I'll pick you up in the morning bright and early. Is seven o'clock all right?"

Sylvia nodded in response and gave Marian a quick, impulsive hug. "See you," she said.

Sylvia drove home to Gran's house, turning on every light when she entered. Nothing seemed odd about the house and no strange voices or lights were anywhere. Shoring up her courage, she walked into the study. The mask was there, and it was just a mask of leaves. She stared at it a moment before sighing with relief that it stayed a leafy mask and turned off the lights and went to bed.

The next morning Sylvia overslept and had to rush to dress before Marian arrived. She had just finished brewing a pot of coffee when Marian knocked at the kitchen door. Sylvia let her in and offered her a cup. Marian accepted and Sylvia poured some coffee for Marian and made café au lait for herself and they both sat at the kitchen table.

"I overslept," Sylvia admitted as they took a sip.

"I'm in no hurry," Marian replied. "Take your time. Can I help you with anything?"

"No, "Sylvia said," But, I would like to get a piece of toast. Can I get you anything?" She asked Marian

"No thank you," Marian said, "but, I would like to see your Green Man."

"Okay," Sylvia said, putting a slice of toast in the toaster. "He's in here," she told Marian motioning to the study and wondering why she said 'he' instead of 'it.'

Marian walked into the study and looked around. Sylvia knew when Marian found the mask because she heard a relieved sigh. Sylvia thought she heard, "Good, he's come back," but wasn't sure. Sylvia had been standing in the doorway and she liked the way Marian picked up the mask of leaves reverently. It reminded her of the way her grandmother picked up stones and shells and such. The toaster popped and Sylvia went to put peanut butter on her toast. Marian emerged from the study a moment later.

"Fascinating," she commented to Sylvia, not saying anything more. "Are you ready?" she asked as Sylvia popped the last bit of toast into her mouth.

Sylvia nodded, turned off the coffeepot and grabbed her purse and house keys.

They drove to a nursery where Marian chose several flats of annuals and several herbs filling her ancient station wagon. On their aromatic ride home, Marian asked Sylvia if she would mind helping her plant some of the herbs and flowers in her garden.

"Of course," Sylvia replied. "I'm not much of a gardener, though. You'll have to show me what to do."

"It's quite easy," Marian chuckled as they pulled into her lane. "You won't have any trouble learning."

Marian's central garden was long and on a small sloped bank outside of the kitchen. She instructed Sylvia to get tall glasses of ice water for them and sit on the terrace. Meanwhile, Marian placed the six packs of colorful annuals where she wanted them planted near the front of the house, some in the kitchen garden and others in a garden near the edge of the property. Marian set small pots of herbs throughout the kitchen garden near the side door of the house. Satisfied with their placement, she went to the shed to get gardening tools.

The day was warm and the air clear of humidity. In fact, it was a perfect spring day with a bright blue sky with only an occasional cloud scudding across its expanse. Everything was green and bright and glowing with an inner light. Marian returned with a trowel and a pair of gloves for each of them and showed Sylvia how she wanted the plants planted. Marian sat down on the grass next to the kitchen garden and went to work. She assigned Sylvia to the planting of the annuals. Sylvia found that she liked taking the small plant plugs, separating the roots and placing them in a little hole, and tucking the soil around the new plants. The sun was warm on her back and her grief was replaced by a feeling of joy as she dug, planted and tucked the snapdragons, impatiens, zinnias, and marigolds. She planted another little plant around the border of the garden that had hairy, somewhat prickly leaves. Marian told her it kept the deer from eating all of the flowers. Sylvia couldn't remember what it was, but she liked the colorful little flowers that bloomed in a bunch. She stretched and sighed with pleasure as she saw the growing number of empty flats. The gardens looked lovely.

She glanced up when she heard a car pull into the gravel driveway with a flourish.

"It's Owen!" she heard Marian cry happily and watched Marian rush over to greet the visitor. Sylvia assumed that Owen was Marian's peer and was quite surprised when a much younger man unfolded himself from the car. Unfolded was a correct description.

From the brief distance, Owen's form enveloped Marian's diminutive form in a bear hug. Marian motioned for her to come over and Sylvia labeled him "geek" in her mind as she saw the glasses and short-sleeved white shirt. She wondered if he had a pocket protector. He was tall and lanky and his hair was a black thatch over rounded black wire rim glasses. When he turned to shake her hand as they were introduced, Sylvia nearly gasped. Behind those glasses were the most gorgeous eyes she had ever seen. They were hazel and a meld of green, brown and gold. Although the geek label seemed to fit the part of him, she was suddenly conscious of his stunning good looks—a little like a young Gregory Peck.

Suddenly Sylvia felt extremely grungy and was painfully aware of her dirt smeared cut-offs and hair escaping her braid. She drew back a step. Self-consciously she brushed back a stray hair or two from her face and hoped she didn't leave a streak of dirt.

Marian smiled at them and after introductions, she said, "Sylvia's been helping me plant my garden this morning."

"It looks great," he stated in a baritone as he looked over their progress.

"Well, you're just in time for lunch," Marian told Owen. "Why don't you unpack a few things from your car." Turning to Sylvia, she said, "Sylvia, can you pick up the empty flats and put them in the recycling container and give those new plants a drink while I fix lunch?"

"Sure," Sylvia replied. She watched Owen unpack a suitcase and some boxes out of the corner of her eye while she cleaned up and watered the garden. After a thorough soaking, she wound the hose back on the hose reel and went into the house. Sylvia stopped by the powder room and checked herself in the mirror. She nearly groaned out loud when she saw a streak of dirt on her cheek and another on her nose. Hair had loosened from her braid and she thought at first glance, that she looked a bit like a scarecrow. Washing her face in cool water helped. She had forgotten sunblock and her nose, cheeks and forehead were a bright pink. The cool water felt heavenly. Sylvia loosened her braid, finger combed her hair and pulled it into a quick ponytail. When she finally returned to the kitchen, she found Owen and Marian laughing over something with cold drinks in their hands. Marian had set out a simple lunch of bread and cold cuts for sandwiches.

Sylvia was quiet during lunch and listened as Owen and Marian caught up on their lives. Apparently Marian's husband had been a mentor to Owen's father. Marian told Owen that Sylvia had very recently inherited her grandmother's house and was seeking employment in the area.

"What's your field?" he asked Sylvia.

Sylvia squirmed uncomfortably. "I really don't have one," she admitted. "I just recently graduated with a Liberal Arts degree."

"That shouldn't be a problem," Owen replied. "I think a lot of companies are looking for employees with a general background so that they can 'mold' them into their model employee," he said diplomatically. "You should find a job quickly."

"That would be great," Sylvia said smiling at him. "I'll be sending out resumes in the next couple of weeks. What is your field?" she asked him.

"Environmental Science with a strong chemistry slant," he told her. "I'll be checking the environmental safety at Thurmont and possibly designing some environmental controls."

Sylvia nodded. She had heard of the Thurmont chemical plant for years from her grandmother. She knew they produced chemicals dangerous to the environment under the façade of safe garden products and other items. Her grandmother had often written letters and made phone calls to protest some of their actions and to support environmental efforts to keep the plant's chemical waste under control. It was an ongoing issue with local environmental supporters. Sylvia knew that at least one Superfund clean-up site in the area was due to one of Thurmont's subsidiaries. She wondered if Owen knew of Thurmont's cloudy history. She held her tongue.

"Owen," Marian interrupted, "I was wondering if you could do me a favor this afternoon."

"Sure, Marian," he replied, "Anything."

"I picked up Sylvia this morning and I wondered if you could take her home. I just realized there are some important phone calls I need to make." She turned to Sylvia and asked, "Do you want to come back this evening for dinner?"

"Thank you," Sylvia said, "but no, not this evening. I have some things I need to get done too," not wanting to intrude.

"Well, you'll need to come back very soon," Marian told her warmly. "Thank you for all of your help with the garden. We forgot about the vinaigrette recipe. I'll show it to you soon. Will that be all right?"

"No problem!" Sylvia told her, "I enjoyed it."

"Let me clean out the car a bit more," Owen said, "and make space for you to sit." He went out to the car and returned with clothes and additional boxes and disappeared upstairs.

Sylvia helped Marian clear the table and load the dishwasher.

"I have something for you," Marian said to Sylvia.

"What?" Sylvia asked, puzzled.

She followed Marian out the door where Marian handed her a large terracotta pot with a variety of green herbs and one purplish black plant.

"What is in this?" Sylvia asked breathing in the fragrant leaves.

"It's several varieties of basil," Marian told her. "Sweet basil, Greek columnar, purple ruffles and 'Sweet Genovese' – a globular basil," she said pointing to each plant in the pot. "You know what the Italians do?" she asked with a twinkle in her eye as if she knew a joke.

"Make pesto?" Sylvia's guessed trying to make a joke as well.

Marian laughed, "Yes, basil is wonderful for pesto," she told Sylvia, "but according to an old Italian folktale, houses with eligible young maidens placed a pot of basil on their front stoop."

Sylvia laughed, "Oh Marian! What are you thinking?"

Marian patted her shoulder and said, "Nothing. Thank you for your help in the garden. Go home and put this on your front stoop and water it well." She gave Sylvia a sly smile and her eyes twinkled as Owen joined them outside. Marian gaily waved them goodbye.

Sylvia sat in the car next to Owen embarrassed at her griminess and the pot of basil on her lap. She sneezed at the sharp minty scent when the tip of the tall columnar basil tickled her nose.

"Bless you," Owen said.

"Thanks," she replied, sniffing.

"You'll have to give me directions," Owen said as they reached the end of Marian's lane.

"Oh," Sylvia said haltingly, "Sure. You'll need to turn right here," she said pointing her finger and continued the directions verbally until they reached Gran's house.

"Wow, that's a hell of a view," Owen exclaimed as they pulled into the driveway which gave way to a view of blue sky and water dotted with sailboats.

"Yes," Sylvia agreed. "I think I sometimes take it for granted. The view is definitely better from the deck if you would like to come in," she offered.

Owen hesitated and Sylvia went on, "I have a cold beer in the fridge," she mentioned.

Owen's eyes brightened and he accepted. Sylvia stepped from the car and took the pot of basil into the kitchen to give it a good soaking. She placed the pot in the sink, opened a couple of beers and handed one to Owen.

"You can come this way," she said, leading him to the living room, through the French doors and out onto the deck.

"This is some place you have here," Owen commented as they stood on the deck looking out at the water.

"Well, officially, it still isn't mine," Sylvia admitted hesitatingly, "...yet." She briefly told him about Gran's recent death, her leaving the house for her and the upcoming visit to the attorney.

"How about you?" she asked. "When do you begin working for Thurmont?"

"Officially," he said with a grin, "next Tuesday. I'll be staying with Marian until I find my own place. Do you know of any?"

Sylvia shook her head. "Gran would have been able to give you some ideas, but" she broke off her voice catching in her throat. She had taken a couple of deep breaths before she continued. "but now, Marian is probably a better one to ask that question," Sylvia told him.

"Do any of these homes rent?" Owen asked.

Sylvia answered, "Many of them used to be summer homes and rentals, but most of them are year-round residences now. It started out as a resort community sometime in the 1940's, I think. My grandparents have been here forever," she told him. "Sorry I can't be of more help," she said.

"That's okay," Owen replied. "I'll pick up a local paper and ask Marian...speaking of which...I should be getting back. Thanks for the beer," he said.

"Anytime," Sylvia said, "Thanks for the ride home," walking him to the kitchen door.

As Sylvia watched Owen drive away, she realized that she was smiling for the first time in several days. Owen's effect on her had been disconcerting. She grinned to herself as she thought of her roommate Gwen. Gwen's comment would have been that he "hit her like a ton of bricks." She briefly considered calling or texting her friend, but still didn't feel like speaking to anyone. Emotions were still very close to the surface.

Feeling much better after showering the dirt and grime from the gardening, Sylvia went into the study to get the phone and phonebook. The mask that had been so lush and green was now looking dry around the edges. Sylvia wondered if she should water it; spray it with water, or something. She didn't know what to do. Remembering the basil in the sink, she gingerly picked up the mask and took it to the kitchen, soaked the basil under the faucet and splashed some water onto the mask and left it in the sink to drain.

Sylvia returned to the den and got her things and went out onto the deck. The day had warmed up, but it wasn't sweltering. There was a slight breeze and the sun felt toasty and warm. She sat and called the local paper for a subscription and also called to set up cable, something her grandmother abhorred. She wanted the service for the Internet and phone as well as the entertainment. Sylvia continued to sit, dreamily gazing at the sky and water, focusing on absolutely nothing. Her limbs were heavy and she didn't feel as though she could move. Sylvia continued to sit – leaving her mind a blank. Quite a while later, she jolted in the chair realizing she must have dozed off. The sun had started to dip and was throwing out its last hurrah of blazing golden light before setting. Her stomach rumbled reminding her it had been a long time since lunch.

Sylvia rose from her chair and went into the kitchen and surveyed the freezer with its variety of meals before choosing one. She popped it in the microwave and took the opportunity to call her mother while it was cooking.

Her mother answered in surprise at her call and informed her she would be picking her up on Thursday to meet with the attorney at 10:30 in the morning. Sylvia rolled her eyes and didn't comment when her mom suggested she wear something conservative, but "nice."

She told her mother she had helped Marian with some gardening chores and had subscribed to the local paper and signed up for Internet service so that she could job search, hoping it would appease her mother for the moment. They hung up and Sylvia retrieved her dinner from the microwave.

Sitting at the table alone, she thought wistfully of the meal Owen and Marian were probably having. Marian had likely whipped up another spectacular gourmet meal. She ate her frozen meal in the silence of the house pressing upon her and the light in the kitchen seemed near blinding. Sylvia sat and pondered what Gran's intention was when she left her the house. Gran knew that Sylvia loved the place, but…a house. Her original excitement diminished and a small flicker of panic grew inside of Sylvia as she sat at the kitchen table. She didn't have a clue as to how to take care of a house—especially an older home with many quirks. This neighborhood was now virtually a retirement community and the houses that had been built since the depression were a contractor's dream. She couldn't remember a time when she didn't see at least two or three contractors flit from house to house like a honeybee fixing leaks and old wires. Her grandmother had often joked that she lived the episode of "This Old House" from PBS and still received the magazine. Sylvia had only shared an apartment with Gwen in the past year and they were never there. She crossed her fingers in hopes that no major repairs loomed shortly. At the moment, it seemed vast and empty. She felt minuscule as she cleaned up her small dinner and realized what the books meant when they said a body was 'rattling round' in a house. Sylvia went and turned on the radio to an oldies station, somewhat louder than her usual. The tunes on the radio helped a little. She sang along with a couple of the most familiar songs and noticed the mask had wilted a bit more. Sylvia stopped singing, stooped to pick up the mask and went to splash more water on it before she returned to the deck wondering if it needed to be outdoors. She took it to the deck and propped it against the railing where it would get the morning sun. It still spooked her a little bit. She wasn't sure she wanted the mask to come to life again, but doubt or hope niggled deep inside and the desire to have the green man speak to her again grew.

CHAPTER FIVE

The sky is filled with stars and the sun,
This earth with life vibrant.
Amongst it all I too have received a home
Out of this wonder, my song is born.
--Rabindranath Tagore

Sylvia awoke with the sunlight streaming in and a fresh breeze coming through the window. She hadn't bothered to look at the bedside clock and was surprised to see that it was just after six when she made a small pot of coffee. Sylvia took her coffee onto the deck to enjoy the pinkish light of sunrise, warming her hands on her cup as she took a deep breath of the crisp morning air, smelling the trees and the sharp, fresh scent of the pines that bordered the property on her right. She loved the way the blue of the water shimmered silver in the early morning light. Sylvia stood a few moments lost in the sunrise thinking of absolutely nothing. When her feet were chilled from the cold wood beneath her, she went back to the kitchen to warm up. The pot of basil was still in the kitchen sink.

Sylvia buried her nose in the fragrant leaves. Feeling a little silly, she tiptoed out to the front door and placed the basil on the top step. Sylvia returned to the kitchen to finish her coffee and have a bite of breakfast. Sylvia realized that her mother would be coming the next day and that she had not cleaned the house as promised. She turned on a local radio stationed and vacuumed, dusted, wiped and mopped until things were sparkling and smelling fresh.

Pleased with herself and her efforts, Sylvia went out onto the deck for a break and perched on the edge of her favorite chair, the adrenalin still pumping from the hustling and bustling of cleaning. The late afternoon sun was blindingly bright. As Sylvia relaxed and settled back into the chair, her eyes fell on the mask which was once again depleted of leaves except one small brown leaf that hung like a curl from a forehead. Sylvia assumed that the other leaves had died, fallen off the mask and blown away by the breeze. She felt a pang of regret that the mask was 'dead' again. Even though her experience with the mask coming to life seemed dream-like and frightening, deep in her heart, she knew it had happened. What was it the Green Man had said? She wracked her brain to remember...he said he had returned, she remembered. Did he have another message? She couldn't remember. Sylvia wondered, with a guilty thought, if she had missed some sort of clue or knowledge to keep the mask alive. Was the Green Man still 'back' if this mask was dead again? She didn't have any idea.

A knock on the door pulled her thoughts away from the mask. She went to the kitchen to see Marian and Owen at the door.

"Hi," she said, opening the door, "Come in."

"We were apartment hunting in the area for Owen," Marian told her as they entered, "and we just stopped by to see if you were home."

"I just finished some cleaning," Sylvia said, "and was on the deck taking a break. Why don't you join me?" she asked politely. "Can I get you something to drink?"

She looked inquiringly at Owen and offered him a beer and asked Marian what she would like.

Marian declined the beer and mentioned that she liked to have a glass of sherry in the late afternoon.

"I think I know where your Grandmother kept it if you don't mind me helping myself," Marian said.

"Of course not," Sylvia told her.

Marian found the bottle of sherry in the dining room buffet and poured a small glass and joined them on the deck. Sylvia perched on the railing while Owen and Marian sat in the pair of Adirondack chairs.

"Any luck finding an apartment?" she asked Owen.

He shook his head. "No, not really," he said. "I like one in town, but thought it could get noisy from the summer tourist traffic," he said. "And the summer places are outrageous until the offseason."

Marian and Sylvia both agreed by sympathetically nodding their heads.

They sat and chatted until Marian suggested they go out for dinner.

"Just give me a few minutes to clean myself up," Sylvia said. She left Marian and Owen on the deck and went to change into a long casual dress the color of butterscotch. It was an odd color, but Sylvia knew it brought out the golden hues in her green eyes and the golden lights in her brown hair. She didn't want it to look as though she was primping for Owen but wanted to look beautiful. She brushed her long hair until it shone and added a little bit of makeup and rejoined them on the deck.

"Any ideas for dinner?" she asked Owen and Marian.

"How does Chinese sound?" Marian queried.

Both Owen and Sylvia agreed and they headed for the local restaurant just outside of town. It was quiet, being mid-week, and there were only two other tables with diners. The waitress sat them near a tinkling fountain with colorful koi swimming in its pool.

They ordered a dim sum platter of appetizers and a variety of dishes to share with each other.

"Do you remember the first time you ate Chinese food with Bran and me?" Marian asked Owen.

"Owen chuckled, "I think I was about seven or eight years old," he replied.

"Yes," Marian said. "Your parents went to a conference and you were staying with us. We ordered Moo Shu Chicken and convinced you it was a Chinese burrito."

"I liked it because it was messy," Owen confessed, "and I still do," he commented as the waitress brought the food to their table.

As they ate, Marian explained that her late husband Bran had mentored Owen's father. They had remained close over the years.

"Yes," Owen said, "Bran guided Dad through the hallowed halls of academia. Phids everywhere," he said shaking his head and laughing a little.

"Excuse me," Sylvia asked, "Did you say 'Phids'?"

"Yes," Owen told her, "Ph.D.'s. Sorry for the academic slang."

"Oh," Sylvia said, understanding dawning on her.

"It was an interesting way to grow up," he admitted. "*Very* interesting dinner parties," he said with a slightly sardonic tone.

Marian laughed at this. "Yes," she said, "Someone always has to expound on his or her ideas, however, boring or bizarre. It certainly stimulates the thinking process."

"Absolutely," Owen agreed and said with humor, "It helped me grow up to be the geek my parents wanted me to be."

"Will you be keeping up with your research, Owen?" Marian asked him.

"Well," he replied, "I'll have to see how this job goes," he said. I still have my theories, but I don't have any way of proving it. I needed a break from school. Mom and Dad don't agree, though. They want me to continue until I have my doctorate completed, and continue with my thesis and more in-depth research."

"What are your theories?" Sylvia asked intrigued.

"I feel that some of the pollutants in the latter half of the century are a catalyst for other problems," he told her. "It was proven with the pfisteria microbe," he said, "but I think it reaches further than that. I have an idea of mapping it somehow."

"Could you do that with a grant or as a dissertation?" Sylvia asked.

"Yes," he said, "That's why my parents are pushing me to continue, but they understand."

"Trust me, I know about pushy parents," Sylvia said dryly.

Owen continued, "That's why I took the job with Thurmont," he said. "If a large chemical corporation is doing its best to protect the environment, it will be a good example and leader for other companies. This could be the start of additional regulations regarding dumping practices. I can still keep up with some of my research as I work with them."

"You've got to be kidding!" Sylvia exclaimed, nearly jumping out of her seat. "Thurmont? You don't think it's a marketing ploy then?" Sylvia asked she fought to keep her voice at a reasonable level. "I mean, I grew up thinking of Thurmont as the 'Big Bad Chemical Plant' down the road," she said. "Weren't they part of huge controversy a couple of years ago?" she asked. "They're *always* in the news for some sort of environmental mess up. Didn't you know?"

"Yes," Marian said, "Actually it was one of their branches that caused two major Superfund clean-ups in the area."

"So Thurmont's going to do its best to come out smelling like a rose," Sylvia stated flatly.

Owen looked a little-taken aback, but Marian nodded grimly in agreement with Sylvia.

"I wasn't aware of that," Owen said. He looked thoughtful. "I guess I jumped at the chance to leave the 'hallowed halls of academia' when the headhunter came knocking on my campus door. I knew you were in the area Marian, and I didn't think of much else. It was my escape."

"I hope you're right about Thurmont," Sylvia told him, "of having the desire to change company policy to be more environmentally conscious. Unfortunately, they have a long history of the opposite. It would be a nice change."

"Owen might be that catalyst," Marian said proudly patting Owen's hand.

The waitress brought their check and their fortune cookies. Marian changed the subject.

"What are your plans for the next few days, Syl?" she asked.

"Tomorrow's the big day with the attorney," Sylvia told them. "Mom's coming down in the morning and we'll be going to sign the papers for the house."

She paused for a moment. "It's still very surreal," she said. "I keep expecting Gran to walk in at any time," her voice catching in her throat.

Marian reached over a squeezed her hand and Sylvia smiled at her gratefully.

"What does your fortune cookie say?" Owen asked Sylvia and Marian, changing the subject again.

They each read their fortunes out loud and laughed over the advice as they left the restaurant. Owen and Marian declined to come in for a drink and Sylvia was relieved, as she yawned several times on the way back from the restaurant. Sylvia picked up a book she wanted to read and listlessly turned the pages. The print danced before her eyes. Sylvia dropped the book on the floor next to the bed. She turned out the light too tired to even read and hugged the pillow tight and listened to the night sounds of insects and the soothing lap, lap of the water against the shore.

CHAPTER SIX

What would become of our souls,
If they lacked the bread of earthly reality to nourish them,
The wine of created beauty to intoxicate them,
The discipline of human struggle to make them strong?
-Pierre Teilhard de Chardin

Sylvia's mother arrived promptly at 8:30 the next morning. She nodded approvingly at Sylvia's choice of a simple black pantsuit and cream silk blouse.

"I still need to put on a little make-up," Sylvia told her mother. "Why don't you have a cup of coffee and I'll be down in a couple of minutes." She poured her mother a cup and freshened up hers.

Her mother went out to the living room and Sylvia returned upstairs to comb through her hair and braided it into a French braid. She added minimal makeup, looked herself over in the mirror and then glanced out the bathroom window and saw her mother at the deck railing looking out at the water.

"I'm ready," Sylvia called out the window.

Her mother glanced up before answering, "Okay, I'll meet you out at the car."

The twenty-minute drive to the attorney's office at the County seat was a quiet one. Both were lost in their own thoughts about the upcoming meeting. When they arrived, they only had to wait for a few minutes.

Their attorney, Mr. Simons, stood up when they entered his office and shook their hands.

"Sit down, sit down," he said, motioning to two high back leather chairs.

"I'm sorry about your loss," he told them as he went to sit behind a gleaming desk and picked up a sheaf of papers.

He looked over his half-moon glasses and spoke to Sylvia, "You're a very lucky young lady," he commented.

Sylvia nodded politely. She didn't feel lucky. She would much rather have Gran back than to have a house, but she kept silent.

He cleared his throat a couple of times. "I'll read the will and then we'll sign the papers," he said.

A lump formed in her throat as he read the will. Sylvia swallowed hard. Her mother took her hand and held it – hard. Her other hand was clutching her handbag. The will stated that Sylvia was granted the house and a small legacy for taxes and some minor living expenses. Her mother received stocks and other investments. It was all very proper and very solemn. And it was probably good that it was dignified and proper to keep their emotions at bay, Sylvia thought to herself.

They thanked Mr. Simon and her mother suggested they go out for an early lunch at a tavern noted for their crab dishes. They ordered bowls of crab bisque and sat quietly sipping iced tea, still quiet. The lump in Sylvia's throat had grown larger. Now she had a headache behind her eyes. It was beginning to throb mercilessly.

Finally, her mother said, "I need to be back at work tomorrow so I'll leave later this afternoon. I thought I would come back Saturday morning for the long weekend," she told Sylvia, who nodded and closed her eyes against the pain in her head.

"I thought we could ask Marian to come over on Sunday for a barbecue," she continued and then visit the graves on Monday—early so that I can miss the boating traffic."

Sylvia nodded, but added, "It will be Marian *and* Owen." She took a sip of cold water and her head pounded harder.

"Owen, who?" her mother asked.

"He's a friend of the family who will begin working at Thurmont on Tuesday. He's staying with Marian until he can find an apartment," she told her mother. "I think Marian and her husband were like surrogate grandparents to him."

"Have you met him?" her mother asked.

"Yes," Sylvia answered, "He's a little bit of a nerd," she told her, "but very nice. He's just completed a masters program."

Their soup came and Sylvia was glad. She didn't want to answer any more questions about Owen. All Sylvia wanted to do was to lie down. She couldn't eat and pushed the bowl away.

"Are you all right?" her mother asked noticing Sylvia's pale face.

"I have a really, really bad headache," Sylvia told her mother faintly and rubbed at her temples. "I think it's turning into a migraine."

Her mother asked for Sylvia's bisque to go and the check. Sylvia was glad her mother drove home. She lay back as much as she could in the car seat and closed her eyes.

When they got home, she took off her good clothes and put on a t-shirt and sweat pant shorts and returned to the kitchen to hunt for some aspirin. She found her mother in the living room and Sylvia sat on the couch and hugged a pillow, looking out the French doors. She looked at the deck and to the sky and water beyond squinting in the bright afternoon light. Something was missing. At first, she couldn't figure it out and then it finally struck her. Her mask was missing! She stood up and went out to look at the deck. It was gone!

"Mother," she asked. "Have you seen my wooden mask?"

"Mask?" her mother replied, "I threw out the dead bit of wood that was on the deck," her mother said.

"Why?" Sylvia asked incensed. Her head was throbbing and her eyes were burning, "Why can't you respect my things? You never ask! You *never* give me a chance!" she shouted. The tears started to flow and she couldn't stop them. All of the pent up emotions and grief of the past few weeks were releasing like an avalanche. She ran up to her room and buried her head in the pillows and sobbed.

Her mother knocked on the door, "Sylvia, can I come in?" she asked.

"No! No!" Sylvia screamed. "Just leave me alone!" she cried miserably to her mother through the door.

Her mother hesitated for a minute and then Sylvia heard her footsteps go down the hallway and down the steps.

It was hours later when Sylvia woke up. She realized raising her head from a sticky, damp pillow that she had cried herself to sleep. Her eyes and face felt swollen and puffy and a dull headache still throbbed away. She lay in bed and listened for several minutes. The house was quiet and still. No breeze blew through the curtains.

She got up and went to the bathroom to splash cold water on her face, avoiding the mirror before she went downstairs. Her mother was gone. She looked briefly through the rooms and found a note on the kitchen table.

Syl,

I'm sorry about your wooden mask 'thing.'

I tossed it out into the yard, but could not find it.

You needed to cry.

I'll call you tomorrow and see you Saturday.

Marian and Owen will be here at 1 pm on Sunday.

Please call Marian to discuss the menu. I thought

I would pick up salmon steaks for the grill.

Love,

Mom

Sylvia put down the note and walked outside. It was twilight and she could barely see in the shadows of the growing darkness. Sylvia stepped off the deck and into the yard looking for the mask. She scuffled her feet in the long prickly grass. She knew she would need to mow it soon. It was useless to try to find the mask. The darkness had settled in around her and a brisk breeze came from the bay. Sylvia shivered in the darkening night. Sylvia returned to the house sad and discouraged.

She ate a piece of toast to quell her grumbling stomach, took more aspirin and drank a large glass of water for her throbbing head, stumbled up the stairs and fell back onto the bed and gratefully turned out the light and closed her eyes. She couldn't remember having a headache that hurt this badly – ever. Her roommate Gwen had frequent migraines and Sylvia remembered her lying in the dark, as still as could be. On those days, she only whispered to Gwen and stayed out of their dorm room as much as possible. Now she understood why. This was horrible.

That night Sylvia dreamed about Gran and thought for a moment that she was in the house. The dream had been so real, but whatever Gran had been trying to tell her in the dream, Sylvia couldn't quite catch. Gran kept repeating something and Sylvia was frustrated that she couldn't quite hear what she said. When Gran started fading away in the dream, Sylvia cried for her not to go, but instead, woke up. She lay in bed trying to think of what Gran's message could be. The pearly pinkish gray light of dawn lit up the bedroom window. For a moment, she was disoriented, wondering where she was and why. Then the memory of the day before –the attorney, the headache, shouting at her mother and the futile search for the Green Man mask came back. She lay still in bed, assessing her head. Her headache was thankfully gone. She breathed deeply the cold fresh air that entered the open windows.

Thinking of the mask, she hopped out of bed grabbed a sweatshirt against the morning's chill and ran down the stairs and outside. The grass was still wet with dew. It chilled her bare feet. Goose bumps dotted her legs like a bad rash. She put on the sweatshirt and began to look for the mask, hugging her arms around herself.

She looked around wondering where her mother might have tossed it. Since the grass was getting long and, it would be difficult to see anything lying flat. She continued to look in the perimeter of the deck area. Finally, she spotted it, near the small grove of trees at the edge of the property a few feet from the side deck.

As she walked toward the mask, a sharp wind blew up. Dust, dirt and sand whirled. Sylvia rubbed her eyes; the flying dirt and sand stuck in her eyes. Through her gritty eyelids, she thought she saw a bright, green flash of light. Dazzled, Sylvia gasped when she opened her eyes. Before her stood what she thought was a great green angel as the air shimmered around the figure in front of her. This time, he was not just living wood and a cloak of brown leaves. Now he wore a verdant green mask of leaves, only now it was a head on top of a six-foot-plus body. Leaves, real leaves that resembled brocaded fabric covered the body that looked like clothing. His skin was a rich variety of browns and grays with a fine, knotty grain polished to perfection. It moved with him. It was living wood!

Sylvia tried to talk, but found her mouth opening and closing, with words that would not come.

"Good morning, Sylvia," the being greeted her with a voice as deep as a bassoon and as rich as a cello.

"Wh-who, who—,what, who?" Sylvia finally stammered, her voice barely above a whisper.

"I am the Green Man," he answered.

"Why are you here?" she asked completely befuddled.

"I have been called, I heard the cry, and I have returned," he stated quietly.

She still looked puzzled and the Green Man looked deep into her eyes.

"I told you before. You are part of this pattern," he told her. "You have a gift we need."

"Me?" her voice squeaked out. "What pattern? I don't understand."

"I'll be with you on this journey," he said, "never fear."

Before she could say anything, the Green Man disappeared. He was simply 'gone.' Sylvia's eyes widened and she looked around her. No one was around. She was on her own.

CHAPTER SEVEN

Sunsets and rainbows, green forest and restive blue seas,
All naturally colored things are my siblings. We have played
Together on the floor of the world. Since the first stone looked up
At the stars.
--Maya Angelou

Sylvia stood and stared at the spot where she had seen the Green Man. The chilling combination of the dewy grass and fresh morning air drove her inside to put on warm socks and slippers. Sylvia pondered the Green Man's words over a cup of her usual café au lait. She had carried it into the living room and now sat, curled up in her favorite spot on the couch, staring out the French doors. The sun had risen now and the sky was changing from pink to blue. As odd as it had been, Sylvia did not feel crazy or that the Green Man's appearance had been a dream. He was absolutely real and surprisingly she felt very much at peace. But, she was puzzled. The Green Man said he had been called. Who called him, she wondered? What cry was he talking about and what pattern was she involved in? What gift? She didn't have any answers.

She grabbed a fuzzy afghan that was lying folded on the couch, wrapped it around her and sat down at the computer. She logged onto the Internet to do some searching. Many, many of the sites discussed the history of the foliate face; others sold various types of artwork depicting the Green Man from jewelry to paintings, sculptures and t-shirts. Videos of ancient carvings in churches were on youtube.com. Mike Harding's website was easily the most complete, but it didn't answer her questions. The consensus was that he was a mysterious figure with only guesses as to why he was carved and blessed and touted in nearly every culture. She watched short videos on youtube.com but no answers came from the mysterious faces filmed with unique musical overlays. The Green Man alluded to a 'call' to him and about a pattern. None of the research gave even a glimmer of understanding about this. Frustrated with not finding the answer she wanted, she picked up the phone and called Marian, to ask if she had books on the Green Man.

Owen answered with a bright, "Good Morning." Unused to hearing his voice, a startled and distracted Sylvia stared at the phone for a second. She heard a hesitant and questioning "Hello?" and finally answered.

"Hi, Owen. It's Sylvia," she said.

"Hi," he replied warmly. "How are you?" he asked.

"Fine," she answered, "Could I talk to Marian for a minute, please?"

"Sure," he told her. "Just a sec."

Sylvia heard him place a hand over the phone and call to Marian telling her Sylvia was on the phone.

It was another moment or two until the extension picked up and Marian said, "Hello, Sylvia. How are you?"

"I'm all right," Sylvia said politely. "I was wondering if you could help me?" she asked.

"If I can," Marian told her, "of course."

"Well, I've become really intrigued by the Green Man," Sylvia told her. "I thought you might have some books about him," and she hesitated before she went on, "and I wondered if I might borrow them?"

"Certainly you can borrow the books," Marian told her. "I have a couple of books and a pamphlet or two from when I was touring England. If you want them right away, I'll need your help in locating them," she told her. "You haven't seen my library yet, but it's *very* disorganized," she told her. She put the emphasis on 'very,' but knowing Marian's tidy home, Sylvia didn't give it a thought.

"Okay," Sylvia told her trying not to sound too anxious, "Is this morning all right?"

"Absolutely," Marian said. "I'll be expecting you."

"I'll be over shortly," Sylvia told Marian as they said goodbye anxious to find answers.

As she showered, another sharp pang of grief struck Sylvia and she let tears flow with the water. Gran would have been someone she could have talked with about the Green Man, no matter how odd or crazy it seemed. Marian had become almost like a surrogate grandmother to her, but Sylvia wasn't ready to share this information with Marian. Not yet, at least. She dressed quickly and rushed over to Marian's.

When she arrived at Marian's, Owen answered the door with a grin on his face.

"Hi, Sylvia," he said, grinning mischievously. "I don't think you know what you've gotten yourself into," he told her as he led her down the hallway.

He was so tall; Sylvia had to tilt her head back to look up at him and returned his warm grin with a puzzled smile wondering what he meant by his comment.

She soon found out. Sylvia had not been in Marian's library. When Owen ushered her into the room, Sylvia stood with an expression of shock and surprise. She suddenly understood Owen's grinning face. Three walls were filled with built-in bookshelves. Shiny warm, golden oak bookshelves crammed with books gleamed in the sunlight from two long windows with diamond-paned leaded glass that let in the morning sunshine. Boxes and boxes and boxes of books that had not been unpacked were around the room. Marian was sitting in a scarlet high-backed wing chair, going through a large box of books. On the fourth wall, a high mantled stone fireplace was paneled in creamy colored wood that added light to the room.

She looked up and smiled at Sylvia when she came in. "As you can see, Sylvia," she said waving her hand that took in the numerous boxes stacked around the room, "This is one of my tasks that I put off when I moved back to the States. Sorry, it's such a mess," she apologized.

"That's okay," Sylvia said. "Where do you want me to start?"

Marian sighed and replied, "The books in these boxes need to be unpacked and put on shelves. They're mostly books on history that Bran used in his teaching," she told Sylvia. "I didn't have the heart to find them other homes. I guess you and Owen could start shelving them there," she said pointing to an area to the left and right of the fireplace. "I have an eclectic collection that can go over there," she pointed. What Sylvia appeared to be a blank paneled wall was actually cleverly built cupboard. Owen walked over and opened one to reveal row upon row of shelves.

"Come on, Syl," Owen said. "No time like the present," he commented. "Let's get started."

A little sigh escaped from Sylvia this time. She hoped no one heard it. She was anxious to find the books on the Green Man. Sylvia scanned titles as she handed books up to Owen.

"Most of these are books on the American Revolution," she commented.

"Yeah," Owen said. "Bran taught early American history to the Brits," he told her. "Bran's field was the revolutionary war and he got my Dad stuck in Civil War history." Owen shook his head. "We have rows and rows of books on the Civil war in my house," he told her. "And, I've been to every Civil War battlefield, monument and museum in existence," he told her. "I learned to walk at Gettysburg," he told her.

Sylvia looked up at him unbelievingly.

"Seriously," Owen told her. "I even have proof of me toddling to a Civil War cannon."

Sylvia shook her head, at a loss for words and turned her attention back to Marian and the quest for the Green Man books.

"Do you have any ideas where the Green Man books might be?" Sylvia finally asked Marian.

Marian looked up at her and answered, "Unfortunately, in one of these boxes," Marian told her. "I had picked up a couple of books when touring Scotland and Rosslyn Cathedral and a couple more in the London area." Marian looked at her questioningly but didn't comment on Sylvia's obvious rush to find the books.

They worked in companionable silence. Marian commented on titles that had special meaning or broke into a hum when she was concentrating. Sylvia scanned book titles by the handful and handed them to Owen to place on the shelf. The number of empty boxes grew. After more than an hour passed, Sylvia was becoming bored, anxious and tired.

"Found them!" The glad cry came from Marian. She triumphantly pulled three or four books from the box near her chair. Sylvia rushed over.

"Basford, the classic," Marian told her as she handed her a large paperback, "Anderson, wordy, but wonderful," she continued giving Sylvia another book.

In the end, Sylvia had a stack of four books by various authors and a pamphlet on the Green man that Marian had picked up on a church tour. She flipped through the books quickly. She was eager to read.

"Hmm," Owen commented looking over her shoulder as she leafed through the many photographs in the Basford book, "He looks rather gruesome, doesn't he?"

Sylvia nodded in response and added, "Some are gruesome, but several are beautiful," she said. "Some of the artwork on the Internet is incredible. Look!" she said pointing, "These were likely bombed in the recent wars in the Middle East," she commented looking at carvings from Iran.

Marian agreed, "You see the Green Man mostly in gardens and decorating older architecture here in the states," she told them. "Look at this pamphlet," she continued, "the art deco pieces are lovely."

"What is this? 'Tetes de Feuilles?'" she asked completely butchering the French.

"I'm a little rusty, but I think it is 'face of leaves," Owen said. "Appropriate," he commented.

They were silent for a moment, gazing at a particularly handsome Green Man.

Marian broke the silence, "Let's finish up here and I'll treat you both to lunch," she said.

"Marian, you don't have to do that," Sylvia protested.

"You helped me out tremendously," she insisted. "If you hadn't asked for these books, I'd have probably left these books and memories for months more," she said.

"All right," Owen said briskly, "You're the boss, Marian," he said.

"Come on Kemosabe," he said to Sylvia. "Let's finish up." He held out a hand to pull her up as she was kneeling beside Marian.

They spent another half hour placing books on the shelves and Owen took the empty boxes to the barn to break them down for recycling. Sylvia went in search of Marian.

"I thought we could go into town to the pub on Main Street," Marian told Sylvia. "I haven't been there in years, but they've rehabbed it from its former glory as the county's notorious biker bar into a decent restaurant. I was reading they had started micro-brewing," she said glancing at Owen with a smile.

He grinned back nodding.

"Sounds great," Sylvia said remembering where the restaurant was. When she was growing up, there would be several motorcycles parked in front, and squeezed into the infinitesimal parking lot at the pub's back alley.

They piled into Marian's ancient Volvo wagon and headed to town with Marian insisting that Owen drive. The pub was quiet and they sat out on the deck and waited for a waitress to come. Since the busy weekend boating traffic wouldn't start until that afternoon, the waitress took her time to coming to their table. Eventually, they ordered their drinks and burgers highly recommended by Marian. They munched on a crab appetizer medley that Marian had ordered. Only a few people strolled from shop to shop on this bright spring day. It was pleasant to sit anonymously behind sunglasses and watch the world go by. The weekend traffic was just beginning to clog the streets as they ate their lunches. They watched the line of SUV's and boats making their way down the narrow main street that parked vehicles on both sides.

"The Pennsylvania Navy," she commented quietly.

"What's that?" Owen asked.

"The Pennsylvania Navy," Sylvia said, "The boaters coming in for the weekend. That's what Gran and Mom call them."

"Look," she said pointing to the license plates, "The majority of boaters are from Pennsylvania, but there are a lot from Delaware and New Jersey too."

"Mom loves to complain about all of them coming into town," she said.

"Knowing your mother, though" Marian commented, "she would likely be hard pressed to deny the positive economic impact on the town."

Sylvia giggled, envisioning her mother's face at this comment. "You're absolutely right," she told Marian.

Curiosity overcoming her, Sylvia asked Marian a question that had nagged at her for a while. "How did you and Gran become such great friends?" she asked her. "I don't remember her mentioning it or ever knowing that you existed for years since you were in England."

Marian laughed as she answered, "Well," she said, "I think we were trying to break the mold in the sixties. I met your Grandmother at a march on Washington, DC. We ended up near one another in the crowd by accident and found we were from the same area. I was 'supposed' to be the model faculty wife," she said adding sotto voce, "and I wasn't." She continued, "Your grandmother was breaking out from under your grandfather's conservative thumb. I'll never forget how angry he was when we got arrested at a sit in."

"What?" Sylvia asked incredulously, "Arrested? Gran or Mom *never* told me about that!"

"Oh, yes," Marian told them. "It was a peaceful demonstration against Viet Nam, but everyone's emotions were running high and we were an example, I think. But, your grandfather! I thought he might consider divorce over that! He found out he couldn't control Holly," she mused.

Marian continued to regale them with stories of how she and Sylvia's grandmother had marched, protested, written letters and worked for various causes.

Their food came and Sylvia was thoughtful while she ate. Her mother had always accused her grandmother of being a hippie or flower child. True, she fit the part in some ways. Sylvia remembered her grandmother's long snowy white hair, kept braided, either long or wound around her head. Gran was flippant towards current fashions and always wore comfortable loose dresses, jeans, clogs or Birkenstocks. She hadn't known of all of her work during the sixties.

"Penny," she heard Owen's voice through her memories.

Sylvia came back to the present with a jolt realizing Owen and Marian were quietly watching her. "I was thinking about Gran," she said, "and the life I never knew about."

"I'm supposed to ask you about Sunday's menu," Sylvia told Marian. "Mom said she would pick up some salmon steaks to grill. Any ideas for the rest of the meal?" she asked her.

"Would you like me to bring a salad with herbal vinaigrette to accompany your salmon steaks?" Marian asked.

Sylvia nodded enthusiastically. "That would be wonderful," she told her.

"What if I bring some French bread?" Owen offered.

"All right," Sylvia said. "Both sound great."

"I have an excellent recipe for a dilled pasta salad if you would like it," Marian told Sylvia. "It's very easy to put together."

"That would be terrific," Sylvia said to her.

When they went back to Marian's house, Sylvia gathered up the books on the Green Man while Marian looked for the cookbook. She came back and handed it to Sylvia.

"I marked the page with the Dill Pasta Salad," she told her. "But, you'll enjoy reading through it. The ideas and recipes are tremendous," she said. "It's too early for dill to be up in the garden, you'll need to pick it up at the market."

"Thanks!" Sylvia said. "It sounds wonderful—and easy for a novice cook like me," she said.

"You'll learn," Marian said. "Just keep experimenting and having fun with it," she advised.

"What are you doing this afternoon?" she asked Sylvia.

"Probably reading these," she said smiling and hugging the books on the Green Man to her. "Thank you again."

Marian hugged her.

"Good," Marian said. "We'll see you on Sunday."

"Sounds good," Sylvia answered. She looked around and not seeing Owen said, "Tell Owen I said goodbye."

"I will," Marian said.

Sylvia settled in her favorite corner of the couch with Marian's books and began reading as soon as she got home. The Basford book had a brief introduction to her theory of the Green Man. It was filled with incredible black and white photos of Green Men throughout Europe and the Middle East. The Harding book was fascinating and built upon his website. She liked his comparisons and theory of how craftsmen traveled from Asia to Europe carving Green Men. Marian had been correct, the Anderson book was wordy but compelling. She read swiftly, feeling comfortable with the history. She was still seeking an answer to something mysterious. Some of her questions were unformed in her mind. The last chapter dealt with the Green Man and his return in the new age as a symbol to protect the environment. In a way, it made Sylvia think of the old Captain Planet cartoons she had seen as a child and the Swamp Thing comic. She wracked her brain, hadn't there been a Swamp Thing television show? She had seen a rerun and thought it pretty lame and dated. Some would probably consider it campy. She went out to the deck and rested her elbows on the railing. She watched the clouds turn into dark purple islands against a teal blue sea. She was lost in thought of the history, theory and mythology she had read. She felt as if she was on the brink of a revelation, but could not quite get to it.

"That's it!" she said out loud and she remembered the Swamp Thing's costume. The Green Man that appeared to her reminded her of the great actor that played the swamp thing. He was like that, yet different. 'Her' Green man wasn't in a mask or a costume. His face was more like the carvings she had seen in the books, and a bit like the masks for sale on the internet, only alive and not frozen into the mask like silence. That was the only revelation she had. She sighed. No answers.

She heard and felt a little breeze. Turning her face to it, she glanced at something out of the corner of her right eye. It was the Green Man.

"Oh, my God!" she said.

Once again, the Green Man chuckled with a deep, rich laughter.

"I told you this morning, some people think so."

"You scared me!" she said. "What are you doing here?"

It didn't feel surreal that he was there and she was surprised that it seemed 'normal' to be having a conversation with this towering green and brown figure. His hand was resting on the railing of the deck. His skin, or whatever it was, looked like polished wood. She had the urge to touch it. She could see the graining along the back of his hand and down his fingers. The brocade-like garment was like clothing, but it wasn't clothing. It was different. It was overlapped and woven leaves in varying shades of green that lent it a rich look similar to brocade.

"Just visiting," he said to her, "and curious as to what you have learned today."

"Not much," Sylvia admitted. "You seem to be a mystery throughout the ages," she said. "Not to be rude, but you're ancient," she told him.

The Green Man nodded, still looking amused and Sylvia continued, realizing he had a great sense of humor. She smiled a small, shy smile in return to his wry expression.

"I feel as though I'm missing a link, but I haven't a clue as to what that link is," she told him. "Actually, there are so many links between the religions, history, mythology, paganism, environmentalism, literature…" she stopped for a moment.

The Green Man stood patiently, still listening.

"The artwork, the renditions are beautiful," she said blandly, "and some grotesque."

"They each have their niche throughout history," he told her. "What else?" he prodded.

"I don't know," Sylvia, said, with frustration tingeing her voice. "An archetype for all?" she queried. "But, how are you a guide, for whom?"

He nodded approvingly at her questioning revelations.

"I don't know what you want from me?" she said with an unusual tone of sarcasm in her voice. "El Khdir guided Moses, for Christ's sake – not a… a…," she hesitated not knowing how to label herself. "You, Gran and, I think Marian," she added as an afterthought, "all believe I'm someone…," she trailed off for a moment. "I haven't a clue as to any '*gift*' that I might have. I'm just trying to get through the day, the week, my *life*, for God's sake! I don't even know *what* I want to do with my life, and you're all hinting at something mysterious *and* beautiful. This is very confusing," she complained.

"Relax," the Green Man said in a soothing tone. "You do have gifts, but you'll need to discover them on your own. Your life," he told her, "is of your own making. Keep seeking," he said in his deep, now quiet voice and then disappeared.

"Great," Sylvia said sarcastically, "I'm supposed to learn *and* relax from a guru who probably doesn't exist and is made from leaves. This is pretty damn crazy," she said to the darkening sky. "Maybe I need to be on Prozac or another damn, fine psychotropic," Sylvia asked the stars and sky. She huffed as she turned to go inside.

"Oh, Gran," she said miserably to the room as she crawled into bed. "I wish you were here. I think I'm losing it."

CHAPTER EIGHT

Nothing can bring you peace but yourself.
--Ralph Waldo Emerson

Sylvia had every intention of getting up early and going to the grocery store before her mother arrived the next day, but she overslept. She had had a restless night filled with dreams of talking Green Men from the books. She had been frustrated in the dreams because they were all talking to her and she couldn't hear what they were saying. "Yap, yap, yap" the bodiless faces spoke to her. In another dream, she had been walking with 'her' Green Man. They were walking down a long road. It looked as though he was comforting her or counseling her. She leaned against him for support. When she woke, she still felt the comforting weight of his arm around her. She closed her eyes and could almost smell the spicy green scent that he exuded; see the detail of the green, leaf brocade on his arm and the life pulsing in the wood-like skin. What had he been telling her?

The bedclothes were a mess. Obviously, she had tossed and turned quite a bit. Pillows were on the floor and the sheet had been pulled out from the bottom of the bed. Sylvia glanced at the clock beside the bed.

"Oh, no!" she groaned. It was after 9 a.m. Her mother would probably arrive in the next hour.

Quickly she left a brief note on the kitchen table, grabbed Marian's cookbook and headed for the grocery store.

After a few minutes of shopping, she vowed she would never go to the grocery story again on a Saturday morning. Screaming babies and fussy, demanding, sticky-fingered toddlers whining for every kind of treat imaginable filled the crowded aisles. Sylvia fought to get down aisle after aisle and eventually gave up. She found refuge for a few moments getting coffee at the store's deli and consulted the cookbook for the ingredients. Hyped up on strong coffee she bravely made her way through the crowded store as quickly as possible. She added some chicken for this evening along with fresh milk and a few other sundry items. Her grocery order was peppered with favorites of hers and her mother's before she checked out.

Boating traffic was thick, and it took Sylvia twice as long to get through town than it usually did. Somehow the large vehicles, towing heavy trailers laden with all sorts of boats, wended their way through the narrow one-way street through town to get to the local marinas. Groups of tourists roamed the streets hanging onto children as they licked and dripped ice cream from cones and crossed the street without looking. Sylvia nearly hit a group that rushed across the street when their party called to them from the porch of the local crab house. She wished there was another way home and gritted her teeth until she left the town behind. When she turned onto Bayside Drive, Sylvia breathed a sigh of relief that she had arrived before her mother.

She put on hot water for the pasta and brewed a pot of coffee and sat down to read the recipe. It seemed easy enough. She was glad the grocery store had fresh dill available in the produce section. She opened the package and touched the feathery herb. It smelled faintly like the dill pickles and looked like an exotic feather. She almost hated to cut it.

She added the pasta when the water boiled and set the timer, drained the dill relish and chopped up the fresh dill and part of a red pepper. When the pasta was done, she could put everything together. Marian had recommended putting it together the day before.

Her mother came in just as she had stirred all the ingredients together.

"Hi," she said. "It smells wonderful in here. What are you making?"

"Hi Mom," Sylvia greeted her going over to give her a perfunctory hug and kiss. "It's a dill pasta salad that Marian told me about. I thought it would be great with the grilled salmon tomorrow."

"I'll say!" her mother said enthusiastically. "It will be perfect. Speaking of salmon, I need to get the cooler from the car and get the food into the refrigerator. It's starting to get warm outside."

"I thought I was just hot from cooking," Sylvia said; now noticing the bright shining sun and the rising heat of the day. "Maybe we should open up more windows to get the breeze through the house."

"I'll go get the salmon and my things," her mother said. "Why don't you get the windows?"

Sylvia covered the pasta with plastic wrap and put it in the refrigerator and went to open the windows. They settled into the living room in front of the open French doors and floor to ceiling windows enjoying the soft breeze. Sylvia looked out at the bay. It was filling up. More and more sailboats dotted the horizon and jet skis and powerboats zoomed back and forth. It would be a busy weekend on the water. Sylvia wondered how the water would be for swimming. Thinking the same, her mother asked if she had been in swimming yet.

"No," Sylvia answered her. "I honestly didn't think of it."

"What did you do yesterday?" her mother asked her, curious.

"Owen and I unpacked and shelved several boxes of Marian's books that had been sitting in her library since her return to the States," Sylvia told her. "And then Marian took us to lunch, I came home and read a bit. It was a quiet day."

"How are things at the bank?" she asked her mother.

"The usual frenetic pace," her mother told her. "But, you know, I love it," she said smiling. "I hadn't realized how much I had missed working," she confessed to her daughter. Instead of grief, her face was happier and more contented.

"It's probably therapy for you," Sylvia told her.

"Yes, I think it is," her mother answered her, surprised at Sylvia's insight.

"Are you getting hungry?" Sylvia asked. "I missed breakfast, rushing off to the grocery store."

"Lunch would be great," her mother told her. "Why don't you clean off the table on the deck and I'll make some sandwiches."

Sylvia went out to wipe off the table and chairs of an umbrella covered table on the deck, clearing off some of the pollen with a damp towel. She went in to get cool drinks and utensils and nearly bumped into her mother coming with a tray loaded with all that they needed.

"I thought we could taste test your pasta salad," she told Sylvia. "It looks and smells wonderful."

"Marian recommended it," Sylvia told her. "She said it gets better each day."

"It's excellent now," her mother commented taking a bite. "Try some."

Sylvia did and found that it was excellent. They ate quietly watching the boats on the water. The heat had risen and the breeze had subsided. It was starting to feel sultry as they finished their lunch.

"What's the plan for the rest of the day?" Sylvia asked.

"I suppose we should get some wine for tomorrow," her mother answered. "What did you decide on for the rest of the menu?" she asked.

"Marian will be bringing a salad with her owns herbal vinaigrette. Owen will bring bread or rolls, we have the salmon and pasta salad," Sylvia stated.

"Good," her mother said. "That leaves getting the wine and some sort of dessert." She paused, thinking for a minute. "Since it's hot," she continued, "what do you think of sorbet for dessert?"

"Fine," Sylvia said.

"Do you want to come with me to pick up the wine and sorbet?" her mother asked.

I'll be happy to come to keep you company and get the wine," Sylvia told her, but I'll probably stay in the car while you're at the grocery store. I had my fill of grocery stores today!"

"Was it that bad?" her mother asked.

"Busy and crowded with screaming babies and fussy, sticky toddlers," Sylvia commented. "The lines were horrendous! Ugh!"

"I'll only be a minute," her mother said when they pulled into the busy grocery store lot after picking up the wine. Sylvia had talked her mother into picking up some of the local microbrew as well, imagining the look on Owen's face when she would offer it. He had raved at the lager the day before at the pub.

"All right," Sylvia said. Sylvia pulled out her book.

"What are you reading?" her mother asked catching a glimpse of the cover.

"Remember Marian's unusual door knocker?" Sylvia asked her.

"No, not really," her mother admitted.

"Well, I was intrigued by it, and Marian loaned me a book about it," she stated.

"Oh," her mother said, clearly not understanding or really caring. Her reading tastes were bent on finances and investments with an occasional gory mystery thrown in.

Sylvia didn't care whether her mother remembered the Green Man door knocker or not. She thought it best that her mother was naïve about the Green Man for the moment.

"Good luck in there!" Sylvia added looking around at the number of cars in the lot.

Her mother made a funny face at her and said 'thanks' sarcastically as she turned to the entrance of the market.

Sylvia paged through the book. Nothing, in particular, jumped out at her. Maybe she was trying too hard. She put it down and looked at the people going in and coming out of the store.

Eventually, her mother came out pushing a cart filled with bags. She put them in the trunk of the car.

"I thought you were only going in for one or two things," Sylvia teased her mother.

"I know," her mother replied, "but, I thought we should have a couple of things for an appetizer too," she said. "I picked up some steaks for tonight, cheese and crackers and fresh fruit, vegetables and dip for tomorrow's dinner. Plus they had some excellent pastries for tomorrow morning that were on sale."

They drove home and spent the day relaxing, not really doing anything. Sylvia lazily watched the boats sail up and down the bay intermittently reading the books on the Green Man while her mother read a popular novel.

Dusk was falling when her mother asked her if she was hungry. Sylvia shrugged.

"I'm not really hungry," she said to her mother, "just munchy."

"Me too," her mother agreed. "What if we put the steaks in the freezer and break into the cheese and crackers and open up a bottle of wine?"

"Mmm," Sylvia answered, "Sounds wonderful."

Her mother went out to the kitchen and prepared a tray of fresh fruit, cheeses and some crackers. She opened up a bottle of pinot noir that she had purchased to drink with the steaks. She took the tray out to the living room and set it on the coffee table. They ate and drank. Sylvia took her second glass of wine and went out on the deck to watch the sunset. Tonight it was brilliant stripes of peach, coral, and fuchsias. It was breathtaking. She watched the stars appear, one by one, as the sunset moved to dusk and onward to the night. When the night had fully fallen, the sky was brilliantly scattered with stars that twinkled in the inky blackness over the bay.

It had been nice to kick back and relax today, she thought. The weariness from her previous restless night caught up with her and she suddenly felt very sleepy. She went inside.

"I didn't sleep very well last night," Sylvia told her mother. "I'm going to turn in."

Her mother looked up from reading her book, "Oh?" her mother questioned her with a look. Are you all right?" she asked.

"I'm okay, just tired," Sylvia replied.

"Okay," her mother said, turning back to the novel she was reading, "Good night," she said vaguely, getting caught up in the book again.

The next morning dawned much too quickly, but Sylvia felt well rested and not disturbed by odd dreams. The Green Man entered into a dream or two again, but his comforting presence felt right to Sylvia. She beamed as she bounced down the stairs to the kitchen.

"Good morning, Syl," her mother greeted. "Did you sleep better? How do you feel?"

"I feel great," Sylvia told her smiling. "What a beautiful day."

She went inside to get a cup of coffee and a cinnamon bun, that her mother had picked up the day before. She rejoined her mother after she heated the cinnamon bun in the microwave.

"What time are Marian and Owen coming?" she asked.

"I told Marian about 5:30 tonight," her mother answered. "Why?"

"Actually, I would like to look for a cordless phone and go to the mall to start looking for a suit or something appropriate for an interview.

"Want company?" her mother asked.

"Yeah, sure," Sylvia answered.

"Let's finish our breakfast and let me read the paper before we go," her mother said. "Here are some ads to check to see if someone has phones on sale."

Sylvia sat cross-legged in the chair and spread the advertisements on the table before her, holding them down with her coffee cup and plate. The breeze was slight and ruffled the corners of the papers.

After an hour or two of shopping with her mother, Sylvia regretted including her mother in the shopping trip. Shopping for the phone had been all right. In fact, her mother had talked her into an excellent cordless set. Their attempt at clothes shopping was another story! Everything Sylvia tried on that she liked was flawed in some way in her mother's eyes. It was either the length was too short or too long. The outfit was the wrong fabric or the wrong color. Sylvia was so frustrated she wanted to scream. She fell in love with a lovely linen sleeveless dress. It was an ankle length, pale sage green linen dress with white leaf designs embroidered around the neckline and around the hem. It was simple, yet elegantly casual. She thought of Owen coming that evening and wanted to wear something pretty. Even though her mother fussed about the price and the color, Sylvia defiantly insisted on buying it and she firmly took it to the counter and paid for it.

It was later than they had expected when they returned home. Her Mom hurriedly worked on the appetizers while Sylvia set the table outside. The lovely day was turning into a perfect evening. The humidity of the day before had dissipated, blown away by the bay breeze. What was left was a warm day, blending the best of late spring and early summer. Sylvia changed into her new dress.

"It's lovely," her mother said. "Don't you want to save it for a special occasion?" she asked.

"No," Sylvia said firmly. "I just love it and want to wear it to-night." She had brushed long hair until it gleamed, left it loose and added dangling white freshwater pearl earrings. She was barefoot and comfortable.

Marian and Owen arrived promptly at 5:30. Owen carried in the salad and a bottle of wine tied with a ribbon. Marian held a bottle of her homemade dressing and a loaf of French bread.

"Come in," Sylvia said, inviting them inside. She introduced Owen to her Mother and giving him a shy smile, took the salad bowl.

"Thanks," he said, smiling at her. He handed the wine to her mother and said, "Nice to meet you," and held out his hand.

"Same," her mother replied shaking his hand.

Sylvia took the dressing and bread from Marian as her mother asked them to come into the living room. She had put the crackers, cheese, and other hors d'oeuvres on the coffee table.

"Syl, will you bring in the wine, please?" her mother asked her, leading Marian and Owen into the living room.

Sylvia took a minute to open the wine before she went in to join the others. Her mother was asking Owen about his degree and the position he would be starting on Tuesday.

He was amiable to the questions and answered with alacrity. Sylvia handed him one of the microbrews. He hesitated a moment and smiled gratefully at Sylvia's mischievous smile and continued to respond her mother's barrage of questions. Sylvia handed wine to her mom and Marian. When she filled her glass, she saw Marian patting the seat next to her on the couch. Sylvia sat down next to her.

"Pretty dress," Marian whispered.

"Thanks," Sylvia whispered back, flashing a smile. She sipped at her wine allowing the conversation to flow around her. She found she enjoyed watching everyone interact. Sylvia pulled herself back to the conversation, refilled everyone's wine glasses and went back to the kitchen to open another bottle from the refrigerator. When she came back, she heard her mother talking to Owen, sotto voce, about her difficulty in pushing Sylvia to find a viable career.

Owen defended her decision regarding a Liberal Arts education, stating for her mother that it made her more employable. She walked in on their conversation.

"I'll be getting my resume together this week," she said quietly, clearly indicating, in her voice, that she had heard their conversation.

Her mother looked uncomfortable.

Owen spoke up, "Once I get my foot in the door at Thurmont," he said, "I can keep my ear out if any positions open up."

"Thank you," Sylvia said, "I may take you up on that." She turned to her mother, "Would you like me to light the grill?"

"That would be great," her mother told her.

"Need help?" Owen asked.

"No, I don't think so," Sylvia said. "I believe I can handle it, but you're welcome to come out and supervise," she told him with a smile.

He followed her out to the deck and she pushed a couple of buttons and ---poof—the gas flame ignited and the grill was lit.

"Hey, I'm sorry if I stirred up something in there," he said referring to the conversation about a job.

"No need for an apology," Sylvia told him. "It's a sore point for my mother and me. It's definitely not a new argument. I wish she would give credit. I have half a brain and I'm not eight years old anymore."

"You know, my Mom complains about the same thing from my grandmother," he said smiling, "so I guess it continues with Moms despite your age."

They stood, leaning against the deck railing, sipping their wine.

"Do you swim from here?" Owen asked nodding to the small stretch of beach at the end of Gran's place. The neighborhood curved around a small cove on the bay with marinas at one end. The other end had a small wooded point that jutted out into the water. The houses that faced the water had a relatively narrow beach and Gran's front yard was perched just above the beach at the center of the cove. Several had piers that stretched out into the bay. Far across the water, you could glimpse the shoreline on the other side of the bay.

"Yes," Sylvia said. "It's quite beautiful. It's a rocky beach, but a few feet out, the bottom is sandy and it goes out at a gradual slope. It's lovely on sweltering days and turns as warm as bathwater in the fall."

"I haven't tested the water yet this year," Sylvia told him. "If you ever want to swim, you're welcome to come over," she invited.

"Thanks," Owen said, "I may take you up on that as the humidity rises."

Her Mother brought out the salmon. "If you two can keep an eye on these salmon steaks, Marian and I will bring out the rest of the food. They shouldn't take too long," her mother told her.

Sylvia nodded in response. She took the salmon steaks out of their marinade. They hissed wonderfully as she placed them on the greased foil that protected them from the flames on the hot grill. Fragrant steam wafted upwards toward them. Sylvia sniffed appreciatively.

"Mom was right. These will only take a few minutes," she told Owen and Sylvia turned the grill down a little bit.

She looked out over the water. A golden glow seemed to settle over everything as twilight began.

"The water traffic has calmed down quite a bit," she commented as only a few sailboats were out in the water.

"There's not much of a breeze," Owen said. "They're likely catching the last bit before motoring into their slip."

"Do you sail?" Sylvia asked him.

"Used too, as a kid," he told her, "Marian and Bran belonged to the yacht club up the road here for years and years. Bran really enjoyed being out in a boat. I don't think Marian enjoyed it much. Usually, it was Bran, Dad and me," he mused. "They sold their boat when then left for England. I haven't had much time or opportunity for the last few years."

She turned the steaks. "Believe it or not, I practically grew up here and I have never sailed," she said. "Boats were one of the very few things Gran did not like."

"I don't have a boat anymore, but if you want to go out sometimes, I could teach you the basics. We can rent a boat at one of the marinas. I'm sure Marian still has contacts at the yacht club," he mentioned.

"That would be nice," Sylvia answered.

She looked at the steaks. "I think these are done," she said. "Can you let Marian and Mom know that everything is ready?"

"Sure," Owen said, "How about a refill of wine as well?" he asked.

Sylvia nodded, concentrating on the salmon and Owen went round the porch to refresh her wine. He informed Marian and Mary that the salmon steaks would be off the grill in a few minutes.

Sylvia double checked that the food was completely cooked and turned off the grill. She put the salmon steaks on a fresh platter that her mother had set near the grill and took the steaming plate to the table.

"Lovely," Marian told her, "and it looks like your salad turned out well," she said.

"Yes," Sylvia answered, "that's an excellent recipe. Can I keep the cookbook for a couple of days and copy out a few recipes?" she asked Marian.

"Certainly," Marian said to her.

The brief moments of tension between Sylvia and her mother melted over dinner with the additional wine. It was relaxed and peaceful. Marian kept them amused with stories when Sylvia remembered what Marian had shared yesterday.

"Mom," she said, "You never told me that Gran was an activist."

"Oh," her mother replied rolling her eyes a little bit, "your grandmother! I grew up being dragged around from rally to rally. She was always going on about one cause or another. It was about animals, the environment, a change in government...," her mother trailed off for a moment. "Your father and I gave her strict directions that she was not to influence you in that way."

"What?" Sylvia cried aghast. "Did you threaten her somehow?"

Her mother looked uncomfortable as the tension rose again. "You could say that your father gave her an ultimatum," she admitted.

"Oh, come now, Mary," Marian said calmly, patting her mother's hand. "Certainly Holly meant no harm. She was trying to share with you a part of her lifestyle that was vital to her and many others."

"Maybe so," answered Sylvia's mother stoutly, "but John and I didn't feel that Sylvia needed to be exposed to that while she was growing up. Basically, we told her to calm down and clam up on the causes or not see Sylvia."

Sylvia couldn't believe what she was hearing. Her parents had threatened to keep her from her grandmother! She had never known about that. It was difficult to hold her tongue, but she didn't want to make a scene in front of Owen and Marian. Usually, she stomped out of a room slamming a door to express her anger. Frustrated, she clenched her hands under the table.

"More wine?" Owen asked seeing her tensing up. He winked at her.

Sylvia gave him a curt nod and looked as grateful as she could as he filled her glass almost to the brim. She took a long drink and continued to listen, too angry to speak.

"Hmm," Marian mused, "Now I know why she backed down on some of her causes. She never said in all these years."

"You have to admit, Marian," Mary pushed the subject, "that some of those groups were somewhat radical and some of the people. My goodness, that local group was full of lunatics! Ted Jamison! That Maureen Davenport woman! Was she a nut case or what? Think of how many times they were in the paper for their demonstrations at Thurmont! Mother was arrested twice. It was so embarrassing!"

"You're right, Mary," Marian told her amicably, trying to make peace.

"I'll clear the table," Owen offered, getting up, changing the subject. "Sylvia, can you tell me where to put some of this stuff?"

Sylvia numbly got up to help too and together they loaded the dishwasher in a couple of minutes. Owen didn't push her into the conversation and she was glad. Owen filled her wine glass again and she took some sips and leaned back against the counter and closed her eyes.

"Thanks," she said.

"No problem," he said. "It sounds as though a lot of this was quite a shock."

"That's an understatement," Sylvia said bitterly. "I never, never knew about how horrible my parents were to Gran!" her voice trailed into silent anger.

"I know you probably don't want to hear this, but they thought it was for the best for you," he said to her.

Sylvia shook her head while she put the coffee on.

"Poor Gran!" Sylvia said, "I'm shocked she let them control her like that. She was so independent! Ask Marian and she'll tell you…" her voice trailed off as emotion swam to the surface once again. Sylvia quickly sipped more of her wine.

"She acquiesced because she loved you," Owen murmured.

"I know," Sylvia said, resigned. The tears were pricking behind her eyelids as a few started to fall down her cheeks. "I'm sorry," she said. "I wasn't able to cry for a long time, and now," she sniffed audibly.

"Now you can't seem to stop, right?" he finished.

She nodded and pulled out a tray from the cupboard. She put the coffee mugs, creamer, and sugar on the tray as well before she said, "I wish you had had the opportunity to meet her. She is," Sylvia paused with a shivery sigh, "She was pretty amazing," Sylvia said.

"I've gathered that," Owen murmured.

Owen returned to the deck while Sylvia went to splash cold water on her face. By the time Sylvia reappeared on the deck, Marian had her Mom calmed down and laughing over another story, but Sylvia couldn't let it go yet. She sat stiffly.

"Coffee's on," she announced when she sat down. She was still a little bristly.

"Thanks," her mother said. "I'll go in and get the dessert in just a minute."

"Marvelous dinner," Owen told them. "Thank you. I'm not used to these excellent meals. I'm getting spoiled between this and living at Marian's," he said.

"You're very welcome," Mary answered, smiling at him. She got up to get the dessert.

"Do you need help?" Marian asked.

"No, I'm fine," Mary told her. "I'll put everything on a tray and be out in just a minute."

"Are you all right?" Marian asked Sylvia quietly. "This must have been quite a shock to you."

Sylvia nodded to Marian, a little afraid to speak due to the emotions welling within her. Sylvia took a deep breath and stared out at the water and the blinking lights from the boats that started to fill the twilight on the bay.

"What a lovely evening," Marian commented as Mary returned to the deck with coffee and dessert. "Just look at the colors in the sky."

They all looked at the apricot and gold colors beginning to lace the horizon.

"The sunsets are spectacular here," Sylvia said. "I never get tired of watching the sky and the water. I try not to think that the stunning color is due to the pollution in Baltimore. I just know the sunsets are so peaceful. They bring happiness," she said simply.

"You are so much like your grandmother," her mother said hearing her comment.

Sensing another possible confrontation, Owen asked, "Would you like to go for a short walk on the beach before it gets too dark?"

"Sure," Sylvia said, finishing her coffee quickly "Let me go and get a pair of sandals." She stood up and took in as many dishes as she could carry. Sylvia placed them in the sink before running upstairs to get sandals.

"We'll be back in a couple of minutes," Sylvia said as they stepped off the deck.

Fortunately, the tide was out and the stretch of beach was wider than usual. It was rocky for the most part. The smooth washed stones of all sizes were a little difficult to walk on. Sylvia picked her way carefully over the rocks in her sandals and avoided some sharp pieces of glass.

"There's been more and more glass each year," Sylvia said, picking her way over the rocks and shaking her head. "It's amazing what you find down here. Some of the trash is a little alarming."

"Have you seen any fish kills?" Owen asked her.

"One or two in the last few of years," Sylvia said. "It hasn't been bad this far north," she told him.

Owen nodded. The sun had started to dip and the sky was turning from a fiery apricot to fuchsia joined with a deep aquamarine. The wake of a couple of powerboats sent small waves lapping at the shoreline in a rhythmic pattern. Sylvia started to calm down, and as she did so, she felt Owen's presence. Sylvia didn't want to admit even to herself that he had an effect on her. She tripped over a rock in the darkening twilight. Owen caught her hand and kept her from falling. Her hand tingled where he had held her hand.

"Thanks," she said, not wanting to let go of his hand. "We should probably turn back. We don't have a flashlight." She looked down at their hands, surprised and amazed how naturally they seemed to fit together.

"Okay," he said letting go of her hand.

They turned to walk back. The sky had turned a dark, dusky blue when they got back to the house and the stars had just begun to pop into the sky.

They were nearing the house and the darkness was gathering quickly. Her mother had lighted citronella candles on the deck and on the table, lighting their way. Owen and Sylvia made their way through the dark grass getting damp with dew. Marian and her mother were lingering over another cup of coffee chatting amiably.

"We should be going," Marian said as they returned. "Thank you, Mary and Sylvia, for a lovely dinner."

"Yes, thank you again," Owen said.

"You're welcome," Sylvia's mother told them. "Come back soon."

"Give me a call soon," Marian said to Sylvia.

Sylvia nodded at her. "I will. Good night," she said to them both, her stomach fluttered as her eye caught Owen's smile.

"Nice young man," her mother commented as they finished cleaning up.

"Yes," Sylvia agreed, "he is."

Her mother was cheerful and the tension gone. Sylvia yawned involuntarily. She was tired and didn't want to start an argument or discussion about the new information on Gran, but felt she had to say something.

"Mom," Sylvia said, "I can't believe you and Dad threatened Gran like that. Why didn't you tell me?"

"Sylvia, you were a child. You wouldn't have understood our reasons. Gran did," her mother answered her wearily. "That's why she complied with us."

"I don't agree," Sylvia said. "I think it was horrible!"

"Look, I don't want to argue tonight," her mother said. "I'm too worn out. I'm going to bed. We can talk about this another time with clearer heads."

Her mother went upstairs leaving Sylvia alone in the bright kitchen light. Steaming, Sylvia paced back and forth between the kitchen and living room. After her fifth time into the living room, she stopped to look out at the stars for a minute and realized she was weary too. Sylvia needed to talk to Marian. She seemed to be the one who knew more about Gran than she. It was surprising that she felt she grew up in this house and knew everything about Gran. Now everyone was portraying a stranger, albeit an interesting one. She was anxious to learn more. Sighing, she turned her thoughts back toward Owen. Her reaction to Owen was entirely different than with anyone she had ever dated and it surprised and frightened her a little bit. She had never been in a really serious relationship. She had never met anyone that she was genuinely interested in spending a great deal of time with. With Owen, it was quite different and more than surprising.

CHAPTER NINE

In God all that is is God.
In Him the smallest creature
Of the earth and sea
Is worth no atom less
Then you or me.
--Angelus Silesius

The humidity returned with the holiday. Sylvia felt sticky when she woke up. Her Mom was in her usual spot at the breakfast table, drinking coffee and reading the paper. Her bag was packed and sitting by the door.

"Morning, Syl," she greeted her daughter. "I thought I would get an early start this morning to beat the traffic. I know I mentioned going to the graves, but I can't. It's too fresh."

Sylvia went to the cupboard to get a mug. She was not awake this morning and was moving slowly. She nodded as she yawned and poured a cup of coffee and peered through slits of eyes in the bright morning light.

"Okay," she said sleepily.

"Can I take you out to breakfast?" her mother asked her.

"No, thanks," Sylvia said. "There are too many tourists."

Her mother nodded, understanding, "Do you want me to make some eggs?" she asked.

"No, thanks," said Sylvia, sipping her café au lait. "I'm going to have some of the fruit from last night," she told her mother, "and maybe a bowl of cereal."

Sylvia got her breakfast and joined her mother. If her mother was leaving early, she thought she might call her old roommate Gwen and see how she was doing.

As if reading her mind, her mother asked her, "Have you heard from Gwen?"

"We've e-mailed and texted a couple of times," Sylvia told her. "I was thinking of calling her today to see if she could come down for a visit. She's just started her new job, so I don't know."

They both chatted, avoiding the conversation of the previous night. After her Mom had left, Sylvia stripped the beds and worked on laundry. She decided to vacuum and dust and ended up mopping the kitchen floor while she had the chance. Sylvia was amazed how quickly a house could get dusty and was surprised at her own domesticity, blaming it on boredom. Knowing Gwen usually slept late, she waited until well after eleven to give her a call.

"Hi there," she said in a voice that still sounded asleep when she called. "I didn't wake you, did I?" she asked teasingly.

"Hey there, girlfriend," Gwen said, waking up as she spoke. "How are you doing, Sylvia?" It was obvious by the rustling sounds in the background that Gwen was moving around in her bed.

"I'm okay," Sylvia told her truthfully. "How are you? How's the new job?"

"It's good," Gwen answered. Hang on a sec while I put on some coffee. Sylvia heard the sound of water running and Gwen picked up the cordless. "I'm just getting to know my way around," she told

Sylvia. "You know, the routine and what I think I should be doing," she said.

"No, I wouldn't know...yet," Sylvia answered her. "But, I'm going to start the job hunt this week. Hopefully, it won't be waitressing or selling retail. I don't think I could do either. Remember when I tried to waitress last year? That was a disaster," she reminded Gwen.

"I agree, serving is not your forte," Gwen laughed and assured her. "Something good will turn up, I know it will."

"Thanks for the vote of confidence," Sylvia said. She went on to tell her how her mother was pushing at her about jobs.

"How's your love life?" Sylvia asked, changing the subject.

"Don't ask," Gwen said. "A couple of guys at work asked me out, but I'm not sure I want to get into that," she said warily. "If something happened, either good or bad, it could get uncomfortable." Gwen was always the practical one. "How about you?" she asked Sylvia.

"Same as usual," Sylvia told her, "Nada, nada, nada...but, I did meet someone that's real," she hesitated, searching for the right words to describe Owen. "Well, I think he's a friend, but I know I'm interested in more," she confessed.

"Ask him out!" Gwen insisted.

"No, I don't think so," Sylvia said.

"It's the new millennium, Sylvia," Gwen teased, "you don't need to wait to be asked out."

"I know," Sylvia said, "I'm just not ready."

"Yeah, celibate, Syl," Gwen teased.

"Hey, that's not fair!" Sylvia cried, "I just haven't found the right person for a decent relationship. Most of the guys at school were goons."

"You're right there," Gwen replied dryly. "Goon or not, you could still ask him out and get out for a change," she reprimanded her friend.

"I'm not ready to do that yet," Sylvia insisted.

Gwen started making chicken sounds and Sylvia laughed.

"When are you going to come for a visit?" Sylvia asked.

"When do you want me?" Gwen countered.

"Please come as soon as you can possible!" Sylvia replied. "Do you want to come next weekend?"

"It would be really late when I arrive," she warned. "Is that okay?"

"Of course, it is!" Sylvia cried to her friend. "That would be great! Bring your swimsuit and we can swim and get the start of a tan," Sylvia told her.

"Any chance I'll meet '*the man*'?" Gwen asked.

"Possibly," Sylvia said mysteriously. "Have a good week. I'll see you Friday night!"

They hung up. Sylvia smiled. She realized how much she had missed her roommate. She looked around the house. It was looking good for her cursory cleaning this morning. She put in another load of laundry and went to sit in the sun. With the heat and humidity building, it took only a few minutes to feel the sweltering heat. Inside the house was much, much cooler.

Sylvia was bored. She didn't want to go out into the Memorial holiday traffic, but she certainly didn't want to clean anymore in the sweltering heat. Sylvia really wanted to call Owen and Marian, but at the same time, did not. She finally guessed that she didn't want to feel lonely.

Thinking she had nothing better to do, Sylvia dragged herself over and turned on the computer and searched through Word to find resume templates and went to work. Using a template she typed up what she thought was a good resume. Without experience, Sylvia really didn't have much to present to a potential employer. She printed out a copy, copied and e-mailed a copy to her mother and to Gwen for their opinions. Restless, she caved in on her resolve not to call Marian and Owen, thinking they could give an opinion on her resume before she took it to the copy place. She dialed, but there was no answer.

She went to the refrigerator to find that it was somewhat barren and grabbed her purse and broke her resolve not to go to the grocery store. Stepping outside, it felt like she walked into a wall. The heat and humidity were suffocating. The lovely spring weather had switched to sudden summer overnight. Inside Gran's house with its thick walls, bay breeze, and ceiling fans, one didn't notice the heat as much.

Crawling gingerly into the hot car, Sylvia turned the air conditioning on high and waited for the cold air to surround her before backing out of the driveway. She took a deep breath of the even cooler air of the grocery store. It was so frigid that goose bumps appeared on her skin right away. She wandered the aisles, picking up fresh fruit, salad, tuna, frozen dinners, yogurt and more of the sorbet that her mother had chosen as a dessert the night before. Fortunately, the store wasn't as crowded as the other day. Sylvia figured that everyone was celebrating the holiday and were busy with barbecues and picnics. It only took her a few minutes to zip through the store for a few things. Sylvia checked out and headed home.

Remembering her mother had picked up a Sunday paper the day before, Sylvia sat down at the kitchen table and spread the paper out before her. Fumbling through Gran's junk drawer in the kitchen, she finally located a black marker. Settled with a pen in hand and the newspaper before her, Sylvia searched for the Employment section. Several openings in the medical field were available and Sylvia vaguely wished she had some sort of medical degree. She tugged at her long braid absentmindedly as she read through the other employment ads. Several telemarketing positions were available, but she had done that part time for a while in college and placed that at the bottom of her list of possibilities. Thurmont was advertising. She glanced through their listings—Assistant to the public information office, secretarial and plant manager. The public information office position sounded interesting and she wondered if she was qualified. It was a definite possibility. Working for

Thurmont made her pause. It had been the arch enemy to Gran for many years, but Owen had a different story. She wondered which was correct. Still, she needed a job and this was something she was qualified to do. She had always liked her writing classes in college. Perhaps it would work. She also checked out advertisements for some temporary agencies.

The telephone jangled and she answered it. Her mother was checking in and Sylvia told her mother, to her delight, about the resume she had emailed and the job possibilities.

"That's great, Syl," she told her. "I'll get online right away and look at your resume. The temporary agencies are a good idea too. I think a lot of them have benefits and most of the employees get hired within a decent amount of time."

"What do you think of the Thurmont openings?" she asked her mother.

"I think you would do well interviewing for the public information office," her mother told her. "You have a decent background in writing and you have good computer skills. When you fill out your application, don't forget to list your web page design skills and your writing classes."

"Okay," Sylvia told her. "Thanks. I'll give them a call tomorrow."

"Perhaps Owen could bring you an application," her mother advised.

"I think I would like to do this on my own," Sylvia told her mother.

"You're right," her mother answered. "It would be better if you would take the initiative. Good luck. I'll call back if I see any drastic errors in your resume."

"Thanks, Mom. I'll talk to you soon," Sylvia ended the conversation.

After several cups of coffee and nervously pacing around the house the next morning, Sylvia called Thurmont's Human Resources office. They said they would e-mail an application and to forward it with a resume as soon as possible. She hung up, breathing a sigh of relief. She wondered how Owen's first day was going. She called a couple more places for an application and realized if she did get an interview in the next couple of days, she had nothing to wear. Well, she had the dress she wore at her grandmother's funeral and the pantsuit she wore to the attorney's office, but she wanted a couple of other things. Her wardrobe of jeans and casual clothes would not fit the bill for interviews. She wasn't sure if she could wait until Friday. Sylvia called Marian for ideas of where to shop since she exhausted the possibilities in the local mall over the weekend with her mother.

Marian was delighted that she called her to go shopping. She suggested they drive to Lancaster, Pennsylvania to the outlets to look for things and it seemed like a good idea to Sylvia.

"I'll drive," Marian told her, "I know a couple of shortcuts to the outlets."

"All right," Sylvia agreed, "But, this time, lunch is on me."

Later, Sylvia went to check her e-mail. The application and information from Thurmont had not arrived in her e-mail account. She quickly emailed Gwen and her mother, signed off and went to pour a glass of wine.

Sitting on the steps of the deck, Sylvia sipped her wine and looked out at the water and squinted to see the edge of the opposite shoreline. It was a faint line in the distance. It was still hot and humid and a drop of perspiration trickled down her neck and shirt. She heard a rustling near her and, startled, jumped when she saw the Green Man next to her.

In Hitchcock-like tones, he said, "Good evening, Sylvia."

"Do you always surprise people by just 'dropping in,'?" she asked him a little testily. With the high heat and humidity, the half of glass of wine had started to affect her and she felt a little tipsy. Having the Green Man appear was an otherworldly feeling anyway, but with wine on top of it, she was questioning herself and her sanity.

"Not always," he told her. His smile was infectious and he looked at her fondly.

"I haven't discovered any of the 'gifts' you spoke about," she told him.

"I didn't expect you to, yet," he told her. "I just wanted to sit with you and look at the world for awhile and to talk."

"I think you have an ulterior motive," she continued.

She waited for a reaction, but all he did was smile enigmatically.

"Why did you come?" she asked eventually.

"Do you remember when you were able to see the life force in things?" he asked her.

"No," she answered and sighed. "I'm not sure what you're talking about. Is it like 'the Force' from Star Wars or something?" she asked unrelentingly.

"It's something like that," he said clearly amused. "Think back," he told her, "Think back to when you were a child."

Sylvia sipped more wine thinking this was a futile effort on the Green Man's part. She didn't have a clue. The Green Man was whispering, now he was reciting a poem. It sounded familiar to her. Sylvia listened.

"I thank you God for most this amazing day; for the leaping greenly spirits of trees and a blue true dream of sky: and for everything which is natural which is infinite which is yes," he murmured.

"e.e. cummings," Sylvia stated, rather than asked. She remembered reading that poem in a literature class.

The Green Man nodded. Sylvia thought about the verse for a moment.

"Leaping greenly spirits of trees," she murmured, "the blue true dream of sky..." She closed her eyes for a moment and suddenly she thought she knew what the Green Man was talking about.

"Are you talking about the trees breathing?" she asked him.

"Tell me more," he asked gently.

"Well," Sylvia began, "when I was little, I used to see the trees breathing. I never actually talked to anyone about it, but I used to draw it in my pictures. I thought everyone could see them. My Mom just acknowledged it as kid art with the colors, but when I was in elementary school when my art teacher ridiculed my drawing in front of the whole class because I had painted the dancing light around the trees. Everyone laughed and made fun of me. I haven't been able to see it since." There was a wistful tone to her voice.

"Some people call them auras. You have the gift of being able to see plant and tree auras, but eventually, you will be able to see the life force in all things. Concentrate," the Green Man instructed. "Look at the trees across the water and focus."

Sylvia looked and looked. "It's no use," she said despondently, "It's gone."

"You don't seem to understand," the Green Man insisted. "It's part of you. You have the gift. Concentrate," he urged her.

Sylvia looked. Twilight was falling. She looked at the tree line. She thought she saw a faint shadow at the top of the tree line. She looked back at the Green Man questioningly who nodded in approval.

"It's a start," he said. "Keep your eyes open," he suggested.

The Green Man vanished in his usual fashion. Sylvia sat and pondered what he had said. Tree auras! It sounded absurd, but she remembered how she used to watch the light dance around trees and plants as a child. Occasionally she had seen colors around people as well. She remembered squealing with delight at Gran and pointing saying 'rainbow, rainbow.' Gran had laughed and scooped her up and gave her a huge hug as she danced her around. She remembered how she thought everyone saw it. Sylvia wondered if Gran saw the auras. She knew Gran had some knowledge of it from her supportive reaction to Sylvia crying out about a rainbow around her grandmother. But something else was nagging at her.

It was something that Gran had told her. She couldn't remember and wished she had not had wine on such a hot day. She rubbed her head and stared at the shoreline more until the trees blended with the dark night sky. Her head ached.

That night she dreamed that Gran was talking to her. In the dream, Gran felt so real and so close that Sylvia wanted to reach out and touch her. Sylvia looked into Gran's eyes. Gran told her everything would be all right. She told her that the Green Man would help her. She told her not to worry. Others joined her in the dream, smiling at Sylvia, welcoming her. Gran hugged her. Sylvia could feel her warm arms around her holding her and comforting her like she did when she was little. Sylvia woke up holding the pillow tightly. The dream had been so real. She wondered who the people were who crowded in with Gran. And then she thought of Gran as tears coursed silently down her face. She wiped away the tears with the back of her hand. Her grief seemed to be leaking out of her in a slow trickle. In the dream, Sylvia had been able to see, hear, and feel Gran's presence. Waking up to the empty room and empty house makes her feel hollow inside. The empty hole in her heart would take some getting used to. Sylvia went to grab some tissues and blew her nose loudly.

CHAPTER TEN

In one salutation to thee, my, God,
Let all my senses spread out
And touch this world at thy feet.
--Rabindranath Tagore

Sylvia wondered if her mother was as emotional about Gran's death as she was or did her mother's crying the day of the funeral satiate her grief. Sylvia couldn't get back to sleep. After tossing and turning for more than an hour, Sylvia got up and looked at the darkness outside. She made her way to the kitchen by feel, not wanting to turn on the bright light, and put on coffee by the night light on the stove. She sat gloomily with her first cup staring out into the darkness from the couch in the living room with her legs tucked under her. Only a few sparse lights were twinkling across the water. She sat for a long time pondering absolutely nothing. Padding her way to the study Sylvia got into her e-mail. Thurmont had sent the application. She filled it out, attached her resume and sent it back to the human resources department. Daylight finally came, the light sneaking quietly over the horizon. Sylvia went back to the living room and opened the French doors to let in the morning breeze. She sat with another cup of coffee thinking about her dream.

She must have dozed because she woke to knock at the door. Sylvia didn't know where she was for a moment. Then realizing that someone was knocking on her door, Sylvia woke up completely. She rushed out to the kitchen to see Marian's worried face peering through the window.

"Marian!" Sylvia cried, "Come in! I'm sorry! I woke up very early this morning and then fell asleep on the couch. Just give me fifteen minutes – okay?"

"It's all right, Syl," Marian soothed her. "We're not on a schedule.

Why don't you get dressed and I'll make us a fresh pot of coffee? This one," she said, "looks a bit thick."

Sylvia breathed a sigh of relief, rushed upstairs for a quick, quick shower and dressed and was back downstairs in 15 minutes as promised earlier.

"I'm still a little damp behind the ears, but I think I'm acceptable," she said to Marian.

"You're fine," Marian assured her. "If you can wait for breakfast," she continued, "I can take you to a place that has wonderful homemade cinnamon and sticky buns."

"Sounds perfect," Sylvia said. "Let's go."

Marian drove the country roads to Lancaster. They passed by picturesque farms and a few Amish buggies on the way. Sylvia stared out the window and the fields and windbreaks. Something was different. She focused not on the trees, but above and away. It was a strange way of looking at things, like looking out of the corner of her eye. There was a pale light that hovered above the tree line. It was the tree's breathing—the auras she had not seen since she was a child. She must have yelped or made a sound as Marian turned to her and asked, "What was that?"

"Nothing," Sylvia said, but she continued to stare out at the horizon in amazement. "Wow!" she said under her breath.

Marian pulled into a grocery store parking lot and Sylvia turned to her, puzzled.

"Groceries?" she queried.

Marian chuckled. "This is the place I was telling you about. Excellent baked goods and free coffee."

Marian had chatted on the way about a fantastic grocery store, but Sylvia had politely nodded and concentrated on the trees rather than listen to Marian's chatter. Now she felt a little guilty. They entered the store and Marian led Sylvia back to the bakery counter. Marian was correct, there were several varieties of luscious looking baked goods. Sylvia chose a bear claw covered in nuts and gooey white icing and Marian wanted a cinnamon bun. In the front of the store, they poured themselves a cup of coffee, paid for their baked goods and were on their way to Lancaster again in just a few minutes.

"Delicious," Sylvia said, biting into her bear claw filled with butter, sugar and nut mixture. Sylvia refused to think of the calorie count in the pastry. It melted in her mouth leaving behind a buttery and nutty aftertaste.

"It's a wonderful store," Marian said. "The meats are premium and come right from the farm. They have an excellent butcher. I believe most of the vegetables are local as well. I should have brought a cooler and we could stop on our way back."

"Perhaps we can pick one up in Lancaster," Sylvia suggested.

They arrived at the outlets at the opening time. Buses were already starting to pull in.

"I haven't been here in years," Sylvia told Marian. "Sometimes Mom and Gran dragged me to the outlets for school or special holiday clothes. Mom makes a yearly trek for Christmas presents with some friends each October."

"I thought you might want to check Ann Taylor, Coldwater Creek and Harve Bernard and some of the other designers for a suit," Marian suggested.

They picked up a map of the outlets and an index and plotted a strategy. Traveling from store to store, Sylvia tried on a variety of clothes and shoes. It was fun and exhausting. Sylvia found a summer pantsuit with a long duster in a lightweight crepe. It was black and very dressy. Marian found a good 'interview' suit for her. She also insisted that Sylvia purchases a little black sheath dress with a matching jacket and a few other things.

After a couple of hours and several packages later, Sylvia thought their shopping trip had been a success.

"I'm starving," Sylvia told Marian. "Let's go and find lunch."

Marian drove her to a small restaurant tucked away in the small town of Strasburg. It was in one of the lovely brick houses along the main street and slightly away from the tourist traffic.

They ordered sandwiches. Sylvia chose a roasted vegetable sandwich and it came with fresh focaccia bread with mozzarella and fresh basil leaves. Marian chose a chicken sandwich with baby spinach and pesto mayonnaise. The waitress brought them drinks while Sylvia looked at the antique furnishings.

While they were waiting for their food, Sylvia asked, "How did Owen's first day go?"

"I think all right," Marian answered her. "He had to fill out all of the entry paperwork and get settled. I haven't seen him this nervous in a long time. Being out of academia is very different for him."

"I just sent an application to Thurmont too," Sylvia told Marian. "There is an available job as an assistant to the public information officer position."

Marian raised her eyebrows. "Oh?" she commented.

"Well, there wasn't much in the paper, and this looked interesting," Sylvia told her. "I have the qualifications, I think. Also,

I'm hoping Thurmont is doing a better job environmentally than it used to when you and Gran opposed their policies."

"I see," Marian said. "It sounds good. When did you apply?" she asked.

"I called yesterday," Sylvia told her, "and they e-mailed me the application. I sent it off this morning along with my resume."

"You sent it off this morning?" Marian asked remembering Sylvia had been asleep on the couch when she had arrived.

Sylvia explained that she couldn't sleep and worked on it during the wee hours of the night before falling asleep on the sofa at dawn. Their food came and Sylvia waited until the waitress had walked away before she continued.

"I had a very strange dream and it woke me up and then I couldn't sleep," Sylvia confessed. "I dreamed Gran was talking to me," she hesitated a moment before continuing, "I thought I would put the time to good use, I guess." She took a bite of her sandwich.

"What did Holly tell you?" Marian asked.

Sylvia wasn't quite sure what to say to Marian. The auras, the Green Man, it all was a little too surreal still.

"Gran told me not to worry," Sylvia finally said. "She said everything would be all right."

"And it will," Marian agreed, nodding her head sagely.

"Have you read any of the books on the Green Man, yet?" Marian asked her.

"Yes!" Sylvia said gratefully. "They're lovely. I'll get them back to you soon."

"No hurry," Marian commented. "Did you find what you were looking for?" Marian asked.

"Yes and no," Sylvia answered. "I learned a lot of history, but…" again she was at a loss for words on whether or not to confess she had met the Green Man.

"Sylvia," Marian said gently. "I know he's back."

Sylvia nearly choked on her iced tea. "What?" she gasped and sputtered. "What did you say?"

"I said, I know the Green Man is back," Marian told her again.

A great sense of relief washed over Sylvia.

"Then I'm not going crazy," she said.

"No, not at all," Marian assured her.

"I have so many unformed questions," Sylvia said, "that I don't know where to begin. Who is he? Why is he here?" she asked.

"I suspect he's here because he's been called in some way or there is some sort of crisis that he can assist with," Marian said.

"Something a little bit like Captain Planet, I think," Sylvia said more to herself than to Marian while she stirred her soda with her straw.

"Excuse me?" Marian asked.

"Sorry," Sylvia apologized. "I think I was talking more to myself. Do you know the cartoon character Captain Planet?" she asked.

Marian shook her head and looked blank.

"It's an old cartoon where five children work to save the earth from ecological destruction and the ultimate superhero is a large blue man with a cape, who comes to save the day," Sylvia informed her. "Each of the children has a gift of some sort…" her voice trailed off.

"Interesting," Marian said. "I suspect he's a little like that. Be patient."

"You know, I'm tired of being patient," Sylvia flared with exasperation. "You're telling me to be patient, Gran tells me to be patient, the Green Man tells me to be patient…what *is it* that you all want me to be patient about?"

Marian reached over to pat Sylvia's hand but, the waitress came over to the table to offer them dessert. Sylvia pulled herself together and tried to quell the emotions.

"Chocolate, please," Sylvia almost growled. "I want something with as much chocolate and sugar as you can muster. Please bring coffee too." Exhaustion from her early awakening and shopping was setting in. Sylvia was feeling grumpy.

"I would like some carrot cake and coffee please," Marian asked the waitress and she went away.

"I know you're frustrated," Marian told her patting her hand, "but I don't know if I have any information to give to you. Like the children with Captain Planet, you must have a gift that can help the Green Man."

She took Sylvia's hand gently between hers. "I know that you walk with the rhythm of the earth. I can see it in your eyes—just like in Holly's. You'll discover your gift one day, but it may take an hour, a day, a year or a long, long time. It may take a lifetime."

"What do you mean by that? By walking with the rhythm of the earth? That sounds pretty 'out there,'" Sylvia questioned.

"Seeing and feeling the energy of the Earth," Marian said simply. "Other than that, I'm not sure I can put it into words."

The waitress brought their coffee and went to get their desserts. She brought Marian's carrot cake and brought a piece of a dense chocolate cake that sat on swirls raspberry sauce and was topped with whipped cream and fresh raspberries.

"Oh, my," Sylvia said as the waitress put it down.

"It's about as dense of chocolate as you can get," the waitress told her. "Take a bite and see if you like it." The server was waiting to see her reaction.

Sylvia took a bite. It was warm and a rich bittersweet chocolate that melted in her mouth. It was a chocolate lover's version of an orgasm.

"This is fabulous," she told the waitress. "However do you make it?"

"Lots of butter, eggs, chocolate and about a tablespoon of flour," she told her. "It's the best."

"Wow," Sylvia commented again.

The waitress walked away with a satisfied smile.

"You were saying," Sylvia asked of Marian.

"I can't be overly specific," Marian said, "but there is something in your eyes, just like Holly's," she repeated herself and then continued, "that I know that you are tuned into the Earth. I see it sometimes in others, but not as often as I would like. I suspect you can see auras," she said.

Sylvia nodded. "I haven't been able to see them in a long, long time," she told Marian. "In fact, today is the first time I've seen them in trees since I've been a child."

"You will probably see them more and more easily if you practice," Marian told her matter of fact. "Can you feel a plant's energy?" she asked Sylvia.

Sylvia shook her head. "Not that I know of," Sylvia returned. "What do you mean?"

"It's difficult to put a lot of this into words too," she said to Sylvia. "But, I know when I touch a plant, I feel joy. It exudes some form of energy. I'm not very good at this. Your grandmother was amazing at it! She could see and feel several different kinds of energy," she told her.

"My Grandmother could see and feel the energy?" Sylvia asked. "I never knew!"

"Well," Marian told her with a quirky smile, "it's not something you advertise. I'm sure many people would think you were quite insane if you went around and told them about their auras and the energy that was coming from the earth all around them. I know it exists in many publications and the few who brave the general population by offering classes and philosophies, but I knew I had to be careful as the 'faculty wife.' I know Holly had to hide it from your grandfather as well. As much as they loved one another, he was too much of a straight jacket to accept anything other than the black and the white," Marian went on. "That's why we—Holly and me, became active in a lot of environmental projects. It was our small way of saving what we cherished. And," she added, "from what your mother said, I'm sure it wasn't even a choice for Holly to share things with you after she had been threatened by your father. Your grandmother adored you and wouldn't let anything come in the way of spending time with you. If your parents had taken you away as they threatened or if they got wind of Holly being psychic—especially with plants, why your father would have locked her up and thrown away the key, it sounds like."

Sylvia shook her head. "Itis difficult to believe Mom and Dad were like that, but it's true." Memories of her father were vague. She remembered the feel of being hugged up against his suit. Her Dad was always busy, busy, and had not had a lot of time with her. When he died, Sylvia had a sore spot in her heart that missed him, but it wasn't the grief that she felt for Gran. Looking back, she couldn't help but feel that she didn't know her father and wondered about his level of caring for her. She turned her attention back to Marian. "Tell me more about Gran and her causes that my parents were so upset about," Sylvia asked, "please?"

"Well, mind you, I was out of the country for a good chunk of the time," Marian told her, "but, your grandmother wrote me some lively letters about what was going on."

"Your mother mentioned some locals, I believe, Ted Jamison and Maureen Davenport. I think they've calmed down on their issues, but your grandmother was active with them and a few others who were very concerned about Thurmont, about pollution and the beaches, and a lot of local causes. Maureen went in for the more radical groups. She wanted national groups to go up against Thurmont. I understand she went to Washington and had to be led away by police she was so vehement."

Marian paused to drink more coffee. Sylvia waited for more.

"Ted Jamison died a few years ago, but Maureen's still around, I think," Marian mused. "I know she and her son were quite active in Green Peace. Last I heard she was on a boat to somewhere. I'll introduce you sometime."

Sylvia took this all in. It definitely gave her a surprising, new perspective on her grandmother. The waitress brought them their check. Marian reached into her purse.

"It's on me, remember?" Sylvia said.

Marian smiled and conceded to Sylvia, "All right," she told her.

They had a quiet ride home. Sylvia had a lot of unformed questions in her mind, but she wasn't sure how to voice them to Marian.

When Marian dropped her off, Sylvia said, "Thanks for talking to me about the Green Man and Gran. I feel a lot better about it."

"Good," Marian said. "I'm glad."

"But, I still have a lot of questions," Sylvia stated.

"I'll be in touch soon," Marian said, smiling, "Take care."

Sylvia waved her off and took her packages inside. The light on the answering machine was blinking and she listened to the message. It was from Thurmont requesting an interview. She glanced at the clock and took a chance at calling personnel after 4 pm. She left a voice message and said she would call in the morning. After that, she called her Mom to tell her the good news. She wasn't home or at work or answering her cell, so she left messages at all three. Thirdly she called Marian who also was not at home to give her the news. Frustrated and wanting to share her news she sent a text message to Gwen. Still restless Sylvia decided to take a walk. She headed out the front door and walked toward the marina about a half-mile away. Sylvia walked briskly, enjoying the warm sun and looking around her. She had not walked down here in a long time. There were the usual dog walkers out and she nodded and said hello as they passed. It felt good to stretch her legs and move after the long drive and shopping.

Sylvia stretched her hands overhead to release the tension in her back. Her walk slowed and she noticed there hadn't been too many changes in the neighborhood since the seventies when the older cottages were razed and more modern homes were put in place. Most of the families kept the charming Arts and Crafts movement cottage style. There were a few exceptions where the older homes had been knocked down and replaced with a new, much larger home of stone and glass that covered two waterfront lots. Somehow the owners had gotten around the laws of building on the same footprint by the bay. She wondered who the new neighbors might be and if they were local or part of what the locals called 'the Pennsylvania Navy.' Gran had mentioned the increase in residents over the years in dinner table conversations. Gran wondered if the land would support everyone with all of the construction and water and sewage needs. Sylvia had listened, but left most of these conversations, which sometimes led to arguments between Gran and her mother, to the 'adults.' She didn't like conflict and would escape out to the beach listening to her mother arguing for progress and capitalism and her grandmother voicing concerns for irrational building and the environment. Perhaps if she had stuck around and listened to the arguments between her mother and her grandmother, Sylvia would have had better insight into the secondary life her grandmother had led and was forced to quell per her parents' directives. When she reached the marina, she turned to walk back by way of the beach. Sylvia was nearly home when she saw a tall figure striding towards her. It seemed familiar and as she got closer she realized it was Owen.

"Hi there, Syl," Owen called down the beach to her.

"Hi!" Sylvia answered Owen, with a surprised tone and gave him a look of puzzlement as to why he was walking on the beach.

"I'm glad I found you," he said when he caught up with her panting a little. Owen had broken into a brief jog when he had seen her. "I thought you might be out walking.

"You're probably wondering why I'm here," he said as if reading her thoughts giving her a warm smile.

She nodded in reply and they continued to walk back toward the house, strolling more slowly on the way back.

"Marian sent me over," he told her, "you left a package in her car and she thought you might need it tomorrow."

"Oh," Sylvia said, "Thanks! You can tell her she's probably correct."

"She said you applied to Thurmont?" he asked.

"Yes," Sylvia answered, "and I missed their phone call today. They're interested in an interview."

"That's great!" he said. "When do you think it will be?" he asked.

Sylvia shrugged, "I'll call tomorrow. I would believe that it would be Thursday or Friday, but I really have no idea."

"How's the new job going?" she asked him.

"So far, so good," he quipped. "I'm really just getting my feet wet," he told her. "Just learning about the place and the routines, you know. There's nothing exciting or interesting so far to report. It's definitely a change from the hallowed halls of academia and I'm enjoying that aspect."

They got back to the house and went inside. Sylvia pulled out a beer and offered it to him while he was talking, taking one herself. They walked back out to the deck and sat on the steps.

"Tell me about the job you applied for," he said.

"It's for a position as assistant public information officer," Sylvia told Owen. "Do you know anyone in that department?"

"I'm afraid not," he said. "Thurmont's a huge place. I haven't had the chance to meet too many people yet. Sorry."

"That's okay," Sylvia said. "I was just wondering."

Owen was sitting so closely to Sylvia on the steps that she could feel the heat from his body. Their conversation lapsed as they watched the brilliant sunset colors collide and melt into the horizon.

"I've seen hundreds of sunsets here," Sylvia murmured. "I never get tired of seeing them."

"There's something magical about them, that's for sure," he agreed. He paused and then looked at his watch. "I should be going," Owen said abruptly, breaking the moment as the sun lowered itself over the western horizon of the bay, burning brilliantly before it settled on the horizon and the air turned from day to dusk.

"Thanks for bringing the bag over," Sylvia said her voice a little husky with unspoken emotion.

Owen pulled up his tall, lean form and went around to his car.

"Good luck on the interview," he told her.

"Thanks," she replied and leaned both elbows on the railing watching him go.

She mentally gave herself a head shake as she watched his car drive away. Sylvia stayed on the deck, musing about Owen until the last dregs of light were wrung from the sky. Twilight fell, and the mosquitoes came out in full force as darkness filled the sky. Sylvia slapped at a few and headed into the kitchen to find something for dinner. She settled in front of the television sitting cross-legged on the couch in the study to eat a microwave meal and flipped through the channels. She couldn't focus. Her thoughts turned to Owen instead of what was being shown on the television.

The next day she called Thurmont at 8:30. A girl name Carol answered the phone in the Human Resources department. Carol asked if she could possibly come at 11:30 that day, Sylvia was surprised, but agreed. After she had got off the phone, she showered and chose one of the outfits she had purchased the day before. It was a nubby golden brown raw silk suit with a gold silk shell. It brought out the gold and brown highlights in her hair and eyes. She neatly French braided her hair, added makeup, and matching brown pumps and hurried out the door to make it to Thurmont on time.

Thurmont was about eight miles from her house. It was a long building in brown and black brick tucked away on several wooded acres. As she drove down the road towards the plant, Sylvia thought it could have been a way to a state park. The parking lot was large and manicured trees and shrubs dotted the islands that were placed strategically around the lot. The building could almost blend in with the trees except the sun glinting off the glass front panels that were, at least, two stories high. Sylvia's heels clicked nervously as she walked up the sidewalk to the front door. A security guard asked her business when she walked through and she waited for someone to come to get her for her interview. While she waited, she tapped her foot and looked around. Glossy photos of Thurmont's products were framed and on the wall. The lunch crowd started to exit through the doors. Sylvia saw a few people sitting at picnic tables in the trees. Two people were coming through the door and were laughing. Sylvia turned to look at them and was surprised to see Owen.

"Sylvia!" he said, as surprised as she, "Hi!" He introduced the woman who stood next to him as "Anna," letting Sylvia know she was a fellow scientist at the plant. She was tall, platinum, almost white blond, with gray eyes. She was wearing a gray suit that matched her eyes which looked coldly at Sylvia.

"How do you do," Anna said to Sylvia in an accent Syl could not quite place.

"Nice to meet you," Sylvia returned politely.

"We were just going to an early lunch," Owen said, "would you like to join us?"

"Thank you, no," Sylvia told him, "I'm here for my interview."

"Oh," Owen said slightly surprised, "That was really fast. Good luck!"

"Thank you," Sylvia said.

Anna looked impatiently at her watch and not at all subtle that she wanted to leave as soon as possible.

Owen finally noticed, glanced at them both and said, "We should be going."

Sylvia nodded. "Enjoy your lunch," she told them and she watched them walk out the door and across the lot.

Her eyes narrowed with jealousy as she watched the slim legs pull into the passenger side of Owen's car that was parked fairly close to the entrance. But her thoughts were interrupted.

"Miss Ash?" a voice asked.

Sylvia turned and a handsome man looked at her questioningly.

"Yes," she said to him, holding out her hand, "I'm Sylvia Ash."

"I'm Garrett Keely," he introduced himself. "I'm the Assistant Director of Human Resources."

"Nice to meet you," Sylvia said, putting on a polite smile and forgetting about Owen and Anna.

"Would you come this way?" he asked her leading her through another set of heavy glass doors. They went down the left-hand hallway of a set of five, that led from a central desk, like spokes on a wheel or rays of the sun. Everything was quiet. Mr. Keely was quiet too and he led her to an office about halfway down the hallway.

"If you will have a seat for a moment," he motioned for her to sit in one of the beige tweed chairs, we'll be with you in a few minutes."

There was a secretary at a computer, clicking away noiselessly. She smiled at Sylvia. She was a perky, black haired woman about Sylvia's age.

"Hi!" she said, stopping to pause for a moment from her typing on the computer. "I'm Carol. We spoke on the phone earlier?"

"Yes," Sylvia said. "Nice to meet you," she said and offered her hand. Sylvia was nervous and sat on the edge of her seat. Her palms were sweaty and she was hoping she wouldn't leave marks on the folder with her resume. She put it down on the chair next to her and discreetly wiped her hands on the arms of the chair. Mr. Keely came out a moment later and asked her to follow him.

Sylvia began to wonder if he purposely made everyone feel nervous and ill at ease as if to test their nerves, before an interview. He led her to a conference room. It was an oval room with an oval table. One whole wall was curved amber glass that looked out at the woods. Sylvia sat on the side so she could look at the trees. He handed Sylvia, a glossy packet about the company.

"Mr. Carter should be here any minute," he said. "Why don't you take a moment to familiarize yourself with the company." He tapped the fingers of his right hand nervously on the polished wood of the conference table and kept glancing at his watch. Sylvia noticed that he had a perfect tan and that his tan nearly matched the color of his hair. He looked a little like a Ken doll. Each hair was combed and gelled perfectly in place. As handsome as he was, for some reason, she didn't really like him.

"Will you excuse me a moment?" his question more of a statement. "I'll see what is keeping Mr. Carter."

"Certainly," Sylvia said politely and she made herself busy looking through the folder thankful he was gone.

A minute later she heard a door and then a brusque voice, "Damn! Forgot about this today," the voice said.

A short, paunchy man, who moved more lightly than you would have thought, entered the room. His hairline was receding and he evidently had been caught eating lunch as he had a napkin clutched in his hand.

"Thanks for paging me, Keely," he said, slapping him on the back. "Damn good of you." Mr. Keely looked pained.

He bounded over to Sylvia holding out his hand. "Jack Carter," he introduced himself. "Head of the public information office," he stated.

She took his hand with a smile. "Nice to meet you, Mr. Carter," she said. "I'm Sylvia Ash."

"Well, we should get down to business," he said matter-of-factly.

Sylvia slid a copy of her resume to him over the table.

"Fresh out of college?" he barked.

"Yes, sir," she said. "All of two weeks."

"What's your degree in?" he asked firing the question at her.

"Liberal Arts," she replied. "I have a strong concentration in English, writing and some coursework in web page design and HTML," she added.

"Good, good," he muttered as he looked over her resume. "I see here you worked on the school newspaper."

"Yes," Sylvia said. "We published hard copy as well as electronic. I know my way around Quark Express as well as Publisher, Front Page and Photoshop," she said. "I think I could pick up on most of the web publishing programs if I had the chance," she said gaining confidence in herself.

"Your qualifications are excellent," Mr. Carter said. "I'll be quite honest with you," he said to her. "We are in a bit of a mess. This is a new position and we're working from the ground up. Anyway, if you're interested in the job, it will be a challenge to create something good and run with it."

Sylvia nodded. It sounded interesting. Mr. Carter was brusque but honest. She liked that. He continued to ask a few more questions and she answered with ease.

"I am very interested," she said plainly at the end of the interview.

"Good," he said. "We have a couple more interviews, and we'll be in touch either way," he told her.

"Nice meeting you," he said, taking her hand in a firm handshake.

"Nice to meet you," she said politely. "I look forward to hearing from you."

Mr. Keely stood up and said, "I'll walk you to the exit."

"Thank you," Sylvia said as he opened the door for her.

Carol was not at her desk when she left and Sylvia assumed she had gone to lunch. She said thank you and goodbye to Mr. Keely at the glass doors and walked to her car.

Sylvia sat in her car and let the air conditioning cool her. She hoped she had felt a lot more nervous than she looked, but, all in all, thought the interview went well despite its brevity.

Sylvia put the car in gear and backed out of the parking space. As she left, she glanced around for Owen's car. Sylvia was disappointed that she did not see it and assumed he was still at lunch with Anna. She was surprised at the sparks of jealousy that she was feeling.

When she arrived home, her answering machine light was blinking madly. It was her mother who said, "Call me!"

Sylvia went upstairs to change from her suit. She put on shorts and a t-shirt and called her mother at work.

"Hi Syl, how did it go?" her mother asked anxiously.

"Very well, I think," Sylvia said. "This is a new position," she told her mother. "They want someone with ideas and who can run with them."

"That's good for you!" her mother was enthusiastic. "You're creative! It sounds perfect for you," she stated with obvious relief that her daughter would be part of the workforce soon.

"I think so," Sylvia answered. "They're to let me know in the next day or two," she finished. "They're to let me know either way. But, Mom," she stated, "It would a surprise to get hired from my first interview. I'm not counting on it, to be honest."

"I'll keep my fingers crossed for you," her mother said. "Thurmont is a major employer in that area. Just think, not too much of a commute! If you don't get this job, you're going to need to look a bit farther from North Bay. I'll talk to you soon."

Her Mom was right, Thurmont was a major employer in the area and one of the few that might have a job for Sylvia. She wasn't interested in the factories that lay outside of the town. North Bay was sort of a quiet, sleepy hamlet. At the town borders and closer to I-95, suburban developments and shopping areas existed. The only other major employers in this area were the hospital and schools. Anything else would be an hour commute into Delaware or towards Baltimore and Washington, D.C. The thought of a two-hour commute each day wasn't pleasant.

Sylvia went and got an old blanket. She put it under the trees in the side yard and lay down looking up at the sky. The earth was just warm under the blanket and the grass a nice cushion. She looked up at the lacy canopy of branches and young leaves against the blue, blue sky. She looked carefully. If she looked a little beyond the leaves and branches and not directly at them, Sylvia could see their auras. She watched, fascinated as the auras moved up and down as if the trees were breathing in and out. Sylvia wasn't sure how long she lay there until her stomach growled. She had been too nervous to eat breakfast and had not had lunch. She picked up her blanket and folded it over the deck railing and went in to get an early dinner.

When Sylvia went through the refrigerator, she finally decided to make a tuna salad sandwich and have it on toast. As she was eating she wished for some potato chips, but did not want to drive up to the grocery store for one item. Sylvia sipped at a cold beer and then went in to check her e-mail. Gwen had replied liking her resume and wishing her luck on the interview, repeating the same as her text message the day before. Sylvia e-mailed her that the interview had gone well. Sylvia knew Gwen had a lot going on in her life. She knew Gwen was caught up in her first few days on her new job. It was a company that had head-hunted her during her senior year and was a prestigious accounting firm. Gwen was more than qualified but had confessed to Sylvia that the corporate world made her a bit nervous. She surfed some more looking at additional Green Man sites. The history of the Green Man repeated itself and she found nothing about his possible return to the earth. She surfed through some of the commercial sites that sold pieces of artwork dedicated to the Green Man. If she got the job, she might treat herself to sculpture, garden art or jewelry. She couldn't decide, but bookmarked some sites.

As soon as she logged off the telephone rang. It was Marian asking when she had the interview.

Sylvia replied that she had already had the interview and was now waiting to hear if she would be offered the job. Marian was positive and said they should have champagne when she got the job. She put the emphasis on 'when' to be positive. They hung up and Sylvia went in search of something to read.

Gran's bookshelves felt like a second home, and they had always surrounded her with comfort. Sylvia hadn't paid too much attention to the titles that her Grandmother had collected, until now. The titles on the shelves showed an eclectic collection of interests of Gran's. Gran's warm presence was almost tangible as her eyes sifted through the titles on the shelves. Finally, Sylvia settled on a volume of poetry by Rilke and took it to bed with her. His words were lyrical and soothing and soon she was off in a dreamless sleep.

CHAPTER ELEVEN

I am circling around God, around the ancient tower,
And I have been circling for a thousand years.
And I still don't know if I am a falcon
Or a storm, or a great song.
--Rainer Maria Rilke

As soon as the dew was dry the next morning, Sylvia put on an old pair of sneakers, shorts, and a t-shirt and mowed the lawn. Since her father passed away when she was in fourth grade, it had been Sylvia's job from her teenage years on to mow the lawn at her house. Her grandmother had had a lawn service come in. Sylvia had canceled it because she enjoyed being out in the sun.

First, she trimmed before she mowed the lawn. The back lawn was a small patch of grass; the front and side yards were long and narrow and went down to the beach. She had worked up quite a sweat by the time she was finished. When the lawn was completed, she put the mower back in the shed and sat out with a glass of cold water. She sat cooling off when the phone rang and she ran to get it. It was Mr. Keely offering her the job.

"Are you all right?" he asked as she panted a bit when she answered the phone.

"I'm all right," Sylvia said. "I've just finished mowing the lawn."

"Oh," he commented, making it sound as though physical work was distasteful. "We would like you to start as soon as possible," he told her. "Would Monday be all right?"

"Monday would be fine," she told him, trying to keep her excitement in check.

He instructed her to come in a bit early, if she could, to work on the paperwork for personnel. They agreed that she would arrive by 8:30 and Sylvia hung up the phone, giving a 'whoop' as soon as she put it into the base.

A moment later she called her Mother. She got her voicemail but left an enthusiastic message. She texted Gwen, and then she called Marian who congratulated her.

"We'll have to celebrate!" Marian told her. "What about this weekend?"

"My friend Gwen is coming in over the weekend," Sylvia told her. "Sorry."

"Bring her along!" Marian suggested. "We can have dinner and champagne here on Saturday night."

"Are you sure?" Sylvia asked.

"Of course, I'm sure," Marian stated firmly.

"All right," Sylvia said. "I'll e-mail her and let her know what's up. If it's a problem, I'll let you know. Is there anything I can bring?"

"Absolutely not," Marian said firmly. "I'll take care of everything."

"Okay," Sylvia said. "Thanks."

They hung up and Sylvia realized how hot and sticky she was. She dropped her clothes by the washer and ran upstairs to shower. The warm water felt wonderful. Sylvia's muscles, unused for mowing, ached. The hot water coursed over her body and eased some of the tightness.

Sylvia got out of the shower and went to e-mail Gwen, knowing full well it would be all right to go to Marian's for a celebration, as she knew Gwen was anxious to meet Owen. Thinking of Gwen's visit, Sylvia sat down and made a list of groceries and things to buy. The next two days flew by with trips to the mall for additional outfits for work and preparation for Gwen's visit. She dusted, cleaned dancing around the house with her favorite CD's, made up the guest room with clean sheets and pulled out a clean towel set. She went to the grocery store to pick up food for the weekend and goodies that she and Gwen liked. She also went to the liquor store to stock up on beer, wine and Gwen's favorite vodka. She added margarita mix to the cart and tequila as well.

Before Sylvia knew it, it was Friday evening and she was waiting anxiously for Gwen to arrive. Gwen had called earlier in the evening from her cell phone and said she was stuck in traffic on the Jersey Turnpike, and would get there as soon as she could. It was sometime after ten when Sylvia drifted off to sleep on the couch to a television program that droned on and on. Gwen eventually pulled in the driveway. The atypical sound woke Sylvia up immediately and she flew out to the kitchen door. Sylvia ran outside and gave Gwen a huge hug as soon as she stepped out of her car. Sylvia hadn't realized how much she had missed Gwen's company. Gwen hugged her back in a bear hug.

"Great to see you, Syl!" she said. She stretched and moaned. "Ugh, I'm not used to sitting in a car for so long! I'm getting old," she said.

"Let me help you get your stuff," Sylvia said and she took the keys from Gwen and got her bags from the trunk.

"Come inside," Sylvia said, anxiously motioning with her head for Gwen to follow her.

"It's gorgeous here!" Gwen said as she looked out at the lights twinkling on the dark water.

"Yeah, it's great, wait until you see it during the day," Sylvia said. "Come on in, we'll get you settled and then we'll grab a cold beer and sit on the deck, okay?"

"That would be heaven," Gwen said.

She followed Sylvia inside and up the stairs where Sylvia put her bags. Gwen took off her shoes, dug in her bag for shorts and a t-shirt and changed into comfortable clothes. Sylvia, in the meantime, had gone downstairs and had a cold beer open when Gwen came downstairs. She took it gratefully as she followed Sylvia out onto the deck. The stars sparkled brilliantly as their eyes grew accustomed to the darkness. A small silvery white sliver of a moon just hung in the sky over the water like a Christmas ornament. Gwen sighed.

"Wow," she said dreamily, "Vacationland."

"How's work going?" Sylvia asked.

"It's a challenge," Gwen told her, "but I love it. You know how I love to crunch numbers."

Gwen had majored and excelled in accounting in school. She had been at the top of her class. She had plenty of job offers during the year and was now working for a high-powered firm in Greenwich, Connecticut.

"How is the corporate environment?" Sylvia asked knowing it had been one of Gwen's concerns about the job.

Gwen yawned loudly before she answered. "It's all a game," she said, "and it's good I like chess. There are a few backbiters, some bullies and a lot of nice people too."

"How about you?" Gwen asked her. "Did you get any more details on the job?"

"Not really," Sylvia said. "It sounds as though they need ideas and a public face."

"Then you'll come out smelling like a rose," Gwen said. "You have a lot of talents with web design and news writing. I always wondered why you didn't major in journalism."

Sylvia was surprised but shrugged "I hope I have some kind of talent," Sylvia returned.

Gwen tossed a cap from another beer at Sylvia where it hit her shoulder, and it bounced onto the deck and off into the grass. "Stop it," she said to Sylvia, "you'll be great."

They talked late into the night, catching up on everything in the last couple of weeks. It was well after midnight when both were yawning considerably, that they went up to bed.

Sylvia slept in later than usual but woke up much earlier than Gwen. She showered and dressed as quietly as she could and tip-toed downstairs to put on coffee. Sylvia didn't know how long Gwen would sleep but suspected it would be late morning if her pattern were the same as in college. Gwen had never scheduled a class before noon if she could help it. Sylvia was restless. Finally, she decided she would make something –a coffee cake or muffins. Sylvia took out the cookbook Marian had lent her and flipped through the pages. Muffins seemed easy enough. She looked through the cupboards for the ingredients, dumped them into the bowl, stirred and put them in the oven, hoping for the best. While they baked, she took a cup of coffee out onto the deck and leaned on the railing.

She thought about the Green Man and wanted to tell him that she could see the auras. As if reading her mind, he appeared at her elbow.

"Wow!" she exclaimed. "How did you know I was thinking of you?

"I just knew," he said in a mysterious tone with the usual humor in his voice.

"I'm able to see plant auras now," she told him proudly. "Quite easily, in fact."

"Good," he said. "That's a step in the right direction. You should work on people aura's next."

"Okay," she said, "Any suggestions?"

"It's the same as plant auras," he said. "You need to focus. Focus your sight beyond the person. Sometimes it's easier if they're against a light background," he suggested.

Sylvia nodded. "Okay," she said. "Will I know what they mean?" she asked.

"Not at first," the Green Man told her. "Just work on seeing them."

They were quiet for a moment and then Sylvia had a question.

"Hey," she said suddenly. "My friend is visiting. What if she sees me talking to you? Will she be able to see you?" she asked in a demanding tone with some concern in her question.

"It depends on the person," he said. "If they're ready to see me, they will," He answered, and then added with a grin, "If they're not ready" he paused, "If not, she may think..." his voice trailed off.

He saw Sylvia's face change from questioning with a look of panic in only a moment.

Sylvia cut him off with an "Ohmigod! The muffins!" and ran into the kitchen.

Sylvia had caught the muffins just before they burned. She used hot pads to remove them from the oven and set them on the top of the stove to cool. Sylvia sighed with relief.

"Sorry," she said breathlessly as she ran through the French doors out onto the deck. But, no one was there.

"Aargh! Men!" she stormed and stomped back into the house to dump the muffins from the pans. Gwen came down a few minutes later.

"What's this I smell?" she asked. "It's wonderful! Are you going all domestic on me?"

"Well, I figured I have to eat my own food, so I thought I had better learn to cook *something*," she said, "other than fast frozen microwave dinners.

"Well the muffins look great," Gwen complimented her and took a bite, "and they taste even better," she said with a mouthful.

"Good," Sylvia told her. "Then I'm not a domestic failure!" she laughed and Gwen laughed with her.

After they had breakfast, Sylvia took Gwen up to the town and they puttered through the boutiques and antique stores. Gwen picked up designer salsas and a candle at two of the shops. She oohed and aahed at some antiques, and wished she had a truck to transport things back to Connecticut, rather than her compact sports car. At a gift shop at the far end of town, Sylvia was surprised to find a decent collection of Celtic music. She looked through the CD's and picked up two that she couldn't resist. One had a picture of a green man on the front and the other had a song about the Green Man. She couldn't wait to listen to them. They walked back to town past the post office and churches and had lunch at the tavern where Sylvia had eaten with Owen and Marian. The town was packed with boaters and tourists, and they had to wait at the bar until their table was ready out on the deck.

"I've got to hand it to you, Syl," Gwen told her. "You live in a great place. I know a lot of people who would trade places with you in an instant."

"It is great," Sylvia said. "I think I take a lot of it for granted because I feel I grew up here," she told her. "But, I'm finding I really enjoy living here."

Their last stop was at the local florist to pick up flowers for Marian. They hurried home to put them in the refrigerator before they wilted.

"How should we dress for tonight?" Gwen asked her.

"Um, whatever you want to wear will be all right, I think," Sylvia said. "Jeans are okay."

"Okay," Gwen said. "Casual sounds great. My poor body has been in shock wearing heels, pantyhose, and suits every day."

They drove over to Marian's a little after six. Owen was on the riding mower, finishing the back portion of Marian's lawn near the meadow.

"There's Owen," Sylvia told Gwen as they pulled into the driveway nodding in his direction.

"I thought you said he was a nerd," Gwen said. "He's a hunk!" and she elbowed Sylvia in the ribs.

They both giggled. Gwen was right he was a hunk. Without his shirt, Sylvia could see his stomach muscles rippling as he gripped the mower's steering wheel as it traversed over a rough patch of ground. A couple of curly black waves hung down on his forehead. He was taking the mower back to the storage shed.

They got out of the car and Sylvia introduced Gwen to Marian, who had come out onto the front stoop. Marian was delighted with the flowers and thanked them profusely and invited them inside. Owen came in from mowing, wiping his forehead with his t-shirt.

"Hi, Syl," he said and she introduced Owen to Gwen. He shook hands with her and when she smiled, he seemed frozen for a second. Sylvia was used to this reaction to her friend. In addition to being incredibly intelligent, Gwen was also stunning. She was tall with long, to die for, blond hair that swung about her shoulders and flashing blue eyes and a body to match. Sylvia used to tell her she should quit college and become a model, but Gwen had no interest in it. Men just stopped and stared and most of the time, she didn't have the time of day for them.

Owen stopped staring for a moment, recovered and said, "I need to go clean-up. I'll be back in a couple minutes."

Marian offered drinks and cucumber sandwiches and they sat outside on the patio to talk. Fortunately, the evening was warm and not oppressive. Owen came back a few minutes later, dressed and apparently fresh from a shower. His hair had curled up with the dampness. His mussed up curls made him look a lot younger and definitely sexier, Sylvia thought, smiling. After a few minutes, Marian excused herself and went to put dinner on the table. Sylvia went inside to help her.

"Thank you, Sylvia," she said, "You needn't have come in. I can handle this."

"Let me help," Sylvia told her. "What do you need me to do?"

"First, you can warm up this milk in the microwave," Marian gave directions, "and start the potatoes beating in the mixer."

"Why do I need to heat the milk?" Sylvia asked.

"For the potatoes," Marian said. "You'll see, they'll become nice and silky when you heat the milk that you beat into them."

Sylvia told Marian about the Celtic CD's she had found. Marian asked her to bring them for some time. Marian took the pork roast out to rest. It was covered with garlic, pepper and what looked like pine needles.

"It's rosemary," Marian said, chuckling at Sylvia's obviously disbelieving look. "It's that lovely fragrance that is coming from the pork roast."

Marian had turned on the broiler. Sylvia watched her as she drizzled olive oil and kosher salt over asparagus spears and placed them in the broiler. Sylvia continued to mash the potatoes and added the milk. They whipped up soft and light.

Marian worked on slicing the roast. "Be a love, and check on the asparagus," Marian asked Sylvia.

"What am I looking for?" she asked.

"Pretend they're toast," Marian advised, "They should be turning a golden brown. Just make sure it's not burning." Marian told her, "and please ask Owen and Gwen to come in for dinner."

Sylvia did as she was told. The asparagus sizzled in the broiler. When Owen and Gwen came inside, Gwen raised her eyebrows knowingly at Sylvia nodding approvingly at Owen's back. Marian asked Owen to open champagne and pour as she handed the platter of meat to Gwen to take into the dining room. Sylvia put the potatoes in the bowl and Marian retrieved the asparagus.

Sylvia had not eaten in Marian's dining room before this evening. She looked closely at the carved oak chairs and saw a stylized Green Man carved into the backs. Two chairs with extremely high backs sat on either side of the fireplace. They also had rather gruesome Green Men carved into the backs. They looked as though they had come from a church. Before Sylvia could comment, Marian winked at her and Sylvia kept quiet. Before she sat down,

Sylvia ran her hand over the chair backs feeling the outline of the carved green man with her fingers.

Marian toasted them all to their beginning journeys and best wishes with their new jobs, and they settled down to eat. Dinner conversation was sparse, but over dessert and coffee, it started up again. They laughed and talked as if they had known one another for years. Full of food and drink, the girls left quite late and returned to Sylvia's to lie on the couch and groan with fullness.

"I don't think I've ever eaten such a wonderful meal," Gwen told Sylvia.

"I know," Sylvia said, "yet she cooks like that all the time. Marian is amazing."

"Owen's pretty amazing too," Gwen said.

Sylvia blushed.

"Girl, you've fallen for him badly," she stated to her friend.

"I know," Sylvia admitted quietly. "Is it that obvious?" she asked worriedly.

"Only to me," Gwen assured her.

"I can't help it," Sylvia told her, "Lord knows I've tried."

"I don't think you need to worry," Gwen told her. "I think he's interested in you too."

"I don't know," Sylvia said miserably. "I feel like I'm in junior high school or something. When I went to Thurmont, he was taking this gorgeous blond scientist named Anna out to lunch. I've dubbed her the 'ice princess' because of her blond hair, silver eyes, and bitchy look. I was so jealous and I have no right to be jealous," she complained.

"Honestly, I feel like I'm mooning over him like the women do in those bodice ripper romance novels."

"Ahh," Gwen sighed. "They are one of my favorite things to read," she said. "Don't knock them."

Gwen had a passion for romances and what she called 'jelly bean' reading. It was her favorite escape when she was stressed.

Sylvia had witnessed her friend disappearing into a book and eating massive amounts of chocolate for hours. Gwen would come out of the trance like state to tackle the numbers in her higher math and management course with ease. It had always boggled Sylvia's mind how Gwen could break out of the book and go back to serious number crunching and tax law with ease.

"Relax," advised her friend. "If it is to be, it will be," Gwen said sagely.

Sylvia half -heartedly threw a pillow at Gwen. "Oh, shut up," she said sleepily to her friend and yawned heartily.

"C'mon," she said, getting up and tugging at Gwen's hand, "Let's go to bed," she groaned and staggered up the stairs.

Sunday, Sylvia woke up later than usual still feeling full from the food and drink of the previous night. She dragged herself out of bed, made coffee and lay back down on the couch in a daze until Gwen got up. She looked at her friend with half closed eyes.

"I'm not used to weekends like this anymore," she told her friend.

"Me either!" Gwen yawned. "Give me coffee!" she demanded, "or a Bloody Mary," she said. "Hell, let's just go for broke and do both."

They sat on the deck letting the sun warm them and sipping coffee and Gwen's requested Bloody Mary's until they were awake and still relaxed. It was a glorious, sparkling beginning of summer sort of day. It was warm, but not too hot, with a gentle breeze off the water. It was later in the morning when they put on their swimsuits and slathered on sunblock and lay in the sun chatting lazily. Sylvia had a large straw hat pulled over her eyes and Gwen lay on her stomach.

"You know we're becoming candidates for skin cancer, don't you?" Gwen quipped to Sylvia.

"I don't know about you," Sylvia replied, "but my 45+ sunblock will help prevent that dreaded disease. I'm just letting the sun sink into these old bones."

"Huh," Gwen answered and turned over so that she was baking her front.

The day passed too quickly with them chatting, snacking and soaking up the sun. Power boats whizzed up and down the bay and personal watercraft scooted along the shoreline. Neither Gwen nor Sylvia felt like braving the chilly water of the bay once they stood ankle deep and shivered, then continued to bake on the deck. Before long it was mid-afternoon and Gwen decided it was time to go back to Connecticut. She gave a long sigh and looked wistfully at the deck and the water when she went inside to dress and pack up her things.

It didn't take her long to pack up. She gave Sylvia a huge hug and wished her well on the new job. "Keep me informed about Owen," she teased her friend.

"Oh, you!" Sylvia cried exasperated. "Don't worry," Sylvia said. "You read too many romances! Safe travels." She wished to her friend and Gwen went down the road back to Connecticut.

CHAPTER TWELVE

Every day is a god, each day is a god,
And holiness holds forth in time.
I worship each god,
I praise each day splintered down,
And wrapped in time like a husk,
A husk of many colors spreading,
At dawn fast over the mountains split.
--Annie Dillard

Promptly, at 8:00 the next morning, Sylvia nervously arrived at Thurmont. Carol, the secretary in personnel, had her fill out several forms, took her to security to get her badge and set her up with the IT gurus for her email account. It was nearly 11 a.m. by the time she arrived in the marketing department office. Mr. Carter came out to greet her.

"Good morning, Ms. Ash," he said heartily and shook her hand again.

"It's Sylvia, please," she said, returning his warm grip.

"All right," he nodded, "This is your desk." He pointed to the desk in the front office.

"I'm afraid you'll be somewhat of an office assistant as well as an assistant information officer. We don't have a secretary so you'll be fielding phone calls as well as taking messages for the department. We're the little brother end of a much larger public information office from the parent company. Mostly, folks have my direct line and e-mail," he told her, "I try to pull my own weight."

As he spoke, he reminded her of the 'Lou Grant' character in the old "Mary Tyler Moore" television series. He seemed to be rough and tough on the outside, but she thought she could see part of a marshmallow core.

"I thought you should read through what's happened in the last few months with the media," he said to her. "Thurmont is part of two EPA Superfund clean-up projects. The community and environmental groups think we're horrible and we're out to change that image."

"Sure," Sylvia said uncertainly.

"Come into my office and get some of this stuff," he told her.

She followed him into an untidy office. His desk had several piles and things looked stuffed into bookcases. It looked as though he had been there for years rather than a few months. He sighed and didn't offer an explanation when she glanced around the office, but rather pulled through what hair he had left on his head. In all of the piles on the desk, Sylvia was amazed to see that he could lay his hands on exactly what he needed. He gave her notebooks and files that were filled with marking profiles, glossy brochures and newspaper articles as well as court litigation. He helped her carry these out and dumped them on her desk and turned on the computer next to it. When they logged onto the Internet, the home page was for Thurmont.

"I'll leave you to look at this stuff," Mr. Carter said. "And, don't worry, I'll take care of the phone and stuff today."

"Thanks," Sylvia returned quietly sitting down slowly and deliberately in front of the huge pile of notebooks.

She spent the next couple of hours reading old promotional brochures, news articles and going through the website. It was nearly one when Mr. Carter emerged from his office. Sylvia looked up feeling a bit dazed.

"Good Lord!" he exclaimed. "You should go and get some lunch! The cafeteria will be closing soon."

"Okay," she told him, "Can you tell me where the cafeteria is?" she asked.

He gave her directions and she set off for the plant. She took one or two wrong turns but finally found the cafeteria. After choosing a sandwich and some chips and soda, she sat down in the cafeteria that looked like an atrium. It had floor to ceiling glazed windows that curved in a half circle and looked out onto Thurmont's wooded property. Sylvia sat down where she could look out. Obviously, many had already lunched and there were only a few stragglers. Sylvia munched slowly on her sandwich and chips. Carol from the personnel office came from the line and looked around. Sylvia waved half-heartedly and Carol returned the wave with a smile and headed over to her table.

"It's Sylvia, right?" Carol asked. "May I sit down?"

"Please do," Sylvia returned.

"How's the first day going?" Carol asked.

"All right," Sylvia answered. "But, I'm a bit overwhelmed."

Carol nodded sympathetically. "I know just what you mean," she said. "I felt the same way and it went on for a couple of months. This place is so big!"

Sylvia nodded in agreement and then asked, "I had no idea about the size of this corporation. It's quite a revelation. How long have you worked here?"

"A couple of years," Carol added. "Mr. Keely is one of the new hires too," she told Sylvia. "He came about six months ago. It's been interesting adjusting to a new boss," she told Sylvia.

"What do you mean?" Sylvia asked.

"Well," Carol confided in her, "my old boss was a love," she said, "and I was so sad when he retired. When Mr. Keely was hired, at first, I thought it would be *great* having such a handsome guy to work for," she said.

Sylvia nodded and motioned for her to go on.

Carol had munched on a couple of Sylvia's potato chips before she answered. "Well, you know he isn't bad to look at. He looks like one of those guys in the underwear ads," Carol said and Sylvia nodded again.

"But," Carol said, "I learned that looks aren't everything. Mr. Keely is an ass," she confided to Sylvia tossing her dark, sleek pageboy.

Sylvia was so surprised at this that she nearly choked on her soda. Then they both started laughing.

"Well, I did think he looked like a Ken doll or something plastic," Sylvia told her.

"I know!" Carol said, "But the problem is that he has the brains of one too!" Then she looked around nervously. "I'm sorry," she said finally, "I shouldn't have said anything."

"Don't worry," Sylvia said. "I know no one and certainly wouldn't pass that on," Sylvia told her comfortingly.

Carol looked relieved. "Thanks," she said.

"Mr. Carter seems nice," Sylvia ventured. "We're supposed to meet to talk later today. Speaking of which," Sylvia said as she glanced at her watch, "I should be getting back. Thanks for sitting and having lunch with me," she said to Carol.

"You're welcome," Carol said. "We'll do it again soon. I'll e-mail you."

Sylvia left smiling. Carol was nice. She found her way back to her office and sat down with the books again. After a couple of additional hours of reading, her eyes were blurry. Mr. Carter emerged from his office again.

"This probably isn't a good time to meet," he asked, "Is it?"

"I would prefer meeting tomorrow morning," Sylvia told him. "My head is spinning with reading all of this stuff," she admitted.

He nodded and said, "Rightfully so. But, I would like to put a thought or two into your head to cook until tomorrow," he told her. "Thurmont's press has been very negative due to the two Superfund clean-up projects in the last couple of years as I mentioned earlier, and no doubt you're reading about it in these notebooks. They're looking for a way to convince the public that we're a good organization that cares about the community. They're looking to marketing to come up with most of the ideas, but it would be nice if we could submit some ideas to 'big brother' company, and show them what we're made of. We can brainstorm this tomorrow morning." He told her. "You've had enough for one day."

"Thanks," Sylvia said. "I'll give it some thought."

When it was time to go, she left and drove home in a haze. She was surprised at how tired she was. She didn't have a clue as to what kind of marketing campaign she could suggest and wondered if she was in over her head. Sylvia poured a glass of wine and went out on the deck to watch the colors in the sky go from brilliant blue to the backlit gold. The sun pierced the rest of the sky from behind the fluffy clouds and Sylvia gasped involuntarily. She had to agree with Gwen, this was a great place to live. The phone rang, interrupting her reverie of the sunset. It was Marian checking in on her first day.

"It was fine," she told Marian. "Although I'm not really sure what I'm doing," she admitted ruefully. "At least…not yet."

Marian murmured assurances to her that everything would be all right, said they would talk again soon and hung up. Sylvia poked about in the refrigerator and freezer looking for something for dinner. She popped a frozen meal into the microwave and ate woodenly a few minutes later wondering what Mr. Carter was expecting from her the next day.

He greeted her heartily when she walked in the next morning, "Hello, Sylvia," he boomed. "I'll give you a couple of minutes to get settled and then we can meet. You should check your e-mail a couple of times a day," he advised.

She nodded at him and put her purse in the bottom desk drawer.

"Do you drink coffee?" he asked.

"Definitely," Sylvia answered.

"Let me show you where you can get a cup," he said as he led her out of the office and down the hallway to a small kitchenette. "Everyone chips in coffee, creamer, sugar, etc.," he told her, "and we all try to keep the place fairly cleaned up. Whoever's in first makes a pot of coffee. When it's empty, you should make another."

"Okay," Sylvia said, making a mental note to pick up an extra can of coffee on her next trip to the grocery store.

He poured her a Styrofoam cupful and handed it to her. "You'll probably want to bring in your own mug," he advised and they walked back to the office.

The phone was ringing as they entered the office. Mr. Carter picked it up and barked, "Public Information Office!" He spoke for a few minutes to whoever was on the other end, and put them on hold and turned to Sylvia, "I'll take this into my office and be with you in a few minutes," he told her.

Sylvia sat down sipping her coffee and looked at her bare desk while the computer warmed up. She didn't have pictures of children or pets to place on the desk but thought she could bring in a small plant or pretty shell or something to make it less sterile. In fact, the entire office was on the sterile side. She thought she would have to do something about that. She turned back to her e-mail. Mr. Carter had sent her a test message and she replied. There was a notice of an all employee dinner meeting at a local facility on Wednesday evening. Sylvia made a mental note that she needed to attend. She quickly emailed her mother and Gwen with her office e-mail account and then logged onto the Thurmont website. It was a somewhat slick site that touted their chemical products and their uses. It wouldn't be overly friendly to the typical Internet surfer. She wondered if they could add a community piece at how Thurmont was working to clean-up their Superfund project problems. She needed to get more details and was thinking about it when Mr. Carter returned.

"Are you ready to meet?" he asked.

"Yes, indeed," Sylvia replied. They took the notebooks and Sylvia took a tablet and pen to a small table in his office. He moved a couple of stacks of papers and sat down. Other than the piles of papers, his office was sterile.

"Public opinion of Thurmont is at an all-time low," he told her blandly. "Our stock is beginning to be affected. Our sister company has all the fancy pants marketing folks for the advertisements for our products, but we need to find a way to come out smelling like a rose to the public."

Sylvia nodded and let him continue.

"This is a new position for me too," he said with a note of discomfort in his voice. "I've only been at this site a short time. They tell me it's a kick upstairs to have this position, but I feel as though it's a kick in the pants," he said. "If I don't come up with something good…" he stopped and left everything hanging.

"I think I understand," Sylvia said. "Can you let me continue to read through this stuff and I can jot down some ideas?" she asked.

"Of course," he said. "I just wanted to let you know what was going on."

"I appreciate your candidness," Sylvia said.

He nodded and returned to his office. She went back to her desk and continued to read articles on the Superfund clean-up. Apparently from this site, chemicals leaked into a nearby stream and killed it. The clean-up took shape to dredge out the stream and place a rock bed beneath it with plastics and wire so that the chemical would not leach back into the water. They recently introduced fish into the new streambed. Another leak of pesticides created havoc with some farmers' fields, ground water and with the livestock. Steps were being taken to rectify the situation. Sylvia read until she felt cross-eyed. About 12:30 she knocked on Mr. Carter's door and said she was going to lunch. He nodded and she returned to the cafeteria. It was noisy today, filled with at least a hundred hungry employees. Sylvia scanned the room for an empty table. She didn't feel brave enough to butt into anyone's conversation. Sylvia lingered around the cutlery area and dawdled getting her drink and condiments. Finally, some people got up and she made a beeline for a small table near a window.

Sitting down with her lunch, she thought about the clean-up projects and wondered how they could improve local opinion. This was a relatively small community area. Even though she had not actually grown up here, she knew the whole county had a small town feel to it. Everyone seemed to know everyone. Historically this was a blue-collar community. The Army post in Aberdeen employed many blue collar workers as well as professionals. Many people worked in nearby Delaware and a few commuted to Baltimore or Philadelphia. It was a nice slice of America in which to raise families. Perhaps something on the angle of America and apple pie might go well here. Family and community and family activities ran through her mind. She thought she could mention this to Mr. Carter. She was lost in her thoughts and jumped when a voice broke through.

"Can I sit here?" It was Owen smiling at her.

"Sure," she said looking up at him. "Please do."

"I didn't mean to startle you," he said as he sat down and took a drink of his soda.

"No," Sylvia replied. "That's all right. I was lost in thought about…" she broke off, not knowing exactly what to say.

She pulled her thoughts together and continued, "I'm looking into the Superfund clean-ups from Thurmont," she told him, "and trying to think of a way to improve public opinion of the company."

Owen nodded. "Have you been on the EPA Superfund site yet?" he asked her.

"No," she said in surprise. "Tell me about it," she said eagerly, leaning forward to listen to the din of the cafeteria.

"Well," he said, "It's a government site that lists all the superfund clean-ups. It might give you some good ideas for other communities."

"Thanks," Sylvia said gratefully. "How do I find it? Do you know the URL?"

"Just type in 'EPA Superfund' on a search engine," Owen told her. "You should be able to find it quickly that way."

"How's your job going?" Sylvia asked.

"All right," Owen answered. "I'm mostly going through paperwork at this point. I'm hoping to get out into the field by the end of the week."

"Is there room for one more?" a voice interrupted their conversation.

Sylvia looked up to see Anna, impeccably dressed once again in a gorgeous pantsuit standing next to Owen. The pale lavender of the pantsuit brought out her chilly silvery gray eyes perfectly. Once again, Sylvia had the childish thought she was dealing with the Snow Queen from fairy tales.

"Sure," Owen said amiably, his eyes brightening when he looked up at Anna, "I'll go get a chair."

He pulled a chair from another table and Anna sat down quite close to Owen. Sylvia had never been a jealous person, but she could feel the green-eyed monster rising within her. Sylvia felt as though she was suddenly thrust into a game of chess with Owen as a pawn. Or so Sylvia thought. Anna seemed to be making deliberate moves towards Owen and trying to see where Sylvia stood. It was somewhat like the politics that Gwen had told her about in her own bit of corporate America. Anna seemed to look at her coldly and triumphantly moved imperceptibly closer to Owen moment by moment until her arm was lightly touching his. The small round luncheon table suddenly felt too crowded and Sylvia suddenly felt like an intruder. She didn't want to play this game. Under the table, she shredded her napkin into small bits and tried to smile confidently at Anna.

"What were you two discussing?" she asked.

"The EPA Superfund clean-ups that are going on," Sylvia answered her

"And what will you do about it?" Anna asked pointedly.

"Working on raising the public's opinion of Thurmont," Sylvia said, meeting her silvery gray eyes evenly.

"Rah, rah, sis boom bah," Anna said with quiet sarcasm, "Quite the little cheerleader for Thurmont."

Sylvia could have slapped her. "Not quite," she said trying hard to keep the sarcasm out of her own voice. "Excuse me," she said. "I need to get back to the office."

"Nice to see you," she said directly to Owen. "Tell Marian I said 'hello.'"

"Will do," Owen said and he started to rise as she left.

Sylvia dumped her tray and walked back to the office with anger and jealousy building with each step. She didn't know what it was about Anna, but something about the woman rubbed her the wrong way. She knew that part of it was the competition with Owen, but there was something else that she couldn't put her finger on.

Sylvia logged onto the Internet when she returned to the office and searched for the EPA site. It was an amazing site with tons of information. She jotted down some notes to take home with her.

When Mr. Carter said good night to her, she mentioned that she would have some ideas the next day. He looked pleased as he wished her a good evening.

Thinking about her empty desk, Sylvia thought a basket of herbs might be a nice aromatic addition to her workspace. She wondered what else she could bring in to brighten up the place. Sylvia would have to ask Carol if she could hang her own pictures or if she could choose prints she liked from the company's cache. She called Marian to ask her if she would want to go herb shopping on Saturday.

"Oh, Sylvia," Marian said, "I'm sorry, I can't go. Owen is bringing someone from work for dinner, and I'll be pretty busy putting it together."

"Okay," Sylvia said, sounding dejected.

"You're welcome to come to dinner also," Marian suggested. "Owen said that he's bringing a scientist colleague. I think her name is Anna or something, on Saturday."

"No thank you," Sylvia declined the dinner offer with a little more vehemence than she meant to express to Marian.

"Do you know Anna?" Marian asked.

"We've met a couple of times," Sylvia answered her truthfully.

"It sounds as though you don't like her very much," Marian prodded.

"I actually would rather reserve judgment," Sylvia told her, "and talk to you after the dinner party."

"All right," Marian said.

"I'm sorry you can't come plant shopping with me, but maybe we can go again soon. I would like to start some pots on the deck and work on the landscaping in my spare time," Sylvia told her.

"We'll go in the next few weeks," Marian promised. "Talk to you soon."

Sylvia hung up steaming at the fact that Anna would be having dinner with Owen and Marian this weekend. She went and e-mailed Gwen with her frustrations and then stomped out of the house and walked down the beach to the marina and back up the road. Feeling only slightly better she took out her frustrations by eating some ice cream for dinner while she watched an old movie. The phone rang. It was Gwen.

"Boy," Gwen said to her after they had said 'hello,' you sounded really upset."

"This is silly," she told her friend. "Owen and I haven't even the semblance of a date let alone a relationship. I don't know why I'm so worked up about it."

"It sounds as though she's a bitch and you like Owen and you don't want him to get hurt," Gwen said soothingly.

"You're right," Sylvia said, "but I think I'm jealous too. Actually, I know I am," she admitted ruefully. "I just don't know what it is about that woman that sticks in my craw," she complained to Gwen.

"And it makes me nervous since I'm the new kid on the block at Thurmont," she admitted. "Anna doesn't seem like the kind of colleague I would want to spill my guts too. She's more of the back-stabbing kind," Sylvia told Gwen.

"I know if I was there you might throw something at me, but if this thing between you and Owen is to be, it will be," Gwen advised. "Give it time and hang in there."

"Oh….you!" Sylvia retorted with exasperation. "Stop trying to make this into one of your cheap novels. That's not what it's about!"

"Yeah, sure," Gwen said in a voice heavy with sarcasm. "Sylvia, do you honestly think I'm stupid or something?" her friend asked.

"No," Sylvia replied, "but, there isn't anything going on with Owen. I have no claims on him. For God's sake, I just met the man. He could be a real creep."

"Do you think Marian would love a creep so much?" Gwen pushed on.

"N, n…no," Sylvia admitted, "but, still, Gwen, nothing is going on nor do I think there will be."

"Right," said Gwen once again sarcastic.

"Thanks for calling," Sylvia said. "It was nice to growl about it with someone. I didn't want to cloud Marian's opinion of Anna until after she has a chance to meet her," she told her friend after she explained that Anna would be at Marian's for dinner on Saturday.

"Marian's a pretty good judge of character," Gwen said. "The ice princess won't pull anything over on her."

"You're right," Sylvia admitted. "So, I need to be patient...and it's damn hard!"

"Yes, I'll agree. You're at 'friendly' with Owen and want to be 'friendlier' and that can be an uncomfortable place to be. Good night!" Gwen said. "I'll give you a call back after the weekend to get Marian's report."

"Okay," Sylvia laughed, "Good night."

Feeling much better, she hung up the phone and tried to focus her thoughts on the project at work. She jotted down a few more ideas she thought would appeal to Mr. Carter before she went to bed.

Mr. Carter was pleased with her suggestions the next morning. She mentioned that with a small town like atmosphere and community that it might be fun to run a fishing contest in the stream that was returning back to health. Also, Sylvia suggested that they start an outreach program to the schools. She suggested that some of the scientists working at Thurmont and perhaps the environmental experts like Owen could speak at schools in the fall to discuss their jobs. Sylvia wondered if the parent company might create some support materials. She also suggested educational grants or contests for environmentally friendly inventions and good news fliers to the community in their community efforts. Mr. Carter nodded with pleasure at her suggestions.

"Good ideas," he told her, "But all of your suggestions couldn't actually start until the fall because the corporate wheels are difficult to turn. We'll also need to do some outreach work this summer," he told her. "Bay Days are coming up in July the weekend after the 4th and we've been asked to run a booth with some marketing items. I could compensate your weekend time by substituting it for a day off during the week," he suggested. "We'll need to man the booth with at least one other person. We can split up the time during the day, but, we can plan that for a couple of weeks. I like your ideas about the 'good news' fliers. Get started researching and complete a couple of mock ups. I have a budget and I can fly that through some of the folks upstairs pretty quickly."

Sylvia agreed. She thought it would be great to have a day off mid-week. He discussed plans for giving her a tour of the plant on Thursday. Mr. Carter wanted her to work on creating a helpful link on the website and design brochures for the public answering questions regarding the Superfund clean-up on top of the fliers and Bay Days. He was working on a standardized letter to have on file when complaints or issues came to the corporation. He also wanted to have some informational brochures available for the booth at Bay Days, so they were under a time crunch. Sylvia spent the rest of the day working on a brochure importing images from the website and pulling together a draft on the history of the company. Before she knew it, the day was over and Mr. Carter was asking her if she would be attending the company meeting at the local fire hall.

"Yes," she answered him. "I thought it was mandatory from the e-mail I received."

"Technically they cannot force you to come, but it is strongly recommended," Mr. Carter suggested. "Be sure to wear your badge and sign in," he advised. "Usually, they provide a decent meal. For a bachelor like me, it's a good thing," he said smiling and patted his ample paunch.

"I guess I'll see you there," Sylvia said. She drove to the local fire hall where parking was already crowded. Sylvia maneuvered into a parking space and went in, surprised at the crowd. After signing in, she went into the queue for dinner. They had provided a variety of sandwiches, salads, chips and desserts. Sylvia chose what looked like chicken salad in a red pepper tortilla, a garden salad, and some chips. She looked around the room to see a friendly face. Mr. Carter was deep in conversation at a full table of other middle-aged men. Sylvia did not want to join that group. She looked for Carol but didn't see her and finally found an empty space at a table near the back.

There was a mixture of men and women at her table. They introduced themselves and then politely ignored her and continued their conversation leaving Sylvia to eat quietly. The meeting began and the gentleman at the podium began talking about financial reports and the company stock. Sylvia was bored. At this point, she really wasn't interested. She looked at the occupants of her table. They politely ignored her, listened to the speaker and quietly commented among themselves. She looked around the room for Owen. Finally, she saw him far across the room with Anna at his side. She had her folding chair as close to him as she possibly could and her slim hand placed on his thigh. She couldn't help herself from staring, her emotions roller coasting.

All of a sudden she realized she saw an aura around Owen. She blinked a couple of times, looked away and looked back at him. It was there, a green and bluish energy around his body that 'breathed' like the tree auras. It seemed to have a different thickness around portions of his body. She looked over at Anna. She had to look hard to see her auras. It was dark compared to Owen's. She concentrated more and realized Anna's aura was a dark red. Fascinated, she looked around the room. If she focused on a table of people, she could see the energy emanating from several of the occupants, but not all. One woman's aura curled up like a puff of smoke another's looked like a wild hairstyle or a crown. Most were a small layer of white energy that surrounded their bodies like the auras on the plants but were thicker around their head and shoulders.

She would love to tell the Green Man about her new skill, but did not want him to appear in the middle of the meeting. The man at the podium droned on and on. He had a small aura, but it could clearly be seen with the lighting in the room. Another man joined him who looked out at the crowd. His eye caught Sylvia's. She supposed it looked as though she was staring at him, but really she was looking for his aura. His aura was large, full of energy and was red with streaks of lemony green. It was almost a sickening combination. Staring at it made her slightly nauseous. She would have to find someone who could tell her what everything meant. He raised his eyebrows and nodded and she knew it was for her. His gaze made her uncomfortable. She thought if she was telepathic that his mental note was 'fresh meat.' She tore her eyes from his gaze and looked down at her empty plate. When she glanced up again, his gaze had moved on.

The meeting ended and Sylvia realized she hadn't listened to a word. She picked up her purse and nearly ran out of the fire hall, wanting to exit before Owen, Anna and the guy at the podium. Sylvia started her car and screeched a little exiting the parking lot quickly. At the stoplight, she took a deep breath and reached to turn on the radio. She jumped and slammed on the brakes to keep her car from rear-ending the one in front of her. The Green Man was sitting in the passenger seat.

"Ohmigod!" she cried putting her hand to her fast beating heart. "You scared me! Do you always just have to 'appear'?" she asked. "Can't you give me a warning, like the rustling of leaves or something?"

"Sorry," he said, but there was clearly a note of humor in his voice, "but I didn't think it prudent to appear in the fire hall."

"You're right," Sylvia said, "But, why are you here?" she asked.

"You called," he said simply.

"Oh," Sylvia replied remembering how she desperately had wanted to talk to him at the fire hall. She started to head towards home when the light turned green again.

"Something like ET's phoning home?" she queried him.

The Green Man laughed a deep belly laugh that resonated through her small car like a tenor singing opera.

"I can see people's auras now!" she told him with amazement. "It was incredible!" she said. "A lot of them were like the plant auras – a layer of white light around their bodies, but some others had color."

The Green Man was calm, "Good, good," he replied in his rich baritone, "that is part of your gift."

She could tell he was pleased by the tone of his voice.

"What does it mean?" she asked. "And what does it mean when there are different colors?"

"What colors are you seeing?" the Green Man asked her.

"Mostly I saw a white light," she said, "and I saw green, blue, red and yellow."

"Hmm," the Green Man, "Very good. If you practice, you'll begin seeing colors more frequently," he told her. "Relax and let it come." He disappeared, this time with a soft sound of the rustling of leaves.

Sylvia rolled her eyes and swore softly under her breath in frustration. At least, he had given her a warning leaf rustle when he disappeared. She assumed he was laughing in whatever cosmic place he went to.

CHAPTER THIRTEEN

Ancora Imparo
"I am still learning."
--Michaelangelo

The next two days at work were too busy for Sylvia to focus on auras. Mr. Carter had arranged a tour of the plant for her and it took much of the day to walk through the facility where her office was located. It was much, much larger than it appeared to be from the outside. Past the front office building, there were two research and development laboratories. Although she did not see her, this is where Sylvia assumed Anna worked. She also did not see Owen or his office and wondered where it was located. On Friday, she took a jitney to get to the manufacturing plant that was down a small road and through the trees. It was almost camouflaged with its tan brick and nestled among rolling hills. She had not realized that a large manufacturing plant was out of sight from the main company facility. Sylvia was surprised at its immensity. It was quite an operation. Trucks carrying bags and drums of chemical fertilizer and pesticide components and completed product came and went in a steady stream. Sylvia found herself saturated with information.

Mr. Carter chuckled when he saw her return late Friday afternoon.

"You look worn out," he said.

Sylvia nodded trying to think of a positive response. She couldn't because she was so weary.

"I know," he said, "This is a huge place that's deceiving in size from the outside. We can debrief on Monday. Go home and have a relaxing weekend," he told her. "I'll see you Monday morning."

Sylvia thanked him. She wasn't sure if she could even speak intelligently at that point.

When she got home, Sylvia flopped onto the couch thinking what a nice boss she had and wondered why he had been sent to Thurmont. He had hinted that it wasn't his choice to change locations and he commuted a good hour or more to and from work. He actually lived in a town fairly close to her hometown outside of Philadelphia. His commute must be brutal, she thought.

She woke up the next morning, stretching luxuriously, and relishing in the fact that she didn't have to go to work. She had fallen asleep on the couch and woken up several hours later, crawled up to bed, stripping off her clothes and falling into a deep sleep. It was a gorgeous summer morning. A soft breeze blew the curtains in the bedroom. Sylvia ran downstairs to put on coffee, took a shower, got a cup of coffee and jumped back in bed naked with a steaming cup and a good book. She felt like a queen.

After an hour or so of reading, she remembered she had wanted to go to the herb farm. She called Marian to confirm the directions. It was about 45 minutes away and through winding roads off the beaten track. Sylvia kept her fingers crossed that she could find it again. She was successful and picked up several healthy plants and two beautiful planters that looked like stone, but were made of a fibrous material. She also picked up a small herb basket with thyme, lavender and rosemary to put on her desk at work. The woman who owned the herb farm urged her to purchase exotic plants for her office when Sylvia explained the sterility of the place. She caved and bought a bromeliad and a peace lily. They were certainly easy enough to care for. She loved the stag's head fern but wasn't sure it would go over well at Thurmont to have a large plant attached to the wall.

On her way home, she stopped in a small town filled with boutiques and antique stores. One of the boutiques had gorgeous clothes in exquisite fabrics. Sylvia fell in love with a lemony yellow linen sundress sprinkled with small purple iris. Sylvia decided had to have it, especially after she tried it on. Usually, Sylvia didn't wear yellow, but when she put on this dress, it brought out the golden brown highlights in her brown hair and thankfully didn't make her look sallow. Sylvia bought it immediately not even caring where or when Sylvia would wear it. She picked up some fresh strawberries and early vegetables at a farm stand, potting soil from a discount store and headed home to work on the planters.

The planters looked beautiful flanking the stairs from the deck filled with thyme that spilled over the edges, tall spiky rosemary, curly tufts of parsley, and mounds of oregano. She breathed in the heady fragrance of the herbs happily. All day she kept trying not to think of Anna with Owen and Marian, but it was difficult especially now that the sun was setting and she knew Anna was surely at Marian's by this time. Sylvia wished jealously and childishly that she had a reason to go or call there.

Anna was a puzzle to her. She apparently sensed Sylvia as a threat with regards to Owen…but was that enough for the cold hatred that she had seen in her eyes? It was disconcerting to have someone who is a stranger dislike her so intently and for no apparent reason.

The weekend passed far too quickly for Sylvia and she moved into a busy week. Mr. Carter wanted drafts of brochures on the company by the end of the week. Sylvia pulled together her notes and worked on a couple of different designs to share with him. Mr. Carter was busy addressing some of the public's concern about the Superfund clean-up. He received several letters of complaint and some hate mail for the company. Any phone calls she received on the subject she thankfully forwarded to his voicemail. Carol e-mailed her about lunch and Sylvia gladly joined her. Sylvia had started to pack lunch, finding it difficult to cook a meal for just one person. Usually, she rounded out her sandwich with a salad from the cafeteria. Carol was waiting for her when she arrived.

"How are you doing?" Carol asked.

"Fine," Sylvia answered, "Hard at work."

"I know what you mean," Carol complained. "I had to work late a lot last week."

"Yes," Sylvia said, "I didn't see you at the meeting."

"I know," Carol said, "I opted to stay here late rather than listen to the boring financial reports. Sometimes it's difficult not to nod off in those meetings."

"I know what you mean," Sylvia said. "I was yawning a lot by the end."

Owen came from the cafeteria over to where they were seated.

"Do you mind if I join you?" he asked.

"No, not at all," Carol said, smiling up at him.

Sylvia made introductions. Carol had met Owen briefly when he was hired and asked how he was doing. They chatted about the lovely weather and the upcoming expected blaze of heat that would hit next month. Carol left in a few minutes needing to get back to work.

"How was your weekend?" Sylvia asked Owen lightly, dying to know where Anna was.

"Good," Owen replied, "Quiet. You?"

"Same," Sylvia replied, "Quiet, but good."

They were both silent for a few moments, not knowing how to continue the conversation. Before the silence became too awkward,

Owen told her that Marian would be calling her soon. She was planning a party in a couple of weeks and wondered if Sylvia would come and also help her out.

"I'd be glad to," Sylvia said. "Do you know when it is?" she asked him.

"June 21st," he told her. He asked how the job was going and she told him it was fine and busy. He had finally started working in the plant and checked out some of the environmental controls. He mentioned he would start some tests either this week or next. They were quiet again. The silence wasn't exactly strained, but it was uncomfortable. Sylvia couldn't help but feel a little prickly towards him. She looked down at his hands resting on the table. The aura was there, just a ½ inch or so of bluish-white light emanating from his skin. She looked at her own hand. It was difficult to see her own aura. She could just barely see the outline of it. She wondered what would happen if their two auras met. Instinctively she moved her hand closer.

"Sylvia," Owen said softly, breaking into her thoughts. "Are you okay?"

Her hand stopped moving. "Hmm?" she murmured and looked up at him, but avoided his gaze. "Sorry," she said, flushing a little. "I was thinking of something I needed to edit." She didn't feel right lying to him but didn't want to explain about the auras. "I'd better get back to the office. Nice to see you," she added politely.

Owen nodded, "Same here," he said.

She returned to the office trying to sort out her feelings about Owen. He had been friendly today, but too polite. She guessed that he definitely did not feel the same way she did about him and decided it was a school girl crush that had to be put to bed.

Hoping that working hard would put Owen out of her mind, Sylvia completed the draft of one of the brochures. She took it into Mr. Carter, who was pleased with the result. She told him the other brochure was nearly completed. He said he would send this first brochure to the corporate folks and let them know a second was coming. He hoped they would send it out for printing by the end of the week.

That night Marian called to tell her about the upcoming party. They chatted and Sylvia carefully avoided asking her about Anna at first.

"Tell me about the party," Sylvia asked her. "How can I help you?"

"Well," Marian began, "It's a midsummer's eve party. We had lots of fun with them in England. We'll be mildly pagan and build a bonfire and celebrate summer," she told Sylvia. "I think I'll refrain from rolling burning wheels down the hill, though," she said with a chuckle, "and quell my deeper pagan roots."

Marian continued, "I am hoping to serve fresh strawberries with champagne," she said.

"Boy! You pull out all the stops!" Sylvia interrupted.

"Well, yes," Marian said matter of fact, "It will be fun. I was hoping I could enlist your help to pick strawberries that morning with me. I'll have most of the food prepared, but we'll need to put on the finishing touches."

"Sounds like fun," Sylvia said.

Not able to contain her curiosity, Sylvia asked, "How was dinner Saturday night?"

"Fine," Marian answered blandly. "Anna is an interesting person. She seems to be a brilliant chemist. Anna and Owen talked about things that were way over my head," she told Sylvia. "She asked Owen a lot of questions for his environmental control plans," she mentioned to Sylvia vaguely.

Sylvia didn't comment and hung up after a few more minutes of chit-chat. She smiled at Marian's comment that Anna was 'interesting.' Sylvia would have loved to have seen her face. Feeling catty, she told herself to stop.

Sylvia finished creating the second promotional brochure the next morning. She e-mailed Carol if she wanted to have lunch together. She did and they met in the cafeteria.

Carol was her usual perky self. She told Sylvia she was going back to school in the fall. She enjoyed her job, she told Sylvia but wanted to go back for some computer classes and possibly a degree.

"Uh, oh," Carol said suddenly, "Look out."

"What?" Sylvia asked.

"Mr. Headly, one of the company executives and the company leach! Don't let him get you in a corner," she advised in whispered tones. "I call him Mr. Dick Head."

Sylvia started to giggle. She couldn't help herself.

"I'm serious!" Carol insisted, "Stop laughing! Here he comes!"

Mr. Headly was the man who stared at her so from the podium at the meeting last week. He was the one with the aura with dark streaks and he made a beeline for their table.

"Hello, Carol," he said. "What's the joke?" he asked.

"Hello Mr. Headley," Carol said politely, nearly blushing. "No joke, we're just silly. This is Sylvia Ash, one of our new hires. She works in Public Information," she said, introducing Sylvia, who was taking long sips of cold soda to calm her giggles.

"Ah, yes," he said. "I'm Richard Headly," he introduced himself. "It's nice to meet you." He held out his hand and Sylvia took it introducing herself.

He held her hand for a moment too long for her comfort.

"I saw a copy of your brochure," he told her. "Nice work. We'll be keeping an eye on you." He leered at her and she truly blushed.

He turned to go and Carol rolled her eyes at Sylvia. Sylvia had to choke back a giggle. She took a calming gulp of cold soda again and looked up at Carol, who grinned at her.

"Okay, okay, I've got it…Richard Headly—Dick Head," she said trying to control her giggles a second time.

"I *told* you," Carol said earnestly, trying to hide a smirk.

They watched him work his way through the cafeteria with his fake smile. He sat down when Sylvia saw Anna come in. She watched with interest that Anna practically sat on Mr. Headly's lap and looked like a cat purring and licking cream. He was definitely interested in her attentions too. In fact, they seemed like old friends.

"Oh, those two," Carol said, bored. "They're all over each other all of the time. Not quite a company scandal, but they're an item."

"Really!" Sylvia said. "She's after Owen too," she murmured—more to herself than to Carol.

"Humph," Carol complained. "She's after anything male in pants."

Sylvia laughed. She loved Carol's bold chutzpah.

"Uh, oh," Carol whispered to Sylvia.

Sylvia looked up to see Owen coming into the cafeteria. He saw Anna cozied up to Mr. Headly and had a look of surprise on his face. Anna totally ignored him and he blanched visibly.

"I'll see you later," Carol said, getting up from her seat. She walked past Owen and said, "There's a free seat over there," and she nodded in Sylvia's direction.

Sylvia didn't know whether to kiss her or crown her with her food. Owen came right over and Carol was giving her the thumbs up behind him. Sylvia couldn't react.

"Hi, Syl," he said, "Can I sit here?"

"Sure," she said ignoring Carol's grin.

She tried to keep the conversation light but noticed Owen frequently glancing over at the table with Anna and Mr. Headly. They continued to have their cozy tête-a-tête in front of the company lunch crowd. Personally, Sylvia thought they should go to an office or something. It was embarrassing to watch. She glanced at her watch and knew she had to get back to work.

"I need to get going," Sylvia said gently.

Owen, who had been lost in thought, glanced at her. "Sorry," he said. "Yup, I need to be going too."

They dumped their trays and left. Sylvia didn't glance back to see if Anna was watching or not. She couldn't help but think that things hadn't changed much since high school with the boy/girl competition thing and wondered if they ever would. Owen walked her back to her office.

"See you later," she said lightly.

"See you," he said, still distracted and waved goodbye to her and headed down the hallway.

She didn't have time to think of Owen and their non-conversational lunch. Mr. Carter was pacing from his office to her desk back and forth and back and forth when she went in.

"Is everything okay?" Sylvia asked as she put her purse back into her desk.

Mr. Carter's face looked worried and he glanced at Sylvia anxiously. It looked as though he wanted to say something and then thought the better of it. She peered at him curiously, waiting for him to say something. Finally, after a minute or two, he did.

"Yeah," Mr. Carter answered and then he stopped and turned. "No, not really. I was wondering if you could help me out?" he asked.

"Sure, I guess so," Sylvia answered, totally puzzled.

"I have to meet with a bleeding hearts activist group about the stream clean-up," he told her. "I was wondering if you would come along also."

"Sure," Sylvia answered. "When is it?"

He looked pained. "It's really short notice," he said. "It's tonight."

"That's fine," Sylvia told him. "I don't have any plans for this evening."

Mr. Carter looked relieved. "Thanks," he told her. "I'm hoping these folks will be somewhat calm. We had some pretty radical folks protesting throughout this project…" he broke off.

"I know a little about this, from a friend," Sylvia said. She didn't tell him that her grandmother had been part of some of the protest groups before she became ill.

He gave her the details and asked if she wanted to join him for dinner before the meeting.

"Sure," Sylvia answered.

She spent the afternoon refreshing her memory about the demise of the stream and the clean-up efforts, trying to get prepared for the evening.

They left just after five to get to an area seafood house. After they had ordered dinner, Mr. Carter thanked her again for coming.

"You need to stop thanking me," Sylvia said. "You're making me nervous! What can these people do? We'll be in the meeting room at the public library, right?"

"You're right," Mr. Carter answered. "It will be fine."

He asked her how she liked the area. Sylvia told him that it was nice to live here and not just visit her grandmother here. She said she was settling in nicely.

"I'm not that familiar with the area," he admitted. "Since they shipped me down here, I have spent most of my time either at the office or on the road commuting. I listen to a lot of books on tape," he told her.

Sylvia nodded. "What do you do in your spare time?" she asked him.

He laughed and looked a little sheepish, "I love trains and model trains," he told her. "I have quite a set up in one room of my house."

"I know nothing about that," Sylvia admitted, "but it sounds interesting."

He told her about his travels by rail in the States and in Europe until their food came. The seafood house was relatively quiet on a Tuesday evening. They finished with some time to spare and Mr. Carter suggested they go to the library where the meeting was going to be held for the remaining time.

Sylvia tried to pay for her meal, but Mr. Carter told her absolutely not. He would submit it for reimbursement from the company, he told her. She assented.

The public library in town was quite small but very cozy, thought Sylvia. They had a great variety of videos and a decent selection of books. She looked around and decided that she should get a card, but realized when she pulled out her license, that she needed to change everything over to Gran's address. That would be something she could do on that day off in July. She told the woman at the circulation desk that she would be back in the next few weeks to get a card.

Mr. Carter had taken a book and went back to the meeting room to wait nervously for the group. He had also taken a couple of display boards that shared photos and captions from the beginning of the stream problem to its current 'healed' state and set them up in the room along with some promotional pamphlets on Thurmont and their products. Sylvia continued to look around until she saw a few people come in and head for the meeting room, then she went to join Mr. Carter.

About a dozen people showed up at the meeting. Mr. Carter introduced himself and Sylvia. One woman, in particular, kept looking at Sylvia as if she knew her. He went over, in somewhat of a droning voice, the steps that Thurmont had taken to heal the stream. After his presentation, he opened up the discussion for questions. A couple of folks started firing questions at him regarding Thurmont and their dumping practices. Mr. Carter fielded them well, stating that he could give them information if they contacted him at the office, but reminded them that they were there tonight about the stream. Sylvia admired how he kept his cool. Others were concerned about keeping the stream healthy and how Thurmont would monitor the progress. The discussion became quite heated at a couple of points, and Sylvia couldn't help but interrupt with a suggestion.

Why don't we set up a stream watch?" she asked. "Couldn't we set up something for the summer and then turn it over to a high school or college group in the fall?" she suggested.

Mr. Carter beamed at her so she went on.

"If you're interested," she pulled out a tablet and continued, "you can sign up with your name, address, phone, and e-mail, and I'll be in touch in the next week or so."

The folks in the room calmed down a little. They liked her suggestion. The Librarian came back to signal that the library was closing and Mr. Carter gratefully brought the meeting to a close.

The woman who kept looking at her came up to Sylvia after the meeting.

"Aren't you Holly's granddaughter?" she asked.

"Why, yes!" Sylvia said smiling at her, "Did you know my grandmother?"

"Yes, I certainly did," she said vehemently eyes flashing with something near hatred. "She will be turning over in her grave knowing you're working at Thurmont," she told Sylvia. "Traitor!" she spat out at Sylvia and stalked out of the room.

Sylvia was shaken. No one else seemed to have noticed the exchange. She wished she knew who that woman was. Perhaps Marian could shed some light on why the woman was so bitter.

Mr. Carter was busy folding the presentation boards and taking them out to his car and had not seen her either. Sylvia tried her best to smile and told the people signing on the tablet that she would be in touch in the next few weeks.

"Thanks for coming," Mr. Carter said. "You saved the day in there. Do you know anything about stream watches?" he asked her.

"I was involved in one of my high school classes," she told him. "I think I can pull it together."

"Good work," he said.

"Thanks," she told him, "Have a safe trip home," she yawned. She didn't envy his long commute home that evening.

Sylvia went home puzzled by the woman with the flashing eyes and apparent hatred of Thurmont. It was after nine and she thought it would be too late to call Marian. She would do it tomorrow.

Restless from the meeting Sylvia logged onto the Internet to research stream watches. She read through several websites and after an hour or so wondered if she would regret what she got herself into.

Tired of the Internet she turned to Gran's bookshelves. They were stuffed with a variety of books, local history, modern literature, classics, mysteries, and gardening. Sylvia was tired and wanted to read something brief and she didn't care on what topic. Jammed between books on gardening was a pamphlet. A spectrum of rainbow color swirled in the front and the title "Auras" was emblazoned at the top. Sylvia stared at it in amazement, suddenly feeling more awake. She leafed through it noting it had headings about the colors of auras and the whole pamphlet was only twenty pages or so. She took it up to bed to read, fascinated. Anna's deep red aura, the book indicated, was of a person who was in turmoil, suffering in some way and domineering, Owen's aura, on the other hand, suggested he was helpful, reliable and friendly. Inadvertently she breathed a sigh of relief. She wondered what color her own aura was. She wondered how much Gran had seen and experienced with auras. Still wondering, she fell asleep.

CHAPTER FOURTEEN

The earth dries up and withers,
The world languishes and withers,
The heavens languish together
With the earth.
The earth lies polluted
Under its inhabitants;
For they have transgressed laws,
Violated the statutes,
Broken the everlasting covenant.
--Isaiah 24:4-5, NRSV

Sylvia was late to work the next morning, careening into the parking lot long past her usual arrival time. She was relieved to find that Mr. Carter wasn't in the office. Breathing a sigh of relief she went to get a cup of coffee before she settled down to check voice mail messages and email. Mr. Carter had sent an email stating that he would be arriving at noon because they had worked last evening and urged her to think about an afternoon of compensation time. She picked up the phone to call Marian to talk to her about last night's meeting. She had no idea who the woman was but suspected it was one of Gran's compatriots on some of the environmental issues.

"There are several folks out there that are still angry with Thurmont. I missed some of the most heated rallies when I was in England," Marian reminded her. "They are quite convinced that Thurmont is out to destroy the area with their chemical poisons."

Sylvia sighed, "I know," she replied. "I had my first taste last night." Sylvia described the woman to Marian, who had no idea who this woman was but said she would think about it.

They hung up and Sylvia searched for website information on starting a stream watch. Revisiting sites she had logged onto the night before, she printed out several pages and worked on a proposal to give to Mr. Carter.

She ran home on her lunch hour to grab a pair of old khakis, t-shirt, and sneakers. She was anxious to check out the stream that afternoon. Mr. Carter was in his office when she got back and she handed him her proposal and let him know that she was going outside. He beamed at her benevolently telling her again that she had saved the day the previous night.

Sylvia changed her clothes and walked towards the woods and stream that were on the Thurmont property. She could hear the stream gurgling away and saw a little of the vestiges of where the stream renewal took place. The warm weather had turned sultry and Sylvia wiped away beads of sweat that formed on her forehead. She went down to peer at the stream. It looked good. Some insects were scooting around and she saw some snails on the rocks. She thought she saw a tadpole or minnow, but it skittered away too quickly for her to identify it. They had placed a bed of rocks at the bottom of the stream and it riffled musically. At a shallow portion of the creek, Sylvia stepped from rock to rock to get to the other bank. The little riffles of water teased her sneakers as she balanced from one rock to another teetering dangerously in one spot.

Once on the other side of the stream, Sylvia noticed that the woods and area around the creek were strangely quiet. She didn't hear any birdsong or scrabble of squirrels. Sylvia walked a little further into the forest, looking at the trees. She couldn't see any auras up close, not yet at least. She wanted to look around, but the ground beneath her feet was strange. It wasn't quite like mud or sand or clay, but something in between.

Sylvia knew there were many natural springs in the area, but the air didn't have the fresh smell of sharp minerals and the clean, wet smell of moisture, as a spring does. When she reached down to touch some of it, a trail of large red fire ants was traversing the muck on their way straight towards her. Sylvia yelped, pulling her hand back quickly. Gingerly, Sylvia stepped out of their way not wanting one to take a field trip up her pants leg.

Thinking she heard voices, Sylvia turned quickly and tripped over a root. Instead of falling, strong leaf covered arms caught her. She looked up and saw the Green Man's face and smiled.

"Thanks," she started to say, but he put one of his brown fingers over her lips stopping her comment.

"Shh," he whispered. "You don't want them to see you."

He held her tightly against him. He was so large that his green and brown figure was like a cloak when she was pressed against him.

"Who is it?" she whispered a puzzled expression on her face as she turned her body slightly to look up and stare into his golden green eyes. His eyes were grave and, Sylvia thought, concerned.

"Look," he murmured, nodding his head in the direction of voices.

Sylvia looked. It was Mr. Headly and Anna.

"What are they doing here?" she asked still whispering.

"Shh," he said again and wrapped his arms tightly around her again so that very little of her showed between his camouflage and a medium sized leafy bush in front of them. She breathed in his woodsy, green smell and watched them walk quite close by, but they didn't notice her. She wondered if the Green Man's magic made her invisible. When the pair had walked past and were fairly far from them, he let her go. She tingled strangely where he had touched her, with joyful little jolts of energy coursing through her body. She stared at the Green Man in wonderment, mouth hanging open a little with wanting to say something.

"Let's go," he said as more of a command than a friendly comment.

"Okay, okay," Sylvia said and followed his command and they walked out of the wooded area. They crossed the stream into the other part of the woods. "Now can you tell me what is going on?" she asked impatiently.

"Actually," he paused, "No."

"What do you mean?" Sylvia was exasperated. "Why were they here?"

"You tell me," the Green Man said.

"W-e-l-l," Sylvia said with exaggeration and a bit of a sarcastic note to her voice, "Obviously they're up to no good," she said using an old fashioned phrase. "Anna is the one with the dark red aura and Mr. Headly," she refrained from calling him Mr. "Dick Head," "has the putrid yellow streaks in his aura. "Both of them are either creepy or bitchy or something," she broke off. "I don't know! Obviously, it has something to do with the clean-up since they were near the stream and pointing at whatever," she finished on a frustrated note.

"It's a piece to the puzzle," he said after listening to her tirade.

Sylvia's reply was a great sigh of frustration. She didn't know how to form her question to him and looked back at him questioningly.

"You're frustrated and question your gifts," the Green Man told Sylvia. "The auras you see are a gift. It's also a step in learning about your other gifts."

"Explain, please," Sylvia said.

"You're ability to see the break down in colors of the auras and know instinctively, simply and clearly what is good and what is bad," he said.

"Something like the way Gran could explain *everything*. She could break everything down to common sense," Sylvia said thoughtfully.

"More than common sense," the Green Man corrected. "It's an ability, just like you can differentiate between right and wrong by people's auras."

"Good and evil?" Sylvia questioned, slightly incredulous.

"Yes," the Green Man said matter of fact. "You have that ability and more."

"Also," he directed her, "don't touch the muck on your shoes. You could wash them off, but I think you should take them off with a plastic bag or gloves and throw them away."

Sylvia looked down at the traces of mud still on her shoes. She looked up with a puzzled expression for an answer only to find that the Green Man was gone.

"Damn it!" she shouted at the trees. She didn't understand any of this. Why her? She asked herself again and again. "I am *not* a patient person!" she half screamed at the trees that surrounded her. Sylvia stomped back to the front door of Thurmont working to compose herself and went back to the office to get her clothes.

Mr. Carter was anxious. "How did the stream look?" he asked.

Sylvia took a deep breath. "Pretty good, I think, from the little experience I've had with this sort of thing," she paused. Sylvia said 'what the hell' to herself and put her thoughts into words, "There's another person who's been hired recently that has a little more experience --well, a lot more experience with this sort of thing," she said. "I thought about asking for his assistance with the project."

"Good idea!" Mr. Carter beamed at her. "By the way, corporate loved the brochures. They've gone to print and we'll have them back in time for Bay Days. Marketing from 'big brother' is putting together some posters, buttons, balloons and that kind of free stuff for kids at the festival. All you'll need to do is to stand and look pretty at the booth."

Sylvia blushed a little at the comment and then nodded. "If you don't mind," she told Mr. Carter, "I would love to get out of these clothes."

"Sure, sure," he said amicably. "Go right ahead." He waved her out of the room.

Sylvia took her clothes and went to the ladies room to change. She didn't have plastic gloves or bags but used paper towels to remove her sneakers and sadly dropped them in the trashcan as the Green Man requested and washed her hands thoroughly with soap and warm water.

Back at the office, she started to organize the information about how to run stream watch. She also searched the company directory, located Owen's email and sent him a message asking for his assistance with the creek watch. She would need his support to figure out what kinds of equipment they needed. She also approached Mr. Carter on how to obtain the conference room, and funding for treats, for an organizational meeting for the stream watch participants. She put the questions about the mud by the creek in the back of her mind.

Owen called later that evening to tell her he would be delighted to help her. They agreed to meet at 10:30 the next day in Sylvia's office to discuss an organizational meeting and training, and explain their ideas with Mr. Carter. Owen said he would dig up some equipment and suggested they order some supplies. He also wanted to take a look at the stream and asked if he could get an idea of the current health of the creek.

After they had hung up, Sylvia remembered that she would need new sneakers and ran out to a discount store. She wondered what Owen would think of the muck and mud that the Green Man warned her about.

The next morning, nervous about her meeting with Owen, Sylvia couldn't concentrate on her work. Owen was prompt and came to the office door with a bag of equipment in his hands promptly at 10:30. She knocked on Mr. Carter's door and introduced them. He smiled and shook Owen's hand expressing his gratitude for Owen's assistance on the project. Mr. Carter retreated back into his office while Sylvia and Owen sat down at the small table near her desk while Sylvia shared her ideas with Owen. He liked her ideas and suggested a plan for training. He wondered out loud if Thurmont would pay for an advertisement in the paper.

"Well," Sylvia said. "Let's ask Mr. Carter. I wondered if we could provide food and drinks for the organizational meeting and training anyway."

She knocked on Mr. Carter's door and said, "Excuse me, Mr. Carter. We had a couple of questions and wondered if you could join us for a minute."

Mr. Carter emerged and they went over their ideas. He said he would check right away with his superiors, regarding a newspaper advertisement for the stream watch volunteers, and funding for the equipment and training.

Satisfied, Sylvia asked Owen if he wanted to check out the stream. They both went to change and met outside the front doors. Owen had a bag of equipment and a couple of nets. They walked through the woods, without talking, down to the stream.

Sylvia led Owen to where she had seen some insect life. He took out his equipment and scooped up some water in a jar to test the Oxygen and PH levels. He took a stick and poked at some of the rocks and pebbles at the bottom of the streambed.

"What are you looking for?" Sylvia asked him.

A thatch of black curls hung rakishly over one of his eyes as he peered into the depths of the stream. Sylvia thought it quite sexy and had the sudden urge to push the hair out from his eyes. She firmly stuck her hands in her pockets and took a step backward, sighing, she hoped not audibly.

"I'm checking for various types of larvae," he told her. He scooped up some the bottom sediment and pebbles in a net and took it over to the ground.

"Look here," he said. "Here's a leech," he started to say and Sylvia screeched "Oooh!" Owen waited a moment and looked through the net. "Here's a black fly larva, a dragonfly larva…Damn! It pinched me!" he cried out. "That tells me that the stream is from fair to poor health. It's something to keep an eye on."

Sylvia wasn't especially squeamish, but the larvae were not attractive to her. She sucked in her breath and bravely looked closer. They were definitely ugly in her eyes. She couldn't believe that the nasty bug like thing Owen pulled from the stream would actually turn into a beautiful dragonfly. Owen put the larvae back into the creek. He stepped out onto the rocks to look some more. Owen was pleased that he saw some tadpoles and told Sylvia to keep an eye out for frogs. He asked if she would walk down the edge of the stream bank as he hoped some would jump in. Sure enough, as Sylvia walked along the edge, one leaped into the water. Startled, she lost her balance and teetered on the brink of the stream. Luckily Owen had come up behind her and grabbed her arm and held her until she got her balance. For a moment, the time came to a standstill. The frog got away.

"Thanks," she told him after the extended moment.

He let go of her arm. "No problem," he said. He took her hand and helped her up the bank of the stream. "I think we can go back now."

"All right," Sylvia murmured.

"Let's go get changed and have some lunch," he suggested.

"That would be nice," she said.

They continued the polite, non-committal chatter before they changed and met back at her office and walked down to the cafeteria together.

"The stream has some problems," he told her. "I'm not sure it's a shining example of a healthy stream to show the community," he said, "but, they could take it upon themselves to make it a wonderful and healthy place. It would certainly be a good project to begin so that they could see decent growth from the time of the clean-up. I wouldn't mind doing a little more research on the clean-up itself so that I could answer any chemical related questions. I want to know if any half-lives of the chemical properties that polluted the stream a year or two ago are affecting its current state of health."

They went through the line and sat by the windows that overlooked the forest. Sylvia was totally oblivious to the lunch crowd around them.

"I would also like to get some additional samples," he told her. "I was concerned that we didn't see more amphibians."

"Which are?" Sylvia prompted.

"Frogs and other aquatic stuff," he said between bites of his sandwich.

"Do you want to go back out again for some samples?" she asked.

"Not today," he told her. "I need to work on another project. Maybe we could do it later this week or early next week – or even on a weekend."

"Okay," she said.

"What is your schedule with the stream watch?" he asked.

"I thought I would clear a date with Mr. Carter, put an advertisement in the local paper and start calling the folks that were at the library meeting this afternoon," she said.

"Whew!" Owen said, "If you get all that accomplished you'll need to put a rush on those kits then," he said.

"All right, all right," Sylvia answered, finally picking up that he was teasing.

They became engrossed in their conversation again and didn't see or hear Anna approaching until she laid a hand possessively on

Owen's shoulder and purred, "Well, well, I've been looking for you everywhere."

Owen was unfazed. "Hello, Anna," he said, glancing up. He must have stiffened or she saw something in his eyes because she dropped her hand. She didn't look flustered, as Sylvia would have felt in that situation, but saw a glint of something that wasn't nice in her eyes. The air conditioning came on full blast –literally and figuratively. Sylvia shivered slightly under Anna's icy gaze.

"Would you like to join us?" Sylvia asked politely trying to keep her composure.

"No thank you," she said, nearly hissing at Sylvia, "Owen and I have some work we need to get completed."

"Sorry, Syl," he said, "I'm starting to take environmental samples. I need to run."

"Thanks for your help," Sylvia said ignoring Anna's icy gaze. "I'll be in touch when I have a few more things pulled together."

Anna turned on her heel when Owen stood up and then she started to walk away. At the cafeteria door, she waited impatiently for him to bus his tray and to join her. Sylvia caught herself shaking her head. He looked like a dog on a leash.

"What did the bitch want?" Carol asked putting her half eaten lunch down on Sylvia's table.

"What?" Sylvia said in surprise. "Carol, you're too much!" she exclaimed. "Owen's starting some of his environmental samplings and she's helping, I guess."

"I'll bet," Carol said dryly.

"Did you just get here?" Sylvia asked looking puzzled at Carol's half eaten lunch.

"No, I've been here for a while, but you two were so caught up in your discussion that I hated to interrupt," she told Sylvia.

"Owen's helping me with a project," Sylvia told her.

"He's a helpful kind of guy, isn't he?" she teased.

"You bet!" Sylvia replied smiling, "although, I hope he doesn't help *her* too much."

"He should watch himself with her, she's dangerous," Carol warned entirely sober. "If you're friends, you should warn him."

"How? Why?" Sylvia asked. "I thought it was just a feeling I got from her. She seems to be jealous of every other female."

"There is that," Carol admitted, "but there's something else that's not right with her. But, I don't have facts on it and I don't want to be the one to spread the rumor. I know for a fact that she slept her way to the top. She admits to that, but she also seems to like to make trouble. The guys that work with her usually end up hating her guts and leaving suddenly or she finds a way to get them fired. Owen needs to be careful."

"Hmm," Sylvia said, "Then I need a way to tell him that information without sounding jealous or bossy. That's going to be difficult," mused Sylvia.

She looked at her watch. "Oh my!" she said, "Look at the time! I need to run!" she said to Carol. "See you."

She hurried back to the office. Mr. Carter was still ensconced in his chair working on some paperwork. She knocked quietly and cleared her throat so that he knew she was there.

"The stream watch is looking good," she told him. "I'm going to start calling people from the Library meeting and set up a date to meet."

He nodded at her and told her to call the local paper to place an advertisement. He had cleared it with the company and also gave her a list of dates when the conference room was available.

"Thanks!" she said and went out to make the calls. Mr. Carter emerged from his office a few minutes later, motioning to her that he was going to lunch. She nodded at him and continued with her phone conversation. This woman was from the library meeting and was concerned about how much time a stream watch would take. Sylvia said that readings are only needed to be taken about four times a year. Sylvia signed her up, and a few others during the afternoon, setting up the meeting date for Thursday the next week. She called the newspaper and searched for equipment on the Internet. Sylvia contacted Owen via e-mail attaching links for the water testing kits and other equipment asking which he recommended. He replied and she ordered them express shipped to Thurmont at their expense.

It was Friday at lunch when she finally saw Owen in the cafeteria. She went over and asked if she could sit with him.

He looked up and saw her, "Sure thing," he said, moving some papers that he had been reading. He looked distracted.

"Are you okay?" Sylvia asked.

"Yeah," Owen said, "I've just got a lot on my mind right now." He changed the subject, "Did you get the kits ordered?" he asked.

"Yes," Sylvia told him. "They're being expressed shipped here and I've set the meeting for next Thursday evening at the Library. Can you make it?"

"I think so," Owen told her. "If you emailed me, I would appreciate it, and then I can add it to my calendar. Just don't set up the training on Marian's party date, okay?" he said with a grin.

"You're right," Sylvia said, "But perhaps we could schedule training and the first watch on Saturday a week after Marian's party. That's two weeks from tomorrow."

"That would be good," Owen told her although she wasn't sure he heard her. He had a faraway look in his eye. "Look, I've got to run," Owen said suddenly. He picked up his papers and walked swiftly out of the cafeteria.

Sylvia's eyes followed him, puzzled at his abruptness and distraction. She could sense something was bothering him, but he certainly didn't want to confide in her. She ate her lunch and returned to the office finishing up what she could before the end of the day. Over a glass of wine on the deck that evening, Sylvia thought about

Owen. She felt they had become friends, but she wanted it to be more. She thought she had seen it in his eyes too the other day, but now she wasn't sure.

The telephone jangled and interrupted her thoughts. It was Marian asking her to come to dinner the next night. Sylvia agreed and asked what she could contribute. Marian asked her to bring a nice pinot grigio for the meal. They had chatted for a few minutes before they hung up. As soon as she hung up, the phone rang again. This time, it was Carol asking if she wanted to go to the movies the next night.

"Sorry, Carol," I just accepted a dinner invitation from a friend.

"Owen?" Carol asked curiously.

"No," Sylvia said laughing, "But he'll be there," She explained the current living arrangements for Owen at Marian's house. "What if we go to the movies tomorrow afternoon or the Sunday matinee?" she asked her.

Carol suggested Sunday so that they could go out to dinner afterward. Sylvia agreed to meet her at the theater that afternoon.

Saturday seemed to drag until it was time to go to Marian's. Sylvia puttered about the house. As she took her regular walk, she wondered if she should get a dog or a cat to break some of the quiet. People certainly seemed to enjoy their dogs she mused, as she saw the regular residents being pulled along the street. A cat would be nice too, to curl up with in the evenings. Her parents had not been big on pets. Sylvia remembered a particularly emotive goldfish that leaped and swam frantically about its tank when she fed or talked to it. She had been crushed when it had died, and her Mother told her she shouldn't get so attached to a pet. Eventually, Sylvia went to the liquor store and picked up two bottles of fume blanc, and brought them home to chill until dinner. She called Gwen and left a message and sat on the deck waiting for the afternoon to pass.

She arrived at Marian's right at 5 o'clock with the chilled wine in hand. Marian was happy to see her and gave her a quick hug.

"It's been ages since Isaw you," she said to Sylvia.

"I know," Sylvia said, "work has a way of getting in the way of fun," she quipped.

Marian opened up the wine and poured Sylvia a glass. They sat under the oak on the side patio. Owen was nowhere to be seen.

"So, tell me all about your job," Marian said.

Sylvia told Marian about her various projects, the pamphlets, the stream watch and the upcoming appearance at Bay Days.

"Nothing overly exciting," Sylvia told her.

"That's probably very good," Marian advised.

Sylvia nodded and finally asked, "Where's Owen?"

Marian sighed and said, "He's upstairs on the computer. He's been very distracted and something's bothering him, but he won't tell me about it," Marian said. "I'm worried about him!" she confided to Sylvia.

"I know," Sylvia told her. "I saw him at lunch yesterday and he certainly wasn't himself. He wouldn't say what was bothering him then."

Marian shook her head, her snowy white curls bobbing up and down. "Hopefully, he'll be down for dinner," Marian said. "I've taken his dinner up to him at his computer the last couple of nights."

"Excuse me," she said, "I think I'll try to get him."

Sylvia tried half-heartedly to stop her, "Don't go and interrupt him on account of me," she said to Marian's retreating form. Marian's step had a determination about it and Sylvia knew Owen wouldn't have a chance. Whether or not Marian heard her, she didn't know, but she didn't turn around or acknowledge her comment. Marian returned a few minutes later walking across to her with a bright smile and confident step.

"He'll be down in a minute," she said smugly.

"What did you tell him?" Sylvia asked looking at her expression.

"Well, I told him that he was quite rude and he needed to eat a decent meal. He can't go on crunching numbers or whatever he was doing without some sort of nutrition," she said.

"You sound like his mother," Sylvia teased.

"Probably worse," Marian admitted as she smiled and took another sip of wine. "And he was listening to some god awful noise, fortunately wearing earphones," she said dryly. "He said it helps him think." Marian shook her head. "I always thought Mozart was good for that."

"I've heard about that theory," Sylvia commented. "It was in one of my classes, general music, I think, but I can't remember the name of the person who wrote about it or the title." She had taken another sip of wine before she remembered out loud, "It was a good class, though."

Marian nodded and said, "I've was raised on the classics and I think I'm too old to change. But, I love other kinds of music too—jazz, folk, bluegrass."

Sylvia nodded. "Gran influenced me in music. She's the one that gave me an eclectic background to music, but she loved folk music the best, I think. Sylvia hummed a lot and we sang together sometimes. I grew up with 'Peter, Paul and Mary;' 'Bob Dylan;' 'the Weavers,'" she said, "it's probably why I tend to go more folk and Celtic now," she commented.

Eventually, Owen came down and said hello to Sylvia. He looked drained and preoccupied. Owen turned down the glass of wine and went back inside to get a beer from the refrigerator. He sat wearily in another chair on the patio.

"What's wrong?" Sylvia asked lightly.

"Number crunching with these environmental samples," he said wearily. "Something's not adding up and I haven't figured it out and why. It's driving me crazy."

"I'm sure you'll get it soon," Sylvia said soothingly. "You probably need a little break so that you can think fresh," she told him.

"You're probably right," he said, but he still stared off into space with a brooding look on his face.

Sylvia sat quietly allowing him to be with his thoughts. Marian brought out a tray loaded with salad, bread, and a seafood pasta dish.

"I wish you had asked for some help," Sylvia scolded her.

"I'm all right," Marian assured her, "But I'll let you two clean-up," she said.

They sat down to another one of Marian's delicious meals. Marian had outdone herself with a pasta dish with shrimp and crab in a light herbed cream sauce.

"I think you missed your calling," Sylvia told Marian. "I think you should have opened up a restaurant."

"There's still time," Marian chuckled. "I should find something to get myself in some sort of trouble. I certainly don't like rattling around here all day."

"How can you say you rattle around?" Owen asked. "You're constantly off volunteering somewhere."

"You're right," Marian answered. "But I would like," she broke off. "I'm not sure exactly what I want to do. I'm feeling a bit restless."

"Do you want to travel?" Sylvia asked her.

"Not by myself," Marian answered. "Save up some vacation time you two and then we can go on an adventure. I'm not one to take the seniors bus trips to Atlantic City. Ugh!" she shuddered.

"You won't know until you try it," Owen said, slyly winking at Sylvia. "You might meet a hot guy on one of those bus trips."

"Oh, you!" Marian tossed a napkin at him exasperated. "Bran was enough of a 'hot guy' for me. You should know that."

Owen nodded and they both had a moment of remembering Marian's late husband. Sylvia wished she had met him. The photos of him showed a large man who looked uncomfortable in tweed, but he had laughing eyes, a brilliant smile and held a pipe comfortably in his hand. Marian admitted that she hated the pipe smoking, but loved him too much to change the ritual. It was better than the cigarettes he had consumed twenty-four seven in their early years of marriage.

Sylvia kept sipping at the wine. It was on the edge of being bubbly and was going to her head with the warm evening air. When she and Owen took the plates inside to wash up, she was wobbly on her feet. Sylvia giggled.

"Here," Owen said, pulling up a chair, "I'll take these," and he took the plates, "while you sit." He helped her into a chair in the kitchen.

"This is embarrassing," she said as she followed his directions nearly flopping out of the chair. "I don't know when the wine has gone to my head like that." She giggled again involuntarily.

"It's probably the heat," Owen told her. "Relax. It's okay."

"Okay," Sylvia said obediently. Her head felt like it was about to spin. "Coffee?" she asked faintly.

"On the way," Owen said as he poured water into the coffeemaker.

Owen put the dishes in the dishwasher and poured her a cup of coffee. She sat in her chair breathing in the fragrant steam from the cup and sipping slowly. After a few minutes, she started feeling a little more like herself. Marian came in and had Owen help her scoop raspberry sorbet into dishes. They returned to the terrace to have dessert, Marian carrying the sorbet, Owen the coffee and Sylvia trailing behind with a plate of tiny rolled cookies walking carefully to the table. She had sobered up a little bit.

Twilight crept in silently. It went from light to purple to a velvety gray cloak around them. Marian lit citronella candles at the edges of the patio and a candle on the table. Sylvia relaxed and looked at the stars popping behind the leaves of the great oak tree and sipping her coffee.

"Do you want to take more samples tomorrow afternoon?" Owen asked her.

"No, I'm sorry, I can't," Sylvia told him. "I'm going to the movies with Carol."

They sat and talked for a few more minutes and Owen abruptly got up, "I need to get back to work," he told them.

Sylvia and Marian looked at Owen and then at each other in the growing darkness.

"Something's definitely not right," Sylvia said.

"I know," Marian returned, "and he wants to work it out himself."

"I should be getting home too," Sylvia told Marian. "Thank you for dinner."

"You're very welcome," Marian told her brightly. "Are you all right to drive?" she asked concerned.

"I'm all right," Sylvia said. "The coffee and the dessert helped tremendously. I guess I didn't eat much today and the wine went straight to my head."

"As long as you're all right," Marian said. "Be careful driving home."

"I will," Sylvia assured her and she gave her a quick hug before she climbed into her car.

She drove down Marian's pitch-black road with her lights on high beam. She heard the wind or leaves rustling but still jumped when she saw the Green Man in the passenger seat. Sylvia slammed on the brakes.

"What are you doing here?" she demanded.

"Making sure you get home safely," he told her.

"Okay, thanks," Sylvia said relaxing a little. "Anyways, it's good to have company. It seems really, really dark tonight," she said peering out the window at the trees on Marian's lane. None of the houses sitting back in the trees had on any lights. It was a little spooky.

"You should call Owen and take samples tomorrow morning," the Green Man advised.

"That's a excellent idea," Sylvia said. "I'll do that."

Sylvia was quiet and the Green Man was too. He stayed with her until she pulled into her driveway and, with a rustle of leaves, disappeared again. She smiled involuntarily at the sound, feeling comforted.

Sylvia went right in and called Owen. She could tell he was still distracted, but he agreed to take samples in the morning. For a moment, he seemed less distracted and even suggested that they go out for breakfast afterward. Surprised, Sylvia accepted his invitation and looked forward to the next morning.

CHAPTER FIFTEEN

Earth mother, star mother,
You who are called by a thousand names,
May all remember we are cells in your body
And dance together.
--Starhawk

Owen picked her up promptly at eight the next morning. It was hot and Sylvia put on shorts and a t-shirt and slathered on bug and sun repellant. He frowned and told her she should be wearing long pants because of ticks and she retorted that jeans were much too hot. He was wearing khakis and a light long-sleeved shirt. They drove to Thurmont's main parking lot that was completely empty. Owen removed a canvas bag, took a large kick seine net, a yardstick and waders out of the car.

"Can I help?" Sylvia asked him.

"You can carry these," he said and he handed her the waders.

They walked through the woods to the edge of the stream where they had observed the stream earlier in the week. Owen wanted to move further down the creek, and Sylvia followed him carefully stepping along the edge of the stream bank. It was relatively quiet with only the occasional twitter of a bird or scrabble of a squirrel. The sun shone through the leaves and Sylvia was getting hot. A trickle of sweat ran down between her breasts and she pushed her damp hair back from her forehead. She couldn't imagine wearing long pants today, and wondered how Owen could look so cool. Owen finally stopped and put down his equipment.

"This looks like a good place," he told her. "Time for your crash course in stream watching," he said.

This part of the creek looked the same to Sylvia as the other part of the stream closer to Thurmont, except being a little deeper, but she didn't argue. Owen removed a small kit, went down to the creek and measured the water at a riffle a few steps away from the shore. He also put a thermometer in the water and asked her to take the yardstick and measure how deep the water was.

"This is to check PH levels," he told her holding up the little kit.

Owen took the kit and put in a couple of drops of liquid from a small bottle. He swirled it around and checked the color of a sliding rainbow of color on the side of the kit. The range of colors indicated if the water was acidic or not. This water was on the edge. Another small kit checked for salt. Owen had Sylvia do this test. No salt, but he wasn't surprised.

"Looks like it's slightly polluted still," he commented. "The question is 'why' since the clean-up was allegedly completed," he commented. "Hmm, it's a real mystery," he said, "and I've always liked mysteries. It's probably why I like science," he continued.

Sylvia nodded but didn't say anything. Owen was obviously in his element. He had a faraway, yet happier look in his eye than she had seen for a week or more.

"Hold onto this side of the net," he instructed her. "We're going to rest the bottom of the net on the stream bed and try not to disturb the sample area," he told her.

Sylvia did as she was told. She stepped out into the shallow part of the stream, balancing on a couple of rocks that did not teeter back and forth when she stepped on them. She held the net steady while Owen stretched it across part of the stream. He reached down to scrub some of the stones in the sampling area and shuffled oddly and sideways towards the net. Together, they lifted the net from the water with a forward scooping motion, and carried it to the stream bank and laid it out flat. Owen carefully examined the specimens in the net. He had a distressed look on his face and she leaned closer. There was a frog in the net that was hopping lamely.

"What's wrong?" she asked.

"This," he said, and he held up a frog that squirmed in his hands.

"So?" Sylvia asked. "What's wrong with the frog?"

"Count its legs," he said grimly.

Sylvia counted, one, two three. It was missing a leg.

"What does that mean?" she asked him.

"It's definitely a sign of pollution," he told her, but it could have been the residue of the chemical before the clean-up. We should keep a count of deformed frogs as well as the PH levels and other water critters."

"Okay," Sylvia said. "I can add it to the list of things we have to watch for."

"Good," he said as he placed the frog gently back into the stream. "And I'm going to take a sample of this water home and check it out under the microscope."

He looked at the macro-invertebrates and made some notes before returning them to the streambed. She watched carefully.

"What's over there?" he asked pointing to the opposite side of the stream.

"Just some woods, I think," Sylvia said.

"Let's go explore," he said brightly, "Race you!"

Owen set off across the stream balancing on the rocks. He nearly lost his balance and Sylvia laughed.

"Uh, oh," he said teasingly, "I must have had some fume blanc this morning."

"Ha, ha," Sylvia replied. "Very amusing," she said sarcastically. Sylvia followed Owen less enthusiastically. She wondered how she could explain the Green Man and the brown ooze she had seen the other day.

"Careful," she warned.

He turned and caught her hand pulling her the rest of the way from the stream and they went up the bank. Just as before, the forest was silent. Dead silent. Owen turned around and around looking carefully up at the trees.

"This is odd," he said. "It's way too quiet."

"I know," Sylvia whispered.

They walked a little bit. The ground was getting mushier.

"What do you think of this?" she asked him pointing to the mushy ground.

"What *is* this stuff?" Owen asked as he squatted down to take a better look at the ooze.

"I don't think you should touch it," Sylvia said warningly.

"Hmm," Owen answered, "You're probably right."

He picked up a stick that was lying on the ground nearby and poked at the ooze.

"I think I would like to take a look at this under a microscope too," he told her.

He removed a small specimen bottle from his pocket, opened it with his teeth, and pushed some of the ooze into the jar with the stick. He closed it tightly and looked up at Sylvia and said, "I don't know about you, but I'm starving! Do you want to go and get breakfast?" he asked her.

"Love to," Sylvia replied.

They made their way back across the stream allowing some of the water to clean off the bits of ooze that had gotten onto their shoes. Owen was quiet and thoughtful as they drove to the restaurant. It was busy with weekend boaters. Owen asked if they could wait for a booth. After a few minutes, they were seated. When Sylvia started to talk to Owen and ask him some questions, he held up his hand to silence her. She squelched her thoughts.

They ordered coffee and breakfast. Once the waitress had left them alone, Owen leaned across the table towards Sylvia.

"I don't like what we saw today," he confided in her.

"What do you mean?" she asked him.

"The deformed frog," he told her, "is a barometer for pollutants. The stuff in the stream rates it at fair to ill health…and I have no idea what that ooze is from. Isn't that the site that was close to the leak?" he asked.

Sylvia had nodded before she said, "I think so. You should check out the EPA Superfund website. It has a lot of information and you'll probably understand it far better than I could," she told him. "It has a breakdown of what happened at this Thurmont site.

"I'll do that this afternoon," he said looking impressed that she had done her research.

He changed the subject, "What movie are you and Carol going to see?" he asked.

"I'm not sure," Sylvia said. "We're meeting at the theater and there are several that show between 1 and 1:30. I don't have any real preference as long as it isn't too scary or gory."

"Not fond of scary movies?" he asked.

She shook her head and smiled as she said, "Only if I can close my eyes and clutch at someone," she said.

"Hmm," he teased, "That's something to keep in mind."

Sylvia glanced up but couldn't tell from his expression if he was serious or only teasing. The waitress interrupted by bringing their meals. Owen had ordered a full breakfast of eggs, sausage, hash browns, toast and a couple of pancakes on the side. Sylvia had ordered buckwheat pancakes and a side of scrapple that had been sliced thin and cooked extra crisp.

The topic of movies didn't come up again. They talked about Marian's upcoming party. Owen told her that in addition to the research that he wanted to do this afternoon, he was also going to chop some wood for Marian's planned bonfire. He needed to look at the weather report and figure out how and when to string lights at various parts of her property.

"She wants those white fairy lights everywhere," he told her with mild complaining in his voice.

"I'm sure it will be lovely," Sylvia said. "When I think of midsummer's eve, I can't help but think of 'A Mid-Summer Night's Dream' and all of the fairies."

Owen nodded in agreement. "Shakespeare," he murmured, "beautiful play, but I could never get that one."

"Did you figure out your problem from yesterday?" she asked changing the subject.

A frustrated look crossed Owen's face, "No," he said, but I'll be looking into it tomorrow."

His voice was so unyielding that she didn't press the subject. The waitress brought more coffee and the bill. Sylvia reached into her pocket to pull out some bills and Owen stopped her.

"It's on me," he said.

"Are you sure?" she asked.

"Absolutely," he said.

"Well, at least, let me leave the tip," Sylvia requested.

"Only if you insist," he said with a grin.

"I insist *this* time," she said, "but, I might not let you off so easy the next time."

"Deal," he said.

He drove her home and left her on her doorstep. Sylvia went into the house and sat down on the couch and hugged a pillow, smiling. She didn't know how long she sat there in the nether world of her daydreams. When she got back to reality, she realized she was running late for the movie with Carol and rushed to wash off the sweat and grime from the morning's expedition. Sylvia pushed the speed limit while driving to the movie theater. She was about five minutes late and Carol was waiting patiently, enjoying the sun on a bench outside the theater.

"Hey there," Sylvia called to her jogging a little to reach Carol a minute sooner, "Sorry I'm late!"

"No problem," Carol said. "I thought I'd work on my tan. Do you have any ideas what we should see?"

Sylvia shook her head. They finally decided on a romantic comedy and purchased popcorn and soda.

"I shouldn't even think about eating," Sylvia said. "I just ate brunch!"

"Did you go out for brunch?" Carol asked.

"Yes," Sylvia told her, "Owen picked me up so that we could take some stream samples, and get a baseline measurement before the stream watch. We went out for breakfast afterward."

"Woo-hoo!" Carol exclaimed. "A date!"

"Umm, I don't think so," Sylvia answered. "This was work."

"You know these nerdy guys," Carol said, "In his eyes it was probably a date."

"I don't think so," Sylvia insisted.

"Did he pay for your breakfast?" Carol asked.

Sylvia nodded.

"You see," Carol said matter of factly, "a date."

"Well, of course, I'm not going to convince you," Sylvia said to her, "even though I would love for it to have been a date. He's too preoccupied with whatever is going on at work to even think about a date, I think," she said. "And no one knows what's going on with Anna!" she exclaimed.

"Anna's probably most of the problem," Carol said. "Mark my words. He's following in the footsteps of many others."

The lights had dropped and the previews had started. Someone 'shushed' them from behind. Carol turned around to glare at them.

"There's flying popcorn on the screen," she hissed back at them. "Give me a break!"

She elbowed Sylvia and giggled. They enjoyed the movie and went out for pizza and beer afterward, Carol taking her to one of her favorite restaurants. Carol waved to the folks behind the counter when they walked in.

"I know, I know," she said. "It's not a 'pretty' restaurant, but the food is excellent. Try their ravioli sometime. There's enough cheese in it, and on it, to clog your arteries, but it's a food experience you'll never forget. I get it when I'm really depressed. It's almost as good as a lot of chocolate."

They ordered a pitcher of beer and a large pizza with extra cheese, extra bacon, and mushrooms. Sylvia had never tried that combination but found it delicious. They tried hard not to talk about work but ended up gossiping anyways, laughing hysterically and placing a bet on how long Mr. Keely would last.

"This was great," Sylvia said. "We'll need to do it again soon."

"Definitely," Carol answered. "See you tomorrow."

"See you," Sylvia said.

She was glad to get back home. She checked for messages to see if Owen had called with any of his results from his microscopic observations. She only found a brief message from her mother. Sylvia called her mother back for her weekly check-in. Feeling sleepy and lethargic from the abundant food she had eaten all day, Sylvia yawned loudly. She sank into the couch and sat back to surf the channels on the television. Finding nothing of interest, she turned it off and looked out at the bay. It was now a subconscious act to check for the auras on the trees. The auras were leaping from the trees and her only thought was that they were happy. "Silly," she thought to herself, "trees can't communicate that way." But, could they, she wondered in the next minute. She wondered if they were picking up on her contentment and happiness at that very moment. She would need to ask the Green Man the next time she saw him.

She walked into the study looking for a good book to read. Funny how she had never actually read the titles of Gran's books. There was a lot of poetry, many classic novels and many books on gardening and nature writing. She ran her hand down the shelves along the spines. She knew Gran had loved books. Each one on the shelf was special to her in some way. Sylvia nearly cried when she found the shelf of children's books. Gran had kept a collection that she read aloud to her on a regular basis. Sylvia pulled out a tattered volume of 'Katy and the Big Snow.' Looking at it brought back so many memories. Gran would have her trace Katy on the page with her finger and they would both chant "chug, chug, chug," as they read the book. There were others. Gran liked fantasy and read chapters of L'Engle's 'Wrinkle in Time' series until Sylvia could read them herself. She pulled out the second volume in the series, 'A Wind in the Door' and took it up to bed to read.

In the morning, Sylvia logged onto her email, hoping to find a note from Owen, and was disappointed to find none. She emailed him asking what he had found in the water samples and continued with her own work. Mr. Carter was at a meeting and the office was quiet. She watered her new plants and worked on the Stream Watch and Bay Days projects. Carol emailed her late morning to say she would work through lunch in her office. Sylvia was disappointed, but not surprised that Owen did not show either. She ate alone quickly and returned to the office, completing the stream watch information, logs for the volunteers and signup sheet and calendar.

There was no message from Owen all day nor on her home answering machine that evening. Sylvia was starting to get a little peeved. He could, at least, have the courtesy to call to tell her if he found anything or not. She paced around the kitchen and stomped out to the deck, walking back and forth there and staring at the wood beneath her feet. Finally, she looked out at the water and walked down to the beach. There she took off her shoes to test the water. It was starting to warm up and felt refreshingly cool. She lifted her skirt and waded deeper. If it had been darker, she would have considered stripping and taking a swim. She turned back to the house, put on her swimsuit and water shoes, grabbed a towel and went to paddle around for a little while in the bay. Refreshed Sylvia toweled off, made some dinner and sat to eat it on the deck. Swallows were swooping low over the water gathering their nightly feast of mosquitoes. She thought she saw a bat or two fluttering as well. As evening fell, Sylvia felt the mosquitoes starting to bite her, and slapped at them for a few minutes until they drove her into the house for refuge.

She didn't hear from Owen on Tuesday or Wednesday. Sylvia, one whose temper was slow to build, was close to peaking by Wednesday evening. She was all set for the organizational meeting and assumed Owen was coming as he had said the week prior, but felt jilted since she had not heard from him. She finally called. Marian answered and said Owen was working late.

"Do you know if he's coming to the stream watch organizational meeting tomorrow night?" she asked Marian, trying to keep anger from edging into her voice.

Marian's calm voice answered, "As far as I know, he'll be there," she said. "I talked about going too, and I thought we would drive together. He hasn't been around much this week."

Still not feeling placated, she said goodbye to Marian and went for a walk to assuage her anger. About a half a dozen cars were parked along the narrow road that led to the Marina. She stared and on her way back realized the crowd was at Mr. Peter's house, the gentleman who had liver cancer. He must have died in the last few days and she had not noticed it in the paper. The feeling of emptiness that had yawned within her for the first couple of weeks after Gran's death returned. She felt sorry for the family as she walked home. Tears of grief, slowly and silently, fell with a few of self-pity from her situation with Owen mingled in. She felt like howling and curled up on the couch, crying herself out. Her grief for Gran came in waves. Tonight everything seemed bleak and empty.

Thursday she awoke with new resolve, that with or without Owen, she would make the project work. She checked and double-checked the handouts and presentation board that she had put together and loaded it into her car. She nervously fiddled with things about the office and waited for the end of the day.

She arrived at the library early and unloaded her things, set up the stark community room and then meandered through the shelves picking up books here and there reading various chapters. People started to arrive at 6:45 and she went to the community room to greet them and have them sign in. There was no sign of Owen and Sylvia thought she would be running the program solo. Marian came in about five minutes before seven and beamed at Sylvia. She was alone and she held up her hands to Sylvia's questioning eyes. Sylvia cleared her throat to start the meeting when Owen walked in. He nodded at Sylvia.

"Are you okay?" she whispered the question while folks were still chatting.

He nodded abruptly. "Are you ready to start?" he asked quietly.

Owen went over basic stream watch procedure using a power point, giving an overview of what type of flora and fauna would be in a fair to healthy stream. He passed out a checklist example and urged people to sign up for training so they could begin as soon as possible.

Sylvia took over again, polling convenient times to meet for training and passed out sign-up sheets.

While people were busy signing up and reading through their information, she sidled up to Owen and asked, "What did you find in the soil and water samples?"

"I can't talk about that right now," he returned curtly.

Rebuffed, Sylvia turned back to the group asking if there were any questions. A few people raised their hands and asked specific questions about stream health about the clean-up. Sylvia deferred the question to Owen. The meeting ended a short time later; the crowd friendlier than at the last meeting. Sylvia had a group of five signed up for a morning training and another group for a late afternoon session.

Marian came up to them, "That seemed to go well," she said.

Sylvia nodded and looked at Owen. He nodded too, but still seemed distracted.

"Thanks for coming," she said to him.

He seemed to come out of his fog, "Sure," he said, "no problem." He smiled at her, but when she looked in his eyes, she could see that he was troubled.

"Look," he said, "I need to go and finish up some stuff. I'll see you later." He turned and left leaving Sylvia standing with her mouth agape.

"I don't know what's bothering him," Marian said. "He's been really agitated this last couple of weeks." She helped Sylvia carry the extra paper out to her car and Sylvia brought the presentation board. Sylvia said nothing. She was still angered by his actions.

"Do you want to go out for a drink?" Marian asked her.

"I would love to," Sylvia answered. "Where can we go?"

"There's a new restaurant on the water that just opened," Marian told her. "Why don't we go and have a drink and a small bite to eat."

"That sounds wonderful," Sylvia said. "I'll follow you."

The restaurant was practically deserted when they arrived and the waitress was not happy when she saw them walk in.

"You can sit anywhere," she said to them and Marian walked over to a small table that looked out over the water.

Marian ordered a Rusty Nail and a hot crab appetizer to share. Sylvia, realizing she had missed dinner, ordered a bowl of crab bisque and a glass of white Zinfandel.

"What is going on with Owen?" Sylvia asked Marian, trying to keep a demanding tone out of her voice.

"I was hoping you knew," Marian replied. "All I know is that something isn't adding up right with the tests for his department and he hasn't resolved the differences in the tests. He's been going over and over the tests and has redone them at least once, I think."

"Can someone have made a mistake?" Sylvia asked.

"I would think so," Marian said, "but he seems really bothered by the inconsistencies in the data."

"Did he tell you anything about the samples on Sunday?" Sylvia pressed.

"No, he hasn't mentioned that at all," Marian said honestly.

"Hmm," Sylvia murmured. If Owen hadn't told Marian, she couldn't very well share the information, but was bothered by his lack of courtesy. She told Marian so as the waitress brought their food to their table. Sylvia stirred up the steaming soup. It was full of chunks of lump crabmeat and had paprika sprinkled over the top. She took a small sip of the hot soup and nodded to Marian. "Delicious," she said.

"The dip is excellent too," Marian said, "Please have some. I don't know what to tell you about Owen," Marian said. "He's always been one to keep difficulties to himself. He's always had a terrible time sharing."

Sylvia didn't comment but spread hot crab dip on the toasted baguette slices that were included with the appetizer. She changed the subject.

"Are you ready for your party?" Sylvia asked.

"I think so," Marian answered. "The weather looks good and I've made a good start on the appetizers. Will you still be able to pick strawberries on Saturday morning with me?"

"Sure," Sylvia answered her. "It will be fun."

"Why don't I pick you up," Marian said, "at 7:30. Is that too early?" Marian asked and Sylvia shook her head. Marian continued, "You can bring your party clothes. Owen or I can take you back to the party."

"All right," Sylvia replied. "I'll endeavor to get organized." She was feeling her sense of humor returning with the comfort of the warm soup inside of her.

"We can pick strawberries and then come back to the house and begin getting ready for the party," Marian said. "The weather looks fine," she continued. "It should be a lovely evening. And I've already worked on appetizers and purchased a few too."

"What?" Sylvia said with mocked shock. "Purchasing appetizers? Come on, Marian, what will it be next? Canned soup?"

Marian chuckled, "I guess my age *is* beginning to show," she said.

"I'm just teasing," Sylvia told her, and then changed the subject.

"Did Owen hang up the fairy lights?" Sylvia asked.

"I think that was one of his projects this evening," Marian said. "Unfortunately, he's been so caught up in whatever is bothering him that I haven't had the heart to ask. Last Sunday he chopped an enormous pile of wood for the bonfire."

"He told me he would," Sylvia said.

They finished their meal and were the only people in the restaurant. The restaurant personnel were making not so subtle sounds that they wanted to clean-up and go home.

"We should be going," Marian said and Sylvia agreed.

"I'll see you Saturday morning!" Marian said. "Good night."

"Good night," Sylvia answered.

That night Sylvia dreamed. She dreamed of Owen. He was angry with her and they had a huge argument, both of them shouting at each other until her ears hurt. Then she dreamed of Anna, laughing triumphantly—mocking her. Anna's laugh was high pitched, cold. Her silvery gray eyes flashed in triumph and Sylvia had Owen tethered to her like a puppet or a dog. Owen looked miserable and she couldn't free him from Anna no matter how hard she tried. She woke up sweating and restless with the pillow held over her ear. Sylvia got up earlier than usual trying to shake the disturbing dreams from her head. As she sipped her second cup of coffee, the last vestiges of the dreams had left her, Sylvia laughed. Her mother had always warned her not to eat rich foods right before bed. The crab bisque indeed gave her nightmares! She showered and dressed for work and arrived quite early.

Still restless and frustrated she vented to Gwen via email about Owen, got a cup of coffee and settled into work. Mr. Carter came in and was surprised to find her at work already. He asked how the meeting went and Sylvia shared what happened with him. He was pleased with the overall timbre of the meeting and happy it had not been a negative event.

"I know this is last minute," Sylvia said, "but do you think I could have this afternoon off as the compensation time you mentioned?"

"Sure," Mr. Carter told her. "We seem to be in pretty good shape with projects."

Relieved, Sylvia thought about her afternoon. She wanted to get a pair of sandals for tomorrow's party and also thought about getting her hair cut. She remembered that she needed to change her license also and called Motor Vehicle to see what she needed.

Carol emailed her to see when she wanted to go for lunch and Sylvia walked down to her office to tell her she was leaving early.

"Lucky dog!" Carol exclaimed when Sylvia told her. "I have some compensation time coming, but I need to finish some of this paperwork," she said. "Anyways, Mr. Keely would never let me leave without significant notice," she said rolling her eyes and putting the emphasis on 'significant.' "Have fun!"

"Thanks," Sylvia said. "I think I will. I'd like to get a pair of sandals for tomorrow night." She had shared with Carol about Marian's party plans.

Carol was impressed. She said goodbye to Carol and then to Mr. Carter and with a happy go lucky 'have a good weekend,' stepped out into the summer sunshine. Sylvia drove off Thurmont's property and pulled into a nearby strip mall to pick up a sandwich at a pizza place. Instead, she saw a salon that advertised 'walk-in's welcome' and Sylvia parked and walked in to see if they could cut her hair. They could and she sat and closed her eyes and relaxed as the stylist massaged her head and washed her hair. It felt lovely. The stylist double checked with her and Sylvia agreed that she wanted her long hair several inches shorter—closer to her shoulders as it was currently at the middle of her back. She closed her eyes and grimaced when she heard the sound of scissors close to her head. As the stylist trimmed and shaped, she asked her where she worked and chatted about topics of general interest. Sylvia had let her hair grow long so that she could be just like Gran. Her goal had been to braid her hair and wrap it around her head, but now she wanted something long enough to French braid, but short enough to look stylish and professional. The stylist had cut her hair on a slight curve so it framed her face nicely. Sylvia left a half hour later pleased with the results and feeling pretty, drove to the Motor Vehicle office to change her license. She went from there to the local mall to hunt for some sandals for the party. After three stores Sylvia had found a lovely soft lavender shawl that matched the color of the flowers on her dress, but still no sandals. Discouraged she walked into the last department store. Strappy cream-colored sandals with gold accents and narrow kitten heels were available in her size. They were light and sexy and she bought them immediately. Pleased with all of her accomplishments for the day Sylvia went to a take-out Chinese food restaurant. Realizing she had missed lunch, she treated herself to shrimp toast. Greedily she ate it on the way home before it had a chance to cool down and gulped large quantities of soda as she ate it. Before she went to bed, she laid out her dress, shawl and sandals over the kitchen chair to be ready when Marian picked her up in the morning and put together a small bag of toiletries and make-up.

CHAPTER SIXTEEN

"Let me bring you songs from the wood:
To make you feel much better than you could know—
Dust you down from tip to toe—
Show you how the garden grows—
Hold you steady as you go—
Join the chorus if you can:
It'll make of you an honest man."
--Ian Anderson, Songs from the Wood

With her usual promptness, Marian came to pick her up at 7:30 and Sylvia in cutoff jeans and a t-shirt, was ready to go.

"I love your hair!" Marian exclaimed. "It's adorable."

"Thanks," Sylvia said smiling. "I definitely needed a little change," she said brushing her fingers through her slightly wavy and slightly shorter locks.

Marian nodded. "Do you have everything?" she asked.

"I think so," Sylvia told her.

She picked up her things from the kitchen chair. They put the things in Marian's ancient Volvo wagon and drove to the U-pick farm. The sun was warm and the strawberries glistened with the bit of remaining dew. They looked like red jewels shining in the sun. Sylvia moved along the rows picking the ripened berries. She filled up a couple of quarts in no time, slipping several ripened berries in her mouth along the way. Picking the berries in the warm sunshine was pleasant. Other women and families were picking and their conversations hummed in the background along with the buzz of insects. Children played along the paths racing each other up and down empty paths and challenging each other to find the largest berries. Sylvia was surprised to see the small auras around the strawberries and the plants as she picked. When she had completed the fourth quart, she looked up to see where Marian was. Sylvia was a couple of rows over, straw-hatted with her head bent over the plants. Sylvia could see that she had picked at least three quarts too. She stood up and stretched in the sun and rubbed at some of the juice stains on her legs and hands before she carried her berries over to Marian.

"I have four quarts," she told her.

"Perfect," Marian said, "I'm just finishing up mine too. Aren't these lovely!"

"They're delicious," Sylvia told her. "I'll have to come back before the season is over."

"Well, they're easy to freeze for winter," Marian told her. "If the weather holds, we could come back next weekend."

They carried their berries back to the farm stand, paid for and loaded them into the car. Sylvia had specifically not brought up Owen, but she was wondering what he was up to. As if reading her mind, Marian told her that Owen was mowing the lawn and putting finishing touches on the fairy lights. She asked Sylvia if she would assist him in getting the bonfire set up in the meadow.

When they arrived at Marian's Owen was on the riding mower just as Marian had predicted. Marian waved gaily in his direction and they unloaded the berries. They washed them off and put them to chill in Marian's extra refrigerator in the basement. Sylvia went out to get her things and Marian led her upstairs to a room where she could change later.

Sylvia walked into the bedroom that had deeply set windows that looked out over the meadow and the forest. The room was like taking a step back in time. There was an antique oak sleigh bed covered in beautiful, snowy, antique linens. Delicate white on white embroidery graced the curtains that framed the windows. Sylvia drew in a breath.

"Marian, this is lovely!" she breathed. "Forget the restaurant idea! You should open a bed and breakfast!"

"Get your things put away and I'll see you downstairs," she said to Sylvia laughingly. "I'm glad you approve."

Sylvia put down her bag and hung her dress and shawl in an antique oak armoire. Then she went over to the window and leaned on the sill. Owen was hanging more fairy lights on the fence near the meadow entrance. She took a minute to lie down on the bed. She stretched luxuriously thinking how lucky she was to have a friend like Marian. It was almost like having Gran around, yet different. Before she began to think about Gran and be sad, Sylvia swung her legs over the side of the bed and went downstairs. She found Marian in the kitchen, sitting at the table checking her list.

"After lunch I'll have you and Owen fetch some folding chairs and tables from the basement and the punch bowl too," she said consulting her list.

As if on cue, Owen came inside. He was hot and sweaty.

"Whew!" he said, "it's starting to get warm out there." He seemed to be in a better mood and smiled at Sylvia. His mood was more relaxed than the past couple of days.

"I have chicken salad for lunch," Marian told them, "fresh fruit and mint iced tea. Why don't we eat and then we can finish setting up."

Owen pulled out paper plates and napkins while Sylvia poured iced tea and Marian brought out fruit, salad and rolls and set them on the table.

"I was asking Sylvia if you two could help get out the folding tables and chairs from the basement after lunch, Owen," she said. "I'll get the linens."

He nodded in response and she continued, "And then you two can set up the bonfire so that it's ready to light this evening."

"All right," Owen answered. "No problem. I'm glad the weather is holding. It's warm now, but I heard on the radio that the night will be a bit cooler."

"Perfect," Marian said.

They finished eating and it took little time to clean-up. Owen and Sylvia made several trips to the cavernous basement that smelled of age and the clay underneath the foundation. They fetched the chairs and tables and then pulled down a dusty punch bowl that was high on a cupboard shelf. Marian pulled linens from somewhere upstairs. She washed the punch bowl while Sylvia and Owen cleaned cobwebs and wiped off the tables and set them on the terrace. Marian brought out the linens and asked them to get the bonfire ready.

"Would you go and get some kindling from the woods," Owen asked her, "while I bring a load of wood over with the tractor?"

"Sure," said she and Sylvia walked off towards the woods.

She picked up kindling but turned abruptly when she heard the rustle of leaves. Not surprised, she saw the Green Man. He looked regal standing among the trees.

"You look like a king today," Sylvia commented as she smiled up at him.

The Green Man chuckled. "In a way," he said softly, but he changed the subject. "You're getting quite good at seeing auras," he said.

"Yes," Sylvia said, "It's wonderful. I found an excellent book at Gran's that helps explain about the colors," she told him.

"Now it's time for your next lesson. You're ready to feel the life force," he told her.

"What do you mean?" Sylvia asked.

"Everything has a life force," he told her.

"Like the one they talk about in Star Wars?" she interrupted.

"Something like that," he told her with a chuckle. "Different cultures call it different things. Put your hands on this tree," he instructed.

"What, am I going to be-- a Jedi knight?" she asked nearly laughing, but she saw he was completely sober and she put her hands on the trunk of a young sapling. A tingling electrical energy surged through her hands, through her arm, up her neck, down her spine, through her loins and down through her body. She gasped and staggered as she took her hands off the tree. The Green Man caught her arm and held her up while the tingling left traces in her core.

"What is it?" she asked the Green Man.

"It's the tree's life force," he said. "You can feel the life surging joyfully through it. You see a different phase of it in the auras."

Sylvia put her hands on the trunk and the tingling sensation went through her body again. She was more prepared for it this time. The tingling filled her body and she closed her eyes briefly as it surged through her limbs.

"This is amazing!" Sylvia said slowly taking her hands from the tree. The tingling stayed with her when she took her hands from the tree for a moment or two and returned when she put her hands back on the tree.

"The life force is in everything," the Green Man told her again. "You'll be able to see and feel it in many things as you grow in your knowledge," he said. "It is one of your gifts."

"Syl," she heard Owen call. "Are you all right?" he called out coming towards the forest.

"Fine," Sylvia called back, "I'm okay! I'll be right there!" she called out to Owen.

The Green Man seemed to melt into the trees. Still tingling a bit, Sylvia gathered up the kindling and walked carefully back to Owen. She must have looked dazed as Owen asked if she was all right again.

"I'm all right," she told him with a little note of annoyance in her voice. She did not really trust her legs and she wanted to sit down to think about what had just happened with the Green Man.

They set up the bonfire. Owen showed her how to build the wood in pyramid shape. After it was set up, they sat down at the edge of the cleared area.

Sylvia tried to keep the annoyance out of her voice, but had to ask, "Can you tell me about the samples now?"

Owen turned and looked at her sharply. He hesitated and then answered, "I'm not happy with the stream samples," he said. "I didn't find high levels of toxicity, but there are still some problems," he told her. "I'm not sure this will be the best marketing ploy to bring up the public image of the company."

"Don't you think we need to give it some time?" she asked. "Since they completed the project this past spring, I don't believe that the stream has had time to recover."

"You're probably right," he admitted. "It's something we should keep in mind and make note of during the stream watches," he said.

"Did you solve your other numbers problem?" she asked.

"Not entirely," he answered and he looked frustrated. "I don't want to talk about it right now," he told her. "I wouldn't want you connected in any way."

"Is that why you didn't answer my emails?" she asked, still hurt and angry.

"It is serious," he said with conviction. "I didn't mean to be rude, but this isn't something you should get involved in."

"Should you?" she asked looking into his eyes.

Instantly Sylvia felt sorry she had asked. His eyes looked troubled and his mouth was set in a thin line. She felt compelled to put her hand on his arm. Tingling shot through her hand, very similar to the tingling from the tree.

"It will be all right in the end," she murmured her annoyance melting away.

"Yeah, I guess so," he sighed. "I hope so," he added more soberly. They sat for a moment and just looked at each other. Sylvia couldn't read him and was wary. "We'd better get back and help Marian," he said.

When he stood up, he seemed a bit more like his old self, smiled a rakish grin and helped her to her feet. He hadn't answered her question, but apparently he felt that whatever he had found was important enough to pursue.

"Is this a typical party for Marian?" she asked Owen, agog with everything they had prepared. She didn't have any experience that would compare to Marian's midsummer's eve party preparations.

"I don't really know," he said. "I was too young to attend before she left for England. My Mom and Dad used to say that Marian's parties were quite memorable, though."

They walked back to the house in silence. Sylvia raised her face to the sun as it was beginning to slant. Even in the early evening, it was changing the meadow into gold and lighting up the backdrop of trees leaving the forest behind in deep shadow.

"There you are," Marian said to them. "Well, what do you think?" she asked them waving a hand at the tables that would hold food and drink.

"Lovely," Sylvia answered as they surveyed the tables in linens set with chunky white candles and flowers and herbs from the garden. "It will look beautiful tonight."

"I think so," Marian said. "Are the lights all set?" she asked Owen.

He nodded, "Oui, Madame, everything's done," he told her with a slight bow.

"Oh, you!" she scolded him, slapping at him good-naturedly, "Good, if you two can help me get some serving platters down, we can wash them up and they'll be ready for the food."

Owen went to get a stepladder and Marian instructed where to get particular platters that he handed to Sylvia, who placed them on the counter for Marian to wash. Once that was completed, Marian thought they should get dressed so that she and Sylvia could start preparing the food and put finishing touches for the party.

They trooped upstairs. Sylvia showered and dressed carefully scrubbing strawberry stains off of her skin and putting her hair up in a simple, classic French twist and returned to the kitchen. Marian was already putting platters into the oven. She was dressed in a lovely, pantsuit of loose layers of chiffon in various shades of blue and green.

"You look lovely," Marian told Sylvia when she came down.

"Thank you," Sylvia said. "You do too, Marian. Your pantsuit is gorgeous."

"Thanks," Marian said, "Now put on this apron so you don't ruin your beautiful dress as we finish up the last minute cooking," she instructed.

"Okay," Sylvia said. "She didn't want to cover up her dress, but knew Marian was right."

As she put on the apron, Owen came downstairs. He looked so handsome to Sylvia that it took her breath away. He was dressed in a snowy white collarless linen shirt and pleated black linen pants. She concentrated on tying on the apron to hide her face.

"Wow," he told the ladies eyeing them both with appreciation.

"Owen, be a love and get the ice in the tubs," Marian told him.

"Yes, Ma'am," he said and saluted her with a smile.

He went to fill large copper tubs with ice and stuck chilled champagne bottles in it. Sylvia piled strawberries into a large cut glass bowl and placed it out by the champagne. She took out the fresh vegetable platters and put the dip on a bowl filled with ice. Marian pulled out a platter of cheeses and trays of crackers. She asked Sylvia to get the bag of sausage and cheese balls from the freezer and a couple of boxes of miniature quiches. They put them in the oven. Owen turned on the fairy lights and lit the chunky candles. Marian had Owen open a bottle of champagne and they toasted one another to a happy midsummer's eve. Guests started to arrive and Marian whipped off her apron and hung it on a hook in the pantry. Sylvia kept an eye on the things in the oven and Owen took the plastic wrap from the cheeses, vegetables, and dips. When the hoer's deourves were cooked, Sylvia took them out to the tables and returned to the kitchen to remove her apron and went to join the party carrying a large platter of shrimp.

It was an interesting mix of people. Sylvia met a doctor, several people that worked at the local university. A high school biology teacher asked if she could call on him in the fall to organize a high school team for the stream watch. She caught glimpses of Owen out of the corner of her eye and Marian was enjoying herself too. Some people were dancing to the Celtic music that Owen had playing on his stereo. She kept an eye on the food and tried to help by refilling the platters as they became empty. Sylvia saw Owen removing empty bottles of champagne and replacing them with additional bottles and ice in the copper tubs. She stood alone finally, slightly giddy from the champagne. The sun had set and Marian's yard looked truly magical with the fairy lights artfully arranged in the trees and on the fence. The fireflies added their own bit of magic. Owen had done a terrific job. She listened to the music and recognized the ancient tune 'Summer is Icumen In' from her high school chorus days. She shivered.

"Are you cold," Owen asked as he came up behind her.

"No," Sylvia answered, "It's so beautiful. You did a great job with the lights. It's perfect." She focused on saying the words correctly so that she wouldn't appear too tipsy.

"It almost makes you want to believe in fairies and magic," he whispered softly.

Marian made the rounds to the guests and told them it was time to light the bonfire. Everyone trooped towards the meadow.

"Don't forget to make a wish!" Marian called to everyone as Owen lit the bonfire. Everyone stood around, silent for a few minutes while the flames licked their way up the pyramid of wood and turned into a roaring blaze. Everyone began laughing and talking and teasing one another about their individual wishes as Marian threw a bunch of St. John's Wort into the fire for luck. Sylvia thought she saw the Green Man through the flames on the other side of the bonfire. She moved her head and there he was. He winked at her, pulled out a panpipe and started piping and dancing and moving towards the forest. People laughed and watched the flames, but didn't notice him.

"Did you make your wish," Owen asked her softly.

Her head was swimming. She started to answer but with Owen standing so close to her he was all she could think about. She shivered again.

"You *are* cold," he said and he put his arm around her. Electric shocks raced through her body from his touch. She had dated in high school and at the University, but no one had ever had this effect on her before. She wanted him to kiss her. She edged closer to him.

"Syl," Owen murmured.

She looked up and turned to him and the next thing she knew she was in his arms and he was kissing her. She felt as though her insides were melting away and she was clinging to him as the kiss deepened and she was kissing him back.

"Syl," Owen said when they broke apart, "I'm sorry. I shouldn't have…" he stumbled over his words trying to apologize when they finally broke apart.

"It's okay," she answered closing her eyes a moment trying to cling to the last vestiges of the magic of the kisses. She was thrilled that he had feelings for her and almost embarrassed at how much she wanted him to continue kissing her and more.

Marian's voice broke through. She was calling to them and Sylvia turned to see her coming toward them. Sylvia and Owen took a step back from each other.

"Owen, I think everyone has gone home, can you work at putting out the fire?" asked Marian.

Sylvia looked around. It only seemed a moment ago that everyone was standing around the fire. She wondered how long they had been kissing.

"Sylvia, can you help me clear the tables?" Marian asked her.

"Sure," she answered uncertainly, a little abashed and certainly sobered up from a short time ago.

Sylvia returned to the house to assist gathering the candles and putting away the leftover food. Owen put out the fire and returned the tables and chairs to the basement and his stereo to his room. Marian poured them each a final glass of champagne and toasted them.

"Thank you for your help," she said and raised her glass, "To a successful Midsummer party!"

They all raised their glasses and drank.

"Now," she said turning to Sylvia. "We need to be getting you home." Marian yawned deeply, "But I don't know if I can drive."

"I can take you home, Sylvia," Owen said.

"Thanks," she told him. "That would be nice. I'll run upstairs and get my things."

She went up to Marian's beautiful room wishing she could stay and that Owen would be with her in that beautiful room. She pulled her things together in their little bag and went back down.

"Thank you again for your help," Marian said giving her a tipsy hug. "I couldn't have done it without you. Whew!" she told her, "that last bit of champagne put me over the edge. Good night!"

"It was fun," Sylvia said.

She went out to where Owen was waiting with the car running. She sat beside him, not saying anything. When he pulled into the driveway, he put his hand gently on her to stop her from getting out right away.

"Sylvia," he said uncomfortably. "I didn't mean to take advantage…" he stopped. "I shouldn't have…" he stopped again.

She turned to him and said, "Owen, it's all right. 'Thou doth protest too much,'" she quoted. "Anyway, I think we were both caught up in the moment and, I enjoyed kissing you." She stopped for a minute. "It's not like the old days when we would become betrothed after a kiss and you would be forced to marry me at gunpoint."

Her comment broke the tension and they both laughed.

"All right," he said, and he looked into her eyes. "I enjoyed it too, but I didn't want to make you feel uncomfortable."

"Don't worry, you didn't," she said. She kissed him on the cheek with a soft feathery kiss, got out of the car and went inside. She watched him drive away

"I guess I got my wish," she whispered to herself as she went up to bed. Crawling between the crisp sheets, she couldn't help but wish Owen was next to her. His chivalrous attitude about the kisses was nice but annoying. She wondered what he was thinking. She hugged the pillow in the darkness, imagining she was laying her head on his chest and fell asleep with many unspoken thoughts and desires.

Sunday morning dawned sparklingly beautiful to Sylvia. She jumped out of bed and couldn't help but smile as she sipped her coffee on the deck. Owen popped his head around the corner of the house.

"Morning, Syl," he said cheerily.

Sylvia nearly jumped out of her skin and blushed realizing all she was wearing was an overly large T-shirt and skimpy panties.

"H-h-Hi," she said shakily when she turned and saw him standing over her.

"Where were you?" he asked.

"I'm not sure," she said, painfully aware that she was clad only in an old t-shirt and her underwear. She maneuvered in her chair to be a little less conspicuous. "Still dreaming, I suppose."

"Marian wanted me to drop off a care package of last night's leftover goodies," he informed her.

"Oh!" she said. "That's terrific. I'll have to thank her." And then remembering her manners she asked, "Would you like a cup of coffee?"

"I would love it," he answered.

She went in and rushed upstairs to put on a pair of shorts before she poured him a cup and brought it back out to the deck. He was sitting and staring out at the bay.

"God, I wish I had a sailboat to use," he said with longing in his voice.

He was staring out at the bay that was filling up with white sails on this lovely summer's day. Other boats motored about and an occasional cigarette boat zoomed by.

"Do your parents still have their boat?" she asked.

"No," he said sadly, "they sold it a long time ago."

"I'm sorry," she said. "That's a shame."

"That's okay," he told her. "Hey! Have you had breakfast?" he asked changing the subject.

"No," Sylvia said. "I was pretty tired from yesterday's party. I just got up a little while ago."

"Would you like to go out for breakfast, or - uh," he looked at his watch, "actually brunch?"

"Sure," Sylvia said, "If you'll give me a couple of minutes.

"Please help yourself to more coffee."

She tugged her t-shirt down and ran into the house and showered and changed quickly into nice khaki shorts, a black scoop neck shirt that showed a little cleavage and her Birkenstock sandals. She had purchased the sandals in a weak moment from one of the shopping channels, thinking of Gran.

"Ready," she said breathlessly, "Where shall we go?"

"I don't know," Owen told her. "I've thought of a couple of places. There's a brunch on the canal or we could head up to Kennett Square and go to Longwood Gardens."

She said, "Both sound lovely. You decide."

"Well," he said, "If you're not busy today, I would vote for Longwood. It's not too hot and it would be a good day to wander through the gardens."

"That would be great," Sylvia said.

They drove what seemed like hours to Sylvia, through winding country roads and then on Route 1 to Route 100. They talked about the party and general subjects. Sylvia avoided talking about the soil and water samples. Her stomach was growling and she was puzzled when Owen drove past the entrance to Longwood.

Before she could say anything, he said, "Marian told me about a great diner up in Chadds Ford," he told her.

"I think Marian knows everything," Sylvia chuckled. "She's an amazing woman."

"I think you're right," Owen agreed.

They drove to 'Hank's Place' and waited for a table. The line stretched out the door but moved relatively fast. Finally, they were squeezed into a tiny table in the back corner and the waitress served them coffee.

"Marian recommended the blueberry pancakes," Owen told her.

"Then I'll have those and sausage," Sylvia told the waitress.

"The same for me, but with bacon," Owen ordered.

They sat and people watched while they waited for the order, not talking too much.

"Marian said Andrew Wyeth used to come here for breakfast," Owen informed her. "It's a hangout for some other artists as well."

Sylvia nodded and wondered if any were there that morning. It seemed to be a mixed crowd of farmers and tourists and some locals who were dressed in extraordinarily expensive clothing. The staff of the diner worked like clockwork. An older gentleman manned the grill and flipped the pancakes with a flourish. The waitresses were busy beyond belief, but kept calm and served customers with ease and patience.

"Have you ever been to Longwood?" Sylvia asked him.

"Not for years and years," he told her.

"Me too," she said. "I think I remember Gran and my Mom taking me there for a theater production once. I remember it seemed to be a magical sort of place."

"I think I went when I was an obnoxious pre-teen and was bored to tears. But, I do remember it being beautiful," Owen said.

Their pancakes arrived and they settled into eating. The pancakes were delicious and they both devoured them quickly and headed up to the gardens. It was a perfect summer's day with the sun shining brightly. Longwood was crowded, but not overly so, at that time of the morning. Everything was glowing with life. The circular arches near the visitors' center were filled with late blooming roses with a scent that was intoxicating. They followed this path past the lakes to the Italian water gardens where they sat and watched the fountains for a few minutes and fed the fish and the geese. Then they walked through the rainbow of color on the flower garden walk, toured the conservatory and the Pierce-du Pont House. After a couple of hours, Sylvia was feeling the effects of the previous late night.

"I'm still full from breakfast," she told Owen, "but, I would love to get a cold drink of something," she said.

"Me too," he agreed. "Let's go up to the cafeteria."

They sat outside with cool drinks and some sinful desserts.

"I know this is a touchy subject," she said to him, "and I don't mean to offend or make you angry, but can you give me any hint or information on the soil samples from the other day?" she asked breaking her vow from earlier in the day.

Here she felt far, far away from Thurmont and safe somehow.

Owen sighed. "I don't really have the testing equipment at home to answer some of my questions or yours," he told her, "and I haven't been able to get to a lab at Thurmont to test my theory, but what I could see wasn't good."

"Is it more toxic waste?" Sylvia asked.

"Possibly," said Owen, "but there were differences. From what I could see, it…" he broke off for a minute. "You see it doesn't even make sense."

"What doesn't?" she prodded gently.

"It's almost like a dinoflagellate," he said.

"What's that?" she asked.

"It's the type of critter that causes pfisteria," he said, "But, dinoflagellates are water based microorganisms and they're not found on land. That's one of the many things that doesn't make sense."

"And," Sylvia asked, "could this stuff or creature mean yet another Superfund clean-up?"

"Very possibly," he admitted. "I don't know really. Definitely some sort of clean-up, but its *alive* Syl. And Thurmont won't like that, I can assure you."

"Things just aren't adding up and I don't know why or how," he said. "It's damn frustrating."

"I'm sure," Sylvia murmured. "I'm sorry I don't know more about microorganisms and stuff," she said. "It's totally out of my league, but I don't mind listening about it."

He smiled at her. "Thanks," he said. "I'm sorry if I've been a bear," he apologized. "This mess is going to get a hell of a lot worse before it gets better. And I need time to research this. Unfortunately, I don't have the access I need for some sites. It's not something I can just *Google* or feel that I can research at work."

"It's okay," she said benignly. Inside she was dying to ask if Anna had anything to do with it, but she bit her tongue.

They finished their desserts and drinks and continued their tour of Longwood. They sat mesmerized watching the fountain show at the central fountain gardens and it was there Owen took her hand. Sylvia was blissfully happy. They continued to walk through the gardens, up through the chimes tower that overlooked a waterfall and through a wooded area. Sylvia just stopped and stared when they came to a grove of Atlas Cedars.

"What magnificent trees!" she cried. "I've never seen anything like them." She went over to one of the trees ducking under the huge branches. "Look," she said to Owen, "you could crawl right into one and sit and read a book. Look at these!" She bent down and picked up something that looked like a wooden rose.

"It's the top part of the cone," Owen said with a grin, "and it certainly looks like a rose," he said examining what she had found.

When Sylvia reached over and touched the bark, she thought she might see sparks from the jolt of energy that met her hands it was that strong. She took her hands away from the tree, and her hands and arms still tingled. Pulling away was hard. As they walked further down the path, she kept looking back at the trees. She wasn't surprised that they had a tremendous aura that seemed to reach out a couple of feet from the tree. Owen took her tingling hand as they finished up their tour. She was surprised at the intensity of the experience. On the ride home, as they continued to talk, Owen occasionally took her hand. He shared more about his childhood and told her about his parents. Sylvia asked him if he wanted to come in for a while when they pulled into her drive, but Owen declined.

"No," he murmured, "I think I'd better get back. Thanks for coming today," he told her.

"Thank you for the lovely day," she said, looking into his eyes seeing only a glimmer of the worry she noticed before.

This time, he kissed her gently, once, twice and then a third time. Sylvia knew it held the promise of many more. It sent a shiver through her insides that was not at all unpleasant. She said good-bye a little breathlessly and went into the house.

After pinching herself for the unbelievably wonderful day, Sylvia checked the answering machine. There were two messages from her mother and one from Carol. She called her mother to say 'hello' and check in for the week.

"You sound different," her mother said, "Are you all right?"

"I'm all right," Sylvia said, "Probably just a little tired from the party last night."

"I don't think it's that," her mother was working on her motherly telepathy, but Sylvia didn't want to talk about Owen and the day today, so she kept silent. After her phone call from her mother, she thought about calling Gwen. Sylvia decided against it, wanting to hold the special feelings of the day wrapped tightly around her like a cozy quilt. She texted her with only two words – 1st date – knowing Gwen would know exactly what she meant. She also emailed Carol that she had lunch for the both of them tomorrow. She pulled out some of the leftovers from the Marian's party that Owen had thoughtfully put in the refrigerator. Sylvia made up a couple of plates for Carol and herself for Monday lunch and heated the rest in the microwave. Then she settled down to miniature quiches, and other treats, with a glass of wine for her ritual of having dinner while watching the sunset over the water. The sun looked as though it had caught fire and was setting with a blaze of impressive orange-red streaks shooting out of its burning edges. She thought of the folktale her grandmother had told her of the Hawaiian god, Maui, which tried to tie the sun down with ropes. The streaks of color certainly looked like fiery ropes of orange and red. Sylvia marveled at the intensity of color.

CHAPTER SEVENTEEN

In May 1963 Dorothy Maclean received an insight from within as she meditated: *The forces of nature are something to be felt into, to be reached out to. One of the jobs for you as my free child is to sense the Nature forces such as the4wind, to perceive its essence and purpose for me, and to be positive and harmonize with that essence.*

Monday morning passed swiftly for Sylvia. She hummed away happily at her desk completing work, laughing out loud when she received a one-word email from Gwen stating 'details!' Sylvia emailed her back the message 'later' and received yet another email stating 'Call you tonight!' Lunch seemed to come quickly and she took the plates of leftovers to the cafeteria where Carol was waiting.

"Wait a minute," Carol said when Sylvia sat down at the table. "What happened to you this weekend?" she asked slyly.

"What do you mean?" Sylvia returned, blushing a little.

"You can't hide it from me," Carol prodded. "C'mon, tell!

"Well," Sylvia said slowly, savoring the suspense of keeping it from Carol a moment longer, "I had a date with Owen yesterday," she told her quietly.

"Great!" Carol crowed. "He seems like a great guy."

"I think he is," Sylvia answered beginning to dig into her lunch. "But, keep it quiet, okay? I don't think the ice princess would appreciate it."

Carol made a face, a rude gesture, and the comment, "Give *this* to ice princess Anna."

They ate for a few minutes with Carol oohing and ahhing over Marian's hors d'oeuvres.

"Can you tell her I'm up for adoption?" she asked Sylvia. "My Mom wouldn't mind as long as I took her the some of the leftovers. Hell, she could adopt my mom too!"

Carol was very close to her Mom, but Sylvia had understood quite clearly that she was not much of a cook. Carol and her Mom had a bunch of local restaurants that they frequented for meals. Home cooking was not something Carol had grown up with.

"Owen is really lucky to be living there," Carol said. "Does she cook like this every night?"

Sylvia started to laugh and then began to answer Carol when she paused. Carol had stopped eating for a moment and glanced around the crowded cafeteria.

"Speaking of the good man," Carol said, "Here he comes."

Owen was coming into the cafeteria and waved to them from across the room. He was smiling until someone put a hand on his shoulder.

"Uh, oh," Carol said again, sotto voce, "Here comes trouble."

Sylvia turned to look and saw Anna coming in after Owen. She walked swiftly up to him, put her hand on his shoulder to make him pause and began talking to him. Owen's face went from happy and smiling to grim. He turned to walk back out of the cafeteria with Anna and did not look happy.

"I wonder what's going on?" Sylvia asked out loud.

"Who knows," Carol said. "Poor guy."

Sylvia finished her lunch and went back to the office. She emailed Owen a brief message "Everything okay?" It wasn't until after 4 pm that she received a terse answer 'No.' Sylvia knew it was related to some of the things they had discussed.

When she got home, the phone was ringing and Gwen was leaving her a message to call her as soon as possible.

Sylvia picked up the phone laughing, "Is this soon enough?" she chuckled.

"Not quite," Gwen growled with a grin. "So tell me, what happened?"

Sylvia gave Gwen a brief rundown of what happened Saturday and Sunday. Without going into detail, she told Gwen about the difficulties between Owen and Anna as well as her own feelings about Anna.

"I said it was tough to have a relationship with someone from work," she chided. "Things can get difficult—fast."

"I know, I know," sighed Sylvia. They talked for a few more minutes and Gwen promised to come again for a weekend soon. Also, Sylvia said she would go north for a weekend in the next month. The expression on Owen's or Anna's faces haunted her. She dialed Marian's number only to find out that Owen was still at work on something. Marian was well, yet concerned about Owen. She hinted that she hoped that Owen would ask Sylvia for another date.

"Are you trying to be a matchmaker?" Sylvia teased her.

"I don't think I need to be in this case," Marian told her. "This is definitely a case of mutual attraction."

Sylvia didn't answer her. She let Marian's words sink in. She told Marian thanks and hung up.

She couldn't help it. She was bothered by the fact that Owen was having problems--she didn't have the correct words for it. The 'not knowing' was frustrating and deep down she knew on some level that Anna was involved. She wondered how involved Owen had become with Anna. Had he kissed her too? Had he slept with her? She called his cell, but only received voice mail. Frustrated, she paced for a while and then went down to the beach. Sylvia sat, throwing small stones into the water, some rather violently, gave up and walked down to the marina and then back to the house. The physical exercise calmed her disquieted mind and she lifted her head to sniff the water-scented air that mixed with freshly cut grass and garden flowers. The sun had started to dip and the bats were coming out for their nightly feast of mosquitoes. Fireflies hovered near tall grasses and blinked off and on leading her down the road. Sylvia loved June.

Tuesday passed and no word from Owen. Wednesday, Sylvia banged around the house and the office with frustration. She tried to focus on the stream watch training and pulling it together for Saturday. Thursday, no word from Owen, but when she met Carol for lunch in the cafeteria, she saw Owen sitting with Anna and her spirits plummeted further.

Carol was watching the exchange between Owen and Anna and said, "They don't look happy."

Sylvia, who had been trying not to stare, turned to look at the two and realized others in the cafeteria were staring at the angry couple. They were discussing something in sharp, short whispers. The cafeteria had turned quiet and bits of the argument floated out to eager gossipers.

Suddenly Anna got up and shouted, "You can't do this to me! You can't!"

"Like hell I can't!" they heard Owen's voice rising. "What you did was wrong!"

Anna got up to leave and Owen put a hand on her arm to stop her.

"Let go of me you bastard," she screamed, drawing all of the cafeteria's attention to her.

Loud silence filled the room as all eyes followed the couple. Somewhere back in the kitchen a loud crash of plates and silverware jolted everyone back and conversations resumed.

Anna stalked out and Owen followed.

"Doesn't look pretty," Carol commented as she and Sylvia and the rest of the cafeteria watched the pair leave.

Sylvia was sick with worry. She had a terrible feeling of dread that she couldn't shake about Owen, and she couldn't concentrate on her work that afternoon. At home, she ripped through the house cleaning and then set off for a walk down the beach to the marina and back to the road. The Green Man fell in step beside her and Sylvia ignored him at first.

"What?" Sylvia finally asked testily.

"Hmm," replied the Green Man, "You're a bit grumpy today."

"Grumpy, frustrated, call it what you want," Sylvia snapped.

"Hmm," he murmured. "Listen well," he told her. "Veriditas," he said breaking off their conversation and looking up the road.

Sylvia looked up too. Owen's car pulled into the driveway. Sylvia gave a small, glad cry and began to jog up the road leaving the Green Man behind her.

"Owen!" she called out eagerly. "I'm here."

Owen was peering in the kitchen door and turned when he heard her call. She jogged breathlessly up to him.

"Hi," she said, panting a bit.

"Hi," he said brushing the front lock of hair back from his eyes.

They stood looking at each other for a few moments, not speaking.

Sylvia asked, "Would you like a beer or something?"

He nodded. He looked miserable—his hazel eyes large and full of sadness. Sylvia thought immediately of a small boy and wanted to comfort him.

"I'll go get it," she said, "let's sit on the deck."

Owen went around to the back of the house. Sylvia let herself into the house, pulled two beers from the refrigerator and went through the living room to join Owen on the deck. He had walked down to the edge of the water and turned when he heard the door to see Sylvia coming onto the deck. She handed him one and they both sat on the steps.

Owen didn't talk for a long time. He sat at the edge of the step, rather nervously, Sylvia thought sipping his beer. Owen finally reached out his hand and took Sylvia's clutching it tightly.

"What's wrong?" she asked after several minutes.

"Anna," he croaked almost choking on a swig of beer, "Anna's been changing the numbers on the environmental tests."

"What?" Sylvia asked incredulously.

"Anna," he said, dryly, shaking his head.

"What's going to happen?" Sylvia asked. She only had a vague idea of the magnitude of his news, but the mere thought of domino effect it would have on the company and with the EPA made her ill.

"I need to report it," Owen went on unhappily. "I suspected it, I couldn't believe it but, I proved it," he said. "Obviously, she's not happy about it from what everyone saw today in the cafeteria," he said sardonically. "She likes to put on quite a show."

Sylvia didn't say anything. She leaned against him.

"I'm sorry," she said finally. "Is there anything I can do?"

Owen shook his head and put his arm around her. They sat quietly for a long time and then he turned to kiss her. First, he kissed her on the hair lightly and repeatedly. She turned her face up to him and she kissed him back. The kisses became deeper and deeper.

When they finally broke apart, Sylvia said, "Let's go inside."

"No," Owen said hoarsely and seriously, looking into her eyes, his one hand cupped against her cheek and the other on her arm, lightly brushing her breast. "If I come inside, I won't be leaving to-night," he told her. "And I don't think either of us is ready for that."

He was probably right, but Sylvia didn't want to agree. Yet, Sylvia's mind and body were not paying any heed to anything that made sense. The smoldering fires within her wanted to flame. She swallowed hard and nodded in agreement with his reasoning. They stood up. His hands lingered on her.

Sylvia leaned her head on his chest and held him as tightly as he held her. Owen kissed her on the top of her head and reluctantly pulled away.

"Thanks. Thanks for being here and for listening," he told her. He said louder with a voice firm with resolve, "I know what I need to do."

Sylvia watched him walk across the deck and over to his car. She held up her hand in a silent goodbye and went back into the house.

CHAPTER EIGHTEEN

O Lord
Let my spirit
Glow so brightly,
That darkness
Will disappear.
-Pakistan, Islamic "a child's prayer."
Peace on Earth

Sylvia watched him drive away and tears welled up in her eyes for no apparent reason. She wondered what he meant by 'he knew what he had to do.' She looked around, hoping that the Green Man would return, but he didn't. Now her heart ached for Owen even more and her frustration level was still high.

She felt she could barely make it through work Friday. She checked and re-checked her e-mail hoping to hear from Owen and looked for him at lunch to no avail. She had a difficult time concentrating and tried, very carefully, to make sure everything was in place for Saturday's training. Fortunately, the kits had arrived by express mail and she double -checked that the appropriate people would be available to open the building and that the catering was in place. Mr. Carter urged her to leave early since she would be working on Saturday, but Sylvia refused. She hoped that perhaps Owen might stop by the office at the end of the day. Reluctantly at 5 p.m., she turned off her computer and the lights to the office. Her car was one of the last ones left in the lot. His car was parked under a tree. She didn't know what kind of car Anna drove. She went home and paced endlessly and finally called Marian. They conversed for a few minutes and Sylvia asked if Owen was there.

"No," Marian answered her. "I haven't seen him. In fact, I thought he might be with you until you called. He didn't get in until late last night and was up and out quite early this morning."

"Hmm," Sylvia murmured. "Okay, thanks."

They talked for a few minutes more and hung up. Sylvia made herself some dinner and picked at it. She turned on the television and channel surfed only staying on a program for a few minutes before switching to another. Sylvia felt like a fool. Even though Owen expressed interest in her, and seemed sincere with his feelings over the weekend, she couldn't help but wonder if he was jerking her around? Was he really involved with Anna. Sighing, she finally went up to bed. She couldn't read. She couldn't sleep. She tossed and turned throughout the night.

The next morning, Sylvia dragged herself out of bed and sat hunched over a cup of coffee. She knew full well she had to be at Thurmont in the next hour and a half, bright, chipper and ready to lead this group on a stream watch. She had hoped Owen might call and say they could go together, but he hadn't. Sylvia washed, dressed in old khakis and a Thurmont T-shirt that had been provided to the company, and set off to Thurmont. The custodian, Ed let her into the building. He was a really nice guy only a few years older than she. He always seemed to be at Thurmont and always had a smile and something nice to say.

"You must live here," she commented.

"Almost," he said. "I like the overtime! The catering's all set up," he told her. "And I started coffee."

"Thanks, you're terrific!" Sylvia said, returning his bright smile. She noticed that his hand was bandaged. "What happened to your hand?" she asked, concerned.

Ed hesitated and then said, "Poison ivy, I think. Stupid of me."

"Gee, I hope you're okay," Sylvia said sympathetically. "It looks like you're really allergic to it."

"Yeah," he replied.

She went to the conference room where she found the caterers had provided carafes of coffee, a variety of teas, juice, muffins, croissants and Danish. Clutching a cup of coffee, Sylvia returned to the lobby to wait for people. She was beginning to feel brighter as the caffeine coursed through her veins. They couldn't have asked for a more perfect summer's day. Sylvia was glad the humidity was down. When Owen arrived a few minutes later, he looked haggard and drawn. She had wanted to be cool towards him but, was shocked at his appearance.

"Owen, you look terrible!" Sylvia exclaimed, "Are you all right?"

"Yeah," he said curtly. "I just need some coffee."

"There's some brewing in the conference room," she said. "Why don't you get some and relax until the people arrive."

"Okay," he said, sounding relieved.

Sylvia couldn't help but wonder why he was in such as state, but she didn't have too long to think, as the Stream Watch team started to arrive. She showed them to the conference room and passed out packets and kits while everyone chatted and had coffee.

She opened the group by welcoming them to Thurmont and passed around a sign-in sheet. She introduced herself and Owen, who stood, sipping coffee and nodding in acknowledgment. Everyone went around the table introducing themselves and then Sylvia went over the facts, why the stream watch was needed and the contents of their packet. Owen used some overhead transparencies and shared the types of life that they might find in the stream. They asked everyone to pick up their things and head out to the stream. Sylvia led them from the front door, through the staff picnic area and down to the stream. The sunlight dappled through the leaves as they gathered at the edge waiting for direction. The stream sparkled in the sunlight and gurgled invitingly over the rocks. Owen gave them step-by-step instructions on what to look for and demonstrated how to test the water and sieve for critters. The volunteers practiced and were enthused when they found larvae and other items listed on their sheet. Owen gave a brief lecture about stream health. He voiced his concerns that the creek's health was relatively poor. He hoped that due to the clean-up that it would improve. Sylvia thanked everyone for their time and handed out Thurmont T-shirts. She said she would be in touch in a couple of months, to return and continue the watch.

She and Owen walked everyone back to the parking area before they returned to the stream area to get the kits. While Owen was assessing each of the kits and making sure they were put together correctly, Sylvia hopped across some stones to the other side of the stream. She stopped and listened once she had climbed the embankment. All was quiet as before. She reached out and touched a tree. There was no life force surging through it. She walked a little and felt another. She felt no life force surging through the trunk. She tried another and another, wondering if her recent gift was lost. As she looked up at the branches overhead, she noticed most of the leaves were hanging limply and realized all of a sudden that the trees had no auras. They were lifeless. Not caring about the muck, she walked from tree to tree, in almost a state of shock, touching and looking, hoping to find some sort of life. Nothing. Dead leaves littered the ground. She looked up and the leaves still attached to the branches were pale, limp and lifeless. It gave her a horrible empty and sickish feeling. Sylvia continued walking through the eerily quiet forest. When she came to a small clearing, there was something that puzzled her. She saw something a short distance away that was pale and white compared to the surrounding earth and woods. Was it a branch or lifeless plant? She walked over to take a closer look. What she saw was a white hand sticking out of the muck. She looked more closely and retched. It was definitely someone's hand, and that meant that the rest of the person was probably buried beneath her. Sylvia screamed—silently inside at first and then she screamed louder and louder, over and over, unable to stop. She shrieked Owen's name and "help" and just screamed.

Owen came running.

"Syl!" he called out, "Sylvia! What's wrong?" His face was pale and worried. He took her by the arms and forced her to look up at him. Sylvia stopped screaming out loud, but words didn't come out. Her body was rigid. Owen held her at arm's length with concern in his eyes. Shakily she pointed to the hand sticking up out of the soil. She held onto her stomach again and buried her head into Owen's chest, her whole body trembling.

"Oh my God," Owen said faintly. He stared at the pasty white hand too, not wanting to get too close.

"We need to get someone," she said shakily. "We need to call the police."

Woodenly she walked back through the trees, across the stream and then started to run back to the building. Fortunately, Ed had left the door open for their group in case they needed anything, but Sylvia didn't see any sign of him. The first phone she could find was at the security desk in the front lobby where she dialed 911, not thinking of her cell phone in her car. Owen had caught up with her and they both sat in the sunshine until the police arrived. It seemed like hours and finally one squad car arrived. Two policemen got out and she explained what she found and led them to the hand. They looked and immediately called for backup as well as an ambulance and they started questioning her and Owen as to why they were in the area and how they found the hand. More police eventually arrived along with the ambulance and the coroner. Sylvia watched from a distance clutching Owen's arm as they exhumed the body. She caught a glimpse of platinum blond hair and gasped. The plain-clothes detective nearby caught her reaction and came right over.

"Do you know her?" he asked demandingly. He was a tall man with hard muscles and the strength of iron, his graying hair was cut in a military fashioned crew cut. He looked down at Sylvia, at her diminutive level, and had to look up at Owen with delving eyes.

"Anna!" she said in a whisper. "I think it's Anna!"

"Anna, who?" prodded the cop more forcefully.

"I d-d-don't remember her last name," Sylvia said shakily. "She's a scientist here."

"Anna Hansen," Owen told them quietly. "She is" he hesitated, "or was a colleague of mine."

"You'd better come over with me to see if you can identify the body," the cop said.

They walked over to where the body had been exhumed. It was Anna. What was horrible was that it looked like something had been eating away at her skin. Trails of flesh had been eaten away and on her arms and legs, you could see the muscles' sinewy tissue.

Sylvia walked over to lean against a tree and was quietly sick. The detective came over with sympathy in his eyes.

"It's never easy," he told her quietly and he handed her a tissue. "Especially if they've been buried for a long time."

Sylvia's head shot up. "But, she was alive a couple of days ago!" she told him.

"Are you sure?" he asked sharply. "Usually bodies with that much decay..." he stopped.

"I saw her in the cafeteria with Owen two days ago," she blurted out unthinkingly and stopped and looked guiltily at Owen. There was a lump of fear in her stomach that started to build into a knot.

"Well," the cop drawled, "I guess I'll need to ask him some further questions," turning to go back to Owen.

Sylvia wanted to sit down, but not in the muck.

"Could I go back to the picnic area to sit down, Officer?" Sylvia asked.

He turned back to her and saw she was still pale. "Sure," he said and he called to another policeman, "Hey, Joe! Come here!"

'Joe,' a tall, young uniformed policeman with a nearly shaved head of blond hair and bright blue eyes walked over to where they were standing and Officer Smith asked him, "Would you take this young lady back to the building's picnic area and let her sit for awhile. I need to talk to her friend for a minute."

As nice as he was, Sylvia couldn't help but catch the note of satisfaction in his voice. He turned to walk over to Owen, who was standing like a statue, unable to take his eyes from the body.

"He thinks Owen killed her," she thought, almost saying it aloud. She walked back to the picnic area with 'Joe.' They sat at the picnic table. As warm as it was, Sylvia felt chilled in the shade.

Joe looked at her sympathetically and said, "It's shock, I'll go and get you a blanket."

He walked back to the squad car and Sylvia sat shivering with her teeth beginning to chatter. Nausea filled her and she rested her forehead on the table. She was grateful when Joe put a blanket around her shoulders.

He started to talk, just in general, asking her name and telling her his was Joe Collins. He told her he had been a cop for five years. He talked about the weather, sports, and any general knowledge. He didn't expect Sylvia to answer and she was grateful. He was trying to take her mind off the horror that she had seen. Some of the chill went away. Her teeth stopped chattering and she started to converse with Joe. It wasn't long before Owen walked back with Officer Smith and another plain-clothes officer. The trail of other emergency personnel followed them.

"It's like a grisly parade," Sylvia thought.

Officer Smith led Owen over to where she was sitting. She was a little warmer now and had let the blanket fall some. She pulled it around her for comfort and looked up at the two with hollow eyes.

"You'll both need to stay in the area for additional questioning," Officer Smith told them. "Thank you for your statements. We'll be in touch if we have further questions."

Sylvia and Owen nodded at him in acknowledgment. He went over their personal information again and where they could be reached and then told them they were free to go. Sylvia folded the blanket and returned it to Joe.

"Thanks," she told him. "Thanks for the blanket, and for sitting and talking with me."

He flashed a smile at her and took the blanket. "Sure," he said, "Take care."

She turned to Owen, who was pale underneath his tan. The police had already brought up the stream watch kits and left them by the building door. Sylvia went over to grab a few and take them to the trunk of her car.

"Let's go," she murmured to Owen.

He walked duly over to the kits and picked up the rest. Sylvia could see the shock was hitting him.

"Do you want to leave your car here and I'll take you home?" she asked.

"No," he said, "I'd rather just get home."

"Look," Sylvia said, "I'll follow you to Marian's or would you rather just come over to my place?" she asked.

"Let's go to Marian's," he murmured. "She might be able to help."

Sylvia followed Owen the few miles back to Marian's house. She wasn't home, but Sylvia went in to get Owen a beer thinking that he might be better off with a straight shot of whiskey. She poured herself a tall glass of Marian's delicious cool spring water. It was so cold it made her teeth ache and she greedily gulped a glassful and refilled it before she went back out to Owen. He was sitting in the sunshine staring at nothing. Sylvia handed him the beer, which he took and drank in thirsty gulps. They didn't speak.

When he had finished, Sylvia finally asked, "He—Officer Smith thinks you did it, right?" Sylvia guessed.

Owen sighed heavily. "I think so," he said. "He didn't come out and say so, but he certainly hinted at it. I'm not sure about the other detective, though."

Sylvia did all that she could not to ask, 'did you?' As if catching her thought, he looked at her.

"What do you think?" he asked her pointedly.

"I honestly don't know," Sylvia replied. "I don't know if you would have just cause, but you would have cause…" she stopped and chewed at her lower lip, "And people have killed for less," she commented uncomfortably. She paused again for a moment and sighed. "But it made me realize that I really don't know you, all that well and that frightens me a little bit," she admitted.

He kept looking at her, those hazel eyes that melted gold and green and brown together. She looked back. As she looked, she thought and thought and listened with her heart.

"No," she said, quietly yet firmly. "I don't believe you killed her, but I wonder who did?"

"I don't know," Owen answered her. "I haven't a clue."

They sat quietly and Owen reached over and took her hand and held it firmly. They sat that way, not talking, not thinking until the crunch of tires came up the drive. It was only after Marian's cheery greeting rang across the lawn that they broke their hands and turned towards Marian.

"Hello, you two!" came her cheerful greeting. "How was the stream watch?"

When she reached them and saw their faces, her cheery smile changed to concern.

"What happened? What's wrong?" she asked with concern when she saw their faces.

Owen and Sylvia looked at each other and then at Marian. It was Owen who spoke first.

"Things turned out a bit differently than we had planned," he murmured.

Marian looked puzzled.

"Maybe you'd better sit down," Sylvia told her.

Marian sat and faced both of them before she said, "Well, it looks as though you have a story to tell me."

Sylvia nodded, "Our morning ended quite differently than expected," she began.

Owen interrupted and stated, "Sylvia found Anna's body in the woods near the stream."

"What?" Marian said incredulously. "Anna? Anna Hansen? That scientist you brought to dinner a couple of weeks ago?" she asked.

They both nodded.

Marian's usually bright, twinkling green eyes shone with a steady light. She looked from one to the other steadily.

"Perhaps you had better tell me what happened," she said seriously.

"Someone murdered her in the last couple of days," Owen told Marian. "I mean," he stammered, "it's been a couple of days since I've seen or talked to her."

Sylvia nodded as well.

"Me too," Sylvia agreed, "And it's possible that Owen is under suspicion," Sylvia said, "because he was one of the last people to see her alive." Sylvia hesitated, "and after they had a very public argument." She had to look away at that point and gazed at the gray and brown bark of the spreading oak over the patio. An ant was finding its way through the crevices and canyons of bark. She wondered briefly where it was going.

Owen had closed his eyes as if in pain when Sylvia made that statement.

"I didn't kill her," he stated again.

"No one's accusing you," Marian said.

"We think the one detective might think he's a suspect," Sylvia stated quietly.

"Do you know how she was killed?" Marian asked.

They both shook their heads.

Owen continued, "She was buried in a shallow grave in the woods. The weird thing is that her skin," he stopped, "her body looked as though it had been eaten away by something."

Sylvia held her stomach. "It was horrible," she told Marian not wanting to relive what she had seen.

"Was it from some sort of animal?" Marian asked.

Owen almost snorted, "Not one that I've ever seen," he said. He went on to describe the way the skin had been eaten away in trail-like lines, some all the way down to the muscle.

Sylvia recoiled and closed her eyes. It still made her feel sick to think of Anna's body. Owen finished telling Marian the rest of the story as Sylvia stared at the bark of the oak again. When he was finished, they all sat silent for a few minutes.

"Do you think you'll need an attorney?" Marian asked Owen.

"I don't know," he answered miserably.

"I think it would be a good idea," Sylvia said, adding her opinion.

"I do too," Marian agreed.

"But, if I hire an attorney now," Owen pondered, "Wouldn't it look as though I was guilty?"

"I see what you mean," Sylvia said and she sighed.

"Well, I think you need something good to eat," Marian told them matter-of-factly. "I'll go and see what I can rustle up for dinner."

Sylvia started to get up to help and Marian put a gentle, but firm hand on her shoulder.

"Sit," she ordered. "Just sit and relax."

Sylvia didn't protest. She felt too numb. Owen took her hand and held it without talking. They sat, not talking, holding hands tightly and looking out over the meadow. The late afternoon sun turned the green meadow into gold and the oak beside them began to spread a deep shadow that reached towards the meadow. Birds began their evening conference as the twilight crept in. They both relaxed a little and Owen loosened his grip slightly on Sylvia's hand. She looked over at him and saw his eyes were closed. Sylvia wondered if he was just thinking of if he was asleep. Before she had a chance to ask, Marian came out to call them in for dinner.

"You are amazing Marian," Sylvia commented as they sat down to another gourmet dinner created by Marian.

"This is nothing," Marian said. "I thought you could use some comfort food."

"Definitely," Owen agreed as he scooped a mountain of mashed potatoes onto his plate.

Sylvia filled her plate but didn't feel like eating. She took a bite or two and exhaustion overtook her. Suddenly she felt as though the effort to bring the fork to her mouth was too much.

"Are you all right?" Marian asked.

"I'm really, really, really tired all of a sudden," Sylvia answered.

"It's the shock," Marian told her. "Why don't you spend the night," she suggested.

Sylvia almost started crying with relief. "Thanks," she said. "Every time I close my eyes," she shuddered, "I see that pale white hand sticking up from the ground. I can see how she was, she was," she hesitated, "how she was eaten down to the muscle tissue. It was....grisly." Sylvia stopped.

"Sorry," she said, "this really isn't dinner conversation." She closed her eyes to the welling nausea from remembering Anna's body, Anna's pale, translucent skin, or the shreds that were left of it and the ragged, bloody trails as the necrosis seemed to eat through the layers. It was worse than anything she had seen on television. It was worse than any horror film she could recollect. Yet, the problem was, real. Finally, she said to Marian, keeping her eyes closed, "I don't think I want to be at home alone tonight."

"The room you changed in last weekend is fresh and ready for you. Why don't you go up and draw a hot bath, have a good soak and go to bed," she suggested.

"I don't think I can argue with that," Sylvia told her. "Thank you."

She picked up her plate and took it over to the sink, went back to the table to retrieve her wine glass and say goodnight.

"Leave your clothes outside the bathroom door," Marian said. "I'll run them through the washer so they'll be fresh in the morning. I think I can scrounge up a clean nightgown too," she told Sylvia.

Sylvia nodded and turned to go up the back stairs. She drew a steaming bath and drained her wine as the bathtub filled. As warm as it was outside, Sylvia felt chilled as though rivulets of icy water ran underneath her skin. She could not get warm. Sylvia climbed in and instantly her skin turned bright pink in the hot water. Sylvia tried to scrub away the horrors of the day until she lay exhausted, soaking in the warm water until it turned too cool to stay in the bathtub. When she stepped out of the bath, her limbs felt heavy and were lobster red. She toweled off and peeked out the door. Her clothes were gone and in their place was a beautiful nightgown of sprigged cotton. She pulled it over her head and went down the hall to the guest room. Marian had turned on the light, opened the windows and turned down the bed. Sylvia slipped between the crisp sheets and turned off the light. A light breeze came in through the window and she could hear Owen and Marian's voices drifting up the stairs. It was a soothing sound. She fell asleep immediately and slept peacefully through the night.

CHAPTER NINETEEN

Earth brings us into life
And nourishes us.
Earth takes us back again.
Birth and death are present in every moment.
--Thich Nhat Hanh,
Earth Prayers

Sylvia squinted in the bright morning that came streaming across her pillow. Her room at home faced west and the morning light was bright yet, diffused. This room faced east and the light from the rising sun was brilliant and filled the room. Sylvia looked around and saw that Marian had laid her clothes, now clean, on top of the bureau. Stretching luxuriously, Sylvia smelled coffee and something that hinted of cinnamon and sugar. She got up, made up the bed and dressed and went downstairs. Marian was pouring a cup of coffee and pulled a second cup out of the cupboard when she saw Sylvia coming into the kitchen.

"Good morning, Syl," Marian greeted. "How did you sleep?" she asked handing her the fresh cup of coffee.

"Wonderfully, thank you," Sylvia answered as she breathed in the aroma of the coffee.

"Sit down," Marian suggested. "I have a coffee cake that just came out of the oven."

"So that's what I smelled," Sylvia said.

Marian brought over a generous piece of coffee cake for Sylvia and one for herself. It was high and light, covered in a crumbly topping, almonds and thin streams of sugary white icing. It looked very decadent and yummy.

"Where's Owen?" Sylvia asked as she cut into the cake with her fork.

"I sent him up to the store for a few things," Marian told her. "He was pacing around like a caged tiger."

Sylvia took a bite of the coffee cake that was still warm. "Yum!" Sylvia commented.

Marian smiled and nodded in response.

"Other than pacing, how's Owen doing?" Sylvia asked.

"He's very upset by the whole thing," Marian said. "We talked a little last night and he told me how Anna was changing the numbers on the government reports for the Superfund clean-up. I know Owen feels betrayed and it certainly made him look like a fool. Apparently he was boastful about the numbers when the agents came to check a week or two ago when he just started his job," she told Sylvia.

Sylvia traced her finger around the rim of her coffee mug absentmindedly before she asked as casually as she could, "Do you know how involved he was with Anna personally?"

Marian looked at her steadily, "I know he took her out a couple of times, but he broke it off," she told Sylvia. "I don't know why. I assuming it was the discovery of the numbers problem."

"By the way," Marian said, changing the subject, "I called your Mother to let her know where you were. Murder is big news in this small community and I have no idea if the news would be picked up in the Philadelphia area. We've had a couple of calls from reporters already," she said.

Sylvia looked at her in surprise. "Really! That's something I never even considered," she said to Marian.

"Well, I think I'll ask Owen to follow you home, just to be safe," Marian said to her. "We clearly have 'No Trespassing' signs in this area, but your home is another story. Someone could be camped out there waiting for some juicy details."

"Great," Sylvia said sarcastically. "Just what I need."

"As I said, this is big news. This is the first murder in a couple of years," Marian told her. "You might want to hire an attorney, too," she advised.

Sylvia asked surprised, "Whatever for?"

Owen interrupted them by coming in and tossing a newspaper on the table with a grimace, "We're famous whether we like it or not," he told Sylvia.

Splashed on the front page was the headline 'Body found on Thurmont Property.' The article beneath it was brief:

Owen Anderson (24) and Sylvia Ash(22), both employees of Thurmont, Inc.,
Stumbled onto the body of Dr. Anna Hansen (26), noted scientist at Thurmont, buried in a shallow grave on the property. Anderson and Ash were walking through the wooded property after a community stream watch effort organized by Thurmont when they found the body. Cause of death forthcoming after autopsy. No comment from Thurmont executives. No comment was available from Anderson and Ash. Investigation forthcoming.

"Great," Sylvia said. "Just what we need, media."

"Now I *am* concerned about you going home," Marian said worriedly. "Owen, will you follow Sylvia home to make sure reporters aren't hovering about?"

"Sure," Owen said. "No problem."

"I guess I should go and face the music," Sylvia said. "Thanks for letting me stay last night."

Marian hugged her tightly and said, "Sylvia, promise me, if it's too crazy, pack a bag and spend the night here. If they come past our 'No Trespassing' signs, I can call the police. You don't have that luxury where you live," she reminded her. "With the road so close to your house, they can lie in wait at the edge of your property."

"Okay," Sylvia said, her feelings of well being suddenly diminished.

She glanced at Owen, "Are you ready?" she asked.

"Sure," he said, "Let's go."

They got into their respective cars and headed down the road. When they arrived at Sylvia's, a couple of cars and a television van were parked along the roadway. Sylvia got out quickly, locked the car and walked as quickly as she could into the house.

She heard the voices, "Ms. Ash! Ms. Ash! We'd like to talk to you a minute."

Sylvia ignored them and went into the house. Owen got out of his car too and there was a murmur of surprise among the reporters. They called after him as well.

When he got safely inside the house, Sylvia said, "This is awful!"

Owen went over and took her in his arms and held her. "I think Marian might be right about hiring an attorney," he said grimly. "This is going to get a lot worse before it gets better."

"I know, I know," Sylvia said resigned. She leaned against him and closed her eyes for a minute. When she opened them, she saw a reporter standing at the door.

"Oh my God!" she snarled, "Won't they leave us alone?"

She strode over to the door and opened it a crack. Camera bulbs flashed and the steady light from a video camera shone brightly in her face. She squinted and said as politely as she could muster, "I have no comment at this time." As she closed and locked the door, she hoped she had done the right thing.

"Let's go to the living room," she told Owen. "Hopefully, they won't come onto the deck."

"You know, I see this happening on the nightly news and now I understand why people get angry with the media!" she said. She grabbed the phone on the way to the living room and called Marian.

"You were right," she told Marian as soon as she picked up the phone. "They're here. We are besieged," she said using an old fashioned term. "This is a private community, but it doesn't have 'no trespassing' signs posted. I guess that gives them the right to barnstorm my property. I don't know," her voice cracked with frustration and tears on the last sentence.

"Pack a bag and come back," Marian told her firmly.

They hung up and Sylvia sat holding the phone and looking out through the French doors at the water for a minute or two before she spoke. The water was as still as glass and devoid of sailboats for the moment. It was the only thing that seemed peaceful to Sylvia at the moment. A seagull wheeled in the sky and a few other birds caught the updrafts from the land and water.

"Marian thinks I should pack a bag and come back to stay for a few days," she told Owen.

"I think it's a good idea too," he said. "You should probably bring clothes for the week, at least," he advised in a serious tone.

"A week?" Sylvia said. She shook her head. "I guess I'm being naïve," Sylvia told him. "I keep thinking this will go away quickly, but I suppose that's not how it works," she said miserably.

Sylvia went up to pack while Owen flipped through the channels on the television. He also walked around checking the locks on the doors and windows. Sylvia came down a few minutes later carrying a suitcase and put it in the kitchen by the door and her dress clothes over a chair.

"You know we could lock your car in the garage," Owen suggested, "and go together to Marian's and to work."

Sylvia thought about it. "I don't know," she said. "I'm worried at leaving the house let alone the car. I don't mind going to work together, but I think I would like to take my car to Marian's."

Owen nodded. "You're probably right," he said. "Are you ready to face the them?" he asked.

Sylvia nodded grimly. They went out to their cars ignoring the shouts from the press about where she was going and what she knew about the murder. The media followed them to the edge of Marian's property and stopped when they came to the 'No Trespassing' signs. Sylvia breathed a sigh of relief when she looked in her +rearview mirror. It was like sharks that had reached an invisible wall and they crowded the road after their cars went through.

"Well, you know where your room is," Marian quipped as they got out of their cars. "Why don't you go and get settled."

Owen took the suitcase and Sylvia took her dress clothes still on hangers and went inside and up the stairs to the room she had slept in the night before. She hung the clothes in the armoire and turned to the suitcase Owen had set on the floor. She started to pick it up to put it on the bed when he took it from her and swung it up so that she could unpack. Owen stood there, seemingly wanting to say or do something, but stood silent.

"You look as though you want to say something," Sylvia stated.

Owen looked at her and then down at his feet and back up at her. "Syl, I have so many thoughts running through my head at the moment, I don't know where to start or how to sort them out," he told her.

She started taking some clothes from the suitcase and put them in an empty drawer in the bureau. She didn't say anything for a few minutes.

"Start from the middle and work your way out," she said as lightly as she could.

He sat down on the bed next to the suitcase.

"Do you think I killed her?" he asked bluntly for a second time.

She stopped what she was doing and looked at him. "I've thought about it," she said, "and deep down, I don't believe you killed Anna. I guess I'm wondering what kind of relationship you had with her and perhaps, how it impacted what happened. I have a lot of questions, too," she told him.

"You can fire away on the questions," he said, "But my relationship with her..." he stated. "It's rather complicated. We worked because it was part of her job to train me for my job. She had been working with the government on the Superfund clean-up as her division created some of the chemicals that caused the problem and is supposed to be part of the solution. We ended up going out a couple of times, but Anna is – or was—a difficult person. She was the type of woman that liked to play with people...flattering you, using you and then taunting you. I think I was one of many."

"Did you sleep with her?" Sylvia bluntly asked the question she had been wondering about for weeks.

Owen blanched. "Yes," he admitted, "once. We were caught up in the moment. I'm a little embarrassed by it."

"Why?" she asked.

"Look," he said, "I don't jump into relationships lightly. Anna made me feel sorry for her and then she made me feel like a fool!" he said vehemently. "And, you've got to know I've feelings for you," he said, "and I..." he stopped.

Sylvia went to sit down beside him. "Owen, you must realize that what you have told me about your relationship with Anna, and probably more, will come out with the police and most likely the media," she said. "As for me," she took his hand and the usual sparks were a steady hum between their hands, "I must say, this has had me think twice about wanting to enter a relationship with you, but then again, I've never felt like this about anyone." She paused, "Ever," she stated, putting all of her cards on the table. "I guess I'm worried about being made the fool too," she admitted, "and I'm a little scared."

He put his arms around her and kissed her gently at first, and then deeper. It was all she could do to pull away and say, "I think we should get downstairs to Marian."

"You're probably right," he said.

He stood up and took her hands and pulled her up off the bed and towards him.

Marian had a pitcher of margaritas, homemade salsa and corn chips waiting for them. They kept their conversation topics light and all finally relaxed. Sylvia realized they had skipped lunch and was feeling the effects of the margarita when they heard a car coming up the lane. Sylvia craned her neck to see a dark blue sedan pulling in beside her car. Two gentlemen in business suits walked over to them.

"Good afternoon," one said, "I'm Detective Rogers, Joseph Rogers," he told them pulling out his badge and showing it to them. "And this is Detective Josephson."

Sylvia judged Detective Rogers to be in his mid-30's. He was of medium muscular build and had black hair and dark eyes. He was married and she wondered if he had any kids. Detective Josephson must be the new kid on the block. He had to be her age or so, but he looked as though he was barely out of high school. He had his light brown hair cut short in a flat top. He looked young, but his blue eyes had a steely look in them. He was a smaller, stockier man than Detective Rogers and looked like a wrestler.

Owen nodded, "You came to Thurmont yesterday," he commented steadily to Detective Rogers.

Sylvia almost giggled as she wondered if the name 'Joe' in part of your name was some sort of pre-requisite for being a police officer. The margarita was definitely affecting her. She tried to pull herself together.

Detective Rogers nodded. "We were wondering how Ms. Ash was making out in the media blitz. Since she wasn't at home, we hoped you could tell us where she was and we're glad to see she's here – safe and sound."

Surely someone in the media tipped the police that she had left her house carrying a suitcase and clothes, thought Sylvia. They probably put in the call as soon as they saw Sylvia's car drive past the 'No Trespassing-Private Property' sign on the lane to Marian's.

"I told Sylvia to come here because of the media," Marian told the detectives, "as I thought it would be less stressful. I'm sorry, we never thought about telling the police," she said. "Can I get you a drink?" she asked, nodding to the pitcher of margaritas.

"No thank you," Detective Rogers said. "We're on duty." Detective Josephson shook his head and still did not say anything.

"Ahh," Marian murmured. "Would you like a glass of iced tea then?" she asked.

"Yes, Ma'am," he said, "We would be grateful for something cool in this heat," Detective Roberts said with a smile.

"I'll go and get it," Sylvia offered, starting to get up.

"No," Marian insisted, "Detective Rogers and Detective Josephson came to talk to you," she said, "Let me go in." Marian got up quickly and went into the house.

"So," he said casually, "How is it that you know Mrs., uh, Mrs...." he trailed off.

"Marian Duir," Marian said as she came out with the iced teas on a small tray with sprigs of fresh mint bobbing among the ice cubes. She bathed them with her gentle and luminous smile.

"Thank you, Ma'am," said the Detective Rogers. Detective Josephson nodded his thanks and kept silent.

"Please call me Marian," she said, "I don't stand on any ceremony and 'Ma'am' makes me feel much older than I'd like to feel!" she said cheerily.

"Marian is an old friend of my Grandmother's," Sylvia told the detectives.

"And a long-time family friend, for me," Owen told him.

"Duir," he muttered, "Duir… The name is familiar," he said.

"Were you at student at State?" Marian asked.

"Yes!" he said, surprised. "How did you know?"

"My husband taught history there for many, many years," she said. "Perhaps you were in one of his classes? His field was history and his specialty was the Revolutionary War."

"Dr. Duir?" Detective Rogers asked in surprise. "He was one of my favorite professors! He really brought the revolutionary history of this area to life!" He slapped his leg happily.

"He was a mentor for my father," Owen added. "Dr. Anderson, my father, specializes in Civil War history. He was at State for a long time too."

The detective nodded and definitely warmed up to them. He took a sip of iced tea and smiled.

"This is delicious," he said. "And refreshing. Thank you."

"Do you live here?" he asked Owen.

"Yes," he said, "for the moment. I graduated with my Masters recently and accepted the job before I found an apartment. It hasn't been easy to find a decent apartment in this area during the boating season and Marian has been kind enough to let me stay."

"Kind!" Marian said with a touch of humor, "It's wonderful for an old woman like me to have your young hands and arms. Owen's been quite helpful around this old place," she told Officer Rogers. "He mows the grounds, repairs things and has been extremely handy."

"Do you do a lot of your work from Thurmont here?" Detective Rogers asked Owen.

"No," Owen answered honestly. "I mainly work at Thurmont."

Sylvia began to feel uncomfortable. These detectives weren't just checking on her state of mind from the media blitz. They came to fish for information.

"Do you know a lot about computers Owen?" Detective Rogers continued, "Is it all right that I call you that?"

"Sure," Owen answered, "I know enough, I guess," he told the detective.

"I'm thinking about buying one for at home," the detective stated. "I haven't a clue as to what I need. Do you have your own system here?" he asked Owen.

"Yeah," Owen said, "It's a pretty decent one," he told the detective. "All the usual stuff that's on most of the basic models, but my friend bumped it up on the hard drive. A friend of mine in school built mine, but there are a lot of good commercially built systems out there."

"Wow!" Detective Rogers said. "It didn't come from a factory? Could I take a look at it?"

"Yeah, sure," Owen said.

They went into the house.

"I have a bad feeling about this," Sylvia said. "I don't think he's here just to look at Owen's computer."

"No," Marian said, "He's scoping out the place, but he seems nice enough. The other one is too quiet, but I think he's just learning the ropes."

Sylvia nodded poured herself another Margarita, wondering if she was doing the right thing. She was feeling a little bit tipsy, but at that point, she didn't care. At one point, as a teenager, she was hooked on soap operas until a friend warned her that if she watched them too much, the world would start to look like a soap opera. She stopped watching them because of some of the outrageous plots but felt as though she was in the middle of one right now. She just wanted to be numb. The phone rang. Marian ran to get it. She walked out with the portable phone towards Sylvia. Marian made hand gestures that the phone was for her and continued to chat. It must be her mother, thought Sylvia.

"Syl!" her mother cried when she got on the phone. "How are you?"

"Okay, I guess," Sylvia told her, "or as well as can be expected." She got up and paced around the patio while she talked.

"Marian's filled me in on what's happened," her mother told her. "You don't need to relive it for me."

Sylvia was relieved and took a long drink from her margarita. Sometimes it was better to be slightly inebriated when talking with her mother. Her mother prattled on and Sylvia wanted to hold the phone away from her ear. She wondered what Owen and the detectives were doing and glanced up at the windows where Owen's room was. Her mother said something about an attorney that brought Sylvia back to harsh reality.

"What?" she asked. "What did you say?"

"I told you I've hired an attorney for you," her mother told her.

"What?" Sylvia cried.

"You *need* an attorney," her mother insisted. "For your own protection," she said.

"But, I didn't do anything!" she almost shouted at her mother.

"I know, I know, honey," her mother said, "but you found a body of someone who has been murdered. You need protection and you'll need advice," her mother said. "Talk to your boss tomorrow. You'll need to take some time off so that you can speak to the attorney."

"Okay, okay," Sylvia succumbed to her mother's wishes. At the moment, it was easier to give in to her rather, than to argue. To be honest with herself, it was nice to feel protected by her mother and Marian.

The detectives and Owen were coming out of Marian's house. She said to her mother, "I need to go now,"

"Okay," her Mom said, "Be careful. I love you."

"Thanks, Mom," Sylvia replied. "I love you too," she returned.

Sylvia hung up the phone and walked back to her chair. She hoped she was walking steadily. The men came over and Owen sat down.

"Thanks for your help," Detective Rogers said to Owen. "And we'll be seeing you tomorrow," he added.

Owen and Sylvia looked at him, puzzled. Sylvia suddenly wished she had not had the second margarita.

"We'll be coming to Thurmont to question people," he told them.

"We gave our statements yesterday," Owen said levelly.

"You're right," Detective Rogers went on, "but I'm sure we'll have further questions for you and Ms. Ash," he said glancing over at Sylvia. "We also need to question anyone who's worked with Dr. Hansen."

"We'd like to talk to Ms. Ash for a few minutes, in private," he said to Marian and Owen.

"Of course," Marian said. She looked at Sylvia and said, "Sylvia, you stay seated. We'll go into the house. I need to start dinner soon." Marian took the almost empty pitcher of margaritas and the glasses and put them on a tray. She turned to Owen, "Owen, how are you at chopping tomatoes?" she asked.

Owen got up and followed Marian into the kitchen. Sylvia felt a rock in her stomach from nervousness.

"Ms. Ash," Detective Rogers began.

"Please call me Sylvia," she said.

"All right, Sylvia," he said. "How well do you know Mr. Anderson?" he asked.

Sylvia was surprised. "Well enough, I think," she said.

"Hmm," he murmured. "Are you sure it's a good idea that you stay here?"

"Yes!" Sylvia exclaimed. "I didn't want to be alone with all of the media swamping my house!"

"Be careful," he warned her and he glanced at her and then meaningfully at the door where Owen and Marian had just entered the house. "If you need to contact us about anything, here's my card." He reached into the pocket of his shirt and pulled out his business card.

"Thank you," Sylvia said, still feeling a little nervous.

"Thank you for your time," Officer Rogers said. "We'll see you in the morning."

The two men got up and walked back to their car. Sylvia stayed where she was until they had gone down the lane and then bolted into the house. Owen was in the kitchen, but she didn't see Marian.

CHAPTER TWENTY

The things, good Lord, that we pray for,
Give us the grace to labor for.
--Saint Thomas More
Earth Prayers.

Before she could say anything Owen stated, "I know, I know. They suspect me. Marian and I agreed that I need to get an attorney. She's calling her friend now."

Marian came from the study and said, "There's been a change in dinner plans. Jon will be coming over for dinner and will be talking with Owen about what's happened. Too bad, I was in the mood for those chicken tacos, but I don't think they're Jon's 'cup of tea.' Oh, well... We're going to have a Mediterranean meal of Lemon Chicken, rice, and salad. Does that sound good?"

Both Owen and Sylvia nodded. "Good," Marian continued. "Owen, I would like you to get out the good china and silver. Sylvia, can you peel some of these small onions?" Marian ordered more than asked this time.

Sylvia was wondering who this 'Jon' was and why Marian, of all people, was jumping through hoops for this dinner. Apparently she wanted things to be good for Owen, Sylvia thought, but there was something more to it.

They set to their tasks and soon dinner was cooking merrily. Sylvia sat, drinking iced tea, hoping she could sober up a little before dinner.

"How can you cook so wonderfully when everything is…is," Sylvia asked Marian, "such a mess," she ended lamely.

"Food is part of life," Marian said. "Food is comfort. Cooking is something I truly enjoy," she said. "It's also one thing I can control in the craziness of all of this."

The margaritas had settled in and she was still a little wobbly. Marian gave her some crackers and cheese and some aspirin, which she took gratefully while Marian chuckled a small chuckle.

"No more Margaritas for you, young lady," she laughed and shook a lighthearted finger at Sylvia.

"Do I look as bad as I feel?" Sylvia asked.

"No," Marian told her, "but you look as though you need a break from the alcohol."

Owen set the table and returned to the kitchen. He sat in the love seat in the breakfast room, leaned his head back and closed his eyes. Marian went up to change into a long, floating sleeveless tunic dress with layers of aquamarine, teal, and blues accented by dramatic silver jewelry. The blue-green color of the dress set off the green of her eyes. When her friend came to the door, they all went out to greet him.

'Jon,' Marian's friend turned out to be Jonathan Adams, Esquire, a distinguished looking gentleman with sharp, bright eyes and snow-white hair which to her surprise, was pulled into a neat queue at the back of his neck. Although he was dressed casually, his clothes were quite expensive, Sylvia noted. She eyed his Ralph Lauren shirt, perfectly pressed khaki pants and open worked leather shoes; that were quite possibly expensive Italian leather—without socks. He brightened when he saw Marian and gave her a hug and kiss on the cheek. Sylvia wondered if he was somehow related to John Adams, former revolutionary president. He sort of had that 'look', she thought.

He brought Marian a beautiful bouquet of flowers with baby's breath, stock, iris, delphinium, and roses – all in blues, purples, and whites wrapped in chiffon along with a bottle of wine. Sylvia also wondered where he had purchased such incredible flowers on such short notice. Marian introduced Sylvia and Owen and asked Sylvia if she would mind putting the flowers in water and the wine in the refrigerator. She offered Jon a drink and served him up her most expensive single malt scotch, neat.

They all sat in the living room, stiff for a few minutes, talking of pleasantries. Marian had set out nibbles of cheese, herb spread, and crackers. Finally, Marian rose and said she would get dinner started and asked Sylvia if she would help. Sylvia rose too, leaving Owen and Jon to talk.

As Marian and Sylvia made their exit, she heard Jon say, "Now, my boy, why don't you start at the beginning and tell me what happened." As much as Sylvia wanted to stay and listen, she scooted out to the kitchen where Marian had started browning chicken in a large skillet. She asked Sylvia to get a lemon and some green and black olives from the refrigerator. Marian measured rice and water and put it on the back of the stove.

"Watch the chicken for me, Syl, and turn on the rice please," she asked her, "I'm headed out to the garden to get some herbs."

"Okay," Sylvia said.

Sylvia stood watching the chicken brown in the skillet. She moved it around with a fork a couple of times and wondered what Owen and Jon were discussing. The screen door banged when Marian came back from the garden and Sylvia jumped.

"Are you okay?" Marian asked.

"I'll be all right," Sylvia said, "I was just lost in thought."

"Apparently!" Marian said. "Let's take the chicken out for a minute and add the other ingredients to sauté. Can you help chop these herbs?"

"Sure," Sylvia said. She was slowly learning the techniques that Marian used to create her herbal vinaigrette. Marian minced the herbs with a sharp little knife and dropped them into a small deep bowl. Sylvia watched as Marian added garlic, capers, a little kosher salt, lemon, and wine. She asked Sylvia to whisk this together while she added a stream of olive oil. Marian put the chicken back into the pan with the vegetables and let it simmer. Then she turned off the rice that had come to a boil and covered it.

"Twenty minutes," she said, "and we'll be ready. Let's have a drink and relax for a moment. I don't know when those two will be done talking."

Marian handed Sylvia a small glass of wine and they sat on the loveseat in the kitchen. Marian had also prepared a small plate of crackers spread with an herbal spread for them to share in the kitchen.

"This murder is all consuming, isn't it?" Sylvia asked Marian.

Marian nodded with a grim face, "Unfortunately it is," she said and added with conviction, "I think Owen is in real trouble. Those detectives were quite suspicious of him."

"I agree," Sylvia said.

The timer's bell rang and Marian jumped up to check the rice.

"Sylvia, please put the salad on the table and ask the men to join us for dinner," Marian requested.

Sylvia walked out to the living room where she heard Jon's voice say, "There's a good chance you may be charged. They'll want to put someone in jail in the first 48 hours whether you're innocent or not." Her stomach flip-flopped when she heard those words. She cleared her throat and knocked.

Two surprised faces looked up at her when she announced, "Dinner's ready."

Owen looked ill and had a difficult time looking up at her. When he did, she saw a pained and hurt expression in his hazel eyes.

"We'll be right there," Jon said and Sylvia turned to go back to help Marian when she heard him say, "Don't answer any questions. Tell them you need to contact your attorney first. Do you understand?"

Sylvia didn't hear Owen's reply. She returned to the kitchen and tossed the salad for Marian and opened the wine and numbly took both to the table. She heard the men's footsteps as she and Marian took in the chicken and the rice.

"This is superb," Jon said as he started eating.

Marian blushed with pleasure, Sylvia noticed. Could there be a budding romance between Jon and Marian? She didn't know. Owen looked tense and Marian and Jon kept up small talk while they ate.

"You missed my party this year, Jon," Marian scolded while they were eating.

"Sorry, love," Jon told her. "But, it couldn't be helped. I had plans to be out of the country months ago."

"All right," Marian teased him. "Just make sure it doesn't happen again," she flirted.

"I assure you it won't," he told her.

Owen and Sylvia stayed quiet. Sylvia took in all of the lively banter between Jon and Marian. It was clear they were old friends and wanting to become more so on both sides. It wasn't an uncomfortable meal for Sylvia, she just wanted to be over as soon as possible. Inside she hoped the whole situation with Anna's murder would just go away, but she knew that wouldn't happen. After they cleared the table and coffee was served, Sylvia volunteered to clean-up and Owen came out to assist her. Jon and Marian took brandy and coffee out to the terrace and sat with the lovely chunky white citronella candles leftover from the party a week prior.

Sylvia and Owen loaded the dishwasher and washed the pots and pans as they cleaned up. Sylvia wanted desperately to ask Owen what he had discussed with Jon but bit her tongue. Owen wasn't offering up any information.

"I'm drained," she commented, "I think I'll say goodnight and go on up to bed."

"I know what you mean," Owen said.

They both went out to the terrace and stood apart from each other.

"It was nice meeting you," she said to Jon. "I'll say good night."

"Same here," he said, taking her hand in a strengthening handshake.

"I came out to say good night, also," Owen said. "Thank you for your advice," he told Jon. "I'm hoping I won't have to take you up on your offer."

"Understood," Jon said to him, gripping his hand also and nodding at him with a tacit look.

"Good night," Marian said to both.

Sylvia and Owen went upstairs. She got ready for bed and changed into her prettiest nightgown and knocked on Owen's door.

"Come in," he said, quietly.

She went inside and he was sitting on the bed. Sylvia had only peeked into the room before and had never stepped inside. It was on the masculine side with dark, furniture—a highboy and a four-poster bed. Owen's computer was set up on an antique library table. It was a spacious room at the corner of the house. One window overlooked the front door and the other over the meadow through the spreading oak. Sylvia went over and sat next to him. Her emotions were a mixture of love, pity, worry, fear, self-pity—she couldn't make up her mind. He had some music playing on his stereo. Sylvia heard what sounded like a rock band mixed with flute and folk type music. And then she heard some of the lyrics, 'Can you see the Jack in the Green,' the singer began. A 'Jack in the Green' was another name for the Green Man. Sylvia listened more carefully. The lyrics described a more bestial type of green man than the Green Man she knew.

"What CD is this?" she asked Owen with wonderment. "I'm not familiar with it."

"Jethro Tull," Owen answered.

"Tull?" Sylvia commented, "I'm only familiar with his hard rock stuff – 'Aqualung' and that sort of thing."

"Yeah," Owen replied, "I love his classic heavy rock, but just felt in the mood for something different tonight. This is kind of rock and folk mixed," he told her, "with something Celtic-like mixed in."

"Hmm," Sylvia answered. "I'd like to borrow it some time."

"Sure," Owen told her, "anytime."

"How are you doing?" she asked him as she sat down on the bed beside him and put her hand on his leg.

Owen shook his head miserably. "Not great," he said.

She moved closer to him and put her arm around him and leaned up to kiss him, but he stiffened.

"What's wrong?" she asked softly.

"Syl," he said, "I told you I don't jump into things—relationships, lightly. I'm not sure I want you involved in any of this. It's already gone far beyond anything I could have imagined. If we..." he broke off. "I don't want you involved any more than you already are!" he said vehemently. "I don't want it to come out in court that we are involved. I don't want you implicated in any way."

"I don't care," Sylvia said. "I care about you and I'm worried." She attempted to touch him again, but he pulled away.

"Look," he said, with anger tingeing his voice, "Jon thinks I'll be charged. I don't want you involved!" He looked at her with a combination of fear and sadness in his eyes.

"I need to call my parents and let them know what's going on," he said, "and what might happen." He stood up abruptly and turned away from her to move towards the phone.

"Okay," she said as emotion free as she could and stood up too. "Good night." Feeling rejected she got up and went back to her room to crawl into bed and stare at the ceiling in misery. She wished she could cry, but the tears wouldn't come. Sylvia tossed and turned. She was hot and got up and opened up the windows as far as she could and pushed the comforter and light summer blanket off of her. Her mind was full of thoughts that would not come to the surface. Sleep only came in snatches throughout the night. It seemed to last forever with waking and listening in the dark and waiting in vain to fall back into a restful sleep.

CHAPTER TWENTY ONE

Everyone is like the moon and has a dark side which he
Never shows to anybody.
--Mark Twain, "Following the Equator."

Sylvia woke up to squint at the bright morning sunlight in her eyes and head hurt and her mouth felt like old socks had been stuck on her teeth and tongue. Damn the margaritas she thought. They had gone down much too easily with the stress of the day. Crawling out of bed feeling ancient Sylvia stood in the shower for a long, long time letting the hot water course over her head until she felt slightly awake. She toweled off but, still felt damp with the onset of the summer's hazy, hot and humid days. The thick walls of Marian's house kept the house at a moderately comfortable level, but even at seven in the morning, Sylvia could feel the oppressiveness of the heat of the day building. She dressed in a light sage green linen and cotton sleeveless tunic dress and pulled a short-sleeved cardigan from the suitcase to guard against a chill from the air-conditioned environment at work. She smelled coffee brewing and gladly followed her nose to the kitchen where Marian was sitting and listening to the morning's news.

"It's to be a hot one today," Marian informed her when she entered the kitchen. "All the heat and smog warnings are up."

Sylvia made her usual café au lait and while the milk was heating in the microwave she asked Marian, "Have you seen anything about Thurmont and Anna's murder?"

Marian hesitated a minute before answering, "Yes," she said. "Apparently the company executives have no comment except they hope to find the perpetrator of the crime."

Sylvia put a slice of bread in the toaster and stood sipping her coffee while it toasted. She wasn't overly hungry but wanted some aspirin to stop her throbbing head. Owen came down and looked grim.

"Good morning, everyone," he said.

Sylvia nodded at him and pulled out an extra cup to pour him some coffee. He accepted it gratefully.

"Did you talk to your parents last night?" Sylvia asked.

Owen nodded. "They're pretty upset," he told Marian and Sylvia. "They said they would come down if…if anything happened."

Sylvia gulped down her coffee and then changed the subject, "Do you want any breakfast?" she asked Owen.

"No thanks," he said. "I'm not very hungry."

"Owen," Marian admonished. "Not eating is not going to help you. Have a piece of toast, at least."

"All right, Mom," he said, with a touch of humor coming back into his voice and face.

Owen went over to make toast and slathered it with peanut butter. He returned to the table with it on a napkin.

"Is this okay?" he asked Marian.

She nodded with a smile, "Absolutely."

Sylvia popped a couple of aspirin and gulped the last bit of a second cup of coffee before she put on the darkest sunglasses she could find as they went out the door. Owen drove them to Thurmont. Still she squinted in the bright morning's light. She gave up and closed her eyes about half way to work. Owen was quiet and they listened to the drone of oldies and traffic reports for Baltimore far south of them. When the news came on, Owen turned it off and Sylvia sat up. They were just pulling into the parking lot at Thurmont and she saw the same television crew vans that had been in front of her house.

"Oh, no," she groaned. "Here we go again."

"I'll drop you off at the door," Owen murmured, "and then I'll park and come inside. Maybe if we divide and conquer it will confuse the reporters."

"No," Sylvia said, "we'll do this together."

He parked as close to the building as he could. They got out, but no reporters came running after them.

"They must be inside," he muttered as he steered her through the front doors, holding her elbow gently. They both nodded to the security guard at the reception desk and Owen walked her to her office. She didn't know what to say to him.

"I'll talk with you later?" she finally asked.

Owen nodded. "Lunch?" he questioned.

"E-mail me when it's a good time," she said.

He nodded. "Hang in there," he said.

"You too," she returned.

He made a move to give her a kiss but stopped himself. Sylvia sat down at her desk a little shakily. She logged onto the company network and onto her email. There were several new messages. Before she could open any, Carol came up to the doorway.

"Hey girlfriend," she said, her face curious and excited. "How are you doing?"

"I've been better," Sylvia told her grimly.

"Well?" Carol asked. "Tell me what happened!"

"I'm not sure where to begin," Sylvia told her. She told Carol an abbreviated story of the Saturday morning stream watch activities and then about finding the body.

"Well, 'ding-dong the bitch is dead!' Carol sang irreverently off key.

"Carol!" Sylvia cried in indignation. "It was horrible! Her body was…" Sylvia broke off.

"What?" Carol persisted.

"It looked as though something had been eating at it," Sylvia whispered. "It was…" she stopped, but could not think of another word but, "horrible."

"You should go home," Carol advised. "You're in no shape to be here."

"I'd like nothing better, but the police…" she broke off when Mr. Carter came into the office.

"Good morning," he said to both of them. "Sylvia, can I talk with you in my office when you're finished?"

"Sure thing, Mr. Carter," Sylvia told him. Both she and Carol watched Mr. Carter go into his office and shut the door.

"I'll talk to you later," Carol said. "Give me a call or e-mail me, okay?"

Sylvia nodded. She cleared her throat and smoothed her dress and knocked on Mr. Carter's door. She heard him say 'Come in' from inside and she opened it with trepidation. He cleared his throat when he saw her standing in the doorway and motioned for her to come inside.

"Sit down," he said kindly. "I understand you had a bit of a brew-ha-ha this weekend."

"You could say that," she answered, trying to keep something like cynicism out of her voice.

"I've heard about it from Headley, now I would like to hear your version," he asked.

Sylvia told her story again. She added a few more details for Mr. Carter than what she had admitted to Carol. Mr. Carter sat and listened quietly while she talked, drinking coffee from a large, stained travel mug that he brought into work with him daily. When she finished, he sighed and ran a hand through what hair he had left and tugged at his belt in what Sylvia knew was a mannerism of his. She waited.

"What a mess!" he muttered. "Are you okay?" he asked.

Sylvia tried to keep her emotions in check and swallowed hard. She couldn't speak again for a minute. "As okay as I can be for the moment," she answered finally.

"Good," he said. "I think one of the best ways to deal with something like this is just to jump on the horse and start riding again." He started talking about a new project and talked about the upcoming Bay Days, but, Sylvia only half listened. She nodded, trying to pay attention and look interested, but it was difficult.

"I'm sorry," she said eventually, "I'm having difficulty concentrating," she told Mr. Carter. "Would you mind following up with an e-mail about all of this."

He nodded. "Go and get a cup of coffee," he suggested, "and get caught up on email. If you could start pulling together a report on the stream watch activity on Saturday, I would appreciate it."

"All right," Sylvia said, "Thanks."

She left and went down to the break room where coffee was brewing. She poured herself a cup and leaned back against the cupboard for a minute. She closed her eyes and sipped her coffee for a moment, before heading back to the office. She was exhausted. Once back she checked her email. There were several from Gwen asking her to please reply, what's wrong and berating her electronically for being out of touch by email, and by phone and text. Guiltily, Sylvia emailed back that a lot had happened in the past few days and informed Gwen that she was staying at Marian's for a few days. She added Marian's phone number and said she would be in touch by cell very soon. Another company email briefly described Saturday's events and asked for cooperation on everyone's parts with the ensuing investigation. A second email from the company informed her of a memorial service on

Wednesday afternoon for Anna. The company would give liberal leave to anyone who wished to attend, and to let Carol in Human Resources know if they planned to attend. Sylvia emailed Carol that she would like to attend and also asked when she was going to lunch. There were no messages from Owen and Sylvia wondered how he was making out.

It was shortly after she finished her email and began to work on her report that Mr. Headley dropped by.

"Good morning, Ms. Ash," he said smoothly. "How are you doing this morning?"

"As well as can be expected, I think," Sylvia answered politely. Something about this man made her skin crawl. He seemed to leer at women and undress them with just a glance. Sylvia pulled her little cardigan around her and refrained from crossing her arms over her chest.

He pushed back a couple of things on her desk and sat down on the edge.

"I'm so sorry for all of the difficulties that you went through this weekend," he said softly and silkily. "I certainly appreciate your efforts to create a good image for the company."

"Thank you," Sylvia said very quietly. She wondered how she could get him to leave.

"I wanted to let you know that the police will be here soon, questioning anyone who was near or involved with Anna," he said.

Sylvia had to restrain herself to not say 'including you', but she held her tongue. She kept her eyes down, hiding her disgust for him.

He continued, "Poor Anna, she was a troubled young woman. It's a shame she couldn't keep out of trouble and make good choices."

His words sounded like a veiled threat. Sylvia swallowed and tried to think fast.

"She was in trouble?" Sylvia asked.

"All the time, personally and professionally," he divulged. "And you," he changed the subject, "seem to be moving along possibly in all the right directions. I'll have to discuss some additional ideas with you when all of this clears up," he said as his hand slid over hers, lingering for a moment as he stood up. She shuddered.

"Sorry," she said, "I'm a little cold."

Before he could make yet another veiled sexual comment, Mr. Carter came out of the office. "I thought I heard voices," he said. "Hello, Dick!" he said, pumping his hand.

"Hello, Carter," Mr. Headley said, pasting a smile on his face as he shook his hand. "I came to offer our Ms. Ash tea and sympathy for her upset this weekend. She seems to be holding up pretty well, though," he said smiling back at Sylvia and patting her hand. After another minute or two of small talk with Mr. Carter, he finally left and Sylvia sighed appreciatively. Mr. Carter noticed how relaxed she became when he had gone. "Good girl," was the only comment he made.

She checked her email again, but with no word from Owen, she emailed Carol regarding lunch at 12:30 and copied the message to Owen. If he had a chance, perhaps he could meet them there. For more than the first time that day, she wished she had brought her car so that she could escape somewhere for a few minutes. She knew it was only natural for everyone to bring up Anna, but she was still having difficulty pushing down the grisly sight of Anna's hand sticking up through the soil and of her mutilated body being pulled from the muck. She kept wondering about the mutilation. All she could think were snails' trails, but they wouldn't and couldn't eat away the flesh like that—or she didn't believe so. And she was so weary of the whole thing that she couldn't even think of an appropriate search term to look it up on the Internet. Finally, she went to lunch. Carol had found a seat away from the trees, as the view from the cafeteria was only a few hundred yards from where the body was found. Sylvia didn't make eye contact with those in line, and perhaps it was her imagination, but people seemed to be giving her a wide berth.

She had taken a bite of her sandwich when Carol asked, "Well? Have they gotten to you yet?"

"What are you talking about?" Sylvia asked when she had swallowed, "Who?"

"The police, of course!" Carol exclaimed, "They've been going around questioning everyone about Anna. I wondered if they were going to question you again?"

"I don't know," Sylvia answered honestly. "Owen and I gave statements Saturday and I talked again to the police yesterday. What more could they have to ask?"

"Oh!" Carol squealed in frustration. "They *always* try to pin it on someone as quickly as possible after the murder!" she said. "Don't you watch t.v.?"

"I guess not enough," Sylvia said. The thought chilled her with worry.

It was then that she saw Owen coming into the cafeteria, and he was looking around. Carol waved to him and he nodded, went to get some lunch and came over to sit down.

"Hi," Carol and Sylvia said at the same time.

"Hi," he said wearily.

Sylvia looked at him questioningly and he said, "The police are here. They're combing Anna's office and starting to question everyone. They wanted to interview me, but I told them I had already made a statement and that they should contact my attorney. They didn't look happy, but I haven't seen them since. They're taking folks one by one into Headley's office."

"Oh, Gawd," Carol said irreverently and affectedly. "He's probably the one who knocked her off."

"Sorry," she said quickly looking at their faces. "I hope they question me about her," she said with fervor. "I could tell them a thing or two."

"Yes," Sylvia said pointedly, "but is it truth or gossip around the company."

Carol looked a little hurt.

"I didn't mean to offend," Sylvia began.

"I know," Carol interrupted, "but you need to realize you two have come in late on this picture," she said. "Anna's been playing games with the men of this company for years. I know that Headley has been her main squeeze for a long time, but he seems to also enjoy her playing her power trip games with a lot of the other men in the company. He appears to get pleasure out of it."

Owen winced at her words as they cut through to the truth. "I need to get back," he said.

"Stop by when you're ready to go home, okay?" Sylvia asked.

He flashed her a very brief smile, "Will do," he said, "See you later, Carol."

"See you," Carol answered, "and I need to get back to or Keely will have my ass."

Carol and Owen left Sylvia alone at the table. She sat and looked outside staring at everything and staring at nothing. The trees closest to the building were pulsing with auras. She stared lost in thought and taking her breaths along with the trees pulse of etheric light. She didn't know how long she stared and was quite startled when she heard, "Ms. Ash?" She turned. Two gentlemen in suits stood behind her. One was Detective Rogers, who had come to Marian's house on Sunday. She felt her heart drop into her stomach.

"Yes?" she answered.

"We'd like you to come with us for questioning due to the events this weekend," Officer Rogers said.

"Of course," Sylvia said. She stood up and dumped her tray and turned to the officers, "I need to let my boss know where I am," she told them.

"He already knows," the other officer said. "We stopped at your office before coming here."

"Oh," was the only thing Sylvia could say.

They didn't march her, but she felt it was close to something like that as they flanked her going down the hallway. They went in the direction of the administrative offices and opened the door that led to Mr. Headley's office. She politely thanked them. They led her directly into Mr. Headley's office where he sat, leaning back in his chair with his leg openly crossed over his other and looking confidently like a cat that swallowed a canary, she thought. The detectives asked her to sit down. Sylvia sat at a small teak conference table in the room, swallowing hard and her palms sweating with nervousness. The detectives sat on either side, turning their chairs slightly so that they could see her while Headley sat across from her.

"Ms. Ash," Detective Rogers spoke formally. "We would like to record this interview, is that all right with you?" he asked.

"I-I guess so," Sylvia said hesitantly.

Officer Rogers took the small tape recorder that was sitting on the table and pressed the record button stated the date, his name, and his badge number. He asked Sylvia again if he could record their interview and to answer 'yes' or 'no.' Sylvia answered 'yes' and they stated that this was an unofficial interview. First, they asked her to relive Saturday morning's events and her finding the body. Then they began firing questions at Sylvia.

"Ms. Ash," Officer Rogers asked, "How well did you know Ms. Anna Hanson?"

"Not very well at all," Sylvia answered honestly. "We met a few times in the hallway and at lunch, but I really didn't know her personally," she stated.

"Don't you get to know someone when you have lunch with them?" asked the other officer superiorly.

"I never actually sat down to eat and talk with Anna," Sylvia stated. "I usually saw her eating with Mr. Headley or met her when she needed to speak to Owen."

Officer Rogers looked up at her. "Mr. Anderson?" he asked. "Did she come to see him at lunch frequently?"

"Yes," Sylvia stated, hoping she wasn't implicating Owen, "Apparently they were working on a project together and she needed him for something—I don't know what," she said.

"Were you familiar with the project?" he asked.

"No," Sylvia said, "not really."

"What type of relationship do you have with Mr. Anderson?" the other officer asked leaning back in his chair and tapping a pencil on his fingers.

Headley sat up and looked at her. She took a deep breath.

"We're friends, actually," she told the police. "We met through a mutual friend, Marian Duir," she paused trying to think of what she wanted to say.

The detective sat up immediately and interrupted her, asking her to state Marian's name, address and phone number. Sylvia did so.

"Owen and I have had occasions to see one another at her home as well as here at Thurmont. We've been working on the Stream Watch project together..." she trailed off.

"Do you have a romantic relationship with Owen?" Officer Rogers asked.

That was difficult to answer. She rubbed her sweaty palms on her dress hoping it wouldn't leave marks on the linen. This is what Owen had worried about last night. She took a deep breath before she answered, "We're friends," she said firmly. "We're friends who decided to go out on one date," she answered them honestly. "We do not have a romantic relationship," she stated leaving out the 'yet' that kept surfacing in her mind.

Headley leaned back in his chair and grinned as well as leered at her. She was too nervous to care about him. They asked her if she knew what Owen and Anna were working on and some details about the lab. She shook her head and they prompted her to say 'yes' or 'no' to the questions. She felt fortunate she didn't know a lot about the training and projects Anna and Owen were working on.

She was feeling a little more comfortable until Officer Rogers asked, "Did you know that Ms. Hanson allegedly changed numbers on reports Mr. Anderson was working on?"

She paused and answered carefully, "Owen shared with me some of his fears regarding that. He said he had just found out that was the case a few days ago and had shared his findings with the people above him. I don't know who they are," she stated, "and what he was talking about didn't make a lot of sense to me. I don't have a science background."

"That's all the questions we have, Ms. Ash," Officer Rogers said, "for now," he added. "Please be available if we have further questions."

Sylvia nodded and he snapped off the tape recorder. She had to admit that the officers were gentlemen. They stood up when she did to exit the room. Headley stayed in his seat just staring at her, challenging her almost.

Sylvia heard him say, "Who's next on your list?" as she left the room. She stepped out into the bright hallway and breathed a sigh of relief. It hadn't been too bad. The administrative offices were near personnel so she dropped by to see Carol on the way back.

Carol took one look at her pale face and knew something had happened.

"What's wrong?" she asked.

"I just came from being questioned. I shouldn't be nervous, but..." she said faintly. "Look, I'm shaking." Sylvia held out her hands.

"Come on," Carol said, "Let's go get a soda and sit outside for a minute." She stood up and went to Mr. Keely's office and said, "I'll be back in a flash," and walked over and put her arm around Sylvia. Carol walked with Sylvia to the break room with vending machines, paid for two sodas, and led her out of the building into the warm sunshine. They sat at the same table that Sylvia had used with the police officer after finding Anna's body. Sylvia shivered.

"What?" Carol asked.

Sylvia told her.

"Was it awful?" Carol asked. "The questioning?"

"No, not really," Sylvia answered. "I mean, I really didn't know Anna. They fished for stuff about Owen. That's what worried me," she stressed. "Headley was there too," she told Carol, "and the way he stares is…is just horrible! You feel as though he's undressing you! His expression looks like he's going to make it seem like torture and enjoy it." She stopped and looked at Carol. "That sounds pretty weird, doesn't it?"

"Not at all," Carol muttered. "He's an ass."

They sipped their sodas. Even with the cool drinks, it took only a minute for them to feel perspiration on their faces. Sylvia's back faced the sun and she could feel it getting damp.

"I should get back," she said. "Mr. Carter will wonder what's happened to me."

They walked back inside and the hallways seemed dark compared to the bright summer sunlight. The air was much cooler inside and they both said 'talk to you later' as they went towards their respective offices. Mr. Carter looked up when she knocked on his door and told him she was back. He asked if she was okay and she nodded, not trusting her voice.

"Do you want to go home?" he asked.

Sylvia shook her head, "It would be nice," she said, "but, Owen and I came in the same car because of the media stuff," she told him.

"Let me know if there is anything I can do," he said, "but I've found the best cure is to jump in and get busy on something," he told her for the second time that day.

Sylvia nodded and went back out to her desk. She checked her messages and her email. Owen said he would be by promptly at

4:30. Her Mom sent her a funny e-card and she smiled at the cute animation on the screen with the line "Hang in there," and some funny birds hanging on for dear life upside down on a branch. It reminded her of one of her favorite picture books as she was growing up –Stellaluna where little baby birds tried to copy their bat friend by hanging upside down out of their nest. She was still smiling when a shadow crossed her desk and she looked up. It was Mr. Headley. Sylvia's smiled faded.

"How are you doing, Sylvia?" he asked, his voice filled with concern that she thought was fake.

"I'm all right," she said. "Thank you," she forced those words out.

He cleared his throat before he started talking and he said, "Um, I was under the impression that you and Mr. Anderson were on friendlier terms."

She looked up at him sharply but, didn't say anything.

"You said this afternoon with the detectives that you had only been on one date with him," he said, "and I was assuming you would tell the truth to the police," he baited her.

Still she sat silently, waiting for what he had to say.

"I was wondering if you would like to go out to dinner some evening?" he asked smoothly.

Sylvia didn't know what to say. Mr. Headley asking her out on a date was the last thing that would have crossed her mind. She opened her mouth to say something and nothing came out.

"Thank you," she eventually said, "that's very flattering but, I'm not sure that would be a good idea, right now," she said carefully.

"You're right," he said, not missing a beat. "Sometime later, then? I would treat a lovely woman like you very well," he said with emphasis on the 'very.'

She flushed under his gaze. As if psychic, Mr. Carter came out of his office.

"Headley!" he said heartily, "What brings you here?" He stretched out his hand and pumped Headley's hard.

"I had a few questions for Ms. Ash," he said, rubbing his hand when Mr. Carter had finished shaking it so firmly.

"Yes, she's a wonderful girl," Mr. Carter said. "Good ideas and a hard worker."

Sylvia usually hated it when people talked about you as if you weren't in the room, but she didn't mind at the moment. She was grateful Mr. Carter had emerged from his office. Sylvia glanced up at the clock on the wall. It was nearly 4:30 and for some reason she hoped Owen wouldn't walk in on this. Mr. Carter again seemed to read her mind.

"Headley," he stated, "Why don't I walk back down the hall with you. I'm on my way to get a last jolt of caffeine before I hit the road this evening." He turned to Sylvia and said, "Have a good night, Sylvia."

"Thank you, Mr. Carter. You too," she said.

Mr. Headley turned to her and said with a meaningful wink, "I'll be in touch."

When they were safely away from the office, she dialed Carol.

"You will never believe what just happened," she stage whispered into the phone.

"What?" Carol asked, eager for news.

"Headley asked me out," she said.

"What?" Carol gasped in surprise. "You're kidding?"

"No!" Sylvia replied. "Can you believe it?"

"Be careful, Syl!" Carol advised, "He's a snake."

"I know," she answered. "He gives me the willies. Ugh!"

Owen came up to the door. He looked tired.

"I've got to go," she said to Carol, "Owen's here to take me home. I'll talk to you tomorrow."

"Okay," Carol said. "Have a good night."

She hung up from Carol and looked up at Owen.

"Are you ready?" he asked.

"Yes," Sylvia said, "Just let me get my things together."

Sylvia logged off her computer, quickly straightened her desk and got her purse. They walked out to the car. It was so hot it was hard to sit on the seat. Owen let the air conditioning cool down the steering wheel before they left the parking lot.

"Itis difficult to believe it's the end of June," she commented. "Time seems to have gone so fast."

"I know what you mean," he said. "It's been great staying at Marian's but I should get back to looking for my own place," he commented.

"I think Marian really appreciates having you around," Sylvia said.

Owen didn't comment but nodded in response. The commuter traffic was building and Owen was focusing on pulling out onto the main highway from Thurmont.

The car cooled and they were at Marian's in a few minutes. They called to her when they went into the house and she answered them from down the hallway. She was sitting in the study, reading, keeping out of the heat.

"Hello, you two!" she greeted them with a smile. "How are you? You look done in. Is it just from the heat?"

"We're okay," Owen told her. "The police were at Thurmont today," he told her wearily. "They wanted to question me again and I told them to contact Jon."

"Good," Marian said. "What happened then?"

Owen shrugged. "They left me alone," he said, "I was trying to get caught up on my work."

"They came to question me," Sylvia said. She looked at Owen guiltily. "It was after lunch, in Headley's office. I'm sorry I didn't tell you on the way home, I had some other things on my mind," she said thinking of Mr. Headley and his lecherous presence.

"What did they ask you?" Marian asked evenly.

"They wanted to know how I knew Anna and how well I knew her," she told them. "They also wanted to know the extent of my relationship with Owen," she said quietly.

Marian raised her eyebrows and Owen looked at her as if to say, 'I told you so.'

"It was pretty straight forward," she continued, "but still it made me nervous."

"I can imagine," Marian said.

"Why don't you two get comfortable and change into cooler clothes and then we'll have dinner," Marian suggested.

"Changing into shorts and a T-shirt would be fantastic," Owen said.

Before he left, Sylvia cocked her head. "What is that noise?" she asked. "Did you get air conditioning?" she asked feeling a soft whoosh of air around her.

Marian laughed, "No," she said, "This house is too old for air conditioning," she told them, "but Bran and I had a 'whole house fan' installed a long, long time ago. It pulls the air through and pushes it out through the attic. It works quite well."

Owen and Sylvia went upstairs to change. It felt good to put on shorts and a midriff shirt. She left her feet bare and padded back downstairs. She had to admit to herself that it was rather nice living at Marian's.

"I kept dinner simple," Marian told Sylvia when she came into view. "We're having a salad plate with some rolls, fruit, and iced tea."

"Lovely," Sylvia told her. "What can I do to help?"

"Fill up glasses with the tea and run and fetch some mint sprigs," Marian said.

Sylvia went to the garden where mint was growing with wild abandon. Marian kept it in check by planting it in a large tub in the garden. She had told Sylvia how invasive it could become when Sylvia questioned the size of the container that was buried in the garden. Sylvia breathed in the sharp, fragrant scent and headed back to the house where the Marian and Owen were at the table. Sylvia placed the mint springs in the glasses and took them to the table. Owen took the salad plates and Marian the fresh strawberries.

"I think this is the end of the strawberries," she said, "but blueberries and blackberries are coming into season," she added brightly.

"They seem to be particularly sweet this year," Sylvia commented as she bit into a large one.

They ate chatting comfortably, Sylvia and Owen relaxing for the first time in a couple of days. Owen joked with her as they cleaned up and snapped the wet towel at her until she ran from the kitchen laughing for Marian to come and save her. Marian came out shaking her head and laughing.

"You two are as bad as two little kids," she said. She glanced out the window and her happy expression changed to one of curiosity, then surprise and then horror. Sylvia followed her gaze. Two police cars had pulled up to the house and Detective Rogers and his partner got out and headed toward the house along with two officers.

Marian headed for the door and waved to the officers. "Come in this way," she said motioning to them with her arm.

Sylvia moved instinctively closer to Owen and he did the same. They stood close, without touching. The four officers came into the kitchen without any particular expression on their faces. Owen had twisted the tea towel and was twisting it in his hands with nervousness and Sylvia stood with her hands clenched at her sides. She noticed that Owen had paled a bit as well as Marian.

The one officer cleared his throat and handed Marian a folded piece of paper. "This is a warrant for Mr. Anderson's arrest and confiscation of some of his personal items," he said.

Sylvia gasped and grabbed onto the counter to hold herself up. It was like a nightmare. She looked up at Owen. His eyes were hollow and she could see the fear in his eyes. The words Sylvia had heard so many times on television throughout her life were being said, right in front of her.

"Mr. Anderson," he said, "you are being charged with the murder of Anna Hanson. You have the right to remain silent, you have the right..."

The words drifted off in Sylvia's mind as if she were hearing them through water. She took Owen's hand and held on as tightly as she could. Finally, the officer's voice came to a stop and through tear blurred eyes she looked up at the police. They wanted to put handcuffs on Owen and she had to let go of his hand. She let go and gave him a hug and he held her for a brief moment in a tight embrace and then he became wooden and unyielding.

"Will you put your hands behind your back, sir?" the one young officer asked him. Owen did so and they snapped on the handcuffs. Sylvia thought she would remember that sound for the rest of her life. Shakily, she stepped back and bumped into the counter. She wiped at her eyes and reached for a napkin from a basket on the countertop to use as a tissue.

"I'll call Jon right away," Marian told Owen and gave him a hug. "Don't you worry."

"Will you call my Mom and Dad too?" Owen pleaded quietly.

Marian nodded, "Of course," she said.

She turned to the police, "Where are you taking him?" she asked.

"Down to state police headquarters, Ma'am," they told her.

"I'll contact his attorney right away," she said.

They led Owen out of the house and to the police car. He got in as best he could with the handcuffs and was becoming even paler. Sylvia felt as though someone had kicked her in the stomach. The two other policemen were waiting patiently. One cleared his throat.

"Excuse me, Ma'am," he said. "Could you show us where Mr. Anderson keeps his personal belongings?"

"S-s-s-sure," she stammered, watching the police car back out and go down the road. She finally tore her eyes away from the spot and looked at Marian who nodded. She was holding the warrant as if it were something nasty.

"Syl," she said, "Take these gentlemen up to Owen's room while I call Jon," she told her.

Sylvia nodded, "This way," she said.

The policemen followed her up the stairs and she took them to Owen's room. They were very interested in his computer and the one went out to get a large box. They loaded in Owen's computer, flash drives and papers. Marian came up behind her and put her arm around her.

"This is awful," Sylvia whispered not knowing what to say, realizing her words were weak.

She put her arm around Marian and they both held on tightly to each other and watched the officers do a systematic search for items in Owen's room. They went through each drawer and looked at every paper.

Finally, Marian said, "I need to call Owen's parents. I'll be right back."

Sylvia still stood watching, not wanting to watch, but not wanting to leave. She was wondering what was happening to Owen. The officers finished up and carried several boxes down to the squad car. Sylvia followed them down and saw Marian was still on the phone. She put her hand over the mouthpiece and said goodbye to the officers and continued to talk. It was evident from the second-hand conversation that Sylvia was hearing, that Owen's parents were in shock and disbelief. She watched the squad car go down the lane and pushed the screen door and went outside. The heat was cooling slightly with the evening coming on and she walked and leaned against the oak tree in the yard, enjoying its cool bark and spreading shade.

A very slight breeze rustled through the thick, humid air. Sylvia didn't pay any attention but jumped when the Green Man put a hand on her arm.

"Oh, my God! You scared me!" she said, putting a hand on her chest.

Her fear turned to anger, "Where have you been?" she demanded. "Do you know what's happened?"

"Let's walk," the Green Man said, "and you can tell me all about it."

Sylvia spilled out everything that had happened since she last saw him on the road to her house. She told him about the stream watch, about finding the body, the mysterious marks on the body, and the problems with the media, the questionings, and Owen's subsequent arrest.

"I feel more lost than I ever have in my life," Sylvia admitted to the Green Man.

"Well," the Green Man said, "that's actually good."

"How?" she asked, "and if you say one word about finding my 'path' I'll...I'll," she stopped and then started to laugh.

The Green Man laughed too.

"Then you'll have a new beginning to work from," he said. "You are experiencing Veriditas," he said.

"What's that?" she asked. "Didn't you use that word the last time I saw you?"

The Green Man nodded. "Veriditas is the 'greening of the soul," he said, "It was a term coined by a medieval nun –Hildegard of Bingen."

He changed the subject. "Do you have any ideas about the murder?" he asked.

"Owen didn't kill Anna," she said, "That's something I feel deep down," she told him. "I think Mr. Headley might be a possible suspect, but I really don't know of any others. I'm definitely not sure about what happened to the body." She shuddered. "It was," she paused, "grisly."

He put his arm around her and pulled her to him in a fatherly embrace. She smelled his leafy green smell of spring, breathed deeply and closed her eyes. Tears filled her eyes and yet, didn't come, but his presence was a comfort and his energy surged through her. It was a healing balm to some of the hurt she was currently feeling. She pulled away eventually and gulped hard trying to think of the formless questions that floated through her head. The Green Man was quiet too. He held her for a few minutes and then told her he had to leave but would be nearby if he was needed. Sylvia nodded. He disappeared and she went back to the house. Marian was sitting in the kitchen. She had poured herself a stiff scotch and was sitting and sipping it. She looked pale and exhausted and Sylvia wondered if this was too much for her. After all, Owen was like a grandson to her.

When Sylvia came in Marian said, "Jon will call as soon as he can," she told her. "And Owen's parents – Phil and Anne will come down tomorrow." Marian sighed heavily. "Let's go into the study and try to relax," she told Sylvia.

Sylvia followed her into the study where Marian turned on an ancient television. They sat on the couch and Sylvia curled herself up and pulled a small blanket over herself. She wasn't interested in what was on television and closed her eyes. She couldn't even think straight. She must have dozed off because she jumped when something startled her. Opening her eyes wide, she tried to remember where she was. Marian patted her leg and Sylvia turned to see that she was on the phone. The ringing must have awakened her. She sat up trying to focus on the conversation Marian was having. It had to be Jon on the other end. Marian talked for a few minutes, asked Jon to send Owen their love and hung up.

She cradled the phone in her hands before she spoke. "They've booked him," she stated. "He's been through the fingerprinting process and they've interrogated him with Jon present. Apparently they found a minuscule drop of blood in Anna's office that they feel belongs to Owen."

"But that could have been from a paper cut or something!" Sylvia said incredulously. "How can they base a murder charge on that?"

"Well, apparently Anna had a diary of her, uh...what could you call it...her exploits. Apparently she also wrote about Owen watching her moves with the statistics." Marian paused, "Oh, I don't know!" Marian said frustrated. "It seems trumped up, but Jon seems to feel he can get Owen released if they can find some other information. He said that booking Owen might make the real killer slip up somehow. It's all very confusing."

She drained her scotch. "Let's go to bed," she told Sylvia. "There isn't much more we can do at the moment. I'm going to see if I can visit Owen in the morning and take him fresh clothes for the hearing. And I need to get the other room ready for Phil and Anne."

"Can I help you get it ready?" Sylvia offered.

"No!" Marian laughed. "I'm way too tired to do anything else tonight and so are you. Let's try to get some sleep."

Sylvia stumbled up the stairs after her, stripped and crawled into bed. Marian had told her to leave her bedroom door open for the cooling of the whole house fan to work. She lay sleepless now, listening to the fan and the creaks and groans of the old house. Sylvia wondered if Owen was getting any sleep and wondered if the jail cell he was in was anything like the things she saw in movies. She tossed and turned, unable to get comfortable. Finally, Sylvia got up and leaned on the windowsill and looked out at the stars. Insects still hummed and she heard an owl in the distance. It sounded spooky. She crawled back into bed and tried to sleep. She wondered what Owen's parents were like. She thought of the Green Man and how odd it was to find comfort in something that wasn't supposed to be real, but was real to her. She doubted her sanity for the millionth time and eventually fell asleep a couple of hours before dawn.

CHAPTER TWENTY TWO

In the life of each of us, I said to myself, there is a place remote
And islanded, and given to
Endless regret or secret happiness.
--Sarah Orne Jewet
The Country of the Pointed Firs

Bumps and bangs woke Sylvia. At first, she thought Owen was kidding around trying to wake her up and then realized with a jolt where Owen was. She jumped out of bed to go and investigate the sounds. It was Marian in the guest room trying to make the bed and move some furniture as quietly as she could manage.

"Marian! You should have woken me up so that I could help you move this stuff!" Sylvia said as she assisted Marian, moving a bureau so that she could dust behind it.

"I know," Marian panted, out of breath from her exertions. "I wanted to get it done before Phil and Anne arrive and, oh, I don't know. I thought it would be a good release of my anger over Owen's situation."

"Constructive, at least!" Sylvia teased her, now fully awake. "What time is it?" she asked.

"It's close to seven, I think," Marian said.

"Ohmigod!" Sylvia exclaimed. "I had better get in the shower and head to work."

Sylvia ran to get into the shower and get dressed. It was another sultry summer's day and she dressed as comfortably and professionally as possible and hurried downstairs to gulp a quick cup of coffee before leaving for work.

"Call me and let me know how things went," Sylvia called to Marian.

She hurried off to work and pulled in just on time. She had rushed so fast she barely had time to think about Owen, but now that she was sitting at her desk, the stress of the past few days seemed to hit her hard—the murder and Owen going off to jail. Her lack of sleep didn't help matters. She told Mr. Carter that she needed a cup of coffee and asked him if he wanted one too.

While she was fixing the coffees in the break room, Ed the custodian came in for a cup of coffee too. He had difficulty pouring due to a heavy bandage on his hand.

"What happened to you, Ed?" Sylvia asked seeing the angry red blotches stretching beyond the bandage boundary.

"Poison ivy, I think," Ed told her, "Itches like hell," he said to her with his usual sense of humor.

"Still? It looks horrible!" Sylvia sympathized. "Have you been to a doctor for steroids or a shot?"

"Nah," he said, "I'm just putting on 'Ivy Stop' and wrapping it up."

"Well, I hope you feel better," Sylvia said, taking the cups of coffee and balancing a Danish from the vending machine on top.

He held the door for her so that she could exit easily.

"Thanks!" she said, flashing him a smile.

"You're welcome," he said, "nice to see manners, not like some of those other bitches," he said muttering the last part under his breath, but loud enough for Sylvia to catch.

She ignored the comment and went back to the office to work on the Bay Days celebration and educational grant specifications while she ate. She looked at the clock frequently, wondering if Marian had gone to the jail and what time the hearing was. Her work seemed meaningless so she started thinking about who might have killed Anna, but couldn't come up with anyone other than Headley. She would have to ask Carol at lunch if she knew of any enemies Anna might have in the company.

When lunch finally came and she asked her question, Carol hooted with laughter so loudly that people turned their heads.

"That bitch made enemies everywhere!" she exclaimed. "You could probably poll a hundred of the guys here and they would all agree. She screwed them royally –literally and figuratively. Headly is the only one who put up with her and I think he got his jollies from watching her make men squirm. It's sick!"

Sylvia fell silent. There went the only theory she had. She chewed at her salad, not really hungry after the Danish that morning. When she got back to the office, she tried to call Marian but received no answer. She drummed her fingers on her desk and tried to concentrate on work. It was no use. She rushed out as soon as she could to go to her home to check the mail and the doors and grab a couple of new outfits. The media were gone for the moment and she thought of telling Marian that she would come back home in the next day or two. She would have to talk to her about it.

When she arrived at Marian's, there was a new car in the parking area and she assumed it was Owen's parents. She walked in and heard voices from the living room.

"Hello," she said, stepping into the room.

"Hi, Syl," Marian said and she introduced Sylvia to Owen's parents.

There was no question that Owen was the product of these two. His father, Phil Anderson, was a near exact replica of Owen. He was a tad bit shorter, she noticed when he stood up to shake her hand but had the same short, dark curling hair, glasses and a nerd-ish look about him. He was thinner than Owen and had the lean look of a runner. His mother, Anne was striking. Whereas Phil looked like Mr. Nerd, Anne looked like a leftover from the sixties. She was tall and had long graying black hair just pulled back from her face and wore a gauzy pantsuit of wide legs and a tunic. Her eyes were the amber and green hazel of Owen's, and she had the vibrant smile he had too. She reminded Sylvia of a flower child and a dancer. Sylvia and Anne looked at each other levelly when they were introduced –assessing one another. Sylvia wondered what Anne was like and if she could be friends with this woman. Anne, on the other hand, was assessing Sylvia's character and wondering what this girl was like who claimed her son's affections. Sylvia sat down near them and asked the group how Owen was making out.

"It's horrible!" his mother told her. "That jail is an awful place. Owen looks like he hasn't slept in days!"

"Well, he most likely hasn't," his father commented calmly.

"I don't know anything about this sort of thing," Sylvia started, "but have they set bail?"

Anne looked tearful and worked hard to control her emotions.

Phil answered, "He was arraigned and he put in a plea of 'not guilty,'" he said quietly, "The judge set bail at a million dollars since it was a murder charge."

"What?" Sylvia gasped, "A million dollars?"

"We've put up our homes as collateral because we need to come up with at least ten percent of the bail," Marian said. "We have some paperwork to take care of tomorrow, but hopefully, Owen can be released on bail and on his own recognizance in the next 24-48 hours. He'll need to surrender his passport and most likely need to stay in this area, but I suspect that those will be his only restrictions."

Sylvia didn't know what to say. It was a numbing experience.

They all sat quiet for a few minutes until Marian remembered, "Isn't tomorrow Anna's funeral?" she asked.

Sylvia said quietly. "Yes, the company promised liberal leave for tomorrow afternoon."

"I'm assuming you're going?" Anne asked.

Sylvia looked across the room at her, "Yes," she said, "I thought I should."

Anne, Phil, and Marian nodded in agreement.

"We should start thinking about dinner," Marian said. "I didn't think of it earlier."

"Why don't we go out," Anne suggested. "Is there some place rather anonymous or quiet in town on a Tuesday night?" she asked.

"Actually, there is," Sylvia said, and she reminded Marian of the restaurant on the water that they had been to a couple of weeks ago.

"Good idea," Marian said.

Phil wanted to drive and they all piled into the Anderson's car. It was strange, Sylvia thought, to get to know Owen's parents without him around. The restaurant was not crowded, as Sylvia had predicted on a Tuesday evening. A few boaters who had docked outside the restaurant were at the table and at the bar. The waitress put them at a table near the water where they could watch the sun set over the water. You could just barely see the landfall line across the bay and its outline of trees and houses growing darker by the minute as the sun painted the sky. Phil asked what type of wine Sylvia liked and suggested they order a couple of bottles. She agreed. Feeling slightly uncomfortable not knowing Owen's parents Sylvia studied the menu carefully. Anne asked how the crab bisque was and Sylvia told her it was wonderful. They each ordered a cup with their meals and talked while they waited for their food. Anne asked Sylvia how long she had been working at Thurmont and Sylvia told her story of inheriting Gran's home finding employment in the area.

"You've had an interesting year then," Anne said sympathetically shaking her head at Sylvia.

Sylvia nodded not wanting to speak at that particular moment with her emotions on the rise. Fortunately, the waitress brought the wine and the soup. Anne asked her other questions in a nice way similar to how her mother had questioned Owen a few weeks earlier. It had to be a 'mother' thing, she thought, trying to find the best person for their baby. It probably wouldn't have been so bad if she or Owen had had siblings, but since they were only children, both sets of parents seemed to be overprotective. It was certainly a type of verbal gantlet. Phil was relatively quiet and contemplative. Marian tried to draw him into conversation, but he seemed lost in thought. Sylvia noticed he had the same habit as Sylvia's mother of running his finger around the rim of the glass. They finished dinner and skipped dessert. Phil, Anne, and Marian told her to put her wallet away when she tried to help pay for dinner. Phil finally won the toss claiming that he indeed owed Marian, at least, a dinner for keeping Owen in the last few weeks. Exhausted they all turned in almost as soon as they returned to Marian's.

Sylvia dropped off to sleep as soon as she crawled into bed. She dreamed of the Green Man and everything glowing with brilliant light – people, plants, trees—everything. It was joyful and very, very beautiful. Unconsciously she sighed with pleasure in her sleep.

Sylvia had gotten up early, surprised to find that Phil had already been out for a run and Anne sipping coffee at the kitchen table with Marian. They were talking quietly. They looked up and smiled when Sylvia came downstairs. She was wearing only the sleeveless portion of the blue suit she had worn at Gran's funeral.

"Good morning," Sylvia greeted, walking over to the cupboard to get a cup and make her usual café au lait.

"Good morning," they both answered.

Phil was still out of breath and was toweling off from his run and paused for a moment for a long drink of water. He was leaning on the counter.

Marian had made her excellent muffins and they were sitting peeking out from a basket on the kitchen table. Sylvia helped herself when Marian pushed the basket towards her.

"Phil, come and have one of Marian's delicious muffins," Anne said to him. "They're tremendous."

Phil stood at the counter and shook his head. "No thanks," he said, "I'm going up to shower and then I'll be down for the usual."

He left the kitchen as Anne said, sotto voce, "The 'usual' is sticks and twigs bran cereal," making a face. She laughed and Marian and Sylvia joined in. He's become such a health food nut as he's gotten older, she commented in a loving, yet complaining sort of way.

When the laughter died down, Sylvia said, "I don't know what the schedule is today," she said. "I haven't a clue when I'll get back."

"Don't worry," Marian said, "You know I can always drop another potato in the pot," she said with a smile.

Sylvia smiled back and then asked her gravely, "I don't know what's happening with the media," she said, "but I can move back home if…"

Marian interrupted her, "Absolutely not!" she insisted. "I suspect that the funeral could be a media blitz and when Owen is released on bail…" she stopped too and shook her head.

"All right," Sylvia answered quietly. "I wonder when things will be normal again."

"Not for quite some time," Anne added her voice, "I suspect. We need to find a way to clear Owen."

Everyone nodded in agreement.

Sylvia looked up at the clock. "I should be getting to work," she announced. "Tell Owen," she paused for a moment, "tell Owen I'll look forward to seeing him soon," she said trying to be positive.

"Hopefully, tonight," Marian said and Anne nodded along with her.

Sylvia left for work only half listening to the radio. She wasn't paying attention until the radio news came on and announced Anna's funeral and Owen's possible bail. They were in the thick of the local news. She made a face at the radio and pushed in a CD. The media were not at Thurmont, but she suspected they were lying in wait at the funeral home.

The morning was long. Even though things were subdued after the past few days, she was still having difficulty concentrating on her work. She sent a long overdue email to Gwen, explaining what had happened in the last week. She stopped by Carol's office where Carol was busy answering the phone with one call after the other. Carol rolled her eyes and jotted a note that she would be taking a break in a few minutes and would stop by the office. Sylvia suddenly realized that her office phone had been strangely quiet. Being in the public information office, she realized her office should be the one to be battered by phone calls from media and the curious. She brought it up to Mr. Carter when she returned to the office. He told her that due to her involvement with the case that Carol received some of the calls, but the majority of the calls were transferred to Thurmont's sister company. He asked her how she was holding up.

"I think I'm still numb," she told him truthfully.

He nodded and said, "Let me know if you need anything."

Carol came in and sat down with a plop in the chair in the outer office. Sylvia heard her and went out to greet her.

"Whew!" she said, "The phone has been ringing off the hook this morning."

"Thanks for taking some of the heat," Sylvia told her. "I understand that you're the one handling a lot of the calls."

"Yup," said Carol. "It's no problem," she said casually. "Most of the calls I can refer up to big brother or say 'no comment at this time.'"

"Are you going to the funeral?" Sylvia asked hopefully.

"No way!" Carol answered. "You know how I feel…uh…felt about Anna. Anyway, someone needs to be here to hold down the fort," she told Sylvia.

"Do you want to grab an early lunch before you head out?" Carol asked.

"Sure," Sylvia said, a little uncertainly. "I'm not sure I can eat a lot. Let me check with Mr. Carter," she said.

Mr. Carter gave his okay and Sylvia and Carol headed to the cafeteria. It was crowded and Carol made a comment that 'great minds think alike' as they hunted for a free table. They noticed that many of the people were in dressy clothes. Sylvia finally found a small table near the exit. She motioned for Carol and they both made a beeline to sit down. Sylvia cleared away the last diners' crumbs and spills.

"Yuck," she said throwing away soiled napkins.

"The people who were here last were pigs!" Carol retorted as they both brushed off their seats and sat down gingerly.

"How are you doing?" Carol asked Sylvia. "How's Owen?" she asked.

Sylvia shrugged. "Like I told Mr. Carter, I'm still numb," she said. "As for Owen, I haven't been able to speak to him. His parents came down yesterday," she said.

Sylvia took a half-hearted bite or two from her sandwich. The food seemed to stick in her throat and she washed it down with her diet soda. Many of the diners were exiting.

"I'm not trying to rush you," Carol said to Sylvia, "but, I think you'd better be headed out soon if you want to get a parking space within a mile of the funeral home," she suggested.

Sylvia looked around at the emptying cafeteria. "I suppose so," she said reluctantly. "Do you know where the funeral home is in Deerfield?"

"Sure," Carol said and gave her directions. "It's the biggest funeral home in the area," she told Sylvia and gave her directions and tips on where to park if the lot was full.

Sylvia threw most of her lunch in the trash, grabbed her soda and said goodbye to Carol. She told Mr. Carter she was headed out and he said, "see you in the morning," and 'Good luck." She hurried to her car. The sweltering summer heat and humidity had socked into the area. Sylvia put on her sunglasses against the sharp glare and turned her air conditioning on full until she could comfortably touch the steering wheel. Most of the folks had already left for the viewing as the parking lot was quite empty. Sylvia drove to Deerfield and tried to remember Carol's directions. She should have written them down. After a couple of wrong turns, she found the funeral home by the media vans parked outside. The parking lot was full and they were interviewing people as they got out of their cars. She thought it was probably good that she was late and had to park a few blocks away. She strode to the funeral home door, dodging reporters. Sylvia was glad she was wearing dark glasses. She kept her head down and went into the funeral home, crowded with visitors. The smell of the flowers and too many people almost made her retch. It brought back vivid memories of Gran's funeral only a few weeks ago. Sylvia stood at the back of the room. There were beautiful flower arrangements and a large blanket of flowers over the closed casket. She was glad it was closed remembering the state of Anna's skin when they pulled her from the mud. She closed her eyes and almost fell into a crying woman.

"I'm so sorry," Sylvia said, "I lost my balance," she told her.

The woman continued to sob and shook her head to communicate that it was all right.

"Are you all right?" Sylvia asked, concerned, as she didn't recognize the woman as being from Thurmont.

"Such a sad thing," she sobbed, "I always knew she would come to a bad end."

"Are you a relative?" Sylvia asked, surprised.

The woman nodded. She was a plump woman who was dressed in a worn black skirt, blouse, and plastic patent leather sandals. She had her gray hair pulled into a bun but, long straight strands were slipping out.

"I was one of Anna's foster parents," she told Sylvia.

"*One* of her foster parents?" Sylvia couldn't help but, comment.

The woman nodded. "Her parents died in a fire when she was eight or nine," the woman told her. "Poor thing, she was severely abused. Sexually, you know. They think that she possibly set the fire, but no one ever knew," she said. The woman blew her nose noisily.

"I'm Grace," she introduced herself as she calmed down.

Sylvia introduced herself and took the hand Grace offered, trying to surreptitiously wipe it on her dress afterward. She looked at Grace puzzled.

"Are you a friend of Anna's?" Grace asked, hiccoughing a little bit.

Sylvia shook her head but realized that Grace couldn't see it as she was staring at the casket.

"I'm an acquaintance," Sylvia told her.

"I'm surprised she had such a good showing," Grace said, looking about the room. "I didn't think she would have this many friends," Grace commented.

Sylvia didn't want to tell Grace that Anna was not well liked and that this was an opportunity to get out of work a little early as well as getting satisfaction for some curiosity. Grace went on with her story.

"She was always such a troubled child," Grace told her. "I think I was the fourth or fifth home she had been to," she said. "Anna always wanted her way and she didn't care how she got it," Grace confessed. "Honestly, I think all my gray hair came when she lived with me."

"What do you mean?" Sylvia asked, curious.

"Oh!" Grace said, laughing and crying at the same time. "I could tell you stories about that one! It amazes me that she made it through her education without landing in jail. But, she was a smart cookie, always on the edge of trouble, but very determined and one of the most cunning individuals I've had occasion to meet."

Sylvia wasn't sure how to react to all of this so, she tried to keep a straight face and just listen. Grace seemed bent on telling her story. She continued to cry and talk about Anna.

"You know, Sylvia, my theory is that Anna was so hurt and angry from her childhood abuses that she wanted to pay back the world somehow by hurting everything she came in contact with," Grace confided. "I felt so helpless. She turned away from any affection whatsoever. I tried so hard with her," Grace said shaking her head. "But, she did everything she could to try to hurt me. I lost my marriage because of her," Grace commented, "but I did love her. I don't think she ever knew that " she murmured.

"I hope she knew," Sylvia said, "But your story…It sounds like something from a talk show," Sylvia commented.

"You're right there!" Grace exclaimed with a bitter laugh, "Something that should be on with that guy who has all the outlandish people."

The service started and Grace stopped talking but continued to cry quietly. Sylvia felt a little sick to her stomach with all of these revelations about Anna. She only half listened to what was being said by the company executives telling everyone what a good employee and excellent scientist Anna was. Sylvia looked around the room to see if she knew anyone. She saw Headley and Keely up front with all of the executives. About seven or eight people down from her was Ed, the custodian. He stood leaning back against the wall. He nodded to her and gave her a brief smile when she glanced his way and she nodded and smiled back. The priest gave a short sermon and the service was finally over. Mr. Headley announced that a gathering in Anna's honor would be held at a country club nearby. Sylvia whispered to Grace if she knew where it was.

Grace nodded, "I want to go up one last time," she said. "Nice meetin' you," she told Sylvia.

"Nice meeting you," Sylvia replied.

She didn't really feel like going to the country club but was curious to see who would show up. She heard from someone, or read somewhere, that the murderer would show up at the funeral of the dead person just to know they were taunting the police. She wasn't really going to play detective, she told herself, but she was just curious.

She escaped past the reporters by having on her sunglasses and leaving with a throng of other Thurmont employees. Sylvia was also surprised that the gathering was being held at the country club. She wondered if Thurmont was picking up the tab or Headley. People had already started drinking from the open bar when she arrived and were attacking the cheese and fruit and crackers. Sylvia ordered a glass of wine and nibbled at some cheese and fruit. She looked around at the welter of faces. So many looked solemn and others uncomfortable. One gentleman looked extremely familiar. It took her a minute before she realized it was Detective Rogers in plain clothes. He sidled up next to her.

"You're not going to give away my secret, are you?" he asked.

Sylvia stared at him, "Don't you think Owen killed her?" she asked.

"I'm always looking for leads," he muttered.

Sylvia nodded. "Have you had a chance to talk with Anna's foster mother?" she asked him.

"Who?" he asked incredulously.

"Her foster mother," Sylvia told him. "She talked to me during the service," she said, "and had a lot of interesting things to say about Anna. She's over there," she pointed to Grace, who had finally stopped crying and was trying to eat a chicken wing gracefully while holding a drink in the other hand. It wasn't working too well. She had already wiped a splotch from her blouse.

"Thanks," he whispered to her and went over to Grace.

"Did you know her well?" a voice asked from behind her.

She turned abruptly to find Ed behind her.

"Ed," she said, "you startled me! No, I didn't know her that well," she told him.

"Me either," he said. "She was an odd one for sure. I thought I knew her a little, but..." he broke off.

Sylvia noticed that the red had crept up his hand. "Have you been to your doctor yet about the poison ivy?" she asked him.

"Nah," he said, "but I should soon," he replied. "It's gotten a lot worse."

"I can see that," Sylvia said. She watched him as he swiped his hand across a sweaty forehead in the highly air conditioned room. She wondered if he was running a fever.

He changed the subject. "How've you been making out since your Granny Holly died?" he asked her.

"Okay, I guess," Sylvia said soberly. "It wasn't easy to be here today." She paused and then asked in surprise, "Granny Holly? How did you know her name?" she asked him. "Did you know her?"

"Oh, I knew your Grandmother," he told her.

"How?" Sylvia interrupted incredulous.

"We belonged to some of the same groups," he said.

"What kind of groups?" Sylvia pressed on.

"Environmental stuff," he said. "In fact, I just got back from an assign..." he broke off, "a trip about two months ago," he corrected himself.

"That's interesting," she said. "I'd like to hear more about your volunteering some time."

Ed nodded distractedly. "How's your friend Owen doing?" he asked.

"Well, not too well," Sylvia said. "They're trying to pin this murder on him."

"He didn't do it," Ed said matter of factly.

"I know," Sylvia said, "but, now we need to prove that. And," she continued, "it seems as though Anna made an enemy of everyone she met, so who knows who did it."

"Yup," Ed agreed and he rocked back and forth on his heels.

Sylvia saw Headley heading their way. "Excuse me," she said, "I need to go."

She darted to the ladies room and scooted inside. She sat on a small padded bench just inside the door and tapped her fingers. Someone came inside and Sylvia pretended to go through her purse as if looking for something. She waited a few minutes and then peeked out the door. Headley wasn't in sight. Sylvia looked through the arched doorways and saw him in conversation with two other people. When he was looking the other way, she went out the front door and to her car with a small sigh of relief.

CHAPTER TWENTY THREE

Thanks to the human heart by which we live,
Thanks to its tenderness, its joys, and fears,
To me, the meanest flower that blows can give
Thoughts that do often lie too deep for tears.
--William Wordsworth
Ode, Intimations of Immortality

Sylvia drove back to Marian's house anxious to see if Owen was out on bail. The Anderson car wasn't in the drive. Sylvia parked and raced inside. Marian was in the study reading. She looked up at Sylvia's apprehensive face when she walked in.

"Not yet," she murmured. "We're in the waiting game. Phil and Anne are hoping to bring him home soon. Why don't you go and get comfortable," she said.

Sylvia went upstairs to change. When she came down, Marian asked if she would water the garden. Sylvia went to the shed to drag out the hose. She stared unthinkingly at the rainbows created by the droplets of water spraying the garden. She was just finishing the last half of the garden when the Anderson's car pulled in. She tried unsuccessfully to see if Owen was inside through the tinted windows and felt her stomach drop as the doors opened. Owen's tall, lanky form emerged and she dropped the hose and ran over to him. He took her in his arms and buried his face in her hair and held her tightly. They stood together for a long time just holding on. Tears leaked from her eyes slowly at first and then tumbled faster and faster. Owen held her as her body shook with sobs and then he took her hands and kissed the tears on her face. He kissed her and her hair and hugged her again. Sylvia looked up and smiled at him through the tears as she attempted to wipe away the tears with the back of her hand.

"I'd better turn off the hose," she said. "Why don't you go in to see Marian. I'm sure she's anxious to see you.

But, he didn't need to go in. Marian came running down the steps to give him a hug and he bear-hugged her in return. Sylvia went back to turn off the water and roll up the hose.

"Let me help," Anne said to Sylvia.

"But, you'll get covered in garden mud," Sylvia insisted. "I can get it."

Anne insisted on staying and helping her roll up the hose before they went inside. While they did, Anne briefed Sylvia on what took place to get Owen out on bail. Owen had disappeared upstairs and Sylvia heard the muffled sounds of the shower running when they stepped into the house. Sylvia went into the powder room to wash her face and clean-up from the garden. When she emerged, she saw to seeing Marian looking slightly harried.

"Sylvia, could you set the table please?" Marian asked, "and put on extra napkins. We'll need them with dinner."

Puzzled, Sylvia followed Marian's directions giving each person a few extra napkins at their place. Anne came in with champagne glasses.

"Marian said she had champagne left over from her party a couple of weeks ago," she said to Sylvia, "so we're opening some this evening. Appropriate, don't you think?"

"Certainly," Sylvia said.

They stood, in slightly awkward silence, in the dining room until Owen came in, wet curls glistening. Both Anne and Sylvia beamed at him. Marian came in at nearly the same time with platters of fresh fruit and cold steamed shrimp.

"Marian, I may have used up all of your hot water," Owen told her. "I felt as though I couldn't get clean enough," he said to them.

"Don't even think twice about it," Marian said surveying the table. "You know, I think I'll need the plates in the kitchen," she told them.

Anne and Sylvia gathered them up and took them to the kitchen where Marian arranged lettuces and crab salad on each.

"Owen, would you cut the bread?" she asked him handing him a baguette and a knife.

"Sylvia and Anne, I need the little finger bowls from the china closet. We can put seafood sauce in those for the shrimp," Marian said.

"Marian, you're pulling out all the stops once again," Owen commented.

"And rightly so," she said. "We're glad to have you home," she told him giving him a hug.

"Where's Dad?" he asked Anne.

"In his glory in Marian's study reading Bran's collection of books," Anne told Owen. "I'm not sure we'll be able to extract him from whatever tome he's poring over," she laughed. "Owen, go and get him for dinner."

"He's welcome to Bran's books," Marian said. "I don't know why I never thought of it before."

"Our house is currently groaning under the weight of all of the books," Anne moaned. "Please, let's break it to him gently by telling him he can have a handful this trip. Is that okay?" she pleaded to Marian.

"Of course," she said. "You'll know where they are when you want to get the rest."

"Thank you," Anne said with relief.

They all went into the dining room. Marian lit the small candelabra on the table and the oak in the room picked up the warm glow. Owen came in and Phil followed, looking a bit dazed from his reading.

"Did you find something good?" Anne teased.

"Oh, yes!" he breathed, not realizing she was teasing him, "it's a beautiful book on the Battle of Brandywine. I don't know why I hadn't read it before. Bran must have been holding out on me," he said with a dazed chuckle.

"It's yours," Marian said. "Please take it home."

"Thank you, Marian," Phil said formally, "I shall treasure it."

They sat down to eat. They toasted Owen's return with champagne and Owen raised his glass "to freedom!" he toasted. Everyone raised their glasses and toasted with him. Owen asked about the funeral and Sylvia told them about Grace and the revelations of Anna's sordid past."

"Poor thing," Anne said. "She must have been horribly abused by her parents. No wonder she was so bitter."

"Mom, you didn't know her," Owen said. "I'm sorry to hear that her childhood was so horrible, but she was an incredibly devious person."

"Marian," Sylvia said, changing the subject, "Do you know of a young man by the name of Ed that might have been in a group with Gran?"

"Ed," Marian said thoughtfully, "Do you know his last name?"

"The custodian?" Owen asked.

"Yes," Sylvia answered. "Apparently he knew Gran through one of her causes."

"Probably ecological," Marian assumed, and she paused.

Owen interrupted, "Ed Davenport is his name, I think."

"Ed Davenport!" Marian exclaimed. "Maureen's son. He was involved with Green Peace, but believe it or not, that was too tame and politically correct so he was part of some other radical organization with an ecological focus. I can't remember the name, but he came to this area to try to convince us to join. It was far too radical for our interests."

"Ed? Radical?" Sylvia asked. "I'm not sure that we're talking about the same person," she said. "He's a very clean cut and conservative kind of guy."

"You never know," Phil commented, "they say still waters run deep."

"Radical enough to kill?" Anne asked in a calm, quiet voice. Silence fell over the table.

"Maybe I should call Jon after dinner," Marian said. "Perhaps he could pass the information on to police or use it in court at least."

"Well," Owen said, "I hope they find the damn emails that I sent out to the executives. Something fishy is going on. If they would only listen to me and look at the copies on my home email, they would see that I was telling the truth!" he stated vehemently.

"Unfortunately, that will probably take some time," Phil said. "That bullshit seems to take forever even if it means someone's freedom lies in the balance."

They finished dinner in quiet. When Marian told Owen to sit down when he started to clear the table, he said, "No, I want things to be as normal as possible," Owen turned to Sylvia, "Help me with the dishes?" he asked.

"You bet," she answered, and she followed him into the kitchen.

They rinsed and stacked the dishes in the dishwasher in silence. After they finished cleaning up, Owen pulled Sylvia to him.

"I missed you," he murmured brushing at a stray hair with his fingertips.

"I missed you too," she started to say when the door swung open and Anne came out with the champagne flutes.

Sylvia pulled away from Owen, feeling like she was in high school and caught kissing on the front porch.

"I thought you were washing dishes," Anne teased lightly.

"All done," Owen said, "except the champagne glasses."

"I'll do these," Anne said.

"If you insist," Owen teased his mother. "Syl, let's go sit out on the patio."

"Are you sure you don't need help?" Sylvia asked Anne.

"Go," Anne ordered. "Phil is back with Bran's books and Marian is on the phone with Jon. I think I can handle a few glasses." She pushed her long dark hair off her shoulders.

Owen and Sylvia went to sit on the patio. He had brought matches so that they could light the citronella candles near them. They sat on the small bench and Owen put his arm around Sylvia. She snuggled into the hollow of his shoulder and gave a contented sigh as she watched the candles flicker in the dusky night. Fireflies were low to the ground twinkling in Marian's yard and out through the meadow to the edge of the trees. The hum of cicadas filled the air. She nuzzled into his shoulder more and was once again totally amazed at how comfortable, and at peace, that she felt when she was with Owen.

"Are you going into work tomorrow?" Sylvia murmured.

"I don't know if they'll want me to come in," Owen said bitterly. "I'll need to talk with Keely in the morning."

She hadn't thought of them not wanting Owen to return. The thought was startling.

"Do you wonder what made those…those tracks on Anna?" Sylvia asked him.

"I think about it all the time," Owen admitted. "I can't get the picture out of my head," he paused, "and I can't figure it out," he said with exasperation.

"I can't get it out of my mind either," Sylvia admitted. "Do you think it has something to do with the soil and the chemical dumping?" Sylvia broached sitting up now.

"Possibly," Owen mused. "But, I've never seen an animal or organism that would do something like that," he said.

"But, if it's something in the soil," Sylvia pushed on, "And it did that to Anna, what is it doing to everything around it?"

Owen shoved Sylvia away somewhat roughly, stood up and raked his fingers through his hair. "Look, Sylvia, don't try to be a fucking Erin Brockovich! Look where it got me!" he exclaimed. He looked at her with a glare that she had not seen before in his eyes. He turned from her and paced the patio.

Sylvia was taken aback and shaken by his vehemence. Anger seemed to fill Owen's body and the air between them was charged. It was a little frightening. Before Sylvia could think of a retort, Marian's voice came from the kitchen door, "Sylvia?" she asked to the night air. "Sylvia, your Mom is on the phone."

"Be right there," Sylvia called back. She stood up to go into the house and still couldn't think of how to answer Owen, still stung by his words. Owen's back was to her.

Sylvia went in to talk to her Mom. She asked how things were going and said she would be down for the holiday weekend.

"Holiday?" Sylvia asked puzzled.

"The 4th of July is Friday, sweetheart," her Mom told her.

"Oh!" Sylvia said, "The days have been running all together in the last week."

"I'm sure," her Mother answered, "Marian's filled me in a bit on what has been happening. Why don't you ask Marian, Owen, and his parents if they want to come to a barbecue on the fourth? You know how we have an excellent view of the fireworks from Gran's front yard."

Okay," Sylvia said, a little distractedly.

"Are you all right, Syl?" her mother asked concerned.

"Yes," Sylvia said, "Yes, I'll be okay. See you."

She hung up and went into Marian and Anne, who were talking in the living room. She asked about the fourth and they both agreed. Then she told Marian she would be leaving in the morning and thanked her for everything. Marian started to protest and looked at her questioningly.

"I need to clean the house before Mom arrives," she told them a flimsy excuse for leaving. "I'm pretty tired, so I'll say goodnight."

She went up to her room to start to pack. She couldn't help but, glance out the window. Owen was sitting on the patio with his head in his hands. She didn't know whether to go out to him or not. She decided not to and went to bed.

Owen was still asleep when Sylvia got up to go to work. She packed up her car after dressing and went back in to have a cup of coffee with Marian and Anne. Sylvia didn't know what to say to them. Marian kept up the conversation about the 4th of July celebrations in town and how it would be wonderful to see it from Sylvia's property. It was soon time to go to work. Sylvia gave Marian a hug and Marian held her tightly.

"Thank you for everything," Sylvia told her and gave Marian a kiss on her cheek.

"If you need anything, you let me know," Marian said.

Sylvia nodded. For some reason, she wanted to cry.

"I'll see you tomorrow," she said to Anne.

Sylvia went out to her car before Anne could stand up to give her a hug. She thought she heard the scrap of a comment between Marian and Anne "I wonder what happened between those two?" Tears let loose in the car and she sniffled at stop lights. Finally, she pulled over, blew her nose loudly and turned up the volume on the radio. She was morose as she continued driving. Mr. Carter had taken the rest of the week as a vacation and it was much too quiet in the office. She banged a few things around and scolded herself. Sylvia and Owen didn't have a fight, but she was as miserable as if they had. She was shocked when he physically pushed her and shouted at her. Sylvia understood only a little of what he was going through and she was frustrated because she didn't know how to help him. She wondered if he was right about his comment. A head peered around the doorway. It was Ed.

"Hi," Sylvia said glad to see another face. She gave him a relieved smile.

"Is it cool enough for you?" he asked.

"Yes," Sylvia said, "I'm all right."

"Good," he said, "there are a couple of women down the hall having hot flashes and claiming the air conditioning isn't on. I'm running through on a quick check," he told her.

Sylvia nodded. Then she remembered about Gran.

"Ed," she called as he turned to go.

"Yes, Ma'am," he said as he turned back to her with a grin.

"You said you knew my grandmother?" Sylvia said.

His face took on an expression that she couldn't quite figure out. Guarded would be a correct word. He nodded. Sylvia wanted to tread carefully.

"I wanted to join some of the same groups that Gran belonged to," she told him, hoping her face didn't give away the lies.

"I don't belong to them anymore," he told her. "I used to belong to a couple of the local 'save the bay' type organizations. I didn't like the politics in them. I wouldn't get involved if I were you," he suggested.

"I'll keep that in mind," she said. "But, I've enjoyed getting the stream watch going," she said, "despite what happened afterward," she stated in a quieter tone. "And I wouldn't mind getting involved and meeting some of Gran's friends. I feel the same as Gran regarding environmental issues," she told him.

"Well, I know that the one group was ineffectual. It involved cleaning up the trash on the shoreline to make it pretty for the high paying tourists, but it never got to the root of the problem," he persisted. "Everyone who wanted to 'be' someone in town would put on their sloppy clothes and pose for the newspaper a couple of times a year as they picked up a piece of trash."

Sylvia wasn't quite sure how to respond, but asked, "What is the root of the problem?"

"Big companies who are poisoning the area and paying off politicians to cover it up!" he said vehemently, anger flashing in his eyes.

All of a sudden, he reminded her of someone, but she couldn't think who it was. Inside she thought, "like Thurmont," saying it silently to herself.

"Is anyone going after them?" she asked.

"Yeah," he said, "but, not so that anyone would notice," he muttered as he stepped inside the office to speak more carefully to her.

Sylvia changed the subject, "How's your poison ivy?" she asked him.

"Not much better," he said, holding up his arm that was now more heavily bandaged. "The doctor put me on steroids. I hope it helps," he said shaking his head. "It's like something is eating away at the skin," he confessed.

Warning bells clanged in Sylvia's head, but she kept on making conversation.

"Ooh, it sounds awful!" Sylvia exclaimed, "You weren't bitten by a brown recluse spider or something were you?" she asked. "I heard that the wounds from them are like that and I know they're in this wooded area."

"Good idea," he said and then he shook his head, "These crazy doctors. I don't think half of them know what they're doing."

"That's why they call it 'practicing' medicine," Sylvia said lightly.

He nodded in response to her and glanced up at the wall clock and said, "Gotta run," he told her. "Nice talking to you."

"Same here," Sylvia said.

Ed left and Sylvia closed the door. She called Marian and asked for Jon's phone number because she thought she had a piece of information. Marian gave it to her but said he was most likely in court at that time of day. She gave Sylvia his home phone number also.

"How are things going?" Sylvia asked in general.

"We're all hot and cranky," Marian told her. "Except Phil, he is as happy as a clam with Bran's books. Owen is moping around the house complaining of the heat and Anne and I were thinking of going some place cool to go shopping," she told her.

"I wish I were going shopping with you," Sylvia said. "It's quite dull here and I can't concentrate," she confessed to Marian.

"I know, honey," Marian said sympathetically, "But as the old saying goes, "It'll all come out in the wash."

"Maybe," Sylvia said.

Carol walked in with a hearty 'hello' and then clapped her hand over her mouth when she saw Sylvia on the phone.

"I need to go," Sylvia said. "See you tomorrow night."

"I'm so sorry," Carol told her, "I'm always opening up my big mouth at the wrong time!"

"It's okay," Sylvia said. "I was on the phone with Marian for a minute. I don't even think she heard you."

"Good," Carol sighed with relief. "C'mon, let's go to lunch."

Sylvia locked up the office and they went down to the cafeteria. It was sparse with employees and so was the food.

"Everyone is on vacation today," Carol complained as she surveyed at the meager choices.

Sylvia didn't know what to choose either. Most of the salads were looking wilted. She finally settled on a sandwich. Carol was waiting for something to be cooked, so Sylvia checked out and sat down. She stared at the trees on the property. You could feel the pressure building outside. Her temples were throbbing. It was cloudy but didn't look like rain.

Carol finally sat down and they both started to eat without much conversation.

"What are you doing over the fourth?" Sylvia asked Carol.

"I'm headed to the beach with my Mom," Carol said. "and I'm packed and ready to go! You?" she asked.

"My Mom is coming down," she told Carol, "she invited Marian, Owen and his parents for a barbecue and to watch the fireworks from the front yard." Sylvia's voice was unenthusiastic.

"What's wrong?" Carol asked.

"Nothing...really," Sylvia said, hesitating.

"C'mon, girlfriend," Carol pressured, "Fess up! It must have to do with Owen."

Sylvia sighed and stirred the straw in her glass. "I don't know," she said. "We didn't exactly have a fight, but...I don't know. It's weird." She shook her head and took another bite of her sandwich.

"Well," Carol said, "he's most likely upset with Thurmont," she told Sylvia. "They won't let him return to work until his charge has been cleared."

Sylvia groaned. "He was afraid of that," she said. She didn't want to divulge what she knew about Anna, Ed or the ooze theory. Carol would think she had gone crazy.

"So you had a lover's spat," Carol said. "Making up will be terrific," she grinned.

"I don't know," Sylvia said. "The cops are keeping a close eye on us," she told Carol. "It's strange to be half in and half out of a relationship, and to have voyeurs hovering all over you, watching your every move."

Carol made sympathetic sounds. "I can't imagine," she said.

"Look," Carol said, "I'm sorry to cut this short, but I want to leave a little early today, so I'm going to scoot back upstairs," she said, "and don't worry!" she demanded.

Sylvia finished her sandwich and drink. The cafeteria had cleared, even more, so she went back to the office. She felt like doing absolutely nothing. She tried to call Jon, but he was away for the weekend. Her spirits flagged. She checked her email, surfed the Internet and wrote a long newsy note to Gwen. As soon as the clock struck four, she locked the door, hurried down the hallway and headed for home.

It seemed strange to be back in her house and all alone. Despite the heat, the house smelled stuffy and Sylvia opened up all of the windows to let it air. She checked messages, but found none of interest and got to work getting unpacked. It was late by the time Sylvia finished her laundry, vacuumed and placed the house in decent order. Then she realized she was hungry. Not wanting to go out, Sylvia called to a local pizza place to deliver dinner. She sat outside in the waning light to wait for the delivery. Boats were filling up the bay and even the water seemed as tired as she as it lapped at the shore lazily. Even the wake from the speedboats appeared to be lackadaisical. Something was different and she couldn't think what it was. She stared at the water until a loud clearing of a throat made her jump. It was the delivery guy and after recovering, she handed him the cash as well as a generous tip before getting a second cold beer from the refrigerator.

She sat in the living room at a tray table, turned on the television and started to eat. After about five minutes of channel surfing, she decided what was on was moronic, and turned it off and stared at the water again. She had to admit to herself that she was lonely. She had become quite used to living with Marian and Owen and had enjoyed their company. Clouds were definitely gathering and she hoped it wouldn't rain for the Fourth of July celebrations. She kept staring out the French doors and the windows. Something was different. It finally struck her that someone had taken the time to cut her grass! Sylvia stood up and walked over to the French doors. Whoever had cut her grass had also taken the time to trim. Owen. It had to have been him. She wondered if this was a form of apology.

CHAPTER TWENTY FOUR

For man is of a quickening spirit and the earth, the strong, incoming tides and rhythms of nature move in his blood and being.
--Henry Beston

"They did a good job," a familiar voice said behind her.

Sylvia whirled around and saw the Green Man, lounging on her couch, one leg crossed over the other and arms stretched out along the back.

"You," Sylvia stated, "Did you cut the grass?" she asked.

The Green Man's laugh was answer enough. It was such an ebullient laugh and even the corners of her mouth turned up involuntarily.

When he had finished laughing and wiped away a tear he said, "I can make the grass grow, but I don't usually cut it," he said with humor. "I usually leave that to humankind who like to put things in neat, orderly spaces."

Sylvia sat down on the couch next to him. "Well then, it probably was Owen," she said.

The Green Man didn't nod or give her an indication of an answer but sat, looking at her steadily.

"Do you drink?" she asked. "Can I get you something?"

"I do drink," he said, "but, I've brought my own elixir," he said and he pulled out a bottle from a hidden pocket of the green brocade of leaves. It was like a hip flask, yet worked in leaves and twigs of a shimmering glass.

"Do you have a glass or two?" he asked.

"Yes, of course," Sylvia said, hopping up from the couch. She went out to the dining room and pulled a couple of cut crystal tumblers from the china closet, rinsed them and dried them quickly and brought them back to the Green Man.

"This is strong stuff," he warned her as he poured it.

"What is it?" she asked, looking at the clear liquid that seemed to be shot through with rainbows. She sniffed it and it was fragrant with honey.

"I don't have a word that you would understand," he said. "It's like a very strong mead," he explained, "Try it."

Mead. That was a honey wine. Sylvia took a swallow and coughed violently. It was the strongest alcoholic drink she had ever tried.

"Sip at it," the Green Man advised with a broad smile on his face.

She took a sip. It was like nothing she ever tasted—honey-like and laced with herbs, fruit, and flowers. It tasted of the earth and of green. It was sharp, heady and sweet at the same time. She liked it.

"It's lovely," she proclaimed, as she took another sip.

"Good," said the Green Man smiling.

They talked long into the night, sipping at the liqueur and talking. It was much, much later that Sylvia woke up with a start and fell off the couch not knowing where she was. She stood up and rubbed her backside and wondered if it was a dream that woke her. A flash of light filled the room and it was followed by a crack of thunder. The smell of ozone filled the room. The curtains blew violently and Sylvia went to close windows and doors. A moment later, torrents of rain began to come down.

She closed and locked the windows on the first floor, then ran upstairs to close the windows against the rain in the bedrooms and bath. Her own windows she left open a small bit, to allow the breeze to come in. She undressed and lay down on the bed to listen to the storm and try to recapture her memory of the evening. She and the Green Man had talked about so many things. She knew she had asked him again why he was appearing and he answered, again, that there was a crisis that he was needed to assist with. He said there had been a united resonance from people concerned about the Earth. "But," she had asked him, "why me?" He had answered her with an enigmatic smile and said again, that she was needed and that it was in her blood. When he had tried to tell her she was on the right 'path,' she had scoffed at him. She knew he had given her some insights about the murder and now she couldn't remember. Details of the many-threaded conversation were vague. She must have fallen asleep talking. Her dreams had been sensual with Owen as well as the Green Man as a focal point, and this embarrassed her. Sylvia tossed and turned on her bed uncomfortably. The heat had risen in the house and she tore off the top sheet and went to open the windows wider. The violence of the storm had passed and the rain poured steadily. Sylvia crawled back onto the bed, hugged a pillow and fell asleep.

It seemed as if it was a dream when she heard her mother's voice calling to her. She woke dazedly and her Mom was at her door knocking.

"Syl?" she asked coming into the room, "are you okay?"

Groggily Sylvia sat up, "Yes, I'm fine," she said to her mother. "Aren't you awfully early?" she asked.

"Well, a little," her mother told her, "but, it's after nine and I was sure you would be awake," she said remonstrating her a little.

"Nine? Really?" she exclaimed. "I was up a bit late last night," she told her mom, "and I tossed and turned quite a bit with the thunderstorm." As she spoke, Sylvia looked outside. There wasn't a trace of a cloud in the sky. There was definitely no sign of the previous night's storm. It was a sparklingly clear summer's day.

"We had a storm, too," her mother said, "but it rolled through relatively quickly."

"Why don't I go down and make you some coffee," her mother offered, "while you get up and dress."

"Thanks," Sylvia said. She went over to shower and dress letting her hair dry naturally in the warm air, and went down to her mother.

She had made the coffee and poured Sylvia a cup as she walked into the kitchen. Sylvia added some milk and sat down at the kitchen table to sit and sip. She definitely liked her café au lait much better, but didn't want to seem rude. She felt as though she had a slight hangover, head fuzzy, and a slight headache.

"What were you drinking last night?" her mother asked her sniffing at the glass that she had brought in from the kitchen. "It smells quite strong. You should be careful about drinking alone," her mother prattled on with warnings.

"I know, Mom," Sylvia said, "I was upset about some things and had a stiff drink, okay?" She was trying hard not to sound petulant and wondered what had happened to the other glass. She couldn't really tell her mother she had been drinking with a mythological archetype!

"What were you upset about?" her Mom pressed.

"Oh, Owen and I had..." Sylvia paused, "I'm not sure what it was..." she sighed.

"He's going through a lot right now," her Mom said in his defense.

"I know," Sylvia said, "and I feel rather helpless." She got up to put a couple of slices of bread in the toaster and pulled the aspirin bottle from the cupboard.

"Just be there to listen to the good and the bad," her Mom advised.

Sylvia stayed silent and continued to drink her coffee. She thought that this time, perhaps her mother's advice should be heeded. Sylvia was glad she didn't feel too hung over from the Green Man's honeyed liqueur, but she was pensive. Her toast popped and she buttered it and took a bite along with taking the aspirin.

Sylvia finished her first cup of coffee and got up again to make a second cup as café au lait and pour her mother another cup of black coffee. Her mom informed her that she was going to have the basic all-American barbecue with hotdogs and hamburgers, potato salad and baked beans. Mary told Sylvia that Marian and Anne were bringing the watermelon, fresh vegetable tray, and a dessert. She prattled on about the evening and asked Sylvia if she would run down to the liquor store near the marina and pick up a case of cold beer and a variety of wines. Sylvia nodded to the conversation and went to get her keys.

"I'll be back in a couple of minutes," she told her mom as she headed out the door.

"Don't forget a couple of bags of ice," her mom called after her.

Sylvia waved in response. She drove to the liquor store in a haze and picked up all of the items. It was crowded with boaters and tourists. She picked her way through the people and loaded up a shopping cart with the requested items for her Mom. She was trying in vain to remember her conversation with the Green Man. Pieces of their conversation would jump into her memory and then quickly leave her. She knew she laughed quite a bit and he also reassured her that everything was all right. Remembering this allayed some of her fear. She drove home. Sylvia heard the vacuum cleaner humming as she unloaded the car and put the wine and beer in the refrigerator to chill and put the ice in the freezer. She noticed her mom had hooked up her crock-pot and the baked beans were bubbling on the counter, filling the house with their savory scent. She went in search of her mother to find out when everyone would arrive. The day seemed to drag at first as Sylvia cleaned and helped her mother with the potato salad for the arrival of everyone at four o'clock.

When they sat down to a light lunch, her mother said admiringly, "You're really getting the hang of mowing the lawn and the trim work."

"Thanks," Sylvia said ruefully, "but, it wasn't my handiwork this time."

"Oh?" her mother questioned, "Whom did you hire to do the lawn?"

"No one," Sylvia answered her. "I came home yesterday and it was done. I noticed it last night at dinner and I suspect it was Owen."

"That was sweet of him," her mother said, "I'll have to ask him and thank him."

"Me too, I guess," Sylvia said.

"What happened between you two?" her mother asked. "I thought everything was hunky-dory."

"I don't know if it's ever been hunky-dory," Sylvia said wearily, "and I can't really tell you what happened except that he seems to be pushing me away. I guess you could say we almost have a relationship."

"Well, I think that's natural after what he's been through," her mother sympathized more.

"I guess so," Sylvia said.

It was after three when she ran upstairs to shower and decided to change into the sundress she had bought the month before. No sense in wasting it, she thought. She wondered how Owen would be tonight, whether or not he would push her away again, or if he was back to being interested in a relationship. It was confusing and depressing.

It was just after four when Marian, Anne, Phil, and Owen arrived. Sylvia made introductions and offered to get everyone drinks as they headed for the living room and the deck. She barely looked at Owen and it was her mother who asked him if he had cut the grass. Owen looked sheepish and nodded that he had.

"Thank you," Sylvia said as she handed him a cold beer avoiding his eyes.

"You're welcome," he told her, trying to get her to look at him.

Sylvia perched herself on the railing of the deck. Anne commented on how lovely the house was and her mother took her in for a tour with Marian trailing behind. Phil sat back in the deck chair and put his hat over his eyes, looking as though he absolutely belonged in that very spot. Sylvia nearly laughed. She admired his way of tuning out chunks of the world at whim. She and Owen were left, sitting and not looking at each other. Sylvia craned her head to look out at the bay and river. Boats headed up toward the town park in droves honking their horns and sending huge wakes rippling over the water. It would be lovely tonight when they lit up their boats in parade formation. She was looking forward to it.

"Would you like to take a walk?" Owen asked her.

Sylvia turned back to face him. "Sure," she answered and hopped down from the railing. "Beach or road?" she asked him.

"Beach," he told her firmly and he followed her down the steps and toward the water.

They walked in silence down to the water and turned towards the marina. Owen started to say something and then stopped. Sylvia didn't know what to say either and so they continued to walk in silence.

"Syl," Owen said, when they neared the marina, "I'm sorry if I offended you or upset you the other night."

"I don't know if I was offended," Sylvia told him uncomfortably. "You scared me a little and you gave me reason to think about..." she started to say.

"Syl, you have no idea how horrible it was in jail!" he interrupted her with a passionate plea. "I can't even begin to..." he broke off and shuddered at the memory, and then said more seriously. "And I don't like being a scapegoat for a crime I didn't commit!"

They continued to walk and went up the road past the house and past the small nine hole golf course, that was built when the community began. Hardly anyone ever used it these days, thought Sylvia as they walked past, but she remembered when it had been dotted with people when she was a child. Now most of the golfers had died, retired or moved to the larger public golf course down the road. It was near the end of the golf course that they turned to head back to the house and Owen reached out and took her hand. Sylvia didn't tug it away. Owen started telling her about being in jail – the lack of privacy, the stench of some of the other inmates, and the drunken priest that made his way from cell to cell by hanging onto the bars, incompetently giving solace. Sylvia let him talk. They reached the house and Owen became quiet again but she didn't get a chance to talk to him about Anna or her suspicions about Ed. They rounded the corner to the deck. Their parents and Marian were sitting, drinking and talking and turned gentle smiles on them. Sylvia could see it in their eyes; they were planning their future. She almost tugged her hand from Owen's just to rebel.

"Did you have a nice walk?" Marian asked.

They both nodded.

"Syl," her mother said, "why don't you get the burgers and hot-dogs and we'll get the grill going," she said.

Owen walked in with her to get a beer. He pinned her to the refrigerator with a long promising kiss.

Sylvia pulled away a little breathless. "Are you sure this is a good idea?" she asked him.

Owen laughed a bitter little laugh. "I'm not sure I know what is or what is not a good idea," he said. "Life certainly has thrown me a curve," Owen said with a hard note in his voice. He raked back his forelock of curls with his hand before he changed the subject. "You wanted to tell me something," he said to her huskily.

"Later," Sylvia said, shaking her head. "I'm not sure if it makes sense," she told him and glanced over to the doorway to see if anyone was about.

He kissed her again and let her go. It was all she could do not to push away. Flustered she opened the refrigerator and pulled out the meats and some of the condiments. She handed things to Owen, who had pulled out a tray, loaded it and carried it out to the deck. Sylvia pulled out other non-perishable goods and took them to the deck hoping she wasn't too flushed from Owen's kisses.

Phil had lit the grill and was presiding over it with tongs in one hand and a cold beer in the other. Sylvia placed the food on the table as her mother and Anne came over to arrange everything. Sylvia paused at the doorway before she went in to get paper goods and more food. Owen was deep in conversation with Marian, who was looking peaceful and lazily fanning herself while sipping her drink. Anne and her Mother were chatting happily and Phil, well, Phil seemed to always live in his own time warp, but he looked contented as he presided over the grill. It all seemed so normal. If someone took a snapshot of the barbecue, no one would even begin to imagine Owen was out on bail on a murder charge, and that they were all feeling stretched beyond their limits. She felt as though she was caught in the middle of a soap opera although no one was dressed as glamorous as the actors and actresses on television. She went in to get more food.

Sylvia felt distracted during the dinner and didn't contribute too much to the conversation at hand. Instead, she continued to watch the boats sailing towards the town park. Several were docked fairly close to the house. There were quite a few parties on board with music and laughter floating over the water. Owen, on the other hand, was almost animated and kept up conversation with her mother, Marian and his parents. They were laughing and talking. Marian tilted her head and looked at her with a concerned look and Sylvia gave her a wan smile. The sun started to dip as they finished their meal. Sylvia offered to clear and clean-up. She wasn't feeling conversational. Owen followed her in.

"Are you okay?" he asked her when they finished putting the leftovers in the refrigerator and started to load the dishwasher.

"Yes," Sylvia answered.

"But, something's not right," Owen pressed.

"I can't explain it, Owen," she said. "I guess I'm still feeling wary about what you had said to me – is it or isn't it a good idea to get into a relationship right now. What really happened to Anna? Who killed her? Who or what made those horrible marks?" Sylvia said with vehemence as she slammed the dirty dishes into the dishwasher.

He took her in his arms and held her and she broke down with tears of frustration. He held her for a few minutes until the tears nearly stopped and she went to get something to wipe her eyes.

"I'm sorry," she said.

"No need," he said leaning against the counter top with his arms crossed.

"I'm sorry I pushed you away," he started to say.

"But, you were right!" Sylvia burst out interrupting. "The police asked me in different ways what sort of relationship I have with you. Headly was there too. He kept leering at me. It was horrible!"

"Well," Owen said, "I don't give a damn about a lot right now. If I learned anything while being in the jail, I learned that life is too short to not go after what you want." He looked at her meaningfully, and Sylvia held his gaze. "I have an idea," he said.

"What's that?" Sylvia asked.

"I've wanted to hike to the lighthouse for a long time," he told her. "and be there as early as possible. Do you want to go tomorrow?"

"Sure," she said,

"Good!" Owen said. "We can have coffee and watch the sunrise over the water. Sound good?"

Sylvia nodded, not trusting her voice at the moment. Marian breezed into the kitchen.

"Hello, you two," she said. "I've come to get the dessert." She went to the refrigerator to pull out a gorgeous cake with blueberries and strawberries to represent the stars and stripes of the U.S. flag.

They followed Marian out onto the deck. Darkness had settled in and the anchored boats lit up the bay.

"Just in time," her mother said. "The band has been playing patriotic music for a while. I think they're going to start the fireworks soon."

Sylvia and Owen took their cake and iced tea down to the beach. They sat on the grassy edge to the beach as the first pop-pop-pop of fireworks filled the air. Owen lay back and pulled Sylvia down beside him. He put his arm around her as they lay on the grass watching the fireworks. It was a gloriously clear night and the fireworks were brilliant against the blue-black velvet of the sky. Oohs and ahhs from the town and the boats carried over the water. Sylvia's breath caught in her throat as the colors burst radiantly before her eyes. Her favorites were the white fireworks that exploded twice in the air with a rain of snowflake-like brilliance. The fireworks display ended in an orgy of sound and light. The boaters whooped and blew their air horns. Sylvia and Owen sat quietly for a minute before heading back up to the deck holding hands. Behind them, the exodus of lighted boats went down the mouth of the bay and toward deeper water and their nightly slips.

Marian yawned deeply and said she would like to get home at a decent hour.

"I can't imagine why I'm so tired," she said shaking her head.

"That's easy," Mary laughed, "the heat and the stress of the last week or two."

Anne nodded in agreement, looking at Marian with concerned eyes.

"I suppose so," Marian said and she looked at them. "Stop looking at me that way Anne," Marian scolded. "I'm not going to fall down dead," she admonished.

Anne put her arm around Marian and laughed. "That's the last thought on my mind," she said. "I know you can take care of yourself well," she continued, "and us too."

Sylvia turned to Owen and asked, "what time tomorrow morning?

"It would be nice if I could pick you up at about 5:30," he told her.

"In the morning?" she asked incredulously. She gulped.

The rest of the group looked at Owen and Sylvia in surprise, wondering what they were talking about. He explained how he wanted to go out to the lighthouse at first light.

Anne sighed, "It's been years and years since we've done that," she said.

"Well, I wanted to share it with Sylvia," he said.

"Of course," Marian said matter of factly, "then it is definitely our time to say 'adieu."

Owen gave Sylvia a one armed hug and a kiss on the top of the head. They called their good nights and went off in their car. Sylvia waved them off, said good night to her mom and went up to the bedroom to set the alarm as well as a backup one. Wearily, she came back downstairs to yawningly say goodnight to her mother and went back up to sleep.

CHAPTER TWENTY FIVE

The bliss of growth, the splendor of beauty,
Fore yesterday is but a dream and tomorrow is only a vision,
But today well spend makes yesterday a dream of happiness
And every tomorrow a vision of hope.
Look well therefore to this day.
Such is the salutation to the dawn.
--Sanskrit Salutation to the Dawn

The alarm sputtered loudly at Sylvia the next morning. She turned it off and looked at the clock that read four a.m. Groggily she hit the sleep button and woke up at five a.m. in a panic. Running to jump into the shower she hurriedly dressed in the khakis Owen insisted she wear, due to ticks, and a light colored t-shirt. She went down to the kitchen to make coffee and sip it until he arrived promptly at 5:30.

He knocked lightly on the kitchen door and she ran to open it.

"Good morning," he said. "Are you ready?"

"I guess so," she said, "but I haven't had much coffee, so I may be grumpy," she said grimly.

Owen smiled, "I have a whole thermos of coffee for us when we reach the light," he told her.

"Terrific!" she said, and scrawled a note to her mother and locked the door behind her.

Sylvia was just starting to see the sky lighten ever so slightly on her left as they drove to the end of the peninsula. Owen was telling her about a second hike that was, at least, eight miles from the ranger station to the light that he would like to do some time.

"Not today, I hope," Sylvia asked with a note of panic in her voice.

Owen laughed. "When the weather's a bit cooler," he told her.

Sylvia sighed with relief. She looked out into the darkness. The road was up and down and almost swallowed by the canopy of trees that arched high and dark above them. They came to the end of the peninsula and to the minuscule parking lot. No one else was around.

"Here we are," Owen said cheerfully. He helped Sylvia out of the car and went to get a backpack. He smiled at her questioning look.

"Treats," he said, "For when we reach the light."

Sunrise was just beginning but, they still needed the large flashlights that Owen had brought to see the path under the canopy of leaves. Sylvia stumbled over a couple of tree roots, glad that the sky was lightening every minute. The birds chattered in the trees with morning conversation. As they came through the trees and into a field, Sylvia drew in a breath. Three young deer were startled by their appearance and took off through the trees at the other end of the meadow. Owen led her to the edge of the field, through some more trees and they were there, at the bluff with the lighthouse. The sun was just rising in a glowing orb of orange to the east and lighting up the blue-gray of the canal below them. A couple of seagulls wheeled in the sky and some hawks soared over the meadow they had just walked through looking for their breakfast. They both stopped a moment before walking towards the lighthouse and setting down the backpack.

Owen had brought a blanket and pulled it out from the backpack and spread it on the bluff. The breeze that was ever constant on that jut of land felt good after their hike. Sylvia pushed the sweat soaked hair up off her neck and sat down on the blanket. Owen stood next to her at the edge of the blanket. They faced the sunrise.

"Remember in the movie 'City of Angels,'" he said, "when the angels faced the sun to hear its music?" he asked Sylvia.

"Yes," she whispered. "I remember."

"This reminds me of those angels standing on the beach," he said as they watched the sun rise higher and higher, sending a golden glow over them in the early morning light.

After a few minutes, Owen joined her and sat down. He pulled out two thermoses of coffee. Opening one he looked inside, made a face at its contents and poured and handed her a cup of coffee with cream.

"Thanks," said Sylvia.

He reached into the backpack again and pulled out some fruit and some muffins that were most likely made by Marian before he poured himself a cup of black coffee.

"You've thought of everything," Sylvia told him, more than a little surprised.

"I tried," he remarked, "but these muffins are leftovers from yesterday."

"You mean you didn't make Marian get up this morning and bake for us?" she teased him.

"She probably would have, if I asked," Owen said.

Sylvia nodded, sipping her coffee. She looked out over the water to see a tugboat pushing a barge slowly down the river and nibbled at a muffin.

He lay down next to her and propped himself up on one elbow and looked up at her.

"How are you doing?" he asked her.

"Okay, I guess," she answered. "Tired right now," she admitted. "I know Marian is an early riser, and I am too, but we got up in the middle of the night!"

"Why don't you lay down here," he suggested, patting the blanket.

Sylvia drained her coffee and lay down beside Owen. They both lay quite still for a few minutes and then Sylvia turned so that they fit together like spoons. Owen put an arm around her and drew her to him tight. It was extraordinarily comfortable even though parts of her body were tingling wildly; her sleepiness overcame the sexual tension. She was warm and comfortable, feeling Owens deep breaths. He was kissing her hair gently. But, in moments, she was falling asleep nestled in his arms.

She didn't know how much time had passed when she awoke, but the sun was much higher in the sky and her face was hot. Owen was still sound asleep next to her as Sylvia woke up and got her bearings. She had not brought a watch with her but noticed there were other people nearby. A child stared at them, but most were looking at the lighthouse and at the view over the bluff. She shook Owen's arm gently.

"Owen," she whispered.

He turned and made a grunt, reaching for her.

"Owen," she whispered more insistently, shaking him harder, "You need to wake up!"

She poured him a cup of coffee and shook his shoulder again. Finally, he opened one eye and when he saw her he sat up so fast he nearly knocked the coffee from her hand.

"Whoa!" she exclaimed.

"What time is it?" he asked her looking into her eyes.

Sylvia shrugged, "I have no idea," she said and showed him her bare wrist.

He pushed the hair out of his eyes as he sat up, took a long draw on the coffee and then glanced at his watch, a was a little-taken aback. "It's after 10," he told her.

"What?" Sylvia said incredulously. "But, it only seemed like minutes ago when we fell asleep. We both must have been exhausted."

"Y-e-s," Owen said slowly, "and it was incredibly good to be sleeping and holding you," he said.

Sylvia blushed before she looked away and changed the subject. "We should be getting back," she said. "They'll be wondering where we are."

"I think we're fine," he told her, but he packed up the backpack and led her over to the lighthouse where they read the historical markers.

"They're trying to raise funds to rebuild the keeper's house," he told her.

"Really," Sylvia said. "That's terrific. Can you imagine living this far out from town with no car or way to get through easily? That road leading down to here is a nightmare. I can't imagine it being dirt and navigating it by horse and buggy."

"Well, I expect most of the supplies came by boat," Owen pointed out.

"You're right," Sylvia said, "I wasn't thinking."

"Are you still hungry?" Owen asked.

"Starving!" Sylvia exclaimed.

"Let's hike back and go out for brunch in town," he said. "The Lighthouse Diner has great pancakes," he told her.

"With sausage?" she asked.

"The best," he replied.

They hiked back toward the car. More people were heading out to the point and they greeted Owen and Sylvia cheerfully as they walked past. Her insect and sun repellant had long worn off and she slapped at stray mosquitoes that kept hovering near her sweaty body. They didn't really talk and Sylvia kept noticing the lush greenness overhead and the change from the vibrant and light spring green to the deep, verdant summer green. The cacophony from the birds had changed to a buzz of insects. Underneath she felt the hum of the forest. It wasn't something she could hear directly, but she could feel the happiness of the trees and life around her. It was a connectedness that she could feel of everything in the forest. It was a nice tangible feeling that made her smile. This was a good place. She glanced up at Owen. He was oblivious to what she was feeling, but he did wear a smile on his face. They sort of burst upon the small parking lot that led to the lighthouse and found it packed with cars. Owen had to maneuver carefully not to hit anyone as he backed and twisted and turned to get his little compact out of its space. They drove towards town in silence. Part way up the road, Owen took Sylvia's hand and just held—not clutching, nor holding tightly, but just—holding. She held on too.

The town was crowded. The Pennsylvania Navy had invaded the North Bay for the holiday weekend and the streets were busy. Shoppers crowded the streets and sat on the small decks to the restaurants. Sylvia and Owen sat inside in the cool air conditioning rather than on the little deck attached to the restaurant and ordered pancakes and eggs and sausages. The waitress was red-cheeked, smiling and missing a couple of teeth, but very nice. She reminded Sylvia of descriptions of a red-cheeked dairy maid from folklore. She left them be and unobtrusively filled their coffee cups when they started to empty.

"I keep putting you off about Anna," he said. "I really haven't wanted to think about it or face thinking about it."

Sylvia nodded and urged him to go on with her eyes as she sipped the coffee.

"I don't know what caused those tracks on her body, but I would like to find out," he said. "The problem is that I'm not allowed back onto the property until this whole thing is cleared up."

"If I got you samples, would that help?" Sylvia asked him.

"I'm not sure you should be out there with a murderer running loose," he said putting his hand over hers. "It's too dangerous."

Sylvia hadn't considered this. Before she could say anything, their waitress brought their food over to them. Owen dug into his pancakes and sausage and Sylvia took her time savoring the nutty flavor of the buckwheat pancakes.

Finally, she asked, "You had some theories, what are they?"

"It's too far out," he said, but I feel it's some kind of organism making those tracks. The question is what kind of organism? There's nothing out there to go on for even a theory."

"What are they referring to when they are talking about the numbers?" Sylvia asked.

"Oh," Owen answered. "As I said before, Anna was manipulating data to make her department look good and then, I learned, she was sleeping with the EPA agents so that they would let some of the mistakes slide by. I'm not sure how cleaned up Thurmont is from the Superfund clean-up," he told her wryly. "It's still a dicey situation."

"Oh!" Sylvia exclaimed softly, her eyes getting wider by the minute.

"Look," Owen said, brushing back the forelock, "I shouldn't even be talking about this—especially in such a public place," he told her with frustration tingeing his voice. "I had planned to tell you this at the lighthouse and more, but we fell asleep," he said and shrugged his shoulders.

"But as you said earlier," Sylvia reminded him gently, "It was wonderful to sleep. I think we both needed the rest," she said.

"And the companionship and the comfort," he finished.

Sylvia nodded her head, "Yes," she told him. "Definitely."

`"I don't know," Owen said, sighing again. "The equipment I have is crude compared to the lab at Thurmont. I'm not sure what to do," he said pushing his hair back again and pushing his glasses up on his nose.

The waitress interrupted again, taking away their empty plates and then came back and asked if they wanted more coffee. Both answered 'no' and Owen asked for the check.

When they were back in the car, Sylvia said, "I think it's important to get those samples. We just need to figure out a way to get them tested," Sylvia said. "And, since you can't go into Thurmont and you can't leave the area, that might be a little difficult."

"I know," Owen said gloomily.

"It's all going to work out," Sylvia said determinedly, "It has too."

Owen took her hand and squeezed it. He drove her home. Her mother was gone. Owen followed Sylvia inside and Sylvia sat down on the couch looking out at the water.

"It's a shame you don't have your swimsuit along," she remarked to Owen.

He had sidled up to her on the couch and had begun kissing her softly on the hair and was working his way down to her lips. It was difficult, but Sylvia pushed him away gently.

"I'm not sure this is such a good idea," she told Owen hesitatingly.

He looked at her a little askance before he asked, "Why?"

"Just as you told me before," Sylvia said, "We need to be careful with everything that has been going on."

"Well," Owen said firmly, "I honestly don't give a damn anymore." He reached out to take her in his arms and she moved away.

"Owen," Sylvia said, "I don't jump into relationships lightly either. We haven't had a chance to talk about this and I don't want to jump into anything with the police and the paparazzi breathing down our necks! The police have already questioned whether you and I have a relationship and I said "No!" Give me a little time," she asked softly and beseechingly, "please?"

Owen moved a little further away from Sylvia on the couch and raked his fingers through his hair. She sat with her hands twisting in her lap.

"Okay," he said finally and looked at her and changed the subject. "You know, Anna was a master. She is still hurting people –even though she is dead," he said gritting his teeth. "She's the reason why we can't be together," he said bitterly.

"That's what Grace said," Sylvia told him.

"Grace who?" he asked.

"Anna's stepmother," she said patiently. "I mentioned her the night you got out of…"

"Jail," he finished.

"Yes," Sylvia said. "She said that Anna was so hurt as a child that she would do anything to hurt someone," Sylvia paused. "Sad," she said.

"Yeah, well…" Owen said losing his train of thought. "She made a lot of enemies. I wonder how the police are cataloging all of this."

"If we can find some sort of laboratory that you can use," Sylvia suggested changing the subject from Anna, "then maybe we can find out what's going on with that muck and with whatever caused… "she stopped and swallowed, "whatever happened to Anna."

"Don't get your hopes up," Owen told her. "I'm barely above house arrest."

"I know," she sighed, "but there must be a way. Have they stated how she was murdered yet?"

Her mother came in through the kitchen calling out a cheery 'Hello!' interrupting their conversation.

"We're in here," Sylvia called back.

"How was the hike?" her mother asked.

"Great!" Owen said. Sylvia nodded in agreement.

"I haven't been down there for years and years," Mary said. "I understand there's a fund to rebuild the keeper's house."

"Yes," Sylvia answered, "We read about it on the sign."

Her mother prattled about her memories of going to the lighthouse as a child. She had been out shopping for some sales at the local outlet mall.

"By the way," she mentioned. "Marian expects us for dinner."

As much as she loved Marian, Sylvia was weary of the social expectations of the last few days. She wanted to be by herself for awhile, but she didn't say anything. Marian picked up on it when they arrived later that day, asking if she was all right.

"I think I'm weary," Sylvia said, "I wish I could sleep for a couple of days," she told her. She had come into the kitchen to help Marian with the salad. Everyone else was laughing and talking out on the patio.

"The stress of what has happened has taken toll on all of us," Marian told her. "And, it will be more than a day or two until you, I mean we, will feel almost normal again. Don't you agree?" she asked Sylvia.

"Did you ever reach Jon?" Marian asked her.

Sylvia shook her head, "No," she told Marian, "His secretary said he was out of town until Tuesday."

"Ahh," Marian said, understanding, "He's probably out on his boat," she told Sylvia. "He has a huge sailboat and Jon loves to meander down the bay every chance he gets."

"Marian," Sylvia asked, suddenly inspired. "Do you still have contacts at the State University?"

"Some," Marian admitted, "Why?"

"Do you know of anyone in the biology or chemistry department?" Sylvia asked.

Marian thought for a moment, "Yes," she said, "One of the biology professors was active in the Greenways project that Holly and I were involved in. Why?" she asked curiously.

"I wondered if there was a lab that Owen could use in the area," Sylvia told her. "He wanted to run a couple of tests and use some microscopic equipment."

"I'm sure he could have access," Marian said, "Especially during the summer. I think their classes are at a minimal level. I could give him a call."

"You would need to talk to Owen to see what he would need," Sylvia said.

"All right," Marian agreed. "I'll do that as soon as I can."

"Thanks," Sylvia said, with a sigh of relief. Maybe they could start to find some answers instead of things lying stagnant while the police figured out what was happening.

She went to get everyone for dinner. It was eminently cooler inside than out with the old house's thick walls. They sat, and Sylvia could hear the hum of the whole house fan. A slight breeze tugged at the curtains at the windows. After talking to Marian, Sylvia relaxed visibly during dinner Marian had made and joined in with the laughter at the table. Looking around the room she was surprised to easily see auras. Anne's aura was a vivid orange color and Phil's a medium blue. Marian's was a mixture of golden yellow and dark blue and her mother's a golden glow around her head. Owen's was a mix of blue and green. Sylvia did not realize she was staring, but Owen looked at her quizzically. She smiled at him and he flashed a grin that made her smile deep inside. After dinner, while they did their usual chore of cleaning up, Sylvia told Owen she had asked Marian about the use of a laboratory at State University.

He was surprised and looked at her with what Sylvia thought was an odd look.

"What?" she questioned. "What's wrong?"

Owen didn't answer at first but just shook his head.

"I think you're assuming a lot," he said. "First, you're assuming that something in that soil is responsible for Anna's condition and or her death. Secondly, you think we're going to find something in the soil. How did you come by that conclusion?" he asked her. "Also, you're assuming I know what I'm looking for and I haven't a clue!"

Sylvia gave a little shrug, surprised at his reaction. "Just a hunch," she murmured.

"A hunch isn't scientific evidence," he said, his voice rising.

"Okay, okay," Sylvia said, "I don't want to fight about this! I thought I was helping."

"Let's get the lab first, okay?" he told her. "Then we can discuss how to proceed."

"All right," she agreed, not happy to wait.

Sylvia was relieved the next morning when her mother left early to get a head start on the holiday traffic. It had been a peaceful weekend with her mother, but she was ready for some quiet time in her own house. Sylvia had finally stopped thinking that it was 'Gran's house' all the time and had started to think of it as her own home. She was still sitting at the kitchen table and as she looked around, loving the house, but thinking of a few changes. She wondered what might be a first easy project, and decided on painting the small bathroom on the main floor. She took her coffee and went into the bathroom to look around. Gran had not updated it because it had been used as a place to dump wet swimsuits and wash off the sand from swimming. Some of the paint had cracked near the ceiling. First, it needed a good scrubbing and Sylvia began the job industriously. Forty-five minutes later, everything was sparkling and she was grimy. She took a second shower and headed for the home improvement store to look for ideas. The tile was still in good shape. It was small squares of polished ceramic in a neutral sand color. Sylvia liked blue and finally chose a soft French blue that would not make the room look too small. The salesperson tried to sell her wallpaper border and tempted, Sylvia took a look through several books. She opted for a lighthouse border that complimented the paint that she chose. Laden with her purchases Sylvia set off for home and turned on the radio at top volume and began to paint. She was just finishing when the phone rang and she ran to answer it.

"Hello," she said breathlessly, hoping not to get paint on the portable phone.

"Hello," a deep voice answered that she did not recognize.

"You sound like you're breathing heavy," the voice said.

"Who is this?" Sylvia asked, annoyed at the plain rudeness of the anonymous caller.

"Sorry," the voice said, introducing himself, "This is Richard, Richard Headley."

"Oh!" Sylvia replied more than a little surprised.

"I was wondering if you were busy this evening," he said, "I thought you might want to go out to dinner."

Sylvia was so surprised at his invitation she almost dropped the phone into the bucket of paint. She finally recovered, "Thank you, but no," Sylvia answered him. "I'm right in the middle of a home improvement project and I'm covered in paint," she told him lying just a little, seeing only one or two specks of paint color on her.

"Another time then," he told her. "See you tomorrow." He hung up the phone.

Sylvia stared at the dead phone line in her hand—surprised, appalled and stumped, not knowing what to do. She put the phone back in its cradle and went to finish up the painting and clean-up her tools. She cleaned herself up and poured herself a tall cold glass of water, and came out onto the deck to sip at it. Headley calling her was a shock and it rattled her nerves. Sylvia changed out of her paint clothes and went shopping for accessories for the new bath. She found new curtains, shower curtain and hand towels all with a lighthouse motif similar to the one in the border. Excited Sylvia returned home to check to see if the paint was dry and to begin to hang the border. She had never attempted wallpapering before, but this border was self-sticking and went on relatively quickly. Sylvia was worried about leaving air bubbles and was grateful the saleswoman had talked her into getting a smoothing tool at the home improvement store. A couple of hours later she hung the curtains and shower curtain and stood back to admire her handiwork. Pleased with the results, she poured herself a glass of wine and nibbled on some pepperoni and cheese. Finally, Sylvia made herself a sandwich for dinner and flipped channels on the television. Vaguely, she wondered what Marian, Owen, Phil, and Anne were doing today. Somewhere in the back of her mind, Sylvia remembered a tour of a historical site nearby. Sylvia went in search of a book, then sat on the deck, propping her feet on the railing. She read until dusk started to intrude, and she was straining her eyes.

The next day, Mr. Carter had taken another vacation day and Sylvia was on her own in the office. Carol was busy, so Sylvia puttered putting finishing touches on the plans for Bay Days. She emailed Carol to see if she was interested in helping out and throwing out the carrot of overtime pay. Then Sylvia asked if and when they could meet for lunch. Ed delivered a bunch of boxes midmorning. His arm was still wrapped and the skin around the bandage was bright red and angry looking.

"Any better?" Sylvia asked when he greeted her.

"Nah," Ed said, shaking his head. His normally smiling visage was clouded. "The doctors can't figure it out," he told her. "They gave me a new medicine and they want me to go for more tests, but I don't have the sick time built up yet."

Sylvia's stomach jumped uncomfortably when she looked at the bandaged hand and angry red skin. She glanced back up at Ed and thought she could see a glimmer of fear in his eyes.

"How's your boyfriend?" he asked her changing the subject.

"Not my boyfriend," Sylvia said ruefully, "but, a friend. Fine," she answered, "for the circumstances."

"Any leads on the killer?" he asked her.

"I wouldn't know," Sylvia told him honestly.

"Hmm," Ed said and paused before he said, "I'd better get back to work," he said.

"Thanks," Sylvia said, "I think," she told him with a grin. "It looks like more work has arrived for me."

He wheeled the dolly with the boxes to a corner and left. Sylvia unpacked the Bay Days pamphlets and looked through the rest of the boxes. There were posters, pencils, and balloons as well as promotional literature on the company. Her pamphlets were among the boxes and she took a couple for herself and a set to send to her mom.

Carol was shocked, but not surprised that Headley had called her over the weekend. She made comments that Sylvia was 'fresh meat' in the company and warned her to be careful. After a long chatty lunch with Carol, Sylvia returned to the office only to stand still in the doorway, staring. A gorgeous bouquet of delphinium, roses, stock and summer flowers sat on her desk. She looked carefully, but there wasn't a card. Immediately she thought of Owen and traced the delicate bloom of a miniature iris with her finger. She picked up the phone to call Owen to thank him. No one was home, so she left a message on the answering machine with a cheery hello to Marian and asking if Owen would give her a call when he had a chance.

It was shortly after Sylvia got home that Owen knocked at the kitchen door. Sylvia ran to open it. When Owen stepped into the kitchen, Sylvia flung herself at him crying with a delighted, "Thank you! Thank you! They're lovely!"

Owen pulled himself away from her carefully to ask, "What are you talking about?"

At this, Sylvia took a step back herself. Confused she said, "Flowers. Didn't you send me the flowers?" She gestured to the bouquet that she had placed on the kitchen counter until she had a chance to water them.

Owen looked flushed and then looked sheepish. "No," he admitted. "I didn't send them, but I wish I had."

Sylvia didn't know what to say, nor did Owen. They both looked at the beautiful bouquet of flowers. Their silence was slightly uncomfortable.

Finally, Owen asked, "Do you mind if I have a beer?"

Sylvia shook her head slightly and Owen went to the refrigerator and took out a beer.

"Want one?" he asked her.

The still silent Sylvia nodded. Then she said more to herself than to Owen, "If it wasn't you, I wonder who sent me the flowers?"

"Secret admirer?" Owen suggested teasingly, with his usual grin returning.

"Not likely," Sylvia snapped slightly sarcastic.

They walked out to the deck and sat in silence again. The airspace between them was filled with tension. A motorboat roared past leaving a wake that lapped frantically at the shoreline. Somewhere nearby a water bird cried out answered by the joyful cry of children somewhere down the beach.

"Where do we stand, Sylvia?" Owen asked her.

Sylvia squinted in the late afternoon sunlight and continued to look out at the water. The glare of the sun made her eyes water and a thin film of tears covered her eyes. She wiped at them absentmindedly.

"I don't know," she said with a slight bitter edge to her voice. "Somewhere between friend and friendlier, I guess."

He reached across the tense bit of airspace from his deck chair to hers and took her hand. The familiar fire started to kindle inside of her.

"I'd like it to be friendlier," he said.

"But, that's impossible right now, isn't it?" she asked and pulled her hand from his.

Sylvia stood up and walked over to lean heavily on the deck. She stiffened at first when he got up and came over, laying a hand on her back.

"Yeah," he said, "I know how it seems but, it's not entirely impossible," he murmured as he rubbed her back.

Sylvia relaxed only slightly. Finally, she turned to him and he kissed her gently and persistently. As their kisses turned passionate, the telephone rang.

Sylvia pulled away reluctantly and ran to answer it. She heard Owen mutter an expletive and she was smiling when she picked up the phone.

"Hello," she answered the phone a little breathlessly.

"Hello," the voice said on the other end. "You sound good all out of breath."

"Who is this?" she asked sharply.

"Did you like the flowers I sent?" the voice persisted.

"Who is this?" she asked again.

"Richard Headley," he answered. "Did you like the flowers?" he asked again.

Sylvia was stunned.

"Sylvia?" he asked.

"Yes," she answered, "They're lovely. Thank you," she said automatically.

"Excellent," he said confidently and comfortably. "See you tomorrow."

Sylvia stared at the telephone in her hand. Finally, she hung up the phone, picked up the flowers from the kitchen counter and threw them in the trashcan with a loud 'whump!' Owen walked into the kitchen just then to see what was taking her so long.

"What are you doing?" he asked aghast, looking at her as if she had gone crazy.

She gave the trashcan lid a satisfied slam before she turned to answer him.

"Headley," she told him flatly. "Headley sent the flowers."

"Headley?" Owen repeated, not quite believing what she had said. "What does he want with you?" he demanded.

Sylvia met his eyes evenly. "He's asked me out," she told him a little defensively.

He continued to look at her questioningly.

"A...a couple of times," she admitted haltingly.

Owen's eye's first widened in surprise and then narrowed with jealousy. Sylvia changed the subject. She didn't want to get into it.

"Come and see what I did yesterday," she said pulling him out of the kitchen to the adjacent powder room.

Owen admired her handiwork. “You did this yourself?” he asked.

Sylvia nodded proudly.

“It looks great,” he told her. He put his arm around her to give her a one armed hug and her stomach protested violently by growling loudly.

“Have you eaten dinner?” he asked her.

“No,” she said laughing, “Can’t you tell?”

“Do you want to go out?” he asked.

“No,” she said firmly. “I haven’t seen any reporters around lately, but I don’t want to add fodder to this craziness.”

“I understand,” he said. “Shall we order take out?”

“Okay,” she answered.

The press had abated and turned to other more current news after the flurry of paparazzi when Owen had been released on bail. Sylvia didn’t want to take any chances and was relieved that reporters were no longer attached to her doorstep at home and at work. They argued amiably over what they wanted and what delivery services were available. They finally settled on a white pizza and waited on the back deck with twilight falling around them. When the pizza delivery guy came and went, they settled down to eat. Over slices of pizza and a couple more beers, Owen told her that his parents had returned home. Owen shared that he was concerned that Marian might be shunned for harboring a charged murderer at her house as she went to her various volunteering efforts.

“Marian wouldn’t care,” Sylvia told him.

“I know,” Owen sighed, “but, she doesn’t need anything like this.”

“Well, I know I’m glad the press has abated,” Sylvia said, “At least until the next phase of the investigation.”

“Don’t remind me,” Owen said. “Jon should be back in the next day or two and then hopefully, we can move on and get this resolved.”

He finished up a last bit of pizza and swigged the last gulp of his beer and turned to go. Before he went to his car, he took her in his arms.

"Look," he said, "When this is all over, we can put the 'friends' part to rest and become much friendlier."

Sylvia looked up at him. "That would be a good idea," she murmured before he bent down to kiss her good night. Holding back from Owen was difficult, but for the moment, she knew it was in their best interests.

CHAPTER TWENTY SIX

For where your treasure is, there your heart will be also.
--Matthew 6:21

Sylvia jumped each time the phone rang or a shadow of someone passed by the office doorway. She did not want to see Richard Headley or hear from him. She was so nervous that when Mr. Carter came out to speak with her, she nearly jumped from her chair.

"Everything all right?" he asked.

"I guess so," Sylvia answered, hesitating. She paused for a moment thinking once again that he reminded her of Lou Grant in Mary Tyler Moore and said in a rush, "No, everything is not all right." She told Mr. Carter about Headley calling and asking her out.

Mr. Carter pushed the few hairs left over his pate back over and over. He looked up at her and shook his head.

"I'm mighty sorry to hear that," he said dismally. "Because I have a new assignment for you."

"What is it?" Sylvia asked, mystified.

He hesitated before he answered, "I have received a directive of sorts," he started.

"The company wants to impress some visitors in hopes to lure them into large sales, and a possible sell out of this division," he said. "They want to give them the full treatment and show them the area," he told her.

"A sale?" Sylvia asked.

"Well, the murder and the bad press from the Superfund clean-up was not a good thing for big brother. Word has come down they're thinking of selling this division and they want it to be as attractive as possible to the potential buyer," Mr. Carter told her.

"What happens if it's sold?" Sylvia asked. "What happens to everyone's jobs?"

Mr. Carter shrugged and pushed back on his balding pate.

"What does this 'show' have to do with our department?" Sylvia asked, "Wouldn't they want the big time marketing folks to come in?"

"We're part of the marketing package," he said miserably. "They would like us to take over with some of the marketing due to changes in personnel, vacations, etc."

"What does this have to do with Headley?" Sylvia asked.

"Headley would like you to accompany him and these visitors," he told her.

"What?" she gasped.

Mr. Carter nodded and said, "They want a pretty girl or two to accompany them on their visit."

"Oh...my...God," Sylvia gasped with ample pauses between her words. "That's barbaric!"

"Right," Mr. Carter said acerbically. "I'm sorry Sylvia, I knew he was..." Mr. Carter struggled for words, "a little eccentric, but I never expected him to pursue you in this fashion. I suppose now that Anna is gone..." he broke off. What went unsaid was the exact thing that worried Sylvia.

Sylvia swallowed hard and said, "When does this little party take place?"

"Friday," Mr. Carter stated, "Friday evening and Saturday."

Hysterically and briefly, Sylvia thought of quitting her job, but calmed down to ask, "What's expected of me?"

"Just go along for the ride as they tour of the area," Mr. Carter told her. "Tell them about the company, our environmental efforts, go out to lunch, and dinner of course," he paused, "and possibly think of some touristy spots to share with them."

"Whew!" Sylvia said. "That's quite a bit! But, it's over the Bay Days celebration. I can't possibly help if I'm to man the booth."

"Well," Mr. Carter said, "It's what I came out to talk to you about. I'll come down for some coverage to free you up."

"There's no way I can get out of this?" she asked meekly.

"I don't think so," Mr. Carter said. "It would be quite awkward at this point."

"All right," Sylvia said. "Let sit down and brainstorm some ideas. How bad can it be?" she asked, speaking more to herself than to Mr. Carter.

They sat and brainstormed possible visitation spots. Sylvia called Carol for some other ideas. By the end of the day, they had formulated a plan that put Sylvia in place for Friday and Headley in for the weekend.

"We'll split up the task of calling for reservations tomorrow," Mr. Carter told her.

"Go home and relax and don't worry."

"Okay," Sylvia said, giving him a rather wan smile.

Headley had not been by all day and she was relieved. She wondered what sort of game he was playing.

When she got home, there was a message from Jon. He said he would call again. Sylvia put on her swimsuit and took a swim. The day was hot and humid and the water felt deliciously cool. She stepped cautiously over the pebbles until she came to the sandy bottom of the bay. A cold spring bubbled up beside her. She stood in the flare of cool water, shivering delightedly, then paddled about to a warmer spot. Finally relaxed, Sylvia turned onto her back and floated looking up at the sky. She wasn't sure how long she floated. Sylvia emerged from the water smiling, still feeling the tug from the wakes and the tiny waves. Slightly staggering up the beach, Sylvia stepped into the shower in the newly renovated bathroom and turned on the steaming water. When she turned off the shower, Sylvia heard the phone ringing shrilly. Throwing a towel around her, she ran to pick it up, praying it wasn't Dick Headley. It was Jon and he wanted to hear her ideas about the murder. In short order, she shared her fears with Jon. He seemed quite interested and warned her to keep the information to herself. He also said to call him immediately if the police had any further questions for her and that he would represent her. Sylvia agreed and hung up the phone.

Sylvia went straight to bed after the call, worn out from the worry about Headley from the day, swimming and the emotional drain from talking to Jon.

It was later than she expected when she woke up the next morning, birds chirping wildly. She rushed to work and trotted down the hallway, not paying attention. She was nearly running by the time she reached the office and rounded the doorway only to bump into Richard Headley as he was leaving.

"Hmmm, I like it," he said smoothly, "when a lovely young woman just rushes into my arms."

Sylvia, quite flustered, stepped back, not knowing what to say.

She swallowed hard, "Excuse me," she said to Mr. Headley.

He looked at his watch and tapped it, "Running a bit late, are we?" he taunted. "Never fear," he said quite low, "you can make up the time with me."

He let her pass and her hands shook when she sat down at her desk to put her purse in the file drawer. Mr. Carter came out.

"I thought I heard someone," he said, looking at Sylvia. "You were fortunate, you just missed Headley."

"No, I didn't," Sylvia said. "I literally ran into him coming into the office."

Mr. Carter grimaced and then told her, "He thought the plans looked great."

"What's next?" Sylvia asked.

"Coffee, first," Mr. Carter grinned, "and then we can split up the reservation making as we discussed yesterday."

The day seemed to go paradoxically slow for Sylvia, but she was surprised how late it was when the phone rang at 3:30. It was Marian asking her for dinner. She gladly accepted feeling, haunted by Headley.

Driving to Marian's was like driving home. Sylvia relaxed when she hit the 'no trespassing' sign on the road that led to Marian's house. Owen and Marian were sitting outside on the patio. Both were reading and Owen had his feet propped up on another chair arm. He swung his long legs down and stood up when she pulled into the parking area. Marian gave her a warm hug and went inside to get Sylvia a glass of wine. Owen held her close for a few moments and gave Sylvia a kiss on her hair before turning up her chin and they kissed slowly and sweetly. Marian returned with the glass of white zinfandel and they sat back on the patio. Sylvia glanced at what Owen was reading, it was an entirely unintelligible text on chemistry. Marian was reading a mystery novel with blood dripping on the jacket illustration. She glanced at the book and then at Marian.

"Not enough murder around?" she quipped to Marian.

"Good author," Marian said after she had taken a sip of her drink, "and good recipes in the back."

"Ahh," Owen and Sylvia answered in unison.

Sylvia felt the peace of Marian's home as it seeped into her like warm, honeyed tea. They sat quietly enjoying the late afternoon sunshine. Sylvia closed her eyes. She was holding her wine in one hand and Owen's hand in the other. The sun started to slip behind the trees in the meadow sending out long shadows and strips of golden sunshine.

Marian had quietly gotten up and gone to the kitchen. She surprised Sylvia when she said dinner was ready, and Sylvia jumped, nearly spilling her wine.

"Sorry," Sylvia said, wiping drips from her hand and the arm of the chair.

"Sorry to have scared you," Marian said, "You're a little jumpy, aren't you?" she asked concerned.

"A bit," Sylvia said, avoiding her eyes for the moment.

They settled to eat in the kitchen where Marian had created yet another memorable dinner of cold cucumber soup, toasted French bread with a chevre Boursin and a Caesar salad.

Marian said, "Jon called. He was pleased with the information you provided him. He's passed it onto the detectives and they're looking into it."

"Have they looked into your computer files yet and checked the emails?" Sylvia asked Owen.

He shook his head. "No use getting any angrier," he said. "I'm practicing patience." He looked at her and they smiled at one another.

"What's been happening with you?" Marian asked.

Sylvia shrugged, "I've gotten pulled into something I really don't want to be a part of at work," she told them.

"What's that?" Marian asked.

Sylvia explained the upcoming Bay Days weekend and her entertaining the visitors with Headley. Owen uttered an expletive or two and then apologized.

"He's never been a nice boy," Marian murmured.

"How do you know him?" Sylvia asked.

"This is a small town," Marian said. "I've been to functions with the Headley's and Richard has always been poor mannered. His parents have babied him beyond belief and gotten him out of every scrape imaginable. He's always been in trouble. Fortunately for him, his parents have had enough money to pay someone off or get him out of his scrape. He thinks he can get anything he wants. He's a big bully."

Owen and Sylvia glanced at each other before they looked at Marian after her diatribe. Their mouths were agape. They had never expected this long tirade from Marian.

"Well that's putting it in a nutshell," Owen said dryly.

His comment broke their mood and they all laughed. Sylvia shared what was going on with Headley's phone calls, flowers, and comments. Marian looked worried and Owen angry.

"Now that Anna is out of his life, he's looking for fresh meat," he muttered none too quietly.

"Funny, that's what Carol mentioned too," Sylvia commented looking at Owen.

Marian just commented 'hmmm….' And they all were quiet as the candlelight flickered over the warm oaken cupboards, table, and floor.

Owen and Sylvia did their usual cleaning up of the kitchen and Marian pulled a cold berry granita out of the freezer. After dessert, they returned to the porch to talk. Sylvia was so relaxed she thought she might fall asleep. The stars sprinkled themselves across a blue-black sky. Black clouds were moving in and snuffing out the stars one by one.

"I think we're due for some rain," Marian commented.

"Hopefully, it will cool things down," Owen said. "The humidity and the heat here are nearly tropical."

Marian chuckled. "England was humid too, only cooler most of the time. I remember many a day of feeling I would never get warm," she told them.

Sylvia lazily wondered out loud what time it was and when Owen told her it was after nine o'clock, she jumped up to go.

"I need to get home," she said, "I have to go to work tomorrow."

"All right," Marian said before she turned to Owen, "Owen, would you follow Sylvia home? I don't trust Headley," she said.

"No problem," Owen said, "I'll go and get my keys."

"There's no need," Sylvia half protested as she thanked Marian for dinner.

Marian gave her a hug.

Owen followed her home in his car and hopped out to open her car door and then the kitchen door. He checked through the house and pronounced it empty before coming back to Sylvia who was sitting in the living room. She had opened the French doors to the breeze that accompanied the front that had moved in. Owen sat down beside her and put his arm around her and Sylvia settled into the crook in his arm. It was only a moment before he was kissing her. There was a rumble of thunder and a crack of lightning. The hair on Sylvia's arms stood on end, but it wasn't from the impending storm.

"Syl," he whispered into her hair, "I'm tired of being patient. I'm sick of worrying if the damn cops will find out. I just don't care anymore."

"Me either," Sylvia whispered back. "I want you," she said, insistence in her voice.

He kissed her deeper, but she pulled away and stood up pulling him by the hand. She led him upstairs to her bedroom. She kicked off her shoes and pulled him down onto the bed beside her. There he started kissing her eyes, nibbling at her ears, and kissing her neck and moving downward. Sylvia thought she would go mad. She wanted to tear off her clothes and his, but he wouldn't let her. He kept kissing her softly and insistently until Sylvia groaned with pleasure. Finally, when she thought she could stand it no longer, he undressed and gently started to remove her clothes. Finally skin-to-skin, Sylvia could feel the fire building, and when they joined she cried out, not only with pleasure but also with the surge of dazzling energy that raced through her body. Much later, she awoke from the deep sleep that had claimed her, she propped herself up on one elbow to look at Owen's sleeping form. Sylvia didn't want to wake him. Gently, very gently, she kissed his shoulder. He moaned and reached out an arm to pull her into him. This time, she began to kiss him. She kissed him awake to start the pleasure again.

Morning came much too soon. Sylvia extracted herself from Owen's clasp. He had been holding her close. She tucked the covers around him and tiptoed downstairs to make coffee. After she made her café au lait, she stepped out onto the deck where it was cool, damp and pearly. It had rained during the night. It had been a slow, steady soughing rain. Now the sky was clear and only the faintest of pink-tinged the horizon. The rest of the world had turned golden in the clear morning sunlight. Sylvia sighed and sipped at her coffee. Her bones felt as fluid as the warm liquid in the cup. She leaned on the railing sipping her coffee and looking out at the water, dazzling in the sunlight. Sylvia showered and dressed and brought up a cup of coffee to place on the bedside table. She whispered in Owen's ear that she had to go to work and to have a good day. He awakened slightly, gave her a kiss, and groaned and rolled over.

Sylvia had never seen Mr. Carter so agitated. He was prancing around, nearly barking orders at her and trying to put final touches on the booth and activities for Bay Days. He was not only concerned about Headley's interest in Sylvia, but it made him nervous that Headley scrutinized everything they did. Sylvia had heard Mr. Carter say under his breath that 'he didn't trust the little bastard." He recruited Ed to head to the town park to set up the tent for the Bay Days celebration on Friday. He re-organized the boxes of handouts. Sylvia just smiled in amusement at him and continued to smile throughout the day.

Carol teased her unmercifully at lunch, "Whoa!" she said and backed away from Sylvia when she came to sit down with her.

"What?" Sylvia asked. "What's wrong?"

"The glow girl," Carol said, "It would knock a person over. I know what you've been up to!" she said slyly.

Sylvia blushed, and then said gravely, "Keep it to yourself, okay?"

"Why?" Carol asked. "When you're in love...and lust," she said the last part for Sylvia's ears alone, "you should shout it to the world."

"But the whole investigation thing," Sylvia said. "We have said we were not involved with one another. And we haven't been until..." she stopped.

"Okay," Carol said and then added darkly, "you'd better stay away from Headley. He'll know right away," she said quietly and emphatically.

Sylvia told Carol about the upcoming weekend assignment. Carol suggested that she roll in poison ivy or something to get out of it and made Sylvia laugh even though the feeling of dread was tightly balled in her stomach.

When she got home, she found Owen was in the kitchen washing and drying lettuce in a salad spinner and scrubbed potatoes glistening on the counter next to a couple of rich looking steaks.

"What's this?" she asked.

"Since we want to keep things low-key," Owen said, "I thought a romantic dinner here would be better than going out."

"Sounds lovely," Sylvia said, surprised and pleased.

Steaks, potatoes, Caesar salad kit and a bottle of wine lay on the countertop. Owen pulled out the wine opener, opened a bottle of rich pinot noir and handed Sylvia a glass. She offered to help, but he told her to sit and relax. Sylvia didn't argue. Owen put the potatoes in the microwave and set the timer. Asking Sylvia to pick up the bottle of wine and an extra glass, he motioned for her to follow him out to the deck where he lit the grill and put on the steaks. Sylvia noticed the table was already set with beautiful fresh flowers and candles.

"Let's sit down," Owen suggested and they sat, looking out over the water. The rain the night before had broken the streak of heat and humidity. The air was warm but dry and it was very pleasant to sit on the deck. Sylvia squinted in the tawny evening sunshine. The river was active with jet skis and water skiers with little gray waves slapping anxiously against the shoreline. It was quite noisy and they had to raise their voices a little over the noise of the boats. Personally, Sylvia thought the cigarette speedboats should be banned, just due to the noise. They roared up the bay without a care and looked like a lot of fun. However, the noise was ear-splitting and grinding as they tried to sit and relax on the deck.

"How was your day?" Owen asked her.

"Fine," Sylvia answered, "Mr. Carter is on a roll getting ready for Bay Days this weekend."

"Did you have any problems from Headley?" he asked her.

She turned to look at Owen, endeared but also amused at his jealousy, "No," she replied. "I haven't seen or heard from him today." She changed the subject. "How about you?" She asked. "How was your day?"

"Same as a lot of others recently," he said. "Quiet. I'm reading a couple of books, helped Marian with some heavy cleaning, mowed her lawn…" he trailed off.

"Busy," Sylvia said feeling like a contented old married couple.

Owen went back to the grill to turn the steaks and back inside to check on the potatoes and work on the salad. This was nice, Sylvia thought. She could get used to this. They ended up eating slowly, savoring their food and each other's company. Their voices were quiet, matching the quietude that had finally settled on the bay. As twilight fell the last chatter of birdsong, the jet skis and boats settled down for the night and everything was hushed. There was a sailboat lazily making its way toward the dock, but if it was motoring, it was quiet. Long shadows from shoreline trees darkened long streaks on the bay's shoreline. Owen lit the candles as lights dotted the bay, the docks, and homes on the water.

"Good news," he said, remembering.

"What?" Sylvia asked him turning her gaze from the water to look at Owen.

"The guy with the lab is on vacation, but will be back this weekend. His colleague didn't see any problem with me using a lab at State next week."

"Great!" Sylvia said. "Let me know when you want me to get samples."

They cleaned up dinner and returned to the deck to sip the last of the wine and watch the sunset. The sun was a bright streak of fiery orange that lasted for a few moments before it sank below the horizon. The sky deepened its blue turning from Cerulean to a dark and dusky blue.

"Do you want dessert?" he asked her in the growing dusk.

Sylvia watched fireflies hover near the water, sending out brief messages to one another. She remembered how many times as a child she had run wildly over the lawn catching them for Gran. It was odd to be feeling all grown up. Part of her wanted to run out and catch those fireflies, shouting in the joy of capture and the even greater joy of letting them go free. But, now she was grown up and she looked at Owen with a different kind of joy in her voice.

"No," she said huskily, "I don't want dessert from the kitchen," she said and Sylvia pulled him up out of the chair and led him up the stairs.

CHAPTER TWENTY SEVEN

It is only when we are aware of the earth
and of the earth as poetry that we truly live.
--Henry Beston

Sylvia couldn't believe how quickly Wednesday passed. She lived for the time when she and Owen could be with one another and worked blindly with a small smile on her face. Mr. Carter was too caught up in the Bay Days preparations to notice that his employee was mooning about, thinking of the previous night or fantasizing what was to come that night with Owen.

She rushed home as quickly as she could and was disappointed that Owen wasn't waiting for her. She heard a car in the driveway and rushed downstairs only to find a dark, blue, unmarked police car with Detective Rogers and Detective Josephson. Sylvia paled considerably and her stomach seemed to fall to the floor. She hung onto the doorframe at the kitchen door. The detectives had started towards the front door and turned when they saw her at the side of the house.

"Ms. Ash?" Detective Rogers said, "Are you all right?" he asked with concern in his voice looking at her pale figure.

They came up to the doorway and Sylvia stood, not moving.

"May we come in?" Detective Josephson asked gently.

"Of course," Sylvia said, recovering, "I'm sorry. I was ..."

"Expecting someone else?" Detective Rogers asked.

Sylvia blushed, "Well," she hesitated, "yes, I was," she admitted.

"Mr. Anderson will be along shortly," Detective Josephson said. He tried to keep the smile from his face.

Surprised, Sylvia led them to the living room and motioned, without speaking for them to sit down. As the detectives sat, she heard more cars and was puzzled. She went back out to the kitchen to see Owen pulling up in his own car, and Marian and Jon in Jon's Mercedes. Owen came with a paper bag and Marian wore a smile. Utterly confused, Sylvia held the door for them.

"Good evening," Jon greeted, "Have the detectives arrived?"

Sylvia nodded and Marian patted her arm. Marian led Jon through the kitchen and into the living room. Owen entered last, taking a moment to kiss Sylvia enthusiastically before they all gathered in the living room.

Everyone was seated and looking solemn. Everyone that is except Owen who was quite jumpy and he would not sit down. Sylvia also noticed that Marian kept looking around. Sylvia looked at everyone quizzically.

Detective Rogers cleared his throat before he said, "Ms. Ash..."

Owen interrupted him with joy in his voice, "Syl, I've been exonerated!" He plopped down beside her and kissed her enthusiastically again and hugged her.

Sylvia couldn't believe it. "What?" she asked.

"Exonerated," Owen told her. "They finally got into my computer and saw my emails to Headley. Also..."

"Also," Detective Rogers said, "Evidence shows that Mr. Anderson could not have committed the murder."

Sylvia looked shocked and then her shock went to joy. She didn't know whether to laugh or to cry. She threw her arms around Owen's neck and hugged him tightly and tears of joy started to stream down her face. Sylvia pulled herself together after a short time. Marian had gone to get a box of tissues and she wiped the tears from her eyes. She looked around at the gathered group.

"Why is everyone here?" Sylvia asked Owen in particular but loud enough for everyone here.

Owen grinned, "Champagne for one thing," he said holding up the brown paper bag.

"And the officers would like to ask a favor of you," Jonathan asked.

Sylvia looked puzzled. Detective Rogers cleared his throat a couple of times before he spoke.

"Mr. Anderson's emails were quite incriminating towards Ms. Hanson," he told her. "In fact, they gave us reason to suspect him originally."

"What changed your mind?" Sylvia asked, curious.

"The autopsy report proved Ms. Hanson's killer was left-handed," he said, "and Mr. Anderson is right handed."

"Ahh," Sylvia said. "But how does this involve me?"

"Mr. Anderson told us that you will be with Mr. Headley this weekend?" he asked her.

Sylvia nodded, still looking puzzled.

"He's a prime suspect, even though his alibi seems air tight," Detective Rogers continued.

Jonathan interrupted, "Owen's emails imply that there are some serious management issues with the environmental dumping," he said, "It's entirely possible that with Ms. Hanson and Mr. Headley's relationship, that they were working together."

"And he's left handed!" Owen said with excited satisfaction.

"We wondered if you would be willing to keep your ears and eyes open in case he slips up," Detective Rogers said. "If he knew that Ms. Hanson was going to be discovered regarding her sabotage, she might think of implicating him."

Sylvia nodded in understanding. "They seemed to have a very odd relationship," she commented.

"Then you'll do it?" Detective Rogers asked.

"Certainly," Sylvia answered.

"You do understand this is all extremely confidential," Jon asked her.

"Yes," Sylvia said, "of course."

"If you start getting some good information," Detective Josephson said, "we may ask if you would wear a hidden microphone so that we can get the information on tape."

Sylvia nodded. While they were talking, Marian had gone to the dining room china cupboard and pulled out some champagne flutes, washed them and brought them in on a tray accompanied by some cheese and crackers.

"Now for champagne," Owen said triumphantly.

He popped the cork and they filled the glasses. Detective Josephson looked at his partner and gave him a knowing wink.

"How about that!" he said, looking at his watch, "will you look at the time! We're officially off duty just five minutes ago," he said. "Thanks!" he said to the offered glass of champagne.

"To freedom!" Owen toasted.

Everyone agreed and raised their glasses in a toast. After drinking and nibbling, Sylvia looked questioningly at the detectives.

Detective Rogers caught her eye and asked, "Yes?"

"I don't know if you can tell me or not," Sylvia began, "but how was Anna killed?" she asked.

"Strangulation," Detective Josephson answered for his partner. "Probably she was strangled from behind. They grabbed her by the throat so hard that they broke her neck."

"Oh, how awful!" Marian murmured.

"But, what about the marks on her skin?" Sylvia asked. "What caused those?"

Detectives Rogers and Josephson looked uncomfortable. Finally, Detective Rogers answered, "We don't know," he said quietly. "The coroner has never seen anything like it. They wondered if it were some sort of cult thing," he said.

Silence hung in the room. Detective Rogers cleared his throat.

"Thank you for your cooperation," he said getting up from his chair. His partner followed suit. "We'll be in touch. Please remember what we discussed does not go beyond this room," he said thoughtfully.

Everyone nodded in agreement. The detectives shook everyone's hand. When they were gone, Marian gave an audible sigh of relief and satisfaction. Jon took her hand.

"More champagne anyone?" Owen asked.

They all held out their glasses for refills and settled back to talk.

"Have you contacted your parents?" Sylvia asked Owen.

"I left them a message that there were new breaks in the case," he said. "I can't even tell them that I'm exonerated yet. The police want to keep it quiet so the killer will slip up somehow."

"They were very serious about the confidentiality part," Jon told them. "It's good of you to cooperate with them, Sylvia."

"There was no choice," she said, moving closer to Owen.

He looked into her eyes and they smiled at each other.

Marian drained her glass of champagne. "We should be going," she said to Sylvia and Owen. She came over to give them each a hug.

"Thank you," Owen and Sylvia said to Jon.

"You're welcome," he returned, "but remember, it's not over yet."

Jon opened the door of his car and helped Marian inside.

"Do you think there is a romance starting to blossom?" Sylvia asked Owen again.

"Possibly," he said, as they watched the car go down the road, "Possibly" as he turned to give Sylvia a long, passionate kiss.

They sat on the couch finishing the bottled of champagne and talking about what was required of Sylvia with Headley. Owen was a little worried, but Sylvia felt better, knowing that the police were keeping an eye on her. "Anyway," she said, "I don't think he's the murderer. Granted, he's a creep and he had motive, but I don't think he killed Anna."

"Who did then?" Owen asked her.

"I don't know," she said, thinking of Ed. She couldn't think if he was right or left-handed. "But, I don't want to think about it right now," she said to Owen turning to him.

"All right, Scarlett. You can think about it in the morning," Owen teased. "Let's go up to bed."

Yawning, Sylvia took the empty champagne bottles and glasses to the kitchen.

Owen brought in the cheese and crackers. They went up to bed and Owen held her tightly for a long, long time.

Sylvia woke earlier than usual. She had been awake, off and on, during the night, not able to shake some of her feelings about who killed Anna. She wondered if there was anyone else who was significant on the list of suspects. The morning was hazy. Mist rose from the bay in a thin layer of fog. It looked mysterious in the early half-light of dawn. It was still humid and Sylvia's thin cotton nightgown clung to her in the moist air. She took her steaming cup of coffee out to the deck. Everything was silent and still. The water gleamed like a piece of mirrored glass beneath the fog. The warmth of the morning air felt good after the chill of air conditioning during the night. Owen liked the air temperature at a near frigid level. Sylvia missed the fresh breeze and white noise of Marian's whole house fan. She sighed audibly and turned when she heard a familiar rustle. It was the Green Man.

"Good morning," she said, "it seems like a lifetime has passed since I last saw you."

He nodded, causing the leaves on his head and beard to rustle more.

"Sylvia, Sylvia, Sylvia," he chanted softly, "Maiden of the woods," he said cocking his head with a sly grin.

Sylvia blushed and started to look uncomfortable.

"Don't fret," he said. "Remember some think of me as the god of fertility." The Green Man chuckled.

"You look quite…" he searched for words, "…content," he said finally.

Sylvia laughed a little and said, "That's a bit surprising considering everything that has happened in the last few weeks, but you're absolutely right. As usual," she added as an afterthought.

She sipped at her coffee and they both looked out at the bay and the rising mist before she spoke again. She told the Green Man about the upcoming weekend with Headley and the deal with the police and how a tiny spot of fear was beginning to grow inside of her.

"I only came to let you know I am nearby if you need me. Don't let fear grow," he advised. "Think joyful thoughts if you can." He took her in his arms to hug her gently and kissed her first on the center of her forehead and gently on each eyelid. The leaves tickled her. "Veriditas," he murmured.

"What did you say?" Sylvia asked in a whisper.

"Veriditas," the Green Man explained, "Remember? It's a term coined by the great Hildegard of Bingen. It means the 'greening of the soul,'" he said stepping back a step but still having a leafy arm cradling her back. "That's something that has been happening to you—recognizing your gift of auras and the ability to feel the life force," he told her. "But you will soon find that your gift is increasing by leaps and bounds."

"Veriditas," she said, trying out the word.

The Green Man smiled. "Call me if you need me," he said and he kissed her eyelids gently before releasing her.

He disappeared and Sylvia shook her head, "How?" she asked the air. And then she blinked. She didn't have to focus for auras, they were brilliant, almost too brilliant as she looked at the bright haze around the plants and the outline of energy on things. It would take her awhile to get used to this new way of seeing. She returned to the kitchen to pour another cup of coffee. When she looked at the vase of flowers Owen had brought to replace Headley's token, she noticed one of the flowers was dying. It was like watching time-lapse photography as she watched the image of the flower dying in a swift, yet minute colored slide show. Sylvia gasped quietly in amazement. She glanced up at the time and hurried to shower glancing first in at Owen's sleeping form. He had moved into the warm spot where her body had been and he was hugging her pillow. His aura was pulsing quietly. She went over to kiss his shoulder and he groaned in his sleep and pulled the pillow closer. She showered and dressed, tiptoed downstairs to get him coffee and brought it back upstairs to the bedside table. She kissed him again on the shoulder and the cheek and said goodbye. He opened his eyes a little and giving her the startled look of a suddenly awakened child, he blinked and pulled her down for a long kiss before letting go.

"Have a good day," she murmured.

"You too," he said.

Sylvia drove to work and couldn't stop thinking of the word the Green Man had murmured. "Veriditas," she would need to look it up on the Internet if she got the chance. She drove, with the darkest pair of sunglasses that she could find, as the auras shone brightly from the life around her. It was difficult to drive. She wanted to sit and enjoy and practice this new way of seeing.

When she arrive, Mr. Carter handed her a typed agenda for Friday and Saturday and suggested that she take the afternoon off to find something 'suitable' to wear to dinner on Friday evening. He waved his hands when he said it and shook his head and she knew he wanted nothing to do with it. "Not my idea," he said.

She looked at him carefully and with her new found sight, she saw that his aura was muddied and slightly gray.

"Are you all right?" she asked him. "You don't look like you're feeling well."

"Oh," Mr. Carter said, "It's just persistent heartburn." He pulled out antacid tablets. "Some people munch on mints," he said, "and I munch on Tummy mints."

She glanced at the schedule and saw that a Limousine would pick her up at her home and they would all be transported to an exclusive Inn and restaurant nearby. Saturday would be brunch, Bay Days, a helicopter ride and then meetings. She was scheduled to be at Bay Days after the chopper ride.

Sylvia sat numbly down at her desk and emailed Carol what was up and spent some time answering email and searching for information on Hildegard of Bingen. She was amazed to learn Hildegard was a 14th century Nun with extraordinarily revolutionary ideas. Hildegard had visions. Sylvia knew from her reading that she most likely was able to see auras. Not having scientific methods, Hildegard matched plants with their characteristics with the illnesses. Sylvia wondered if she could match the auras of the plants with the people…an interesting hypothesis. Sylvia was also fascinated to learn that Hildegard of Bingen wrote and published music and plays. An initial search on the Internet led Sylvia to several recordings. Groups around the world devoted themselves to her choral works. When Mr. Carter told Sylvia to 'shoo' and go off shopping—bosses orders—she thought she might stop by the book and music store to pick up a CD of Hildegard's music and a book on her theories. Sylvia drove carefully to the mall, but she didn't have her heart in looking for an attractive dress to wear in front of Headley. Sylvia found a simple, tailored sleeveless black crepe dress with an interesting neckline and matched it up with black high-heeled sandals. She knew Gran had had some simple dramatic gold and onyx jewelry that would set off the dress well. Satisfied with her purchases Sylvia made her way through the mall to the book and music store. They only had one book on Hildegard of Bingen, which she bought and ordered another. There were several CD's available and Sylvia ended up closing her eyes and making a choice. Leaving the mall, she popped the CD into her car's player and, listened to ethereal women's acapella voices. Sylvia stepped out of the car at home in a daze, the music still in her ears. She automatically went in through the kitchen, dropping her purse on the countertop and walked through to the deck. Owen was there with his feet propped up on the railing, reading. He looked up at her when she came out and jumped up to give her a kiss.

"Are you okay?" he asked looking at her dazed face.

"Yeah," she said softly, and then shaking her head, "Yes," she said. "I was just caught up in a new CD," she told him.

"What was it?" he asked, curious.

"Hildegard of Bingen," she said.

"Who?" Owen asked.

Sylvia gave him a brief rundown on Hildegard and on her music. He went out to get the CD and they sat and listened to it while they had a drink.

"It's not really my cup of tea," Owen admitted, "but, it's not too bad."

"Hungry?" Sylvia asked him.

"No," Owen said. "Not really, it's too hot. What do you have in the bags?"

Sylvia rolled her eyes. "An 'appropriate' outfit for tomorrow night," she said exaggeratedly. "We're to go to the Old Mill Inn for dinner," she told him.

"Wow," he said, "They're pulling out all the stops for these folks.

"They want to sell the company," Owen said. "Do you know who the potential buyers are?" he asked.

"Not a clue," she said.

"Let me see the dress you bought," he said.

She pulled out the little bit of black crepe. Owen asked if she would try it on and when she did, it clung in all the right places.

"Wow!" he commented when she walked into the room. "You look fabulous, I'm not sure I want you to wear that for Headley," he told her.

She walked over to him and he unzipped her in one swift movement and the dress fell to the floor in a little puddle around her feet. She stood in the black high-heeled sandals and her black lingerie as Owen breathed "Wow" again and sent tingles up her spine.

CHAPTER TWENTY EIGHT

The gloom of the world is but a shadow;
Behind it, yet within our reach, is joy. Take joy.
--Fra Giovanni

Sylvia was surprised that Headley had not been a pest this week. She wondered what was up or if he was trying some weird form of reverse psychology. Sylvia was still wary of him and worried most of the morning about the dinner that night. She spent her time going to the local park to scope out the tent site for Bay Days with Mr. Carter. He still didn't look well to her, his aura even grayer than the day before. The intense heat and humidity certainly didn't help and she urged him to drink cold water instead of coffee or caffeinated soda. Ed wasn't looking much better either. He and a co-worker, Joe, had driven a company truck to the site and worked to set up the tent and tables they would use the next day for their display. Ed's arm still had not healed and he was clearly in pain. She helped unload some of the parts and held poles in place while the men heaved and worked to get the tent in place.

They set up tables and Ed said he would be back in the morning with the boxes of materials, display boards and air tank to blow up the balloons.

"Don't forget a couple of chairs!" Mr. Carter called after him.

"God, I hope he heard me!" Mr. Carter said. "I can't imagine being out in the heat like this tomorrow and need to stand the whole day."

"I'll throw a couple in my car when I get home," Sylvia told him, "as a backup."

"Thanks," Mr. Carter replied. "Let's get some lunch," he said and he nodded at a restaurant that was next to the park and on the water. Sylvia gratefully sank down into the seat of the booth and let the cool air conditioning waft around her. They ordered cold drinks immediately and Sylvia drank the glass of water before the iced tea she had ordered even arrived.

"Is it always this hot here?" Mr. Carter asked.

"I don't think so," Sylvia said. "It seems particularly bad this year, especially with the humidity."

"Horrible," he said, wiping his face with his handkerchief even though they had been sitting in the cool for several minutes. "You know I only live about fifty miles away, but that fifty miles makes a tremendous difference with the humidity."

"I think it's because we're on the bay," Sylvia commented.

"Nervous about tonight?" Mr. Carter asked her, changing the subject.

Sylvia nodded.

"You should be," Mr. Carter said, "Off the record, I think Headley is an asshole. Be careful."

"I'll do my best," Sylvia replied.

"Wish I knew how to get you out of it," he said, shaking his head.

Their food came and they were silent while they ate. Mr. Carter asked for a rich dessert, but Sylvia declined. Between the heat and her nerves, she wasn't very hungry.

Mr. Carter told her to go home after lunch.

"I'll be seeing you in the morning," he said when they walked out to their cars. "Here, don't forget to wear this T-shirt in the morning." He tossed a T-shirt to Sylvia. Thurmont was going patriotic this year and decorated the navy blue T-shirts with Thurmont emblazoned in red and white across the front like a baseball team.

"Thanks," Sylvia said, "See you in the morning."

She drove home trying not to think about the evening with Headley. Owen wasn't at her house and she called Marian. Marian invited her over for the afternoon and Sylvia gladly accepted.

Even though the sun was blazing, the heat seemed to slightly abate with the shade of the forest driving to Marian's house. Owen and Marian were sitting on the patio, Owen's legs propped up on another chair. She gave Marian a long hug and turned to Owen for a long kiss. A little breathless, she sat down and Marian poured her a tall glass of homemade lemonade.

"You're out of work early," Owen commented.

"Mr. Carter told me to go home so that I had ample time to get ready for this evening," she said.

"I don't like it," Owen said. "Even if you are doing this for the police, I don't trust Headley."

"I know," Sylvia sighed, "neither do I."

"Why don't you go back to Sylvia's house with her, Owen," Marian suggested. "That way you'll be available if Sylvia needs you when she gets home this evening."

"Yeah," he said, "I've always wanted to do that bodyguard thing," he quipped flexing his muscles.

Sylvia laughed, "You can be my bodyguard anytime," she told him. She glanced at her watch. "I should be going," Sylvia said. "Will you be coming too?" she asked Owen.

"Definitely," Owen said. "Let me get a couple of things." He went back into the house and came out with a small duffle bag and a thick book clutched in his hands.

Sylvia gave Marian a hug. "I'll talk to you soon," she said.

"Be careful," Marian advised, "and keep your ears open."

Sylvia rushed to get ready while Owen hovered about.

"You don't need to look too nice," he said worriedly as she slipped into the clingy black dress and was putting on make-up.

"Jealous?" Sylvia teased.

"You bet," he said.

A female detective arrived in an unmarked car and helped Sylvia hook up a wire underneath her clothing. She showed Sylvia how it worked and gave her some tips.

"We'll be close by if you need us," she said. "Don't worry, I've been through this a hundred times."

"Owen, you should probably stay out of sight when Headley arrives," Sylvia said.

Owen nodded. They went downstairs to wait for Headley. Sylvia was nervous and paced. She checked her make-up and glanced at the clock for the millionth time.

She was startled when the back door bell rang. She had become so used to everyone using the kitchen door, that she nearly forgot there was a back door. Even after living at Bayside full time, it was still a little confusing that the 'back' door faced the road and the 'front' door faced the bay. She kissed Owen quickly and went to answer it.

The limousine driver was waiting and said 'Good Evening' to her and motioned for her to get into the car. Sylvia closed the door and nervously went to the stretch limo that filled her driveway. The driver opened the door and she got in. Headley was sitting there, grinning at her like a Cheshire cat.

"Oh!" Sylvia gave a little cry, startled that he was in the limo.

"Good evening, Sylvia," Headley said. "You look lovely," he told her taking in the little black dress.

"Thank you," Sylvia replied.

"Champagne?" he asked her.

"Why yes, thank you," she said, still nervous, taking a flute from him. She took a sip. "Mmm, champagne, I never get enough." What a stupid thing to say she thought to herself. It sounded like something from an old movie. She thought she heard Headley mutter something like 'you will tonight.'

"Excuse me?" she asked. "Did you say something?"

He held up his glass to toast her, "to the lovely Sylvia." He cocked his head to look at her. "There's something different about you tonight. I can't quite put my finger on it."

Sylvia clicked her glass with his but couldn't look him in the eye and drank the champagne much too quickly. He quickly filled her glass again while he was talking about the evening. As he talked, he moved closer to her and she felt stuck like a rat in a trap. She wasn't frightened of him any longer. Now she was angry at his audacity to think that he could push her around. She didn't think that he killed Anna, but probably had felt reason to if he was jealous of her sleeping around. Personally, like Carol, she thought he got a kick out of it. She glanced slightly past him and saw his aura. It was still strongly streaked with yellow. He was quite close to putting his hand on her leg when the driver of the limousine turned sharply into the hotel and Headley had to catch himself to keep from spilling his champagne. Sylvia thanked the driver in her head.

"Damn!" he muttered, "clumsy driver."

They waited a few minutes until the guests from the other company arrived. The door opened and a sandy hair young man stepped in to say, "Good Evening, Headley."

His name was Jim Tucker and he nodded to Sylvia and before he said, "I'm sorry to tell you there has been a change in plans. Peter was unable to make it, so the company sent Natalie in to pinch hit. The sandy-haired gentleman backed up and motioned for someone to get in. "Natalie" stepped into the car and Sylvia almost gasped aloud at her beauty. She flashed a smile at Headley and Sylvia, bright white teeth against perfectly tanned skin. She was, in fact, tan all over and a white chiffon halter dress and gold sandals set off the tan. Her hair was brown with gold highlights in a very chic pageboy. The sandy-haired gentleman climbed into the limo and made introductions. He introduced Natalie Browne to Headley and Headley introduced Sylvia to Natalie Browne and to Jim Tucker. Natalie extended her slim hand to be shaken. Headley opened another bottle of champagne and served it to everyone while they drove to the small restored inn near the Maryland/ Pennsylvania line.

The Mill Race Inn was a restaurant Sylvia had only read about. It was a restored mill where the wheel side of the restaurant was completely glass so that everyone could see the workings while the water spilled over the wheel and into the pond. It was candlelit and decorated with beautiful artwork and antiques. Headley had reserved a prime table where full view of the powerful wheel turning just a few feet from the table.

Jim had apparently known Headley for a while. He gave his condolences regarding Anna and gave a brief account of Anna's death to a shocked looking Natalie.

"I'm so sorry," she said, putting her hand over Headley's.

That was it. He was hooked. Sylvia thought the other company had sent Natalie instead of the masculine sales counterpart, as probably, Headley's reputation as a ladies man had gone around in some corporate circles. She began to relax. Natalie and Jim asked about her and her job. She didn't have a lot to say other than the basics, but Headley gave them glowing reports of her stream watch efforts and innovative marketing ideas. They drank and ate a few appetizers. Sylvia couldn't even imagine eating dinner after the delightful tidbits that had been brought to the table. Headley and Natalie obviously hit it off and were deep in conversation. She thought she could see a slight smirk from Jim, and asked him about his job. He told her briefly about his position and his employer, chemical company. He also told her about his wife and three kids before he sighed.

"What's wrong?" Sylvia asked.

"I'm missing my kid's game," he said, "being away this weekend."

"Oh, I'm sorry," she said. "Perhaps tomorrow when you stop at the Thurmont booth at Bay Days, we can put together a bag of goodies for your kids," she suggested.

He brightened and said 'thanks.'

Dinner was served. The restaurant was famous for their seafood dishes and each one of them had ordered something different. Delicate miniature vegetables adorned the plates and fresh hot breads were brought to the table. It was obvious that Natalie was making moves on Headley. Sylvia would have laughed out loud if she could have. Instead, she looked out the huge window and was mesmerized by the falling water over the water wheel.

"This is a pretty amazing piece of architecture," Jim stated to her, "and engineering. I'm impressed!"

"Hmmm?" Sylvia asked, "Oh, yes, it is lovely," she said.

Jim asked her some questions about the company and Sylvia apologized again stating that she was not part of the scientific end. She knew that the company combined organic and inorganic materials to produce a stellar fertilizer used worldwide, but she did not know the actual components to the fertilizer.

Jim asked about the Superfund Clean-up sites. Sylvia was able to discuss the strategies that were used with the stream and her efforts to bring about community support with the stream watch efforts. She also mentioned they were working on stricter environmental controls with one of the recent hires, not mentioning Owen by name.

By the end of dinner, Jim and Natalie seemed interested in Thurmont. They wanted to discuss things further at the hotel and Sylvia begged to go home as she had an early day with Bay Days.

Headley, completely smitten, looked forward to spending additional time with Natalie and was eager to drop Sylvia off at home. They said good night, and she wished them all a pleasant evening. Chuckling, she let herself into the house where she nearly ran over Owen, who had heard the limousine and was standing in a shadow, waiting for her to come in.

"What's so funny?" he asked.

"Headley!" Sylvia laughed, finally letting herself to roll with laughter. "He's…such…an…ass!" she laughed in spurts as she talked.

"I don't understand," Owen said, baffled.

"I know," Sylvia said, "and I know I'm a little tipsy," she said.

She went to the kitchen to pour herself a tall glass of water. After she controlled her giggles, she and Owen went out to the deck where the hot air had cooled considerably with the slight bay breeze. Owen lit the citronella candles and they sat in the chair and waited for the police to show up. Detective Josephson came with the female officer. The female officer helped her get the wire off.

"Tell me about your evening," Detective Josephson said.

"I don't know where to begin," Sylvia said. "Headley thought he was going to put the moves on me, but this company threw a curve ball!" She started to laugh again. She told Owen and the detectives about Natalie and said she could and would lay bets that Headley would be sleeping with her tonight.

"That company has Headley pegged," Detective Josephson said.

Officer Brown did not add any information but smirked a little with a quirky smile.

"Do you still need to go tomorrow?" Josephson asked.

"As far as I know," Sylvia said.

"Don't worry about a wire tomorrow," he told her. "It sounds as though Headley will be otherwise occupied."

"Thanks," Sylvia said.

They said good night to the officers. Owen had his arm around her protectively and they went to lock doors and turn off the lights.

"I'm tired!" Sylvia said emphatically. "C'mon. Let's go to bed!" she suggested.

She pulled Owen up and together they blew out the candles. Still chuckling, she pulled him up the stairs where he gently pulled off the bit of black jersey that she called a dress and then stood back to admire his handiwork before she pulled him to her.

The forecast predicted hazy, hot and humid for Bay Days. Sylvia couldn't remember it being different any other year. Bay Days to her were some of the most uncomfortable and stickiest days she could remember every single summer. She always wondered why they would not change the date to a more comfortable season. Sylvia was glad that she didn't have to dress up for Bay Days. She put on a pair of fairly short white shorts and topped it off with the navy blue T-shirt emblazoned with 'Thurmont' in large red and white letters. Sylvia added a pair of socks and tennis shoes and pulled her hair back from her face with a headband. Mr. Carter had asked if she could arrive fairly early so that they could set up before the crowds started to arrive. Owen promised that he would help too. She showered, dressed and took coffee up to him, prodding him in the shoulder and wafting coffee fumes at him. He reached out and pulled her down beside him in the bed, tickling her until she asked for mercy.

"C'mon!" she cried, "You promised you would help!" she said as she tried to pull away.

Owen made a grunting sound and pulled her down beside him again and began kissing her.

"Come on!" she said again. "I need to be there in a few minutes."

"You're no fun, you know that," he accused her teasingly.

"I know," she said, in mock despair. She pulled him out of bed before he pulled her back into bed. She could not give in to the desire fluttering in her lower abdomen this morning.

They drove to the town park and walked hand in hand to the Thurmont booth to find Mr. Carter frantic.

"Look!" he cried. "Look at what happened! Damn it!" He was red with anger and sweating profusely in the heat that had started to build.

Sylvia and Owen looked. Emblazoned in paint across one part of the tent were the words "Thurmont sucks." Another message was "Thurmont kills" and "Murderers."

Sylvia was shocked. At first, she thought the 'Thurmont Sucks' might be from teenagers, but the more esoteric graffiti was clearly by some sort of group that hated the company. Sylvia never imagined that it might come to Bay Days, thinking that the letters and calls they had been dealing with, in the public information office were rather benign. She could almost feel the hostility from the spray painted signs and it took them several minutes to stop gaping at the graffiti. Finally, Owen took things in hand.

"Look," he said, "I'll run to WalMart. They're open 24 hours, and I'll buy some green spray paint that matches the tent. We'll spray over the graffiti and set up, okay?"

Sylvia and Mr. Carter nodded. They were still speechless. When Owen left, Sylvia finally started to move, putting covers on the tables and starting to unload the pamphlets. She felt so naïve. Where had she been all those years at college? Sylvia thought she must have been living in a bottle stuffed with cotton. It was if she was just beginning to wake up and this was quite a surprise to find that the world was not such a nice place sometimes. It was something that she had avoided since her father's death so many years ago. She stopped unpacking and thought for a moment. It was silly to unpack and set everything up if Owen was going to spray paint. The residue from the spraying paint would likely land on all of their materials. She looked over at Mr. Carter heaving a box onto a table to tell him so and noticed he was grayer than usual and sweating profusely.

"You don't look so good," she said, looking beyond and seeing the muddiness in his aura.

"It's this damn humidity with the heat," he said, pulling out a large handkerchief and mopping his forehead.

"Look," Sylvia said, "We really can't unpack anything until Owen sprays the tent." She explained about the flying residue.

"You're right," Mr. Carter puffed.

"Why don't you sit down," she told him, pulling out one of the lawn chairs she had brought along. She glanced over at the parking lot. "Owen has my car. If you let me borrow your car, I can run and get us coffee or something cold," she said.

Mr. Carter sat down in the lawn chair gratefully. He fumbled in his pocket and finally pulled out his keys and tossed them to her. "Here you go," he said. "Coffee and something cold, please," he told her. He started to reach into his other pocket for cash, but Sylvia stopped him.

"It's on me," she said lightly. "I'll hurry," she said.

His health really began to worry her. She adjusted the seat in Mr. Carter's car. It was filled with empty coffee cups, candy, and fast food wrappers. She knew he lived on the road. She drove to a little grocer in town and grabbed some large bottles of cold water, a hot coffee and caffeinated sodas for Owen and herself and hurried back to the park. Owen was already there and Mr. Carter had moved his chair away from the tent and was squinting in the morning sunlight watching Owen. Sylvia handed him the coffee and the large water.

"Thanks," he told her.

Sylvia popped the top on her soda and drank greedily. The sun that rose was hazy. She looked around the park. It was busy with vendors setting up tents and unloading cars. The regular walkers and bike riders were making their loop through the park along the path at the water's edge. One young mother already had her children playing on the playground. Ducks and geese wandered in packs looking for handouts and a few fishermen were on the rock jetties that reached out into the bay. She was finally getting used to seeing a glow around everything. If she focused on an object, the aura would become more brilliant and easier to see. She turned to look at the tent. Owen's efforts had helped. If you looked closely, you could still see the words, but faintly, under the green paint.

Carol came up with her coffee and said, "Hi Syl! It's a hot one, isn't it?"

Sylvia nodded and without missing a beat Carol asked how the previous night with Headley went. Before Sylvia could answer, Carol noticed what Owen was doing.

"What the hell happened?" she demanded. She had pulled her dark pageboy back into a high ponytail and it was bouncing wildly as she gaped at the tent.

"Someone vandalized the tent last night," Mr. Carter explained.

"Some of those friggin environmentalists," Carol assumed.

"We don't know," Owen muttered, "but, that's a good possibility."

"Yeah," Mr. Carter said, "We had some minor threats this week, but I ignored it. Maybe it wasn't such a smart idea, in hindsight." He sighed.

Sylvia looked at him, surprised. "No, I didn't tell you," he said. "I thought we had enough to worry about.

Sylvia asked Mr. Carter to stay seated while they unpacked and set up. He didn't argue, which Sylvia thought was a bad sign.

"Keep an eye on him today, okay?" she asked Carol when they had gone to retrieve a box. "He doesn't look well to me."

"I agree," Carol said, "He looks a little gray around the gills."

"So tell me about last night!" Carol said.

Sylvia went into a description of the night and how the executive from the other company pulled Headley's attention away from her.

"Smart people," Carol commented.

"That reminds me, I need to pull a couple of bags and goodies for Jim," Sylvia said.

"Who's Jim?" Carol asked.

"He's another executive that came to have dinner last night. He's missing his kid's baseball playoffs for this sales meeting and he's feeling really guilty," Sylvia told her. "He's a decent guy too," she added.

They put together some promotional bags. Owen was busy blowing up balloons and tying strings onto them and hanging them around the booth to disguise the vandalism. When Sylvia looked up, she was surprised to see how quickly the park was beginning to fill.

"I haven't been here in years," she commented looking around.

"People are getting here early," Carol said, "so that they can get seats for the water ski shows."

"What time are Headley and the crew coming by?" Carol asked.

"They're coming here just before lunch," Sylvia said. "We have reservations at the crab house in town," she told her and then a helicopter ride over Thurmont property and the area before we come back to have dinner and sail on Headley's boat."

"Whew! Full schedule!" Carol said.

"No kidding," Sylvia said.

"Sorry I couldn't get you out of it," Mr. Carter commented from the back of the tent. "Short of breaking your leg, I didn't think of anything," he joked with her.

"I'll be okay," she said. "I wasn't kidding about the charms of Natalie Browne! Wait until you meet her!"

The crowds drifted by slowly. Owen and Sylvia worked at blowing up balloons and tying ribbons on to hand out to children. Most people walked by. Sylvia noticed it was the freebies and the children wanting to have the pencil or balloon that actually brought most of the adults to stop by the booth. Carol worked at pre-stuffing car litter bags with brochures and information while Mr. Carter fielded questions. The morning went by quickly—too quickly for Sylvia's sake. It was nearly lunchtime when she sent Owen away to grab lunches for Mr. Carter and Carol and to keep out of Headley's way. He gave Sylvia a quick kiss and hug and told her he would see her at home. He left just in time as coming down the path from the opposite direction was Headley, with Jim and Natalie.

"There she is," Sylvia stage whispered to Carol.

Carol put on her sunglasses and peered down the booths while pretending to adjust the balloons but, looking at Natalie.

"You weren't kidding!" she whispered back. "She's just his type. All glitz and glam and probably as poisonous as a man o' war."

Headley and the crew came up to the booth. Headley made introductions and Sylvia pulled out the goody bags and handed them to Jim.

"Thanks for remembering," he said to her and he gave her a warm smile.

"You all right with holding down the ship?" Headley asked Mr. Carter.

"Of course," Mr. Carter boomed. "I have a trusty first mate by my side," he joked back to Headley indicating Carol with a wave. "Besides, the crowd will settle down with the water shows."

Headley nodded curtly to Mr. Carter and turned to Sylvia. "Ready?" he asked.

"Sure," she said. "Let me get my bag."

Carol went to the rear of the tent where they had put their handbags. "Good luck," she whispered, pretending to get a lipstick out of her bag.

"Thanks," Sylvia whispered back.

She scooted around the table and fell in step with Jim. They walked to the crab house. Headley ordered pitchers of beer and an enormous amount of crabs. They talked and cracked peanuts and threw the shells on the floor. Natalie looked uncomfortable with the casual atmosphere at first, but after a couple of beers, she was cracking peanuts and throwing shells on the floor with everyone else. Headley made it his personal job to teach her how to crack and eat crabs. The luncheon was much more relaxed than dinner the previous night. Apparently Jim and Natalie had given Headley all of the information they requested and now they were relaxing and enjoying the day.

Practically rolling out of the restaurant, they walked back to the park to pick up the helicopter Headley had hired for the afternoon. Other helicopter rides were being offered for $20.00 per trip. Sylvia knew that Headley had some local pull and was catered to by many of the businesses. The pilot jumped out of the copter and shook Headley's hand. He quickly observed the group. Headley and Natalie volunteered to be in the back and Sylvia and Jim were by the doors. Flutters of nervousness swam through Sylvia's stomach. She had never been in a small plane let alone a helicopter. It seemed so open and much too tiny for five people. The rotors began to turn, sounding like a giant insect above their heads. The co-pilot gave them instructions on keeping their arms down, how to secure the seatbelts and put on headsets for communication.

Sylvia held her breath while they started to rise up from the ground. She gave a gasp. The pilot asked if she was okay.

"It's incredible!" she told him. "This is fantastic!"

The pilot smiled and nodded. Jim nodded in agreement as well.

It seemed only a moment when they were hovering above the park and the Bay Days celebration. The world was crystal clear and the bay was sparkling. The sailboats looked like toys and the park full of colorful small moving bodies. She tried to pick out the Thurmont tent and thought she had spotted it when the helicopter turned and buzzed away towards the plant.

Sylvia could see the trees pulsing with energy as they flew. In her imagination, she thought she could feel their energy as she flew above them. She was mesmerized and couldn't stop looking all around. When they got above Thurmont, Sylvia did a double take and gasped at what she saw. In the woods where they had found Anna's body, there were marks on the land that looked like a spreading stain. Her skin prickled and she could feel the hairs standing up on her arms. The stain had a pulsing aura. It was muddied and difficult to see against the dark landscape, but it was entirely different from the light filled auras of the vegetation on either side of the woods. She knew it was something horrible, but didn't have a clue as to what it was.

"What's wrong?" Jim asked, slightly concerned noticing her change from elation of the experience of the helicopter flight to one of concern.

"Down there," Sylvia said pointing. "What is it?" she asked.

"What is what?" Jim asked unconcerned. "I see Thurmont and the surrounding trees. It's a lovely bit of property with the wild open space down to the stream."

"Does Thurmont own the stream area as well?" Jim asked turning to Headley.

Headley turned his attentions away from Natalie and talked to Jim. He pointed out the boundaries of the property promising to drive them over later that day. Sylvia stared down at the ground. She saw the stain of brown, pulsing with life and knew that was growing—slowly—but it was growing and moving all the same. It seemed to be centralized in the wooded area where they had found Anna's body, but snaky tendrils were moving away from the company grounds. It was clear now that she was the only one who was able to see whatever it was. She thought it must be part of the new vision the Green Man spoke about. They started to fly south towards town again, and now Sylvia craned her neck to see outside to follow the snaky tendrils of brown. It went towards town and down towards the bay. Looking at it gave her a sick feeling in the pit of her stomach.

"Are you okay?" Jim asked her, noticing her pale expression.

"Yes," she said. "I think I drank one too many beers," she lied quickly.

He nodded with understanding. "Wonderful lunch," he said, "but, I'm not sure this roller coaster ride was such a good idea right after a meal," he murmured.

They were heading back to the park to land. As disturbed as she was by what she saw at the Thurmont plant, she couldn't help by smile to the pilot.

"Thank you, the ride was fantastic," she told him warmly, "I can understand why you love to do this. If I had your job, I don't think I would ever want to land!"

The pilot grinned at her. "That's the idea," he replied.

The pilot helped her out of the copter and she wobbled a bit as she got her land legs back.

"Thank you," she said a little shakily to Mr. Headley.

He nodded, barely acknowledging her now that Natalie was in sight. He was extremely attentive to her, taking her hand.

"What's next?" Jim asked quietly.

"Umm, sailing, I think," she murmured back to him.

Behind Headley's back, she saw him grimace and stifled a laugh. Looking for something to divert her attention she glanced around the park. Somewhere near the Thurmont booth were flashing red lights.

"I wonder what's going on?" she asked the group.

"Where?" Headley asked.

"Looks like the Thurmont booth," Jim said without a doubt.

Concerned, Sylvia ignored Headley and started towards the booth. Jim followed her quick pace while Headley and Natalie came up behind. The red lights proved to be an ambulance and a separate paramedic truck. Paramedics had Mr. Carter on a gurney, with an oxygen mask over his face, checking his vitals.

"What's wrong?" Sylvia cried when she saw her boss with a pasty looking face looking still as death.

"You a relative?" the paramedic asked.

"No," Sylvia said, "but, as close to one as you could get at the moment," she told him, trying not to sound belligerent. "I'm not sure he has any family left. I'm a good friend," she said.

Carol and Owen, standing nearby nodded in her direction, confirming what she said to the paramedics.

"Possible heart attack," he stated.

"Oh, no!" Sylvia gasped. "He hasn't looked well for a couple of days, now," She told them.

"Are you able to come to the hospital to fill out some paperwork?" he asked her.

"Sure," Sylvia said, "Whatever you need."

She looked at Carol and Owen. "Okay?" she asked, knowing it wasn't a problem before she said anything. She looked at Headley too who nodded.

Jim piped up, "Look," he said, "if it's a matter of handing out brochures and stuff, I can help with that." He turned to Natalie and Headley. "You two don't mind if I stay and help out, do you?" he asked. "Honestly, I don't think you'll find me to be a very good sailor."

Natalie sort of glared at him, but covered it up when Headley glanced at her for confirmation. Sylvia went off in the ambulance with Mr. Carter and made a hand gesture to Owen and Carol of "I'll call you." Headley and Natalie turned to go towards the boat slip and Jim turned to introduce himself to Owen and Carol.

Sylvia had never ridden in an ambulance. She was in a jump seat of sorts and it was a very bumpy and uncomfortable ride. The paramedics were working on Mr. Carter, communicating to the hospital and trying to stabilize him. One of the paramedics told her they would be arriving at the hospital in a few minutes. He told her they would check Mr. Carter over in the ER. Then, likely, he would be admitted and send him to the heart unit on the second floor. Before she knew it, Sylvia was handed a stack of forms to fill out for Mr. Carter. She did the best she could, putting down the particulars and called Carol regarding health plans and policies on the cell phone. She wracked her brain to think if he had any other relatives. There were none in the immediate area, but Sylvia thought he had said one time that he had a sister in California.

She handed the forms back to the receptionist and hoped for the best, giving them a weak smile and lamely trying to explain her position and knowledge. They told her it would be a while until he was transferred to the heart unit and suggested she wait in the waiting room. Sylvia sat and leaned back, closing her eyes. What a day! Her mind was racing. She was so relieved Natalie Browne drew off Headley's attentions. Then she remembered the brown spreading stain starting from Thurmont and spreading down the peninsula and wondered what it was. Opening her eyes, she looked around surveying the waiting room. One woman was waiting for treatment and moaning, holding her stomach. There were people in shorts over bathing suits pacing up and down and a young woman holding a small baby. She looked around the sterile waiting room area. A few old magazines were lying on end tables. Sylvia got up and paced along with the others. She had never been a patient person. She started to think of Gran and thought that her Mother must have waited patiently or impatiently when Gran had chemotherapy and other appointments and treatments. Her respect for her mother grew at that moment. She sat down again and leafed through an old news magazine, not reading and then through an old woman's magazine, looking at Christmas cookie recipes and snowman crafts. Just when she thought she could stand it no longer, she heard her name being called by the receptionist. They told her that Mr. Carter was being transferred to the Coronary Care unit and that she could go up to see him in a few minutes.

The receptionist looked at her pale face and said, "It will take them, at least, a half an hour to get him set up and situated. Why don't you go to the cafeteria and get a snack?" she asked sympathetically.

"Thanks," Sylvia replied and then asked, "Can you give me directions?"

Sylvia purchased a soda, chocolate, and some crackers. At that point, she felt like she could main line chocolate without a problem. She sat at a table. The cafeteria was quite empty except some tired interns that were downing large quantities of coffee and having a rather heated discussion of some sort of procedure. At least, that's what she could make out. Finishing her snack, she headed up to coronary care. The nurse told her she could see Mr. Carter for fifteen minutes.

Sylvia took a deep breath and walked into the ward. Mr. Carter was awake and hooked up to an astonishing number of machines. He tried to give her a wan smile and she sat down and patted his hand.

"You know you didn't have to go to these lengths to keep me out of Headley's clutches," she said lightly.

"Don't make me laugh," he croaked hoarsely and tried to smile again. "You okay?" he asked.

Sylvia nodded. "Actually, I am," she said, "Except I'm a little worried about you." She looked at him and noticed that his aura was a bit brighter and she knew he would be okay. She gave him a better smile and filled Mr. Carter in on the fact that she had filled out the paperwork for him and wasn't sure if everything is correct. She told him about the last few hours with Headley and Co. and that Natalie had drawn Headley's attentions away from her and how nice a guy Jim was.

"How about you?" she asked.

"Heart attack," he stated bluntly and hoarsely.

"I think you were lucky," Sylvia said. "Is there anything I can get you?" she asked, seeing the nurse about to come in and kick her out.

"No," he said.

"I'm going back to Bay Days and help them clean-up and then I'll be back," she told him.

She leaned over to give him a kiss on the cheek and turned to go. When she was outside his room, she realized that she didn't have a car.

"Don't panic," she told herself, "Think." Sylvia hoped Marian would be home as she dialed. Briefly, she stated to Marian what had happened and Marian said she would be happy to pick her up and to sit tight.

The heat was intense outside. Sylvia went back into the hospital to look for a vending machine for a cold soda and went to wait by the large plate glass window and keep an eye out for Marian.

Thankfully Marian pulled up a short time later. Sylvia climbed into the car and was nearly blown away with the air conditioning on full blast.

"Thanks for picking me up," Sylvia told her.

"No problem," Marian said, "Sounds as though you've had quite the day."

Sylvia nodded. "Not one I would like to repeat, actually," she said, "although it wasn't terrible, just…" she was at a loss for words.

They were both silent for a few minutes and Marian asked how Mr. Carter was doing. Sylvia filled her in as much as she could and told her she would be going back that night.

By the time they got to Bay Days, the crowds had thinned out in the heat and Jim, Carol and Owen had started to pack up things that were left. They were surprised to see her and she gave them a report on Mr. Carter.

"Thanks for pitching in, everyone," she said wearily and leaned against Owen with a huge sigh. Sylvia thought if she closed her eyes she would be asleep in an instant. Instead, she tried to glance around as Owen started to rub her neck and shoulders. Sylvia groaned in pleasure and pain. "Can I hire you?" she whispered to him.

"Free of charge," he said smiling and paused a moment before he said, "today."

"What happens with the tent and all of this stuff?" Owen asked.

"Ed or one of the other guys is to be coming with the truck soon," she told them.

"Have you seen Natalie or Mr. Headley?" she asked Jim.

"Nope," Jim said, "and I don't expect we will. Can someone give me a ride to the hotel?"

"Sure," Carol said. "I could do that. Okay if I go boss?" she said jokingly to Sylvia.

Sylvia smacked playfully at her. "Go!" she ordered. "Go and have a cold beer for me," she said.

"And a refreshing shower, I think," Carol said. "To think last week I was on the beach..." she sighed.

"It was nice meeting you Jim," Sylvia said sincerely. "I hope your kids like the stuff. Thanks for helping out," she said again.

Jim shook her hand and Owen's too. "Nice meeting you," he said to Owen. "Good luck."

Sylvia sat down on the stack of boxes and watched Carol and Jim go.

"I would love to get a shower and something to eat before I head back to the hospital," Sylvia told Owen.

"Mind if I tag along?" he asked.

"I was hoping you would say that," she sighed and leaned her head on his shoulder. "I'm pooped!"

Ed came rattling up with the truck. He was surprised to see Owen and asked him how things were going. Owen shrugged.

"Any word on the murder investigation?" he asked Ed.

"No," Owen said carefully. "I know I'm innocent, but I'm not out of the woods yet," he said.

"What happened to your arm?" Owen asked Ed, noticing the bandage.

Sylvia leaned closer.

"Some sort of skin infection," he told Owen. "Thought it was poison ivy, thought it was this, that and the other thing. Now they're telling me it's a form of cellulitis. I feel like crap," he said. "You don't want to see what's under the bandage. It's gross. My Mom has it too," he said.

They worked together to take down the tent and load up the truck. Sylvia was thoughtful and Owen asked her a couple of times to hand him things.

"Sorry," she said, "I think I'm tired."

"Me too," Owen said. "I'm looking forward to a cold beer."

"Sounds good to me too," Ed said.

Sylvia was hoping Owen wouldn't ask Ed to go out for a beer or to come back to her house for one.

Instead, Owen said, "Yeah, but we'll have to wait on that. We need to get to the hospital," he said and gave Ed a brief account of what occurred that afternoon.

"Mr. Carter's an okay kind of guy," Ed said, "I'm sorry he's feeling poorly. Give him my best, all right?"

"I'll do that," Sylvia told Ed. "Thanks for transporting the stuff."

"No problem!" Ed said, "I love the overtime!"

They waved him off and went to Sylvia's car. She was thankful it was only a couple of miles to her house.

"How about a quick swim before a shower?" Owen asked her.

"Sounds great," Sylvia said.

They both waded out into the water that was almost as warm as a bathtub that night. Sylvia walked around until she found the updraft from a cool natural spring and floated.

"Thanks for helping out today," she said again to Owen.

"No problem," Owen said. "Maybe it will earn me brownie points to get back to work sooner."

"If it were up to Mr. Carter and Carol, I'm sure that wouldn't be a problem," she said.

She floated on her back and looked at a wisp of a cloud that drifted slowly across the clear sky. It floated and slowly dissipated as it traveled from west to east. Finally, she put into words what had been bugging her.

"I guess Ed is no longer a suspect," she said tiredly.

"What do you mean?" Owen asked.

"I thought that stuff on his arm was like the tracks on Anna. I've been dying to look under that bandage!" she said.

"Maybe you should leave detective playing up to the police," Owen advised.

Sylvia shot him a pissy look. "Look," she said, "do you have any better theories?"

"No," Owen said, "but I think your lead on Ed is a bit thin."

"I guess so," Sylvia said, "But, I felt so sure..." she trailed off.

"But if his mother has it too, it's probably not that stuff on Anna," Owen confirmed.

"You're right, you're right," Sylvia said petulantly. "Let's get a shower."

They waded into shore and washed the bay water off of them. Owen wanted to go to Marian's for clean clothes and they headed back to her house. Jon's car was in the parking area.

They entered through the kitchen door calling out "hello!"

"In here," they heard Marian call from the living room.

They walked to the front of the house where Marian seemed surprised to see them. They greeted Jon.

"I'm surprised you're here," Marian said.

"Just to get some clothes," Owen said.

"Do you need dinner?" Marian asked.

"No thanks," Sylvia said, "We're headed out again," she told Marian and Jon. "I'd like to get back to the hospital to see Mr. Carter before visiting hours are over."

Marian nodded in understanding. Owen came down in clean shorts and shirt and was ready to go.

When they got out to Sylvia's car, she said, "Is Jon pursuing Marian?"

"I think so," Owen said, starting up the car and turning on the air and turning down the CD they had listened to on the way over.

"He's tried a couple of times since Bran has died, but Marian hasn't been ready," he told her. "I think she's now giving it consideration," he said.

"Wow," Sylvia said softly. "Who would have guessed?"

"He's a decent guy," Owen said, "But he'll never be Bran," Owen told her.

"You were close to Bran, weren't you?" Sylvia asked.

Owen nodded, "He was like a grandfather to me," he said to her. "But," he changed the subject, "Marian seems to be happy. That's what's important and I think it's good for her."

"Absolutely," Sylvia said. She took his hand and squeezed it. She was happy for Marian but didn't think anyone could feel the way she and Owen felt about one another. It felt so singularly wonderful that she didn't think anyone else could feel this way. They drove to the hospital to check on Mr. Carter stopping first at a large grocery store for a floral arrangement. He had definitely been diagnosed with a heart attack was him scheduled for an angioplasty and possible heart catheterization the next day. He thought he would be going home for a few days.

"You'll have to hold down the fort on your own," he told Sylvia.

"It's okay," Sylvia said. "There's not a lot going on anyway, is there?" she asked.

"Not really," he said. "I just hope no one gets wind of the vandalism this morning."

Sylvia had forgotten all about it and shrugged. "Whatever it is, we'll deal with it. Don't you worry."

"I won't," he said, "And still be wary of Headley," he advised.

He started to look fatigued from their conversation.

"Don't worry!" she told him. "I'll stop back tomorrow," Sylvia said, "to make sure you're not giving the nurses any trouble."

"Where do you want to go for dinner?" Owen asked her when they left the hospital.

"I don't care," she said.

"Okay," he said, "then it's up to me." He drove her to a small café near the state university. It was usually a college student hang-out, but with summer session going on, fewer people frequented it. They had good beer and excellent sandwiches. It was dark, cozy and cool. Sylvia relaxed.

"I can't imagine why I'm so tired," she told Owen.

He laughed sardonically. "Come on Syl," he said. "Look at the last twenty-four hours. Eat up and I'll take you home and tuck you in bed." He pushed her plate a little closer to her.

"Promise?" she said.

"Promise," he told her.

Sylvia couldn't finish her sandwich and took most of it home in a 'to go' container. They walked out to the car.

"I'm driving," Owen insisted. "You are way too tired."

Sylvia didn't argue. She answered by yawning deeply, practically staggering and apologizing to Owen. Owen opened the door and she crawled into her seat. About half way home she dozed off. When they got home, Owen pulled her gently from the car and took her upstairs.

"Come on, Syl," he said. "Help me out here."

He helped her take off most of her clothes, tucked her in and she heard him go downstairs. After that, she didn't hear another thing until morning. She woke up with Owen standing over her with a steaming cup of café au lait.

"Slide over," he said.

Sylvia wiped the sleep from her eyes and moved over. He handed her the coffee and she sipped it with tiny sips.

"Too hot?" he asked.

She nodded and put it on the bedside table to cool.

He was dressed, but crawled under the sheet beside her and held her. With her head on his chest, she listened to his heartbeat and her breathing, which was slowing and rising and falling with his heartbeat. Owen stroked her arm with light fingers. She turned to kiss him and began to stroke him gently.

She felt so relaxed when she woke up a couple of hours later. Her coffee was cold and she made a face when she took a sip. Sylvia stretched luxuriously and went downstairs to make a fresh pot of coffee. Owen came down a few minutes later and held her in his arms lightly while the coffee perked. They took fresh cups out to the deck. The humid air had moved through and it was warm but dry and crystal clear. Sylvia smiled and was genuinely content sipping her coffee and staring at the water.

"What are your plans for today?" she asked him eventually.

"Nothing special," he said. "Unfortunately, it will be that way until we get everything resolved."

"I was so sure it was Ed," she said emphatically. "Just a feeling I had."

"Hmm," Owen said. "We still need to check out that muck."

"I know," Sylvia said. "I thought I could get some tomorrow night after work. What do you want me to collect it in."

"Oh, any sterilized jar will do," Owen told her. "I won't need a lot to make some tests," he said.

Sylvia nodded. "All right," she said.

The day passed far too quickly. They lazed around for most of the day. Sylvia dropped Owen off at Marian's and went in to visit with Mr. Carter, but he was off having some tests completed. He had left the keys to his car and a note asking her to pick it up from the park and move it to a safer location. Sylvia and Owen parked it in her driveway.

When Monday rolled around, Sylvia found herself answering question after question about Mr. Carter to people who stopped by the office. It seemed like a never -ending stream. She emailed Carol a complaint as she pasted a smile on her face and explained for the millionth time about Mr. Carter and his heart attack. Actually, he was doing well. She had spoken to him. He was out of coronary care and the angioplasty and ensuing catheterization had gone extremely well. They had reduced the blockages and put in shunts. With medication, change in diet and some rehabilitation he was going to be just fine. Sylvia offered to drive him home when he was released. He laughed and said he hoped to drive himself home, but thanked her all the same.

CHAPTER TWENTY NINE

"Courage isn't having the strength to go on—it is going on when you don't have the strength." --Napoleon Bonaparte

It was just before lunch when Headley came in. He sat on her desk and reached out and chucked her under the chin.

"You're cute, you know that?" he said to her. "Miss All-America, "A" apple pie. You are the all American sweetheart."

She tried not to recoil but to look him in the eye. "Really," she said coolly. "I have never thought myself as that."

"Oh, honey, you are," he said. "But, I won't hold that against you."

Sylvia wanted to punch him. Instead, she asked, "What do you want?"

"Just checking to see how Carter is doing and ask you out to dinner," he said raking his eyes over her.

Sylvia tried not to squirm in her seat. She felt like the fly that was about to be eaten by the spider.

"Mr. Carter is fine," she said. "He hopes to be out of the hospital tomorrow. As for dinner, I'm afraid I'm busy tonight."

"No need to be afraid," Headley cooed. "That comes later." She barely heard the last part and wondered if she had imagined it.

She cleared her throat. "How did things go with Natalie and Jim?" she asked. "Are there offers to buy the division?"

"Things went just fine with Natalie," he said, putting the emphasis on the word fine. "She was a lovely dalliance, but now I can turn my attentions to home matters."

"How can you do this?" Sylvia said, finally losing her cool. "What about Anna? What about Natalie? Are they just people to be played with?"

Headley was unfazed. He sighed and said, "Anna. I do miss her. But we were adults and we played with each other as adults," he said. "Natalie, as I said, was a dalliance, and like I said, and she was," he hesitated, "…a business proposition. You, on the other hand, are a piece of sweet, ripe fruit ready for the picking," he told her looking as though he wanted to eat her up like a gooey dessert.

Sylvia sat stunned and disgusted. Of all the women in the company, why her? Before she could think of a snappy answer, he was gone. Moments later Carol came to the door asking if she wanted to go for lunch but stopped mid-sentence when she turned around the corner of the door and saw Sylvia's face.

"What's wrong?" she asked concerned. "It's not Mr. Carter, is it?" she asked.

"No," Sylvia said bitterly, "guess again."

"Headley?" she said astounded. "Is he after you again?"

Sylvia nodded her head. She wanted to cry and scream and hit something at the same time.

"I guess I shouldn't be too surprised," she said. "C'mon, let's go and get some lunch."

Sylvia wasn't hungry, but Carol kept pushing food at her. Finally, she ate a few bites and took a soda and candy bar back to the office.

At four o'clock Sylvia locked up the office, put her purse in the car and took out a couple of bottles and went towards the woods where the muck lay. She also had brought along some plastic gloves and snapped them on after she teetered across the stream and headed into the woods. It was silent as before. The phrase 'silent as a grave' kept popping into her head. "Stop it!" she scolded herself. "You're perfectly safe." She kept saying it to herself like a mantra. She scooped up some muck into the jars and took the plastic gloves off and put them in a plastic bag that she had brought along.

"Hello there," a voice said behind her.

Sylvia whirled around, her heart beating wildly. It was Headley.

"What are you doing here?" she demanded. "Jesus! You scared me!"

"Au contraire," Headley said, "I'm the one who should be asking what are you doing here? You are my employee, you know. You are on the edge of trespassing since it's technically after your work hours."

Sylvia stood silently, not wanting him to know his bullying was frightening her.

"What have we here?" he asked, pulling at the plastic bag that held the gloves. One of the bottles was still clutched in her hand.

"What is this?" he asked silkily, "Collecting samples for your boyfriend? What difference will it make, he's going to fry for Anna's murder."

"He's innocent!" Sylvia cried.

"Really," Headley said in a lazy sort of voice that was more frightening than his threats. "That could change," he chuckled. "Evidence could be found if you're not nice to me."

Sylvia was startled. What kind of game was he playing at? She was almost afraid to ask, "What do you mean?"

"You know what I want," he said huskily. He pinned her to a tree with his hands locked on her breasts. "Feel this," he said, pushing his pelvis into hers.

"Let…me...go!" she said loudly, nearly screaming.

"Not on your life," Headley chuckled. "I'm going to make Miss "A" Apple Pie into my little sex slave. You'll love it," he said, nearly drooling and pushing her harder into the tree.

"You're nuts!" Sylvia cried.

"Maybe," he said, "or maybe just a nymphomaniac," and he laughed a wicked sounding laugh.

His hands were under her shirt now and he was trying to pull her bra off. One strap snapped painfully. She attempted to struggle, but he pushed her against the tree harder. She thought she was going to throw up. Sylvia couldn't breathe. She pushed again but he was too strong and pinned her against the tree ripping away at her shirt.

"Good, I like it when you struggle. This is going to be fun." he breathed heavily on her and stifled her scream with a horrible kiss. She screamed inside, the horror of the moment bursting in her brain. He unzipped his pants and then reached up her skirt to pull down her panties when there was a flash of brilliant green and white light. The next thing she knew she was in the arms of the Green Man and she was sobbing. Golden sunlight filtered through the green leaves of the trees. It felt like a golden blanket yet, Sylvia couldn't stop shaking.

He held on to her tightly. "It's okay," he kept murmuring. "You're all right."

She was still shaky. Her lips were bruised and her bra strap broken, her shirt torn and skirt muddied. He kept holding her and talking to her like a mother to a child who had had a nightmare. It had been a nightmare. It seemed surreal.

"Where's Headley?" she asked shakily.

"Don't worry," the Green Man said, "and don't ask questions."

"How did you know I needed help?" Sylvia looked at him wonderingly.

"You called," he said simply, "and I came."

She digested this for a few moments and didn't ask any more questions. It felt good just to sit near him and feel the pulsing of the earth. Her breathing started to calm down moment by moment.

"Can you drive?" he asked.

"In a few minutes," she said.

"Good," he said. "Go home."

Sylvia wasn't sure how she made it to the car or made it home, she just did. She drove automatically. Sylvia couldn't remember if the Green Man was beside her or not. When she got home, she slumped over and put her head against the steering wheel accidentally beeping the horn. Owen came running out.

"Syl," he cried. "What's wrong? What happened? Were you in an accident?"

She couldn't answer him. He helped her out of the car and held her in his arms. She started sobbing again. "H-h-Headley," she blurted out after a couple of tries. It was Headley."

"Bastard!" Owen cried. "I'm calling the cops. This needs to be reported," he said grimly.

Sylvia didn't answer. They waited until the police arrived and she gave a report. They kept asking her where Headley was now, but she didn't have a response.

"I think I fainted," she told them. "He went away. I don't know where " she said dully. Owen had also called Marian who came right over. She made Sylvia a cup of strong, sweet tea.

"Drink this, child," she said. "It'll help a little."

Sylvia took a couple sips and retched. "I'm so cold," she said to Owen and Marian, her teeth chattering away.

Owen ran to get a blanket and put it around her shoulders. The policeman looked at her sympathetically and said he only had a few more questions. He asked if she needed to go to the hospital and he asked all kinds of embarrassing questions.

"Will you be done soon?" Owen asked the policeman.

"For now," he said. "Get some rest."

Owen led Sylvia up to bed and helped her into her nightgown while Marian showed the police the way out. Just before she dropped off to sleep, Sylvia remembered the bottles full of muck. They were in the car and she told Owen where to find them.

"Go to sleep," he said, kissing her hair, just above the ear. "Go to sleep."

And go to sleep she did.

CHAPTER THIRTY

"Wait until it is night before saying it is a fine day."
French Proverb

Sylvia didn't wake up until almost noon and shot out of bed and down the stairs.

"Whoa, whoa!" Owen said when he heard her clattering down the steps. "Where do you think you're going?"

"Didn't you see the time?" she cried, "I'm really late for work!"

"You're not late, you're not going to work today," Owen told Sylvia.

"What?" she asked.

"Sit down," Owen said. He made coffee and brought her a steaming cup. She sat at the kitchen table and looked perplexed. After she had taken a few sips, Owen started talking.

"They picked up Headley," he said, "and charged him with sexual assault. I understand when they searched his apartment they found some drugs and paraphernalia."

"How did you find this out?" she asked disbelieving.

"Jon," Owen said, "Jon called and told me and said he would represent you when the trial came. It won't be for awhile," he said gently. "Yeah," he went on, "apparently the cops thought Headley was really high on something when they picked him up. He was incoherent and muttering about flashing green lights and a giant green man. Pretty weird to see the Jolly Green Giant, eh?"

Sylvia nearly choked on her coffee. She remained silent.

Owen patted her on her back to stop her coughing and refilled her coffee cup.

"Go up and get a shower," he said, "I'll fix you breakfast and then we can go to State to look at these samples."

Sylvia didn't argue. She spent a long time in the shower scrubbing off any vestige of Headley. Now she was angry and she was glad he was caught. What a bastard!

She pulled on khakis and a t-shirt and padded downstairs in her bare feet. Owen was just finished scrambling eggs and was busily buttering toast.

"Thanks," Sylvia told him, "Do you hire out?" she asked teasingly.

"Only for you babe," he told her and she smiled at his response.

While she ate, Owen talked about the possibilities in the muck. He suspected a micro-organism but didn't know what kind.

Owen drove Sylvia to the State University. He seemed to know the campus well and pulled into an available parking space and fed the meter. Grabbing the bottles he motioned for Sylvia to follow him. They went to the Science Center and Owen pulled a card from his jeans pocket and looked for a directory. Finding what he wanted, they went to the second floor. The smell of chemicals and formaldehyde was strong. Most of the offices and classroom doors were closed. Owen walked down the hallway reading names and numbers. At an open door, he stopped and began to talk. Sylvia caught up to him. Sitting in a very messy office was a red-bearded man with bright blue eyes. Owen introduced her and she learned this was the acquaintance Marian had mentioned, Dr. Bill Gutzman. He was wearing a faded "Save the Bay" T-shirt. Posters and environmental bumper stickers decorated the walls of his office. One of the small glass enclosed ecosystems was on a shelf at eye level. He and Owen talked for a few minutes in with scientific detail that confounded Sylvia. It was like another language. Finally, Bill stood up and led them to a lab where Owen could work. Bill unlocked a door from a large ring of keys and let them in.

Sylvia looked around. It smelled like a science lab. Owen took a deep breath and sighed with contentment. He was in his element. Owen took the samples and prepared some slides. He looked at the slides for a few minutes and then moved them from one microscope to another. He was muttering, but Sylvia couldn't make out what he was saying. He went over to a computer and turned it on and logged onto the Internet. Owen logged onto a site and then went back to the microscope. He kept pushing back his hair in the familiar gesture. Sylvia knew he was frustrated, but didn't want to interrupt. He finally looked up and remembered she was there.

"This is so strange," he said. "I can't figure it out."

"What is?" Sylvia asked.

"Well," Owen said, "It is difficult to explain because it's not making sense. Would you go down the hall and ask Bill if he could come up to take a look at something please?"

"Sure," Sylvia said.

She went down and delivered the message. Bill followed her to the lab and he and Owen an intense discussion. Bill looked into the microscope and became very excited. They went over to the computer again and accessed a couple of different sites. Bill pointed out some examples on the Internet. They both checked the computer screen and then went back to the microscope. Bill moved the slide to another microscope attached to the computer. Owen turned to explain to her that they would show the micro-organisms on the screen and be able to save them to a file as well as print out the image. Bill got a couple of shots and printed out some pictures of the slides. He and Owen took the copies and marked up some of the pictures with circles and arrows.

"This is amazing!" Bill commented.

Owen excitedly said, "I know! I know!"

"Excuse me," Sylvia said, "Can someone let me know what's going on?"

"The micro-organism," Owen said, "it's like nothing we've ever seen before."

Bill was staring into the microscope, "Vicious little bugger," he said.

"What do you mean?" Sylvia asked.

"It's eating everything in sight. Kind of like the 'blob' in those old horror films, only this blob has vicious teeth."

"It reminds me of the pfisteria organism," Owen said, "but, that's impossible," he said out loud.

"Why?" Sylvia asked. "Why is it impossible?"

"Pfisteria is a water-based organism," Owen explained. "It doesn't exist on land."

"But, why can't it have a land counterpart?" Sylvia asked. "You know, an evil twin."

Bill and Owen looked at each other and Bill raised his eyebrows to Owen.

"Smart girl," Bill said. "Possible...possible," he muttered.

Owen took out a pad of paper and started to make some notes. His pen flew across the paper. They worked long into the afternoon and Sylvia's stomach was growling loudly.

"Do you guys want to go and get something to eat?" she asked, trying not to sound plaintive.

"Yeah," Bill said, "A short break would be good. Let's go to the pub down the street and we can brainstorm about this."

Sylvia refrained from rolling her eyes. They were men on a mission. Not that she minded terribly, but they were definitely two peas in a pod. Bill carefully placed signs, "Experiment in Progress, Do Not Touch!" and made sure he locked the door behind him.' They walked out into the late afternoon sunshine. The warmth felt wonderful after the highly air-conditioned lab. Sylvia rubbed her arms to warm up. They walked to the pub a couple of blocks away and settled into a corner booth. After a pitcher of beer came, Owen took out his notepad and started taking additional notes.

Owen commented on the chemicals in the soil. "Looks like we found the dump site," he said.

"Yeah," Bill said. "Another clean-up project for Thurmont. You would think they would get a grip, but they're big business and all they care about is money, money, money."

"Well, also, the current director is partially at fault, too," Sylvia commented.

"Headley?" Bill asked and Sylvia nodded.

"He's an ass," Bill stated emphatically. "If they found someone who actually cared about the environment, the Superfund clean-ups might end and community support would build. The company with Headley running it is poison to the environment."

Sylvia looked at him sharply. "Are you part of a group that protests Thurmont?"

"Nah," he said, "I'm active in the conservancy organizations in the area. The hothead protesters don't seem to get anywhere," he said, "Unfortunately, they just get arrested."

"Have you heard any rumblings about Thurmont lately?" Owen asked.

"There are always rumblings," he said quiet and with meaning.

Both Owen and Sylvia looked at him sharply. Both wondered about the vandalism at the Thurmont booth at Bay Days. Owen shook his head and Sylvia nodded.

Bill caught the last part of the silent conversation and said, "What's going on? Do you two have a secret code?"

Owen laughed. "Okay, I'll come clean," he said. "Someone vandalized the Thurmont booth at Bay Days."

"How?" Bill asked, openly shocked and surprised.

"They spray painted 'Thurmont kills,' 'Thurmont sucks' and other tomes," Sylvia quoted the graffiti.

"I haven't heard anything lately, but I'm not surprised that it happened." Bill said, "I'll put out a couple of feelers if it would help."

"Thanks," Sylvia said, "I would appreciate it."

They finished their beer and nachos. Owen asked if it would be okay to return the next day. Bill agreed easily and said he might surf the Internet for additional research.

Owen took Sylvia's hand and squeezed it. He was happy to be getting somewhere with the samples. He wished out loud to get into his files at Thurmont.

"Well," Sylvia said, "if you can give me your username and password, I could email them to you. I don't know why we didn't think of it before."

"Great idea!" Owen said and he leaned over to kiss her.

"I hope it helps," she said fervently.

They found their car and headed for home. Sylvia was thinking about the micro-organism they had seen. She had a lot of questions for Owen.

"By the way," she asked, "How are the chemical fertilizers put together at Thurmont anyway?"

"Actually, it's quite a unique process," Owen told her. "It's a mixture of organic and inorganic materials, that produce quite an excellent grade of fertilizer for farms and gardens."

"Wasn't the pfisteria organism related to an organism in fecal matter?" Sylvia asked.

"Something like that," Owen said, "from the chicken droppings and the runoff into the rivers is one of the theories."

"So-o-o," Sylvia said, "I know I'm not a scientist or anything, but if that could cause the pfisteria problem, couldn't the wrong mix of organic material and chemicals create a new, and potentially dangerous micro-organism?"

"Possibly," Owen mused. "I hadn't thought of it that way." He looked as though he was far, far away in thought. He turned to grin at her. "Have you ever thought about going into science?" he asked her.

Sylvia looked at him, "No, not really," she said. "I never thought I had an affinity for it."

"Well, you have a great way of putting things together," he told her. "You're thinking out of the box."

"Thanks," Sylvia said.

"You know, I need to call Mr. Carter," Sylvia said suddenly. "I totally lost track of the day."

She called as soon as she got into the house. Mr. Carter was definitely more cheerful. He asked how work went and she explained what happened the day before.

"What a bastard!" Mr. Carter said shocked. "I never thought his sexual harassment would lead to assault."

"Are you okay?" he asked her.

"I will be," Sylvia sighed.

"By the way," Sylvia told him, "We parked your car here at my house. I hope that's okay."

"Sure," he said, "Thanks for not leaving it in the park."

He went on to tell her that he would likely be able to go home tomorrow. They discussed the particulars of getting his car and him home. Sylvia told him she would be returning to work the next day and to call her there. She hung up from Mr. Carter and went to ask Owen about the next day. She also checked to see if Owen was available to help her drive Mr. Carter back to the Philadelphia area.

In the middle of her question, she remembered he was going to work on the research at State. She stopped mid-sentence and said, "Forget it."

"Why?" Owen asked.

"Your research," she said. "Maybe I can ask Carol."

She dialed Carol's home phone number. Carol answered.

"What happened to you today?" she asked cheerfully. "Did you and Owen have a hot night?" she teased.

"I-I guess you haven't heard," Sylvia said.

"Heard what?" Carol asked.

"About Headley," she paused, "and me."

"What?" Carol said, "Are you going to tell me you're engaged or something?"

Sylvia was quiet for a minute.

"Syl?" Carol asked. "What's up?"

"Headley assaulted me last night, Carol," she told her quietly.

"Oh my God!" she said, "I'm sorry I was teasing you Syl," she told her.

"What did they do with him?" she asked.

"I guess he's still in jail," she said. "They also picked him up for some drug and drug paraphernalia charges."

"Wow!" Carol said. "I'm amazed the rumor mill hasn't been frothing at the mouth!"

"Me too," Sylvia said. "I think someone's trying to cover it up."

"I don't believe they want any more bad press for the company," Carol said.

"You're probably right," Sylvia said. "I'm thinking a little darkly these days."

"Who could blame you?" Carol replied grimly. "Are you okay?" Carol asked her.

"I will be," Sylvia said.

"Well," Carol said, "A lot of women here will want to give you an award."

"Why?" Sylvia asked.

"For nailing Headley and putting a stop to his asshole behavior!" she told her.

"I don't think I could ever do that," Sylvia said, her humor returning. "I don't think he'll ever stop being an asshole," Sylvia laughed ruefully.

"True," Carol said, laughing with her, "but, he's stopped for a little while, at least. He'll be fresh meat for those prison guys. Now he'll know what it feels like."

Sylvia didn't want to think about it. Sylvia asked her about the transport of Mr. Carter and Carol agreed easily.

"Another day away from Keely is always wonderful," she said.

They said good night and she went out to Owen in the study. He was reading a rather complex article on micro-organisms.

"Find anything?" Sylvia asked.

"Nothing that matches what we saw," he said. "I would like to isolate one of the micro-organisms tomorrow," he told her, "and see how it reacts with fresh soil."

He was in his element and she let him be and browsed among the bookshelves for something to read. A wave of tiredness came over her. She took the book and lay on the couch in the living room. It was very late when she woke up. She thought she heard a noise and realized a light was still pouring from the study. She stood up to turn on a light and ran smack into the Green Man.

"Oh!" she said, "I'm sorry!"

He put his arm around her to steady her before she sat back down on the couch.

"Thanks for saving me last night," she said.

"All in a day's work," he said lightly, his mustache of leaves curling with his smile.

"You're something like a superhero, aren't you?" she said.

He just looked at her steadily and with his usual sense of humor said earnestly, "No cape."

Sylvia left out a loud "Ha!" in laughter and then clapped her hand over her mouth, concerned Owen might hear her and come out to investigate. She stifled another giggle at the thought of it.

The Green Man reached out and took her hand. She could feel his energy pulsing through her, healing her internal pain.

"Sylvia," the Green Man said as he took one of his fingers and stroked her cheek gently. "You're going to be just fine," he said.

Sylvia smiled, relieved, but not understanding.

"Syl?" Owen asked coming out of the study, "Are you awake?"

The Green Man vanished in an instant.

"Who are you talking to?" Owen asked.

"No one," Sylvia lied.

"Hmm," Owen said, "I must be fatigued. I could have sworn I heard voices. Let's go up to bed."

He pulled her up off the couch and they went upstairs. It was a quiet night and Sylvia lay in bed listening to the night sounds. Most of the boaters had returned to their homes and daily jobs. There was a soft lap, lap, lap of the water on the shoreline and the sound of a crazy mockingbird wanting to mate deep in the night. A rustle of leaves filled the air with the gentle night breeze that pushed the curtains in a dance at her windows. Owen was already asleep. She sighed deeply. She curled up next to Owen and fell asleep too.

Sylvia was busy at work the next day, fielding questions about Headley to people that stopped by. Executives from the sister company came in, all in their dark blue suits, to apologize to Sylvia. They said they would take care of things, but gave no details. Carol said that they wanted to make sure she didn't sue for sexual harassment as well as assault. It was late morning when she was able to log in as Owen, and email his files to him at home. Mr. Carter called to say he was ready to roll. Sylvia and Carol got their things together and went to pick him up.

Mr. Carter was still a little pasty looking, but his sense of humor was back. He made several jokes about hating to leave the nurses at the hospital but didn't mind being taken away by two beautiful young women. They drove back to Sylvia's house to get his car. Carol drove her car and Sylvia drove Mr. Carter in his car to his home outside of Philadelphia. He lived in a quiet, tree filled neighborhood in a Cape Cod house with a stone porch. His neighbor had been watching the house and gathering the mail, but the grass looked overgrown. Sylvia asked him if he wanted her to cut it.

"No," Mr. Carter said, "but thanks for the offer. I have a young man in the neighborhood that can take care of it."

He apologized in advance for the state of his house. "I'm an old bachelor, you know," he told Carol and Sylvia.

He had piles of books and magazines about trains lying around. It was cluttered, but not dirty.

"Will you be okay here on your own?" Sylvia asked.

"I'll be okay," he said, "I can't thank you enough for everything you've done."

"Make sure you check in with your family doctor," Carol advised.

"Yes, Mom," he joked to Carol.

"Can we go and get you some groceries?" Sylvia asked.

"I'll be fine," Mr. Carter said again. "Shoo! Get back to work or I'll tell your boss," he quipped.

"Okay," Sylvia conceded.

She gave Mr. Carter a gentle hug and a kiss on the cheek. She could have sworn that his eyes filled up. She was emotional, too, after everything that had happened in the past week.

He gave Carol a quick hug too, and they waved goodbye. Unfortunately, they hit prime rush hour traffic and sat on the interstate for over an hour. Between an accident that had happened a few miles south of them and the daily rush hour, it was well after six o'clock when they were near Thurmont. Sylvia's cell phone rang. It was Owen.

"Where have you been?" he asked. "I was starting to get worried."

Sylvia explained about the accident and the traffic delays.

"Since you're headed back to Thurmont to get your car, would you do me a favor?" Owen asked.

"Of course," Sylvia said.

"Would you go down to the lab to get my green notebook? I have some notes in it that I need access to," he asked her.

"How will I get in?" Sylvia asked. "What do I do if your office is locked?"

"Ed's a decent guy," Owen told her. "I'm sure he'll unlock the door if you ask."

"Okay," she said, "I'll find him and meet you at home."

"No, wait," he said, "Bill and I are still in the lab. Can you meet us at the pub and we can all have dinner?"

"Sounds great," Sylvia said and hung up.

Carol had a hair appointment and was running late due to the traffic so she dropped Sylvia off at the entrance to Thurmont and waved goodbye. Sylvia went in to look for Ed. It was a little creepy to come into the company after hours. The lights were still bright, but it was too quiet for Sylvia. Her footsteps echoed as she walked down the hallways. She stopped briefly by her office and checked messages and then went to look for Ed. She wasn't quite sure where his office was located and wandered through the halls looking for him. She found him vacuuming.

"Hi Ed," she shouted.

Ed jumped and turned off the vacuum.

"Sorry," Sylvia said, "I didn't mean to startle you."

"No problem," Ed replied, "What can I do for you little lady?" he asked with his usual grin.

"I was wondering if you could let me into Owen's office, please?" she asked. "He needs a notebook that he left in there."

"Well, seeing that it is you," Ed told her, "I'll do it."

She followed him to Owen's office and noticed that his arm was still red and the bandage loose.

"Are you still having problems with your arm?" she asked him.

"Yup," Ed replied. He stopped. "I can't seem to remember anything these days." He tapped his head, "A senior moment. What was it you wanted to get again?"

"The notebook," Sylvia said again, "from Owen's office."

"Oh, yeah, right," Ed said, pausing between each word.

He took out a large ring of keys and sifted through looking for the right one.

"Here we go," he said and he opened the door and turned on the light for Sylvia.

"Thanks," she said.

Sylvia looked around Owen's office which was extraordinarily neat. She looked on the bookshelf by his desk and there, in a neat row, were several notebooks. She looked until she found a green one and pulled it off the shelf.

"I think this is it, thanks," she said turning to Ed.

The loose bandage had slipped off of his arm and she could see the skin infection that had been plaguing him. His arm looked like Anna's body. Along his forearm were spidery tracks of red that looked like snail trails. They were oozing and looked sore. Realization struck her and it must have shone in her eyes.

Ed looked at her and then down at his arm where the bandage had slipped. He let out an expletive.

"Damn it! I wish you hadn't seen this," he said wearily.

"But..." Sylvia couldn't get any words out. Finally, she said, "You...Anna..."

"I didn't kill her," Ed told her. "I just buried the bitch."

Sylvia still couldn't speak. "But that makes you an accomplice," she whispered to herself finally, still in a state of shock.

"What did you say?" Ed asked warily.

"Nothing," Sylvia said, shaking her head.

She couldn't take her eyes off of his arm. He had started to wrap the bandage tighter and fasten it so that it wouldn't slip. What would he do now? Would he kill her too? But, he said he wasn't the killer. Who was? Wild thoughts went through her head. She glanced around Owen's office for something to use as a weapon in self-defense if she needed it. Nothing, she could see absolutely nothing.

"I need to go," Sylvia said.

"You aren't going anywhere," Ed told her in a level tone. "I need to think. I can't remember anything these days," he said frustrated. He rubbed his head. "I need to think," he said again.

Suddenly he told her, "Move!" in a rough voice.

"What are you going to do?" Sylvia asked in a small voice, panic beginning to set in.

"Nothing, yet," he said, "except put you in a safe place until I can figure out what to do."

She hesitated, and Ed prodded her with his good arm.

"Move!" he said again. "Keep your hands where I can see them," he ordered.

He led her down the hall to a part of Thurmont that she had never been. He opened up a pair of heavy double doors. It led to the boiler room.

"Get in here," he ordered.

He pointed to a large utility closet that was filled with cleaning supplies. Sylvia was reluctant and Ed pushed her so that she stumbled and fell into the closet. The door clicked shut and he locked it.

Sylvia wanted to scream, but there was no one to hear her. It was dark in the closet. She had been clutching Owen's notebook when she remembered that Owen would be waiting for her at the pub. She remembered her cell phone and fumbled in her purse to get it. When she looked at the read out it did not have a signal. She tried anyway but heard the familiar beep-beep-beep and the mechanical voice that said the call could not be placed. Sylvia sank down to the floor. She wanted to cry.

A small sliver of light came in from under the door and a tiny bit of fresh air. The utility closet was beginning to get stuffy.

Sylvia thought about Ed. He said he hadn't killed Anna, only buried her. It made her wonder who had killed Anna. Was it Headley? She wondered what Ed would do. Would he or his accomplice kill her too? It seemed as though the police weren't any closer to finding the murderer than before. How long would it take Owen to realize that she wasn't going to make it to the pub? If he came to rescue her, would it be too late or would they hurt him too? Would the Green Man come? She had too many questions to which she had no answers. It made her head ache terribly. Sylvia rubbed at her temples. She called silently to Owen in her head. She called to the Green Man.

Sylvia lost track of time. Nothing happened and no one came. Panic came in waves and Sylvia worked hard at keeping calm. She thought she dozed off and she woke up aching from her cramped position. She heard voices outside the door. Sylvia pressed her ear close to the door to try to hear the conversation. Was it Ed? She waited breathlessly, listening.

Suddenly the door opened and she tumbled out. Ed stood there and an older woman. Now she knew why Ed had looked familiar. It was the woman with the flashing, angry eyes from the meeting at the library. She was the one who told her she was a traitor. It must be his mother because they looked so much alike. She, too, had bandages and they were on both arms.

"You little bitch," she said to Sylvia vehemently. "What did you think you were doing?"

Sylvia didn't answer. She didn't see any point in antagonizing this woman. She was clearly crazy.

"How did she know?" she demanded of Ed.

He said wearily, "Sylvia found Anna's body and saw the tracks on me. She put two and two together."

"Stupid!" she said to Ed. "How can you be so stupid." She raised her arm as if to cuff him on the side of his head. Ed flinched and she dropped her bandaged arm that was clearly bothering her.

The woman started pacing up and down in the boiler room muttering to herself. She was a scary sight with her bandaged arms, wild eyes and white hair sticking up on end.

"Lock her up again," the woman ordered Ed.

"Why Ma?" he said, "What are we going to do?"

"Dig a grave," she said seriously.

Sylvia felt faint and she reached out to grab onto something. She swallowed hard and said, "Wait! Why kill me? I'm trying to help! I'm working with the scientist to clean-up and take care of whatever attacked your arms and Anna!"

"It's true, Ma," Ed said.

"But she knows," the woman hissed to Ed. "She knows we killed the bitch who was poisoning the world!"

"You can't get away with this," Sylvia whispered. "People know I am here to retrieve some valuable notes. They'll look for me."

"Get the keys to her car," she said to Ed. "We'll have to get rid of that too."

She paced some more, "I've gotta work this out. It'll be all right," she talked to herself as she continued to pace. "I can't think. I can't t-h-i-n-k in here!" she screamed at her son.

"Give me your keys, Sylvia," Ed said to her.

Sylvia had tears in her eyes and she couldn't see very well. She wiped them away and fumbled in her purse. There wasn't an exit nearby and she didn't think she would make it to the door. She was too slow. Ed's mother grabbed her purse and shook out the contents. Sylvia's keys clattered as they hit the floor.

"Ed, please, please don't do this," she pleaded.

"Get a shovel, son," said his mother. "We'll need a flashlight too, it's starting to get dark."

"Don't you move a muscle," she threatened Sylvia.

The look in Maureen Davenport's eyes chilled Sylvia to the bone. Ed went to fetch the shovel and flashlight from the closet adjacent to where she was kept prisoner. The older woman continued to pace but kept an eye on Sylvia.

"Do you have any rope?" she demanded of Ed.

"I don't know," he said, "What do you need rope for?" he asked in a whining voice.

"To tie up her hands, stupid!" she shouted and this time, she did cuff him on the side of his head.

"Ow, Ma!' he cried. "You didn't have to go and do that."

The protest sounded like an old argument. Ed searched through the closets and came up with a dirty piece of old clothesline.

"Will this do?" he asked sarcastically to his mother.

"Fine," she spat out at him and to Sylvia, she said, "Hold out your hands."

Sylvia did as she was told. She kept thinking that when they reached the door to the outside, she could make a run for it. The old woman tied her hands so tightly that the rope cut into her wrists. Sylvia wondered what time it was. A big clock hung on the wall. It was 8:35. Owen must be thinking something happened by now. She called to him in her mind. She called to the Green man. She was beginning to get confused as well in her panic and didn't understand why no one came. The older woman pushed her towards the door.

"March, little lady," she said.

Ed followed her with the shovel and the flashlight.

"Whack her on the head with the shovel if she gives you any trouble," the woman said.

Near the door, the older woman took Sylvia's arm and motioned for Ed to take the other.

"Don't even think of running," the woman warned.

They sloshed her through the little stream into the woods where she had found Anna and where Headley had assaulted her. Sylvia now hated these woods. She walked as slowly as she could, praying again for the Green Man to come and rescue her. Where the soil was extremely mushy, his mother ordered Ed to start digging as she held on tightly to Sylvia with her left hand. Her left hand. The pieces fell into place like bricks falling into a shallow pond. Maureen Davenport was amazingly strong. Sylvia suddenly remembered Maureen had snapped Anna's neck. She closed her eyes for a moment and swayed.

"Stand up," Maureen tugged at her and stated with a bitter tone. "Pesky little do-gooder, just like her granny."

It was easy for Ed to dig because the soil was so soft. Sylvia noticed that he tried to keep the muck from his skin area and dug an area large enough to put in her body.

Thc older woman started muttering again. "Should I break her neck like the last one?" she asked herself, "Or whack her with the shovel."

Sylvia felt faint but willed herself to stay on her feet, breathing air in through her nose and out through her mouth. She willed herself to breathe and to stay on her feet.

After Ed had dug a sizeable hole, Maureen said, "Whack her on the head, Ed."

Ed looked at his mother blankly.

"With the shovel, stupid!" she yelled at him.

"Oh, Ma!" he said, "I don't want to kill her!" his voice had a plaintive whine to it.

"Why do I have to do everything!" she spat at him. "Hold onto her!" she ordered, "and give me that shovel." Her voice had risen an octave and was thunderous.

From what seemed far, far away, Sylvia thought she heard voices.

"Over here!" she shouted wildly, "Over here! Over here! Over here!" as loudly as she could when Maureen hit her in the mouth.

Sylvia pulled away from Ed, blood streaming from a cut lip and stumbled toward the stream. She rolled down the embankment and landed in the water.

"Syl!" Owen cried catching up with her, "Sylvia, are you all right."

Sylvia couldn't speak, she nodded and then started sobbing. He picked her up out of the edge of the stream and held her. Bill was behind Owen looking distraught. A couple of policemen had followed them.

"Up there, I think," Owen told them. "Be careful," he warned, "Don't get any of that mud on your skin!"

"Ed, right?" Owen asked Sylvia.

She looked up surprised, "And his mother. How did you know?"

"Thank, Bill," Owen said. "We were talking about the vandalism and the tent set up and somehow Ed's name came up. He said that Ed belonged to a pretty radical environmental group, but his Mom was way out on a limb," Owen told her.

"She killed Anna," Sylvia said, "His Mom thought Anna was poisoning the world."

"Well," Owen said with what little sense of humor he had left, "in a sense she was."

They could hear expletives coming from the wooded area. Ed and his mother were in cuffs. Maureen was screaming at them, calling them murderers and then became totally incoherent.

"Do you think I could get out of this?" she said and she held up her wrists.

"I don't know, Syl," Owen said with a grin on his face. "It could be fun, you know."

Sylvia stared at him. "I can't believe you're joking at a time like this," she said.

"Who's joking?" he said with a grin.

They crossed back over the stream. Bill followed. The police wanted them to make a statement before she was able to go home.

CHAPTER THIRTY ONE

"Namaste"

Months later…

It was December and a Friday. Sylvia was trying to get the office area into the Christmas spirit. Carols played as she decorated a small tree in the office. Mr. Carter came out and smiled benevolently at her. He was about twenty-five pounds lighter and was eating better and exercising. He looked much better than he had the past summer. She hummed along with the radio.

Owen came in to pick her up for lunch. He had a book in hand. He had been reinstated in his job and was taking graduate classes at night at State University to work on his doctorate. They wanted him as a full-time doctoral fellow for his research on the micro-organism, but he wanted to work at Thurmont and try to clean things up and do onsite research at the same time. The micro-organism had been created from the mixture of the organic and inorganic materials somehow transfigured into a dangerous protist. Like the pfisteria organism, it mimicked a plant and then attacked flesh and plant life alike and sucked the life out of whatever it could sink its little microscopic teeth into. It was the horrible stain that had spread across the region from Thurmont reaching fingers towards the bay. No one would understand what she had seen, but she was glad it was being cleared through Owen and Bill's research. They had no name for it yet, but Owen was hoping to name it himself since it was his discovery. He had already written one paper on it that had been accepted well by the scientific community. They went to lunch and talked about Marian's solstice party the next day. The weather had turned cold, but no snow covered the ground. Marian and Jon were headed to England for the holidays and they were celebrating early with a solstice party. Marian planned for hot buttered rum, lots of candles and a bonfire.

Carol joined them with a bowl of soup and a sandwich. She told them all the company gossip, and who they should talk to, and who to avoid at the company Christmas party the next week. Headley had been fired and the interim director seemed very nice. Sylvia had only met him a couple of times. Once when Owen was reinstated and honored for his discovery of the organism and his work to study and eradicate it. The other time when he stopped by the office for a handshake and a smile.

Sylvia was glad it was Friday. She still had some last minute Christmas shopping to do.

She had told Owen about the Green Man, but she wasn't sure he believed her. Marian supported her story, but his scientific mind just wouldn't open to the possibility of an archetype coming to life. Sylvia was a little sad, but it was something she could live with. She hadn't seen the Green Man for awhile and that made her kind of sad too. She knew she was still growing in the knowledge that he wanted her to discover, but was sorry for his absence of late.

Saturday dawned bright and cold. A few flakes of snow drifted down. The water and the sky were steely gray and it looked like snow. She brought a cup of coffee up to Owen.

"Time to get up sleepy head," she teased.

"I'm cold," he growled and he pulled her down beside him.

"No! We can't do this," she protested as he kissed her. "Marian is expecting us to help her set up for the party." She got out each word between Owen's kisses.

"Spoilsport," he murmured in her ear.

"Just wait," she teased, "and I'll give you an early Christmas present."

They packed up a few things because they would be spending the night and taking Marian and Jon to the airport the next morning.

Marian hugged them tightly when they arrived. Owen and Jon moved tables to the dining room where Marian had gold netting to place over snowy-white cloths. Marian had been cooking for weeks and keeping things in the freezer. Sylvia pulled out the chafing dishes and put the small sterno cans in place for lighting later.

It was much later when the party was in full swing when the Green Man appeared. Sylvia had gone up to the bedroom to fix her make-up and saw his reflection in the mirror. She turned and rushed to take his hands and he pulled her into a hug. She felt his joyful life force through her.

"Sylvia," he said, brushing his hand against her cheek. He seemed to get choked up and could not speak.

They sat on the bed and she told him everything that had happened since the last time she saw him and he smiled down at her.

She cocked her head to one side, "You knew all about it, didn't you?" she questioned him. Noticing his crown of holly and oak she commented, "You look like a king tonight," she said.

He stood up and straightened to his full height. He looked regal in his brocade of leaf suit and his living wood skin polished smooth. Tonight he wore a crown of holly atop the oak leaves on his head regally. "It's a special day," he said, "the Solstice. It's the one day when I will go to be renewed and reborn."

She gave him a puzzled look but, he didn't have a chance to answer her unspoken questions.

"Syl," Owen called, "Where are you? It's time to go to the bonfire."

"Will you join us?" she asked the Green Man.

He nodded without speaking and followed her out of the room. Owen gasped when the Green Man stepped into the hallway. Sylvia introduced Owen, took a hand from both and headed outside. Owen was not able to speak but kept gaping at the Green Man's regal form. Sylvia couldn't help but grin. At least now he would believe her.

It was a clear, sparkling winter's night. A full moon was in the sky, but its light could not shadow the brilliance of the stars that shone brightly in the blue-black sky. Marian had lit a bonfire in the meadow. Its flames leaped up trying to touch the sky, higher and higher in a mixture of brilliant white, gold and orange flames.

When the Green Man appeared, several people cheered. He nodded, king-like, acknowledging his patrons. Sylvia stared up at him with surprise and pleasure that so many saw and recognized him. They all waited and watched the flames.

Finally at the right moment, the Green Man said, "Goodbye, Sylvia. Veriditas."

"What?" Sylvia whispered, dragging her attention back to him. She had been caught up in the magic of the starlight and the flames.

"I'll always be nearby if you need me," the Green Man whispered and kissed her, his oak leaf mustache tickling as he kissed. It was a kiss from a friend, a mentor, but passionate at the same time. Sylvia caught her breath. "Keep looking and listening and learning," he told her.

Sylvia shivered. The Green Man stepped into the welcoming flames and Sylvia gave a little cry of "No!" Tears coursed down her face even though the Green Man was smiling as though the flames were like a cozy blanket. People around her were cheering and shouting, "May your days grow longer."

"Goodbye," she whispered through her tears.

Owen stood with her for a long time, his arm around her shoulders as the party guests left one by one to return to the house for warmth, and food and drink. Sylvia couldn't take her eyes off the space where the Green Man had stepped into the flames. Owen kept urging her to come inside, to get warm, but Sylvia wouldn't move.

Finally, the bonfire died down. All that was left were a few pieces of wood. Owen came out and kicked at a few to cool the embers and spread the ashes with his boot.

"Look at this," he said, kicking at a large piece from the center of the bonfire and shining a large flashlight on it.

Sylvia gasped when she saw it. It was the wooden mask that she had found months ago after Gran's funeral. Battered by wind, water, weather and fire, its rough edges had been worn smooth. Sylvia picked it up. She knew it was a last gift from the Green Man.

And she knew he would return. Owen took her hand and they walked together back towards Marian's house with the stars singing around them.

The End

Dear Reader,

I hope you enjoyed reading *The Greening.* More intrigue and adventures await Sylvia, Owen and the Green Man in The Leafing and The Blossoming available at www.amazon.com and various retailers. More information on books by Sharon Brubaker at www.sharon-brubaker.com

If you enjoyed The Greening, please leave a review at www.amazon.com or at www.goodreads.com. Reviews are so very important. It helps other readers find books to enjoy. Thank you in advance for taking the time to leave a review.

Also, a little gift. Scan the QR code below for a complimentary recipe from Marian's Oakwood Manor Cookbook:

Thank you for reading.
Sincerely,
Sharon Brubaker
www.sharon-brubaker.com

What they're saying about <u>The Leafing:</u>

""The Leafing" was just the right blend of mystery, excitement, romance and environment. I enjoyed being brought again to the Chesapeake Bay. Once I started, it was hard to put down. This book was just as great as "The Greening" and I anxiously await the next book in the series."

"Sharon Brubaker has done it again, another page turner. The characters from The Greening are back, once again tangled in intrigue. Super mystery intertwined in a love story. Can't wait to follow their story in book three."

31671140R00269

Made in the USA
Middletown, DE
08 May 2016